VERATH THE RED

BOOK 3 OF THE DRAGONWALL SERIES

MELISSA MITCHELL

For Katrina Cozens, with her keen eye for detail and love of all things Dragonwall.

DRAGONWALL
Dragonfire Sea
Shadowkeep
Belness
Eagle Lake
Mistport
Redport
Squall's End
Three Horned Man
Scattered Islands
Kastali Dun
Bay of Bandu

engr Gate
Northedge
The Gable
Forest
Kaljah
incastle
South Sea

PROLOGUE

Isabella waited alone, shielding her gaze against the sun. She surveyed the empty landscape and sky above, chewing on the inside of her cheek. This was a mistake. She shouldn't have come.

Dissatisfaction bloomed in her chest like a night flower opening at sunset. She pressed a hand against her abdomen, trying to calm herself. Nearly a year had passed. Would he look the same? Act the same? Would he look upon her as he once did? Her mind raced back to their first meeting, to the days when he had been nothing but a dragon. She recalled the reverence in his telepathic voice, the awe in his piercing gaze. A huff fell from her lips. He'd been a dragon—yet had beheld *her* as the greater being. She *was*, of course she was, but what dragon would admit to that?

She glanced about. Perhaps it wasn't too late. She could slip away, pretend she'd never received his invitation. Vigilance had requested she wait beside the monstrous boulder that pointed south, like a finger, towards the very tip of the Eigaden Peninsula. Shielding her gaze against the sun, she saw the sparkle of cerulean blue beyond the land. Her eyes watered. It was too much—too bright. She already missed the muted light of the forest.

A sigh escaped her lips. She clenched her teeth together. Never take orders from a dragon. Not even a request made politely. She had considered refusing, her thoughts like a pendulum swinging back and forth. She knew what it might mean, seeing him again.

The war was over, and against all odds, Rage had been defeated. She owed the beasts of the sky *nothing*. Yet, a smug smile of satisfaction crept across her face. What would they think— those beasts? How would they react when they discovered what she'd done? Perhaps they wouldn't realize it...not until much later, tens of thousands of years from now.

And still, a sense of obligation tugged at her gut even now, but an obligation to only one beast...not all. She felt pulled—tugged. With Vigilance, she had always struggled against some invisible force tying them together. He was—in a way—her creation. That alone made her fond of him.

She looked for a sign, taking in the landscape, trying to understand why Vigilance had wanted to meet here—alone. Klide waited patiently beside her. She stroked his soft mane, whispering reassurances. Unicorns were not servants of her people, they were companions. Klide had been her companion for many years, offering his back countless times. His unbelievable speed allowed her to travel throughout the countryside, far and wide, faster than any horse could possibly match.

Klide's mind touched hers, humming with the gentleness of the forest. She could almost smell the night flowers and foliage, the soft dirt. His presence was different from a dragon's. A dragon's mind—*drengr*, as they preferred to be called now—was overly complicated. There was still too much dragon and not enough human in them. She should have done a better job. Dragons, even the drengr, would never be simple and pure.

Still, the magic she'd worked was impressive.

The back of her neck prickled. Klide whispered a warning, brushing against her. She glanced at the sky and found the glitter of deep blue scales on the horizon, moving towards her. She exhaled, relaxing her tense shoulders. Her fingers reached for Klide's mane again, for comfort. His hair was silky against her skin. He nuzzled her side before turning his attention to the grass beneath his hooves. It never tasted as sweet as home...

She felt his thought like a forlorn sigh. And yes, she had to agree with him. Nothing seemed as sweet outside their forest world.

A penetrating drumbeat filled the air, a pulse pressing firmly against her ears. *Dom...Dom...Dom...* A smile spread across her lips at the sight of him, of his beautiful form. Even *she* could admit it left her breathless. With each measure of distance he covered, her heart felt lighter, easier, more relaxed.

She quickly replaced her smile with a frown. He shouldn't make her feel like this. It was...dangerous.

The drumbeat stopped. Vigilance tightened his wings, diving towards her. *"Queen Isabella."* His rich, velvety voice sounded in her mind, unbidden.

The first time he'd done it, she'd been infuriated, years ago when she discovered him in her forest. That he could enter her consciousness in the form of speech was unfair, to say the least. An ability she carried with her like a weakness. One that did not translate to all sprites, only a select few. It had taken much practice to shut them out.

"I'm glad you have come," he added.

She did not respond.

He slowed his descent, bringing his body upright with mighty back wing sweeps. His massive form was just out of reach. He transformed mid-air, warping and rippling, shrinking in size, her magic at work, and landed on two feet.

He stalked towards her. The sight of him made her falter. Even as a human, his hulking form towered over her.

"Good afternoon, Vigilance." She bowed her head as propriety dictated, one monarch to another. "I hear you go by the title of *king* now."

"King Eymar," he said, his gaze wary. His eyes were pools of glittering blackness, his face a tableau of handsome sculpting. That had always irked her. She'd never given his human form permission to be handsome. It felt like a personal attack of her own magic. Few of her other creations looked like him—godlike.

"Eymar?" She couldn't help her frown. "You changed your name?"

"It has a pleasing ring to it, yes?"

"Oh, yes. Very fitting. *King Eymar*," She let the title roll off her tongue, failing to hide her sarcasm. "Didn't you go to war over the very idea? That none should claim kingship over the dragons. Yet, here you are." She studied him, his finely wrought clothes. "You have done nicely for yourself."

"We went to war with Rage for more reasons than *that*, as you well know." His voice was sharp like the edge of a blade.

She snorted.

"As if you are one to judge," he scoffed. "How dare you interfere as you have done?! How could you go against me?" He took a threatening step towards her and stopped himself, fists tightening at his sides.

"Me?" She placed a hand against her chest. "Against you? Since when have *my* actions been accountable to you? You may be king of your people, *King of Dragonwall*, but we sprites remain independent. There is only one power to which we answer."

"Oh! Of course." He glared down at her, jaw flexing. "And I suppose it was your *king tree* ordering you to turn every damned dragon into a drengr?" She pressed her lips together. It wasn't, but she wouldn't say otherwise. "Gods, Isabella! You even turned those who fought for Rage! Now I must rule them all, the good *and* the bad!"

She snorted. "Those *dragons* you speak of were more than happy to take up human form. How dare you deprive them of the opportunity?! Such a privilege should not be reserved for you alone —you and your little *cadre* of drengr fairtheoir." Her tongue tripped over the words of the asarlaí language, hating it for its oily dirtiness. She took a deep, steadying breath. The longer she spent outside the forest, the further her control slipped.

"You betrayed me, Isabella. You went against me. You did not so much as ask."

A bark of laughter burst from her lips. "You should be thanking me. My meddling has given you people to rule—a kingdom. You think the dragons would have accepted a drengr ruler? Bah! You still have much to learn, young Vigilance."

He growled in warning. The low sound sent chills racing over her skin. Just because he looked human, didn't mean he was.

"Stop," she snapped, her words like a slap. "Control yourself. Such outbursts are unbecoming of a king." This time he snorted, but more quietly, as if agreeing. "Now," she said, "am I to understand that you summoned me here to chastise me? What's done is done. There are fewer dragons than ever. The Ice Clan has been banished, what little of them remain." She sighed, weariness taking hold of her. He looked tired too, jaded. Perhaps he was learning the truth of ruling.

"No, I did not summon you here to berate you," he said at last. "I summoned you for a different reason entirely." His gaze turned soft as it traveled over her, eyes tracing the curves of her body. A pleased shiver raced down her spine, bringing with it a seed of fear.

Vigilance turned toward the land and sea beyond. "Look before you. What do you see?"

She gazed in the same direction, as she had earlier. "A whole lot of nothing." Open land had never appealed to her, nor any sprite. Give her tall trees and security, a closeness to nature that could not be substituted for a wide open sky.

He chuckled. "You say that now, but I was blessed by the gods with a vision." Her breath caught. "This desolate and lonely place will become the greatest city Dragonwall has ever seen. There—see that rocky outcropping? That is where we will place the great keep. You will help me, of course, for I cannot build it alone. We will call it *Kastali Dun*."

A heaviness settled in her chest, a deep sense of *knowing*. "We? Oh no, my dear Vigilance—"

"Eymar."

"You will always be Vigilance to me. But if you wish...*Eymar*.

You are mistaken. I will not support any more of your wild ambitions. I helped you defeat Rage, much to my people's dissatisfaction. A rift has been created among the sprites, as you well know, between many elite families in Esterpine. I dare not create more strife within my kingdom."

His eyes gleamed, but he said nothing. She frowned. What was he hiding? She looked back out over the land, trying to calm the rising turmoil within her.

"Isabella…" The way he said her name, coaxing, like a spell, with the power of the dragons ringing in his voice, left her flushed. "This land is our future. Let me show you." He held out his hand, inviting her to partake in something only he could offer. She regarded him. "Fly with me."

"Fly?" The invitation gave her pause. She regarded him, glancing up at the sky. "I would do better on the ground."

Despite the claim, something of a thrill took hold of her.

He chuckled. "You say that, yet you build platforms in the tops of your trees to gaze at the stars. Come."

Without another word, he dropped his hand and transformed into his hulking dragon form. He really was one of the largest dragons she had ever seen, larger, even, than Rage. She glanced at Klide. Her companion snickered, as if granting her permission, but did not look up from his grazing. "Oh, very well," she mumbled, unable to stop herself.

In all her time spent working with the dragons, not a single one had ever offered to carry her. To take her flying. They were proud creatures, after all. For most, it would be a great honor to see what flying was like. Even her.

Despite her excitement, each step towards Vigilance felt heavier than the last. Something was happening here. He gave a satisfied hum as she stepped up beside him.

"*I suppose there is no elegant way for it?*" she asked, eyeing his extended forearm and height. She glanced down at herself. Her silvery gown shimmered in the sunlight, its sheen rolling across the fabric in waves.

"*You will know soon enough.*" There was something more to his words, a hint, a promise. She faltered. Her fear deepened into an abyss, yawning before her. *"Do not fear me, Isabella."* Once more, his use of her name was like magic, as if he had the ability to control her when no others could. It left her feeling childish—weak, even. But, that was silly. She was not weak. Nor did she have a reason to fear him.

Squaring her shoulders, she reached for him. Her hands made contact with his scales and the world around her vanished. She gasped, plunging into the confusing depths of an expansive mind that was not her own. A sense of betrayal took hold of her. She tried to struggle free, to keep her mind separate. *"What have you done?"* she sputtered, attempting to breathe. Was he trying to control her? To conquer her? To manipulate her?

"No, my beloved."

Beloved? The word gave her pause.

"I would never seek those things. This is something entirely different," he said. *"We are mates, you and I. Surely you knew? Surely this was your doing, when you made me. Surely you understood the consequences of your actions? Of your own creation?"*

Ice slid into her veins. *"What is this magic?"* she whispered into the confines of their shared mind. There, within his thoughts, she saw the answer. While he was away in the north, a strange thing had started happening to the male drengr under his command. They began forming unmistakable bonds with human females, taking them to mate for life. The females of her creation, it seemed, were unaffected. That alone was something she didn't quite understand. She shook her head. *"It was never...never my intention."* Her palm remained firmly against him. *"I never intended for something like fated mates."*

"No, your intentions were far darker." A fond chuckle sounded deep in his chest, as if he couldn't be angry with her no matter *how* horrid her intentions had been. *"You hoped to ruin us, Isabella. You hoped to force us into a form that would eventually result in the dwindling of the dragons. As half-humans, you hoped to shorten our lives."* His chuckle deepened. He saw everything laid bare within her mind. Her intentions. Her deceit. Her betrayal—for that was what

it had been. *"And look how your plan backfired."* Despite his words, there was an overwhelming sense of love for her, for everything that she was, her strengths and her weaknesses. He wanted all of her—exactly as she was. *"The irony of it is, you shall now be queen of the creation you detested. Not just any queen. My queen."*

There was no fighting it. No fighting what her heart yearned for —this creature she had created was to be hers. In that, she delighted. The feelings of her heart betrayed the common sense within her mind.

"Come, my dear Isabella. It is time to look upon the location of your new throne." His voice was like pure light, chasing away the darkness she had seen rolling in. The world within her mind flared bright. The gleaming of Vigilance's thoughts filled her own. So she stopped fighting him and let him claim her.

CHAPTER I
AN UNSCARRED KING

Kastali Dun

Claire narrowly dodged a blow intended to sever her head from her shoulders. She cursed under her breath, putting distance between herself and her attacker. He lunged again.

She wasn't prepared for the fate looming over her, but she would do whatever it took to change that, even if it meant subjecting herself to this form of personal torture. She had allies, friends who had promised to help her, but they couldn't fight this battle for her. Neither could the king. This responsibility was hers and hers alone—

"Stop that!" Jovari snapped. They were supposed to be sparring. "You're distracted today. Focus."

The practice grounds were located on the second level of the great keep. It was early, but the grounds were already full. She took a deep breath, the cool air a balm to her heaving lungs.

Jovari came at her again, swinging his practice sword overhead. She parried, meeting his blow. Their weapons clashed with a dull thunk. Her sword's grip slipped beneath her sweaty palms. She clenched her teeth, muscles straining to hold him at bay.

"Breathe! You are not breathing!" Koldis shouted from the side-lines. She threw him a glare.

Smack!

She groaned and spun away. That one was deserved. She knew better than to take her eyes off Jovari, even for a second.

"You left your side exposed," he scolded.

"I'm aware!" Frustration bunched her shoulders. "I was too busy focusing on Koldis's instructions." Several strands of hair had come free of her braid. She angrily swiped them off her sweaty forehead, glaring at both of her trainers. "How am I supposed to focus on everything all at once?"

"Practice—that's how." Jovari lifted his brows in challenge. "Your footwork is…deplorable. You glance down too often. And your mind isn't in the right place. If you must, then move like this." He demonstrated. "Keep your eyes on me—remember? Here. My sword. Right here." He took a swing for emphasis, then came at her again.

She dodged a series of attempts, hands firmly gripping her practice sword. Blow after blow rained down on her. She studied each of Jovari's movements. They were quick. Upper cut. Right sweep. Left lunge. Downward stroke. A pattern emerged. Her confidence grew as she memorized the motions. Time seemed to slow.

His sword swept in, aiming to deliver a deadly strike on her left. Seizing the opportunity, she brought her blade around and whacked his exposed flank. "Argh!" He jumped back but his face split into a grin. "Well done! Did you see the pattern in my movements? Yes? Good. Some swordsmen grow lazy. They develop habits or patterns. Always look for them."

They began again.

Soon enough, she was gasping for breath. Jovari was a difficult opponent, with a traditional fighting style that straddled the line of precision and elegance. He moved with quick, efficient thrusts and sweeping blows that tested her strength.

Koldis was a different story. He liked to fight dirty. Besides basic self defense, he'd taught her how to fight with her fists, how to throw a proper punch, and the sensitive places on a person. At one point, she'd nearly broken his jaw with the heel of her palm, or so she liked to think. She'd injured herself in the process, but she'd healed thereafter. Her magic made her more than human, allowing her to take a harder beating.

That's how it was for anyone with magic. It granted long life and the ability to heal. But it couldn't make a person immortal.

Not even Kane could claim immortality. Unlike a mage, an asarlaí sorcerer could live for thousands of years, fueled by their power. Something in the way their intent twisted their magic allowed them to live much longer. But even the asarlaí could be killed, and they had been, long ago. The dragons had done it. Now, she just needed to figure out how.

Strength and power grew with magical ability, and magical ability grew with knowledge, practice, and skill. The more powerful she became, the stronger she would be physically. The same was potentially true of her sprite blood, assuming she had any. But of course she did, because there was a luminescent sprite mark on her body to prove it.

"Watch where you step!" Jovari scolded before tripping her. She grunted, hitting the ground. Pain erupted as she rolled to break her fall. That was the first thing they'd taught her, how to fall properly, taking the brunt of her weight on the back of her shoulders and the side of her buttocks.

She swiftly lifted her sword in time to meet Jovari's downward blow. He nodded and lowered his weapon. "Good block. But next time, do it standing up. That shouldn't have happened." He tapped her right foot with the tip of his practice sword.

"Sorry," she grumbled.

He grabbed her hand and pulled her up.

A flash of movement caught her attention. Desaree sat on the grassy slope watching them. Affection welled up in her chest at the sight of her handmaiden. If it hadn't been for Des, she wouldn't have adjusted to Dragonwall's way of life as easily.

"Who's that?" she asked, squinting at the unfamiliar man approaching. Desaree stood to greet him. They shared a few hurried words as he removed something from his satchel. Desaree took it and dropped a few coins into his hand before he rushed away.

"Looks like a letter from the relay." Jovari stood beside her, watching.

"The relay?"

He gaped at her. "How do you think letters get delivered over long distances? Humans have to communicate somehow. They certainly can't like we do."

She didn't miss his use of *we*. Like the all drengr, she had telepathic abilities. She could hear and speak to every single one of them. She could even overhear private conversations between them. For months, it had been a curse more than a blessing, until Reyr helped her learn to control it.

Her chest gave a sharp pang at the thought of Reyr. She regretted their parting words. Regretted how she'd behaved. But, there was nothing she could do about it now. She pushed him from her mind.

"Who'd be sending Desaree a letter?" she wondered.

Jovari looked bemused. "I do not think it is for Desaree."

Koldis materialized beside them. "I think that's enough for one day. I am tired of watching Claire get pulverized."

"Agreed." Jovari grinned.

"Any places that need healing?" Koldis studied her, his features etched with concern.

"I'm fine," she said. "Really."

While she could heal herself using magic, she preferred to avoid that, even if it meant having bruises. They never lasted long, anyway.

"You sure? I could—"

"I'm not a fragile doll, Koldis!" she snapped, then stifled her irritation. Gods, when had he become such a mother hen? She glanced over at Desaree and added, her voice softer this time, "My ailments will all be gone by tomorrow, but thank you."

"Fine. Fine. Give me your practice sword. Off you go."

She bid them goodbye and rushed off.

Desaree met her half way, her face aglow. "A letter from the king! I checked the seal. It's from Ellia."

"Ellia...?"

"The outpost."

"Oh!" Her heart skipped a beat, excitement coursing through her.

"Ellia is occupied by both sprites and humans," Desaree explained. "It's on the southern border of the forest."

Claire took the letter, double checking the seal. It was unread. Desaree prattled on, but she hardly heard a word she said, too caught up in her racing thoughts.

King Talon had departed exactly seven days ago, which already felt like an age. If her calculations were correct, this letter would be dated approximately four days prior, which meant it had passed through many hands to reach her so quickly. Her fingers itched to break the seal.

She and the king had once shared a very strained relationship. She'd despised him, and rightfully so, after the way he had treated her. Once he had finally apologized, things between them changed.

It helped that he'd rescued her from Kane's clutches. She saw him differently now. They were finally beginning to understand one another. Sharing letters, in a way that surprised her, brought them closer.

And then...he'd left for Esterpine.

"You aren't going to read it while we walk?" Desaree asked. "Don't you want to know what it says?"

"I...I do. It's just..." She reached into her pocket and caressed the parchment.

"Ahhh." Desaree's eyes glinted. "You want to take your time with it."

"Yes, perhaps." She chewed on the chapped skin of her bottom lip.

"Oh!" Desaree stopped, grabbing her arms. Her face turned mischievous. "I think I know what you need." She dragged them through the dim corridors of the keep's lower level.

Her guards' footsteps echoed close behind. It was King Talon's doing, to keep her safe. They followed her everywhere. There was even a pair stationed outside her chambers. It seemed excessive, but she'd grown used to it.

Besides, there were always the secret passages through the castle.

They reached a deserted corridor and stopped before a closed door. "Remember when I promised to show you King Talon as he once was?"

"You mean the painting?" She'd completely forgotten about it. She glanced over her shoulder. Her guards stood at a distance, hands casually resting on their sword hilts.

"Yes. It will only take a minute." Desaree reached for the latch. It was locked. "Can you...?"

"Oh." She lifted her hand and covertly hovered over it commanding it to open. Fatigue immediately surged through her. She took a gasping breath, steadying herself. Her endurance had gotten better, but she still couldn't manage a simple cantrip without wavering. How was she supposed to kill Kane?

Desaree pulled her into an abandoned storage chamber, quickly closing the door behind them. Claire's nose tickled, then twitched. She sneezed, taking several deep breaths. The air was dusty and smelled stagnant. There were only a few small windows to let the light in, so she used more magic, fighting against her fatigue. An orb of light flooded the space with illumination.

Scrabbling claws signaled the retreat of mice. It seemed that whatever magical protections the keep used against vermin didn't extend to forgotten places like this.

"Gods," she breathed, taking in the heaping piles that loomed over them. Fabrics, bed frames, chairs and more, stacked atop each other. She looked at the nearest tower. Just a gentle poke and the whole thing would topple over.

Forgotten or not, it was a treasure trove.

"I think it is over here...somewhere." Desaree led them down an aisle. "Not many people come here. Most of the stuff is really old, cleaned out of chambers because it needed repairs, or replaced by later styles."

There was so much to look at.

"Here! This is it." Desaree took hold of an object covered in cloth, leaning against an old desk, and moved it away. "Are you ready?"

"I..."A nervous thrill skittered down her arms. "Let's see it then."

A cloud of dust came away with the cloth. They both coughed. The dust cleared.

Claire's lips parted. "It's...he's..."

She moved closer, lured by an unexplainable force. He was exactly what she'd expected. The same prominent features, the same silver eyes, the same messy hair, yet, his skin was flawless. Perfect. This was Talon as he'd once been, handsome enough to take a person's breath away. There was something else too, something captured in his expression. Her hand lifted, fingers caressing the piece. "He's so sure of himself."

There was none of that haughtiness left in him now. So much had changed. Yes, he was still confident, but for different reasons, and in a different way. He knew his own power and strength. His own abilities. None of that had to do with a handsome face.

"It is a shame, is it not?" Desaree's voice cut through the silence. "To be scarred in such a way."

"I wouldn't call it a shame," she decided, caressing his letter again. "He is exactly as he should be." Not that she would ever tell him that. He hated his scars. She knew that.

Desaree looked as though she might argue, then pressed her lips together.

"I think I've seen enough." She reached for the sheet, tossing it over the painting. "Let's go back."

Back in her chambers, Desaree rushed them through her morning routine. Breakfast was delivered just as they finished. They sat down, both breathless, both eager for a moment of respite.

She picked at her food. Talon's young face was haunting her, tangling her emotions. She took one more glance at her food, then discarded her spoon.

"That's it?" Desaree eyed her. "You've hardly eaten anything all week. Please tell me you're not trying to starve yourself."

"Desaree," she warned.

"Someone has to take care of you, if you won't take care of yourself," Desaree snapped.

Claire exhaled, squeezing her eyes shut, then said, "I'm sorry. I'm just not all that hungry."

She had a creeping suspicion as to why.

"What's wrong?" Desaree reached for her hand and squeezed.

"I don't know. I…I feel restless," she whispered. "Something inside me feels stretched thin. Sometimes it's hard to breathe." Desaree's eyes darted down to her bodice. "No, it's not from my corset—I know what you're thinking. The only thing that comes close to this feeling is the unbreakable promise I made."

"And you are sure it is not that?"

"Pretty sure, yes. This is different."

"Well," Desaree said, "Be that as it may, I insist you eat a little more. Please. Give my poor nerves a break."

Claire sighed, reaching for her spoon. Each bite of porridge went down like a heavy lump. "There. That is all I can manage. I did my best. Besides, Marcel was expecting me over an hour ago."

"Fine." Desaree stood and adjusted several ties on Claire's gown. "Good luck today."

"Thanks. I'll need it."

She left her handmaiden, shutting the door behind her. Her guards waited, ready to follow her through the keep. Still, that invisible force pulled her. She placed a hand over her stomach and breathed. Then breathed again. It was no use. Perhaps it was finally time to admit why, even if she wasn't ready to say it out loud. Gods! She missed him.

CHAPTER 2

LESSONS AND A LETTER

Kastali Dun

Claire worked with Grand Mage Marcel after breakfast. He was a squat older man, always dressed in robes of black that belted at the waist. Kind of like a medieval monk. He just needed a barrel of wine.

Their lessons were unconventional. Quests for knowledge, more than anything. They'd spent nearly two weeks focused on the vodar, working to uncover information about their magical abilities, ways to destroy them, secrets that might offer protection.

Marcel's study was half library, half common room. Tables, chairs, chaise lounges, sofas, a wall of books, and two fireplaces—one at each end of the room—lent to its inviting nature. Currently, they were sitting at one of the large work tables.

Their search had been mostly fruitless. The vodar could be banished in three ways: by fire, beheading, or stabbed with their own poisonous blade. She had yet to test the third theory, but it was the only bit of extra information they'd gained.

Marcel shuffled through several books. "Find anything useful?"

She frowned, looking down at the book in front of her. "No. Unless you count a graphic description of how they drag their souls around." She shuddered. "Looks like the only efficient way to defeat them is with *sprite fire*. I am the only one that can do that. So, yeah."

Marcel chuckled. "Is that what you're calling it now? Sprite fire?"

She smiled. "Has a nice ring to it, don't you think?"

"Indeed!" He'd learned about her sprite fire after the vodar attack. Not that they knew much about it. She couldn't even explain how she'd done it.

Marcel's magic fit neatly into a box. Hers had no such place. While mage magic was spoken as a command, using words of authority, hers had been sung in a coaxing manner. It had been instinctual, coming to her with no prior knowledge, or even training. Just like when she'd attacked Caterina, except she hadn't said a word, then.

They'd practiced, in hopes of better understanding her abilities. The first few times, it hadn't gone well. He'd replaced three sofas and a table. While her control had improved, they were still no closer to understanding why she could do it.

She pulled another book forward and began thumbing through it. The minuscule handwriting was difficult to read. An overzealous religious text about the ways wicked souls were tortured after death. She snorted, shutting it. "I hardly think a vodar wraith is going to snatch me up if I pilfer an orange." She grabbed another, but it wasn't much better. "It feels *useless*," she said at last. "How are we supposed to help the villagers in Celenore if we can't find a way to permanently destroy them? They'll just keep coming back."

That was ultimately the reason they were doing this. To help the villagers from Lormont, Osbourne, and Swinston. They had come to the king's court a little over a week ago, just before Talon's departure, begging for an audience. A child's blackened body had been placed before the king, shocking everyone including her. It brought back memories of Cyrus that were better left buried.

Soldiers had been sent to the region for protection. An outcome that pleased everyone except her. She knew that wouldn't be enough.

"We must keep looking," Marcel said. "That is what the king has asked of us."

"What if there isn't any other way?" She slumped in her chair.

"There is *always* another way, and we must find it. People are dying."

"Or you could just send me," she said.

"Oh, my dear girl, I admire your bravery. But I think we all know what the king would say about *that*." He returned his attention to his studies. End of discussion. Case closed.

Her next lesson with Mage Joren was more engaging. He was fairly young compared to the others. Despite being nearly one hundred years old, he didn't look a day past thirty. His dark skin was smooth and youthful, with a few faint creases around his eyes from smiling. His curly brown hair was cropped short. And his eyes always danced.

Joren was from Austar, known for its vast deserts.

Their lessons centered around Dragonwall's geography as it pertained to magic. She took a seat at the table in his study, folding her hands in her lap. "You look bothered," Mage Joren said, eying her as he rose from his desk.

"Hmm? Oh…" She chewed on the inside of her cheek. "I suppose."

"What's on your mind?"

She hesitated. "I know we're supposed to study Alnore today and the Woodport Rebellion, but perhaps we could focus on Celenore instead?"

Joren regarded her. "All right." He went to his cabinet and shuffled around before removing a different map than the one already on the table. It was tightly rolled. He spread it before her, using paperweights to hold the corners. "I suppose you have something specific in mind?"

"What can you tell me about Lormont, Osbourne, and Swinston?"

"Ah. I had a feeling. This has to do with the recent attacks?"

"Yes. What can you tell me about the region and its people?"

"As far as magic?" He shrugged. "The people in those villages have little, especially compared to other places we have studied. There is a mage in Lormont, but she is only of the third level."

"Oh..."

Mages used levels to distinguish their abilities. Complete fluency and control over the old language merited the highest distinction: a mage of the tenth level. Some mages found rarer types of magic, dabbling here and there in strange practices, and moved arguably higher, but no further distinction was earned.

She scanned the map and frowned. "What I don't understand, is why these three villages? Why haven't the vodar moved to other settlements? What's so special about them?"

"Well..." Joren looked thoughtful. "The king does have ties to that region."

"Ties?" She sat up straighter. "What sort of ties?"

"Queen Ahelessa, the king's own mother, was born in Osbourne. She grew up there before King Tallek discovered their mate bond. By the time King Talon was born, whole generations of her family had already come and gone. Our king visited there once. I think."

She blew out the breath she'd been holding. "But if his mother grew up in Osbourne, why the other two?"

Joren shrugged. "As a whole, the villages are isolated, making them an ideal target. The king's mother would have visited them in her youth, perhaps making friends. Likely, it made sense to attack all three, especially given how superstitious the villagers are."

"Superstitious?" She frowned, eyes darting over the map. "Is there a reason they're so isolated? It makes them harder to defend."

"That area has never been populous. The three villages make up what is called the *Three Horned Man*."

"The...what?" She snorted. "Let me guess, there's a story behind that?"

Something she'd learned from Joren: Dragonwall had stories for everything. Most were absolutely absurd, built on mythological creatures, magic, and superstition. "There is. But I wouldn't say it's all that entertaining." He took a seat across from her. "There was once a man named Muga—"

"Muga?" She repeated the name, her brow furrowed.

"—who stalked the marshes on the northern shore of the Flat River. Muga killed three men who had cheated him in a game of Rue, and with—"

"What's Rue?"

Joren sighed. "A card game. Hardly important. The three deaths weighed on his soul. As a result, Muga grew a horn of evil for each kill. These horns made him ugly. He knew none would wish to associate with him after that, so he decided to establish three villages named after the three men he killed, all in hopes of redeeming himself. With each village built, a horn was shed from his head, making him easier to look at, but he always remained beastly. Anyway, that is how the villages came to be, according to the story. Muga was forever known as the *Three Horned Man*. The only problem is, no one has ever seen him." Joren smiled. "Anyway, the story remains. The people in that region are very superstitious of Muga."

She pressed her lips together. "Well, that's silly. What about the Mage in Lormont?"

"Mage Sidra." He frowned. "Not sure she is qualified to do much, I'm afraid. Not with the vodar."

"Then Marcel was right, we really are the only ones who can help."

Joren fixed her with his gaze. "Let us hope we uncover the answers we need—and quickly."

Her final lesson of the morning was with Mage Sepia. The woman was always in good spirits. She was aging, her smooth olive complexion developing small wrinkles, her hair, once raven black, now silvered. "Today, we shall move to healing brews," she announced.

"Thank the gods!" Claire muttered, then quickly covered her mouth.

Mage Sepia's eyes sparkled in response. "Yes. Yes. I know you're impatient. You young ones always are."

After spending weeks learning how to properly chop herbs, crush beans and seeds, and turn various roots into powders, they were finally going to do something. Mage Sepia led her into the workroom. The walls were lined with shelves of bottles, ingredients, books, and all sorts of trinkets with magical qualities. The tables were covered with glass beakers and other instruments. It looked more like a scientific lab than a potions workroom. Then again, after filling her head with so many books growing up, she had preconceived notions about what a witch's workshop ought to look like. A dungeon filled with cobwebs and dust—a messy place, shelves overflowing with strange ingredients. A direct opposite to Mage Sepia's tidy space.

Sepia removed a book and they began working through a list of ingredients. The hardest part was getting the techniques correct. "Ginger essence can be tricky if not done properly," Sepia warned. "For this brew in particular, see how it recommends adding the ginger powder in small batches? If you add it all together, it will not mix correctly."

Ginger essence was a popular remedy for upset bowels, sold in apothecaries throughout Dragonwall. This particular brew seemed more like a home remedy than anything. But she didn't complain; it was still better than chopping and dicing.

She continued to stir the small cauldron over the flames, making sure it did not boil too vigorously. "Just a slight bubbling around the edges," Sepia advised. "Nothing heavier. No rolling boil. That will harm some of the ingredients."

The mixture looked mostly clear and only clouded when the contents were stirred. The smell reminded her of ginger tea.

"There now, the last and most crucial step. You must stir it in a counterclockwise direction while you speak the words of healing. This will allow you to imbue the brew with the ability to heal beyond the ingredients we have used." So...there was magic, after all. "By way of test, and without looking at the recipe, what incant might you use?"

"Um..." She wracked her brain. "*Ender mein*, I suppose?"

It's what Jovari and Koldis usually used to heal her bruises. Talon had used it once, too.

"Close, but no. You cannot use the basic cantrip here. You are not healing the brew, you are healing the person who will *drink* it. You will need an incant, at minimum, perhaps even an incantation, if you wish."

She fell silent, considering all the words she knew. "How about, *Vetal eiga afla ender mein?*"

"Hmm. It's crude, but it should work. There now, do as I have instructed."

She followed Mage Sepia's instructions, stirring counterclockwise while speaking. As the words flowed from her mouth, she felt the same uneasy prickling sensation paired with exhaustion. She clenched her teeth and hid the feeling.

The cauldron glowed light blue, just like Saffra's aegan when mixed with water. Sepia bent over it, examining the result. The color faded. "That's how you know you have succeeded," she advised. "When it cools, it will be mostly clear again. Very well done. Let's bottle it, and you can take some with you, if ever you have need of it."

Claire and Desaree met for the midday meal. She was relieved to be more than halfway through her lessons. Her eyes immediately scanned the dining hall. "Saffra's not here." Disappointment riddled her voice.

The king's prophetess had been through a lot. Who could blame her for hiding away? With Commander Daxton's memory damaged, he no longer remembered anything, not even his betrothal. That alone had hurt Saffra the deepest.

"She just needs time," Desaree said, also scanning the hall. They sat down to a full table. Claire chatted about what she'd learned that morning. As usual, it was difficult to work up an appetite, despite the rich bowl of creamy potato soup and hot bread sitting before her.

Her final lesson started after lunch.

She dreaded lessons with Mage Targa. Not just because he was insufferable, but because of his little teacher's pet. Lady Caterina had suffered under the delusion that she and King Talon would be married one day; it was an arrangement made by her traitorous father. But that wasn't the worst of it. Caterina had done horrible things to Desaree and Desaree's family. Until Verath could gather enough evidence to prove it, there was nothing they could do.

Mage Targa's lessons were on the old language, performing simple cantrips, incants, and incantations. There were five students, two male and three female, including herself. The only two she liked were Devmont and Jaycel, both much younger than her. Renna was Caterina's friend and almost just as bad.

As soon as her lesson was over, she rushed back to her chambers, greeting Desaree on the way to her desk. At last, she unfurled her letter.

Dear C,

After three days of travel, we've reached the forest. Despite our haste, we still took longer than I'd hoped. It is well past dark, making the trees ominous. I would never admit it to anyone else, but I am uncomfortable. Scared of a bunch of trees. You won't let me live that down, will you?

The envoy awaits, so I must hurry. I do not wish to say more, in case this letter is intercepted.

I cannot help but wish you were here. Perhaps we would feel less like outsiders?

As for all else, the past few days have been trying. B claims that I am unpleasant—that my temper is short. Me? A short temper? But he is right.

Nearly all our traveling companions avoid me. I

cannot blame them. I am irritable and eager to be rid of my burden. I do not envy you those weeks you traveled across the kingdom. I understand, finally, the weight of your burden.

I digress.

Hopefully, we'll be no more than a week here. I am looking forward to my return, especially to the tournament's ball. The sky can be a lonely place, as much as I love flying.

How are your lessons? I hope you are working hard? And behaving yourself?

The people here in Ellia agreed to deliver your response, should you be inclined to send one. I look forward to hearing all that transpires in my absence. Please be discreet.

Yours truly,

T

THE *T* WAS A CALLIGRAPHIC FLOURISH. She smiled, reading the letter twice more, lingering over certain words. She was hesitant to admit to it, but she also looked forward to the upcoming tournament and ball. Mostly because they were going together.

She pulled out her writing things and got to work. Once the ink was blotted and dry, she addressed and sealed it. Then she set it neatly on the desk, with instructions for Desaree to send it off tomorrow.

A loud knock startled her. "Enter," Desaree called.

A messenger boy burst in, breathless. "Pardon, my ladies." He glanced between them and held out a bit of parchment. "Lord Verath sent this—to be read immediately."

The parchment was a mere scrap, simply folded in half.

Lady Claire, the king's tower at once. More attacks in Celenore. Burn this.
—Lord V

HER STOMACH DROPPED. "MORE ATTACKS?" she whispered, glancing up to meet Desaree's gaze. She strode to the fireplace and tossed it into the flames.

More attacks could mean one thing. The soldiers were not enough to save the villagers. They needed more help—a lot more help. And King Talon wasn't around to do anything about it.

CHAPTER 3
A DANGEROUS DECISION

Kastali Dun

Claire entered King Talon's tower, Desaree on her heels. Verath sat by the fire with Jovari and Koldis. All three stood by way of greeting and dismissed the handful of tower servants lingering in the shadows.

"Wine?" Verath asked.

"Yes, please," she and Desaree said in unison, sharing a smile.

Verath busied himself at Talon's wine cabinet before handing around goblets. There was a lingering tenderness in his gaze whenever it fell on Desaree. For the first time since coming to Dragonwall, a small bit of envy crept into Claire's heart. She missed the feeling of being cared for—loved the way Verath appeared to care for Desaree.

Once settled around the fireplace, Verath said, "Thank you for making yourself available. We received a letter from the relay, expedited." He fiddled with a bit of folded parchment. "It's from Celenore, dated two days ago. As you know, King Talon sent reinforcements to Lormont, Osbourne, and Swinston. Unfortunately, the soldiers and mages did not last the night."

"What?!" She leaned forward. "You're...you're sure? All of them?"

"Unfortunately."

"What happened?"

"Their presence was detected. As soon as darkness fell, the vodar swept in and annihilated them. The villagers write that their screams did not last long."

"How many did Talon send?"

"*King* Talon sent two hundred—"

"Two hundred?!" Her hand went to her stomach. "Two..." There wasn't enough air in the room.

"—split between three villages. They were accompanied by six mages of the seventh and eighth levels from the college. None survived."

"And..." She swallowed. "The villagers?"

"The villagers remain undefended. Deaths of their women and children continue each night."

"How dare he?" she seethed. That Kane would involve innocents in his petty quest for power left her shaking. "May I see the letter?"

Verath handed it over. Desaree sat beside her, face pale, lips pressed into a tight line. She read through the contents. There wasn't much else beyond what he had said. The final lines were a desperate plea. She chewed on the inside of her cheek. "They have called for more aid." She handed it to Desaree who quickly glanced through it. "Do we have more to send?"

"Our previous reinforcements were no match. But...we do have more to send. Much more. King Talon's forces are vast." Verath stood abruptly and flicked his fingers. "Come with me."

They followed, Jovari and Koldis trailing behind.

Verath led them to the war room. She'd been here once before, not too long ago, when she had requested Talon make Desaree her handmaiden. It looked no different than it did before.

A large table took up the center, a huge map stretched across it. There were pieces on the map—figurines—similar to those on a chessboard.

Verath ushered them over to a section of the map outlining Celenore, one of Dragonwall's twenty dragondoms. He pointed at a cluster of figurines—soldiers, each holding a sword in one hand and a shield in the other. They were no taller than the length of her finger.

"Each piece represents a company of one hundred," he explained. "As you can see, we have approximately three hundred within twenty leagues. They can be assembled in...two, maybe three days."

"But," Koldis added, "we would need more mages to flank them."

"Yes. True." Verath nodded, turning back to her. "You see? There are options." He slid each piece into place. "What do you think? Shall we send what we have?"

"You're asking *me*?" Her voice took on an unusually high pitch. "Didn't Talon leave one of you in charge?"

"He left Verath in charge," Jovari said, crossing his arms.

"But, technically speaking, Lady Claire, you are the highest ranking individual in the king's absence. Therefore, I thought it prudent to seek your advice. What say you?"

She opened and closed her mouth. "It's...it's hopeless." Her eyes darted over the pieces on the map. "What's the point? If I tell you to send them, then I'm sending three hundred men to their deaths. It's absurd, you ought to know that."

Given Verath's expression, he *did* know. Perhaps he merely wanted to hear her say it. "That may be true," he said. "Have you and Marcel discovered any other way to defeat them?"

Her cheeks flushed with embarrassment. "Sprite fire. It's...it's the only reliable way for this many of them."

"I see." Verath turned to Jovari and Koldis. "That settles it. You will be ready to leave at dawn?" They nodded. "Good. Make sure you select wisely from the fort's drengr."

"Wait!" She stepped forward, looking between them until her gaze settled on Verath. "You...you're sending *them*?"

"I am. They will do better than any of our mages at present, and especially better than the villagers."

"Give us some credit, Claire." Koldis pinned her with his gaze. "We fought the vodar well enough before."

"But not properly!" She turned to Verath. "What about me? You'd send them before considering me?" It stung that he hadn't factored that in. "I can destroy them better than any of you."

Verath hesitated. "You really think you could destroy them?"

"You doubt me?" She stared at him, a silent challenge. "I didn't have trouble when they attacked this tower, did I? Do you need me to prove it?"

Before he could answer, words flowed from her mouth. The sprite language was like liquid sugar against her tongue. It took but a single sentence for the padded chair beside Verath to burst into green flames.

"Gods above!" He jumped aside, cursing.

Jovari shot forward, muttering a cantrip that sent the chair sliding across the room and into the corner. A moment later, and it would have engulfed the table and map. The flames smoldered into nothing, leaving behind a pile of ash.

She crossed her arms. "Proof enough?"

"Impressive." Verath's brows lifted. "Perhaps I was wrong. You may yet do better than Jovari and Koldis."

She crossed her arms. "Then you'll send me?"

"No, Claire!" Desaree spoke for the first time, taking hold of her arm. "You wouldn't *dare*! You wouldn't dare abandon the keep's protection with King Talon away. He made you promise to—"

"Desaree!" Verath gave a low warning growl.

Desaree looked up at him, defiance written on her features. "Well, it's true. She promised."

"Desaree *is* right," Jovari said, affording Desaree a grin by way of apology.

"Oh, great. Not you too." Claire glowered at him.

Jovari shrugged. "The king charged us with guarding you above all else. You *are* safest in the keep."

"That's not necessarily true. The castle may be safe, but two shields are better than one." She looked at Verath. "No offense."

He shrugged. "None taken."

"Be that as it may," Jovari said. "King Talon will murder us."

"Only if he finds out," Koldis added, offering a wicked grin. "And if he does, we tell him it was Claire's idea. She's the only one here he won't burn to a crisp."

"Wait a minute...." Her jaw dropped. "You...you guys planned this whole thing, didn't you? You knew Talon would be angrier with you than with me." They glanced at each other. "You knew sending more soldiers wasn't an option. You brought me here just to get me riled up, just so that I would suggest going myself! You...you *manipulated* me."

She had to give them credit. It was smoothly done.

Koldis said to Verath, "I told you she would figure it out," then winked at her.

"Unbelievable!" she muttered.

"All right. Fine. You caught me." Verath shrugged. "The hope is that King Talon will not find out until after you return. And if you hurry, you will be back before him."

She glanced down at the map. "How long will it take us to get there?"

"If we fly quickly," Koldis said, "two days. Two days there and two days back. Plus however long it will take to actually eliminate the wraiths. It will be risky. King Talon hopes to return in a week."

Already, ideas were swarming her mind. She strode from the room, making them follow after her. They resumed their seats around the fire. She lifted her goblet, if only to wet her dry throat at the sudden idea of leaving. "Do any of you have a plan yet? Since you clearly orchestrated all this?"

"No plan," Jovari said. "We'll need your assistance on that matter. You understand your magic far better than we do."

"Right. And what about the fort's drengr? Will they accompany us?"

"Aye," Koldis said, "to assist us and keep you safe in the process."

"How many?"

"At least twenty?" Verath looked at the others for confirmation. They nodded.

"It's risky," she said at last. "But worth a try."

These people needed her. How could she sit back and do nothing while they died? Even if it did mean breaking her promise to Talon. Desaree was right on that front. But...these people were Talon's people. These villages were once his mother's home. She couldn't leave them to fate.

What was more, she felt partly responsible for what was happening—not that she voiced this. She had angered Kane not once, but twice. Her coming to Dragonwall had upset all of his plans. He was doing this to rile her as much as Talon. To send a message. Her guilt brought an all-too-familiar voice into her mind.

You cannot hold yourself accountable for Kane's actions, Cyrus said. *His choices are his own, not yours.*

He was right, but knowing it didn't make it easier. She exhaled, perhaps feeling a little better. Cyrus had an uncanny way of knowing when she needed him the most. And he also showed himself at the most random times, complements of the Gift he'd given her. Implanting his soul into her very being. An act that was as simple as sharing a dying kiss, which he'd done back on her lawn the first time she'd ever faced the vodar.

For that reason alone, she owed it to Cyrus to kill these things. To seek vengeance for his death. His voice was the reminder she needed.

"I can see that you are weighing your options." Verath broke the silence. "That's good. You would be a fool to agree without consideration. This could be dangerous for everyone. I cannot promise your safety."

She barked a laugh. "I've been in danger ever since setting foot in Dragonwall. But, if we succeed, we will gain the upper hand."

"I should hope so." Verath leaned back to regard her.

"Then it's worth it. Completely worth it." A thrill shot through her. The idea of dealing Kane a setback, especially after all he'd done. But more thrilling was the idea of flying off on an adventure. Of doing something proactive. She missed flying. She missed the freedom of it. The wind in her hair...

"Is it proper, though?" Desaree blurted, looking for another excuse to keep her safe. "Only mates fly with their drengr. How are you planning to get her there?"

"Desaree," Claire chided. "I'll be all right. Really. I'll be careful."

"Ah...yes," Koldis said. "About that. I might have been against it once, but I've come around. This is important. People's lives are at stake. Besides, we plan to keep out of sight from the general public. No one will know she's left the keep."

"We will leave before dawn," Jovari added.

"And the villagers?" Desaree asked. "What will they think when they see her sweep in on the back of a dragon?"

"Perhaps we can keep her hidden from them, too. I cannot be sure how we will go about it, but our secrecy will be a top priority."

"I..." Desaree fumbled with a stray thread on her sleeve. Apparently she had no more protests. "Fine."

"Claire?" Verath pinned her with his gaze. "Let us have your answer, then."

Claire's stomach somersaulted. Desaree's jaw was clenched. She hated going against her handmaiden's wishes. Desaree took excellent care of her, and *how* was she repaying that? By placing herself in danger. When Desaree's eyes did not meet hers, she turned away and said, "I'll do it."

"Good." Verath sounded relieved. "Desaree will help you pack. Bring only what you need. You must fly far and with great haste."

AFTER DINNER, she removed her Osprey hiking backpack from beneath her bed. She hadn't used it since traveling across Dragonwall. The moment she pulled it out, memories began flooding back. So much had happened since finding Cyrus.

She sighed, glancing over everything she removed. As much as she wanted to go down memory lane—looking at old items like her iPhone with its dead battery—she didn't have the time. Nor did she want to confront the emotions that bubbled to the surface whenever she thought about her parents. Were they searching for her, even despite the note she'd left them?

Desaree was unusually quiet, helping her pack. It hurt to see her upset. "I'm the only one who can do this, Des. There is no other way."

Desaree rounded on her. "Oh? Is that how you're justifying it? It's bad enough that you have an asarlaí sorcerer to defeat. But now, you decide to go traipsing across—"

"Flying, not traipsing."

"Gods above!" Desaree tossed a tunic across the room. "*Big* difference! Look, Claire, King Talon's problems are not yours to solve."

"While that's true, I'm not going to sit back and let innocent people die if there's something I can do to help."

Desaree clenched her jaw, then exhaled. "I know. It's just...I have a bad feeling."

"I'll be careful. I promise." It meant a great deal that someone cared enough about her to be worried.

After Desaree retired for the night, she gravitated towards the entryway. A box sat on the decorative table near the door. It had been a week since Talon had given it to her, and yet, she hadn't worked up the courage to open it.

There is no need to be afraid. The sword is as much a part of you as I am...

Her chest tightened, hearing Cyrus's voice. "What if I'm not ready?" she asked, her voice a raw whisper. "What if I'm not able to bear its weight?"

Its weight is as it ought to be. You will bear it just as you have borne many things, just as you bear me. It is time...

Her fingers trailed the lid. "I only hope I can wield it as honorably as you did."

In all the time I have known you, Claire, you have never disappointed me. That will never change...

"Thank you," she whispered, blinking to clear her vision. She lifted the lid. Cyrus's sword rested on folds of silk, glittering up at her in its scabbard. The pearls that decorated both the scabbard and the cross-guard held her gaze. How ironic that such a lethal weapon could be so beautiful. She caressed the large pearl that sat in the pommel—Leeana's bonding jewel.

Blowing out a breath, she lifted the sverak from its box. Her mind went back to the night she had rescued Cyrus. Suddenly she was at the farm again, standing in her living room, studying Cyrus's belongings. Her heart tightened. She blinked away the tears that came. Wrapping her hand around the sword's grip, she drew it. The blade rubbed against the scabbard before breaking free. She held it up into the light, admiring it for what it was.

There. You see? You have done it...

Something akin to wonder washed over her. It wasn't the first time she'd held it, but this time it was different. It was hers.

Desaree woke her an hour before dawn, helping her dress in a tunic and pants. She also wore a sturdy pair of boots, a pair of leather gloves, a heavy woolen cloak, and a fur-lined hat.

"It isn't very elegant, is it?" she said, eying the hat in her reflection.

"Rightly so. I do not know how riders tolerate them. No one will see your beautiful hair." A six-stranded plait traveled over the top of her scalp and down her back. "Now, I have only packed you two changes of clothes, so treat them gently. I'll not have you looking like a pauper."

"I'll do my best to make you proud." Claire's throat tightened. Their argument seemed all but forgotten.

As they gathered up the remainder of her belongings, Desaree turned to her. "I wanted to apologize for my behavior last night. I shouldn't have made things harder. Your burden is already hard enough. I...I was just scared." Her throat bobbed. "I still am."

"Oh, Des!" She flung her arms around Desaree's neck. "It will be all right, you'll see." Their hug was exactly what she needed.

They departed for the keep's lower level, making their way through darkened corridors. When they arrived, Saffra stood by, waiting beside Talon's shields. Saffra rushed over and hugged her before whispering, "I hope you did not think you would leave without saying goodbye!" Then Saffra squeezed her tighter and added, "Desaree wrote me a note last night. I wanted to be here to see you off."

"Thank you." She gave Saffra's shoulders a final squeeze before stepping away. "I'll be careful."

"She'll have no choice but to be careful," Verath said, stepping up beside them. "Claire? Are you ready?" She nodded, too emotional to speak. "Good. You will be flying with Koldis first. They drew straws."

She glanced at Koldis, searching his face. There was no disgust there. In fact, he was grinning. *This will be my first time flying with someone,* he said in her mind. *For what it's worth, I am glad that it is you.*

"I'm honored." She gave him a friendly smile before turning back to the others.

"It's time." Verath's voice held a sense of urgency. He stepped away.

She said a few more rushed goodbyes, hugging Saffra and Desaree again. "Take care of each other," she whispered. "And when I get back," she added so that no one else heard, "we will explore the cave beneath the keep. I want to figure out how to open that door!" Her offer brightened their expressions. "In the meantime, I give you leave to explore it without me. See what you can find." They both nodded.

A throat cleared behind them. It was time to go. She went to Koldis. He and Jovari had already transformed. She stared at them, mesmerized by the way the torchlight sparkled upon their scales. In the darkness, they looked nearly as black as Talon.

Koldis wore a padded leather harness, though she had no idea how it had gotten there. Moving quickly, she made sure she had a strong hold on her backpack, then she climbed up on his forearm and used the straps to pull herself up. The harness sat in the dip of his neck where his shoulder joints came together. She strapped her pack to the ties behind her so it rested atop the curve of his body.

"*I'm ready.*" She said the words so that all three shields heard her.

Koldis roared, letting his bellow echo from the walls of Kastali Dun's keep. Every slumbering patron probably jolted from their beds, but she didn't care. She had just enough time to smile and wave at the three bodies silhouetted against the torchlight before Koldis jumped. Her stomach dropped. His emerald green scales rippled as the muscles beneath them contracted. There was a rush of wind and a heaviness that forced her head to drop. She looked around to find the ground falling away. The next thing she knew, they were airborne.

CHAPTER 4
FLYING NORTH

Claire shrieked as Koldis swerved. A draconic rumble vibrated against her legs. *"Just avoiding the seagulls."*

"Seagulls?!" she demanded. "What seagulls?!"

"You know, the ones over... Oh, they must have flown off."

She smacked his scales, instantly regretting it. She rubbed the palm of her hand. *"Seriously?!"*

"Apologies. I will warn you next time. If I see any seagulls, I mean."

She rolled her eyes—

Her stomach jumped into her throat. She was weightless for several heartbeats. *"Koldis!"*

"Sorry. Just had to change altitude."

"Yeah, right! You're doing it on purpose!"

There was a brief hesitation. *"Maybe just a little. If you stopped cawing like a bird about it, I'd be less tempted."*

"Ugh, that's enough! Wipe that smugness out of your voice."

"Yes, my lady. At once."

"I'm serious! I'll jump off your back if you don't warn me next time. And you'll have to come catch me. Or explain to Talon how you're responsible for me splatting all over the ground."

He grumbled, perhaps a laugh. *"Tighten the harness around your legs. You're not going to fall off."*

She did as he said, pulling the belts tighter and adjusting the fastenings.

Hours had come and gone since departing Fort Kastali. The sun was well into the sky, blanketing the land in a glow like spun gold. She inhaled, letting the cool autumn air sting her nose. She would have frozen to death in the sky were it not for the furnace of scales beneath her. Koldis was a living, breathing heat radiator.

"Banking right." Koldis broke her train of thought. She tightened her grip on the harness just in time. He dropped his right wingtip and the ground below tilted. Her stomach lurched. She soon found herself sideways in the air. They adjusted their direction and Koldis straightened out.

A smile teased her lips. *"At least you warned me this time."*

"You threatened to jump off my back if—"

"Yes, yes. I was just teasing-arrahhh!" Her words ended in another screech as her stomach flew to the top of her ribcage. Koldis abruptly dropped ten feet. She groaned, trying to shake the sudden onset of nausea. *"Okay! I get it! No teasing. But it's not like you're any better. That was unfair and you know it."*

"Fine. Fine. I shall warn you next time," he said, his voice laced with smug amusement.

"Gee...thanks."

Beneath them, the northern coastline of Galadhal sailed by. The Scattered Islands were to their left, clusters of land sprinkled like freckles over the water. The Eigaden Peninsula was to their right, with its vast sprawling plains covered in long amber grass.

They were heading north, to the marshes where the Flat River drained into the sea.

"Dropping altitude," Koldis said, gradually angling his body downward. He performed this maneuver smoothly, which told her all she needed to know.

As their angle changed, she had a direct line of sight to the ground. Her heart pounded, watching it approach. Blood rushed to her face. It was hard to keep from smiling, from spreading her arms as if she were riding the wind.

"*How did I do?*" Koldis asked, flattening out.

"*Much better this time. Thank you.*"

"*As my lady commands.*"

"*Shut up.*"

She loved flying. She'd missed it so much. But it was more than flying that boosted her mood. She was glad to be doing something proactive. To be useful and needed. Best of all, she was on her way to destroy the creatures that had killed Cyrus.

Twenty of Fort Kastali's pairs flew with them, making two tightly packed V-formations around her. They moved in sync. Every time Koldis changed his position, they followed.

Each drengr was unique, with scales that glistened in the sun. Their colorful hues ranged from deep purple to red, spanning the spectrum. Like all dragons, they had unique characteristics that set them apart. Traits passed down from their ancient clans, like the shape of their tail, or the types of spikes upon their head.

Jovari flew directly in front of her with his group. She could easily make out his clubbed tail. Others were tipped with long spikes or barbs. She wouldn't want to be on the receiving end of *any* dragon's tail.

She glanced over her shoulder at the pairs behind her. There were ten. "*Koldis?*"

"*Yeees?*" That smug voice again.

"*I have a question.*"

"*Of course you do.*"

"*Do the drengr always fly in a V-formation? Or are there different patterns?*"

"*We almost always fly in a V-formation of some variation. Like a tight V or a loose V, unless we are in battle, in which case the formation changes. For flying like this, long distances at a moderate pace, a loose V is best.*"

"*So, like geese?*"

"*Ha!*" His chest rumbled. "*Yes. Like geese. It is the most aerody-namically efficient. Those in the lead make it easier for those behind,*" *creating lift. Notice the formation in front of us? Each pair sits a little lower in the sky than the pair before them.*" He paused. "*Do you know why the leader of a formation rides in the front?*"

"*He's got the hardest path to carve?*"

"*Exactly.*"

She smiled. "*What about each of the pairs? Do they get to choose their position in the formation? Is it a rank thing?*"

"*At times. Not today. Watch everyone in Jovari's wing. Watch closely.*"

"*Why is it called a wing?*"

"*Well, when a dragon's wing extends, it forms a V shape. See?*" Koldis turned to regard his own right wing. She did the same, looking at the wing joint and how the bones angled away from it. "*Anyway, I would have thought that was straightforward.*"

"*Straightforward?*" She snorted. "*Maybe for a dragon.*"

"*Maybe so. As I was saying, if you look at the wing in front of us, watch their movements.*"

She studied them. "*What am I watching for, exactly?*"

"*Patience...*"

It took nearly ten minutes before she spotted it. The pairs directly behind Jovari dropped out of the flight pattern and went to the back of the formation. After that, the positions rotated, everyone moving forward by one.

"*They take turns,*" she realized. "*But, what about Jovari? He isn't switching. Won't he get tired?*"

"*It takes more than a little flying to fatigue him. Besides, he isn't carrying anyone.*"

"*But you are. You're carrying me and you haven't rotated. Aren't you tired?*"

"*Not one bit. You know, I was admittedly anxious to carry you. Now that we are in the sky together, I am thrilled to have a companion.*"

Her chest exploded with warmth.

"*We will land soon so that you might stretch your legs,*" he added. "*Is that favorable, my lady?*"

"*I...of course. Yes. And stop calling me that. You never do.*"

She sensed his wicked grin, but he didn't say anymore.

"There is a copse of trees ahead." Koldis broadcasted his statement to the entire company. *"Prepare to land."*

"We follow," came the response of twenty voices. She flinched as each struck at once. But she did not close her mind. As long as they kept their voices to a minimum, she'd be okay. The headaches only came if the talking grew excessive.

As one, both wings angled downward. Her stomach tightened as the ground drew closer. Then it rushed right up beneath them and she jolted forward. They landed beside a cluster of trees. They looked much larger from the ground. She had to blink several times to adjust to the change in perspective.

Around her, riders dismounted and drengr changed form. Being on land was a relief. She almost wished they might linger. Already, a dull ache was forming in her thighs. She'd forgotten how sore flying made her. At least this time she had a harness.

Koldis gave everyone a few minutes to tend to their needs before calling everyone to attention. "Form up," he ordered. The reaction was instant. "Thank you," he said, gazing at them. "I'm sure you are wondering why we're here. We hand-selected you because this is a highly complex, highly important mission, and you're a damned good bunch." His praise left some of them grinning, as if they shared a secret knowledge of past adventures.

She studied her companions. Nearly all appeared young, except for three pairs. Their skin showed signs of aging, their hair riddled with streaks of gray. One pair looked old enough to be grandparents.

Since arriving in Kastali Dun, there had been few opportunities to interact with the drengr and riders of Fort Kastali. They did not often visit the keep, and when they did, she was usually tied up with lessons. Riders wore their hair similar to hers, in braids with caps over their heads, or cropped short to eliminate the fuss altogether. She couldn't help but envy them as she wondered what their lives were like.

"Now then," Koldis was saying. "I would like to introduce you to Lady Claire. You've heard of her, I'm sure? Good. Claire, allow me to introduce our companions for this mission."

She plastered on a smile. "Right. Uhm. Nice to meet you all."

Koldis began naming pairs. There was Briza and Astrid, Faedrol and Hannah, Gradyr and Leila, Nokin and Serena, Til and Darcie, Hiondel and Lily, Celill and Eva... Oh, gods! How was she going to remember everyone? Forty names in one go was a big ask, but she was determined to know everyone as soon as possible. Especially if these people were here to keep her safe.

"Now, on to our mission," Koldis said. She almost sagged with relief. Before he went on, everyone was required to swear an oath of secrecy.

"*Minn verger ordun ut yaas. Elle heiit et hirla luth.*" Words in the old language that made her skin brake out in goosebumps, which roughly translated to, "My word of honor is yours. I pledge to uphold it."

Then, Jovari and Koldis took turns explaining their mission.

"It is a matter of honor that you never mention Lady Claire's involvement. Everyone in Dragonwall must believe—and go on believing—that she is comfortably situated in the capital under Lord Verath's protection."

If Kane knew she'd left the keep, he was sure to come after her.

"She's here because she is the only person capable of vanquishing the vodar. *Permanently.*" Her companions shared confused looks. "Beheading a wraith will only send it back to the underworld, where it can be summoned again. She's found a way to keep that from happening."

Vithran, one of the younger drengr, stepped forward. "Forgive my ignorance, my lords. How do we plan to keep Lady Claire's presence a secret? The villagers will see her once we arrive."

"We will keep her presence hidden, allowing her to act from afar. I know it's not the best answer, but we must trust Lady Claire and her plan."

Her plan? They'd asked for her help. Now they made it sound like it was entirely up to her.

After a painfully long silence, she realized they were waiting for her to say something. She cleared her throat. "Uhm. I think I have a solution, but it still needs work." She explained what she had in mind. Talking about it helped solidify her ideas, until she felt more confident about what they would accomplish. "If all goes well," she finished, "I will remain in the sky, overlooking the villages, hidden by darkness. The villagers will never see me. They will only see the product of my accomplishments."

Elaine, Ardoweth's Rider, stepped forward. "Pardon, my lady, but how will you know what is happening if you're up in the sky? Even with a rider present, yelling information back and forth seems unreliable."

"We will use direct communication. The information will be relayed to me telepathically. You will speak to me as you speak to each other."

No one said a word. They merely gaped at her.

"Truly?" Hiondel stepped forward. "But that's...impossible."

She swallowed. "It might seem so. But I possess a unique ability to communicate with all of you."

Hiondel's eyes widened.

She'd once hated her ability. Now, she took secret pleasure in telling others simply to see their surprise. After her kidnapping, Talon had done what he could to discourage the rumor, that she'd somehow used telepathy to aid in her rescue. If information like that fell into the wrong hands, it could be bad.

Her companions began to mutter, sharing looks of doubt and confusion. Jovari and Koldis had removed themselves, stepping back behind her. Their position was clear—she was to handle this on her own.

She caught a smirk of amusement from Koldis and offered him a glare in return.

"Listen!" she said, raising her voice. "I know it sounds incomprehensible, but yes, I can hear you speaking—if you address me."

"Impossible." Celill stepped forward. "You aren't a drengr."

"Try it." She flashed him a daring grin. "All of you." She regretted her words almost immediately as twenty voices bombarded her, all asking the same thing.

"*Yes, I heard all of you,*" she said to twenty minds at once.

Heads jerked. Eyes widened. Voices swore.

"Look," Koldis said, *finally* stepping forward. "Claire's plan is the best we have. Yes, you will have to speak directly with her, but I'm confident she can do what she claims."

She lifted her chin.

"Now, we must make haste. We will stop sparingly. Riders, sleep in the sky." He straightened, making his full height more apparent. "Drengr, are you with us? Riders?"

"We are with you!" they cried.

She grinned. Within minutes, the drengr transformed, riders remounted, and everyone returned to the sky. She found herself comfortably seated in her harness.

She reached into the pocket of her cloak and removed some of the dried meat rations one of the riders had slipped her. There hadn't been time for breakfast, and she wouldn't have wanted it anyway. She was too anxious.

Giving the jerky a try, she bit off a hunk and chewed. It was softer than she expected. A peppery spice gave it a kick that soon made it addicting. She found herself demolishing the three slices, wanting more.

"*I didn't think to bring any food,*" she admitted to Koldis. "*Should I have?*" Even though they'd likely hunt on their journey.

"*You knew this was a long journey, yet you brought no food?*"

"*I...I don't recall packing any.*" She scowled.

"*Didn't Desaree help you pack? Did you check your bag?*"

"*I...no.*" Her cheeks flushed hot. Now that she thought of it, she'd let Desaree do most of the work. Her chest tightened. Desaree was meticulous.

"*No need to fret. Our riders brought more food than they need. Besides, we will catch plenty of game.*" He paused before adding more smugly, "*You think we would let you starve, my lady?*"

"*No,*" she said all too quickly. "*Now, help me learn their names.*"

They spent the next several hours going over each pair. Koldis quizzed her relentlessly. He pointed out a drengr or rider, describing a few characteristics like the color of scales or neck spikes or hair. She was responsible for their names. It helped the time pass faster.

Koldis also taught her the wing formation positions in the process. *"That rider behind me in third—what's her name?"*

"That's Rachel. Her mate is Odrick."

"Good."

Third position was directly to the back right of first, which was the point of the V. Second was back left. Even numbers were to the left, while odd numbers were to the right. It made identifying the drengr and their riders even easier.

THEY STOPPED mid-afternoon for a quick meal. She was relieved to find a store of food, which Desaree had placed in the front pocket of her pack. Meat jerky, two dense loaves of bread in a funny flat shape—"We call them rounds," Koldis said when he saw her eying them—and a bundle of dried fruit wrapped.

Most of the drengr preferred their dragon forms when traveling; they hadn't bothered to transform. But Koldis had shifted to keep her company. She eyed the loaves he called rounds, turning one over in her hands.

"They are dense for a reason. A little goes a long way. If I'm not mistaken, those there were made by Thomas. You'll know because the taste is a little sour, and he puts sunflower seeds in the dough."

"I take it that's a good thing?"

"You will be glad you have them, believe me." He winked and walked away.

She wrapped the bread back in its cloth, then she rummaged around deeper. Near the bottom she found a couple of honey cakes, and at the very bottom, something in a silken fabric. A smile spread across her face. A drawstring bag of candy. "Oh, Des! Bless you!" she whispered, eying the toffees inside. Even though Desaree had been frustrated with her, she had still been considerate. That left her feeling warm all over.

CHAPTER 5
A RARE UNICORN

The Gable Forest

Jeanine stood in the shadows, peering through an overgrowth of lush foliage, utterly bewitched. Right in the middle of the clearing, a black unicorn, possibly the rarest creature of all, grazed on a patch of grass. She'd seen plenty of white unicorns, but never one like this.

She watched, afraid to breathe. It was the second time she'd encountered him. The first, he'd bolted before she got more than a glimpse.

"If you stare long enough, he might humor you out of boredom." She jumped, cursing under her breath.

The unicorn's ears pricked, head lifting in her direction. She didn't move—didn't blink. After a few long moments, he returned to his grazing.

"Are you mad?!" she hissed, rounding on Prince Feowen. He was cloaked in shadow behind her. "What are you doing?!"

Two days. She hadn't seen him for two days, and he chose now, of all times, to make an appearance.

"Trying to help, obviously."

"You? Help?" She narrowed her eyes before turning back to the clearing. "If by *help* you mean scare it away, then sure, you're helping a lot."

"Just watch." He stepped forward, wicked grin blazing, and parted the foliage before him.

As he stepped out, the unicorn's head swung in his direction, but did not bolt. She cursed Feowen under her breath. He held out his hand, his movements slow and deliberate. "Gehtalla...gehtalla..." The unicorn's ears pricked. "Taventah vah'lia. Gehtalla... gehtalla..."

She watched, unblinking. The creature lifted his head higher and acknowledged Feowen with a loud snort, like a horse, but did not move away.

Feowen glanced in her direction, his expression triumphant. The unicorn sniffed his fingers with mild interest before lowering his head to graze again. He brushed his fingers over the creature's neck, moving cautiously before petting it with both hands.

A smile came unbidden to her lips. Was it truly that easy? It shouldn't have surprised her. Feowen was good at nearly everything. Why not this?

He continued to stroke the creature. "I believe he will let you pet him now." His voice was a low murmur. The unicorn merely shifted to enjoy a new swath of grass. "He already knows you are hiding. Come here."

She pushed the foliage aside and stepped into the clearing. It was done less gracefully than the prince, with a good deal more noise. The unicorn had already gone back to snacking, but his left ear swiveled in her direction. She crept over.

"Here—" Without invitation, Feowen grabbed her hand and moved it forward. "Let him sniff you first."

The prince's hand was warm against hers. She dared not move. The unicorn lifted his head and sniffed her fingers before turning his attention to her palm. She giggled, the sound slipping from her lips before she could stop it. The whiskers and hairs around his mouth tickled.

"There. See?" Greeting finished, Feowen guided her hand to the creature's coat, inviting her to copy him. He began along the neck, stroking the unicorn's hide with slow, languid movements.

She did the same and gasped. "He's softer than a horse!" The sleek coat was more velvety than anything she had ever touched. Like an expensive fabric from her childhood days, back when she and her mother lived in Lincastle. That felt like an age ago—a dream more than a memory.

"Does he have a name?" she whispered.

"We may never know what he calls himself, nor what other unicorns call him. But to us, he is known as Tourmaline."

"Tourmaline," she whispered, keeping her voice gentle.

Tourmaline lifted his head and nudged her, as if recognizing the sound of his own name. Then he gave them a snicker of farewell and plodded away, disappearing into the underbrush, leaving them alone in the forest. She blinked after him.

There and gone.

She exhaled, as if she could breathe again. "So…Tourmaline. As in black tourmaline gemstones?"

Feowen smiled. "Exactly. Do not ask me who came up with it."

"Who says I was going to ask?" She lifted an eyebrow.

"Insightful guess? I'm quite certain you were about to ask."

"You think you've figured me out, *Prince Feowen*. I assure you, that is not the case."

"Yet—" A mischievous grin spread across his face. "Not the case *yet*. I am determined to make it so."

There was truth to his words. He had made it obvious from the start that he was determined to make sense of her. To figure her out.

Shortly after arriving in Esterpine, she had caught him spying on her. It wasn't until he offered to train her that she discovered there were no boundaries to his probing questions. He had asked about everything from what her home life had been like in Kaljah, to her aspirations, to questions about human culture, traditions, and beliefs. Humans intrigued and even baffled him.

Yet, she got a deeper sense that she alone confused him above all else.

"Well," she said, "you won't understand me better if you avoid me. It's been two days. Where have you been?"

"I knew you would ask that too," he said. "So, I have come up with a well-rehearsed explanation."

"Oh? The truth? Or something you made up?" She took a seat in the grass, pulling a few blades to twirl around her fingers. Sunlight was difficult to come by here. She cherished it on the rare occasions when she found it.

"You doubt my truthfulness?" He came to crouch before her, his gaze intent on hers. "We sprites do not lie, remember?"

"Yes, you ooze honesty by speaking in riddles. Half the time I can't make sense of what you're saying. I suppose you aren't so bad, but your sister..."

Princess Taylynn was notoriously cryptic. It was said she was a great sprite prophetess, speaking to the trees, learning many things before they happened. Maybe that explained it.

She and Taylynn had only interacted a handful of times, and each left her more confused than the last.

"Well, I shall be plain then," Feowen said. "Even if I was sworn to secrecy."

Usually there were weapons between them, and a sparring ring. Sitting this close, with his full attention upon her, was...a bit much. She could make out the tiny details of his eyes—flecks like glitter within the depths of them. His long lashes. The arching shape of his eyebrows, not a blue hair out of place. His lips. The smoothness of his skin.

She looked down at the grass in her fingers to avoid him. "If it's secrecy you seek—you'd best not tell me."

"But circumstances have changed. Now you're involved, so there is no more hiding it."

She stared at him. "You realize you're not making any sense... right?"

He grinned. "Let me be plain. Dragonwall's king has come to Esterpine."

The sounds around her faded. Dragonwall's king? Here? Was this a joke? Was he toying with her?

"We had hoped to hide his coming. My mother implemented a number of measures. She wanted to be discreet until negotiations were well underway. That did not... Anyway, he wishes to meet you, so we can hide it no longer."

"What?!" She all but choked. "Wait, you're serious? And just to make sure I understand you correctly, by Dragonwall's king, you mean King Talon the Black?"

"I should have thought it obvious."

"I... There must be some mistake." She blinked.

"No mistake. He is here."

A rough laugh fell from her lips. "So, I guess Tourmaline is no longer the rarest creature in the forest?"

Feowen's eyebrows drew together. Then a smile split his lips and he laughed. The sound sent warm shivers through her. Birds around them erupted into song. She simply stared, studying the way his face lit up, the dimples in his cheeks, his frustratingly perfect teeth. There were times he seemed human, and then there were times like this...

"Rare. King Talon. Yes. I suppose so. So when you meet him, do not lurk in the shadows as you did with Tourmaline. Hmm?"

"Meet him? You...you *were* being serious?" Her heart pounded. "But...why would he want to meet me? I'm just...just..."

"Is it not obvious?"

"Why would it be? I'm no one. I have no rank, no titles. I cannot possibly think of a reason."

He snorted. "Humans..."

"What is *that* supposed to mean?!" She jumped to her feet, glancing about, trying to make sense of things. To make sense of this moment. The king—here!

Feowen stood up after her. "It means... Oh, never mind! I would hate to deprive you of the opportunity to figure it out. Now come. We cannot keep him waiting."

Her jaw dropped, all sense of modesty abandoned. "Like...like right now? Why didn't you say so before?! And, you're not going to tell me *why* he wants to meet me?"

He merely smirked and slipped into the forest.

"This isn't a game, Feowen!" She glared in his direction. When he didn't answer, she was forced to follow after him.

It took nearly twenty minutes to reach Esterpine. During that time, Feowen updated her on everything that had happened with King Talon's visit. The king and a party of drengr were escorted to Esterpine. They had entered the city in the dead of night. Their party was given lodging in the Crystal Palace with the queen. This was all done in an effort to keep them out of sight. Even still, the rumor had apparently circulated the city.

"Why didn't I hear about it?" she asked.

"Probably because you spend all your time exploring the forest outside the city."

The king was here for negotiations with Queen Jade. The state of Dragonwall's affairs were in disarray. Goblins weren't the only threat to the kingdom, as she was just now learning. There were rumors of pirate attacks along the coasts, and even wild dragons in the north.

Much of this came as a shock. "You really think wild dragons have returned?"

"You villagers don't get out much, do you?"

"As if you sprites are any better!" He grinned at this. She chewed on the skin of her bottom lip, thinking. "How long will the king be here?"

"Perhaps another five days, longer, if need be. So far, everything has gone smoothly. Our negotiations are nearly complete, aside from the finer details. Petty things, really."

"So, the sprites will help Dragonwall in whatever war comes?"

Feowen's next words were measured. "King Talon has our support, but not in the way others would expect."

They reached the Crystal Palace and she stood frozen before the steps, suddenly horrified with herself. "I cannot meet Dragonwall's king looking like...like *this*. Look at me!"

"Why not?" Feowen looked her up and down.

Her jaw dropped. "Have you no sense of propriety? Look at what I'm *wearing*."

King Talon was...well...a king. He was used to fine women who pranced around his castle in beautiful gowns. She knew enough about court life in Lincastle to know that.

She was wearing a pair of trousers and a long tunic, her father's sword strapped to her belt. Everything was worn and dirtied from hours of tromping through the forest. She probably had dirt on her face and in her hair too.

Feowen shrugged. "I imagine the king has more important concerns than your attire." He snapped his fingers and stepped forward. "Come along."

There was no getting out of it, appearance or not. The time had come to do something she never would have imagined doing. Not even in her wildest dreams. It was time to meet Dragonwall's king.

CHAPTER 6
TAYLYNN'S WORDS

Esterpine

Talon fidgeted with his ancient coin, eyes flicking over his surroundings. He and Bedelth occupied a private sitting room provided by Queen Jade for their own personal use. Those among his entourage had been likewise accommodated with spacious quarters.

Like all the rooms in the palace, everything was made of crystal. It was as cold and calculating as those who had constructed it. But the furnishings were warm—small comfort that was—in hues of green and brown.

"Maybe they aren't coming," he said, rolling the coin between his fingers. He and Bedelth were waiting to meet the young woman credited with rescuing refugees from Kaljah. "You would think Prince Feowen was traveling halfway across the kingdom to find her."

"Patience, my king," Bedelth said. "It has not been that long."

He grunted.

Nearly ten more minutes passed before he heard voices. Then a loud knock at the door. He slipped the coin into his pocket and stood, adjusting his crown as the doors swept open. Bedelth came to stand beside him.

Prince Feowen entered, trailed by a woman huddling behind him. "As promised," the prince announced, bowing his head. "The woman we discussed." He stepped aside. "Jeanine, this is King Talon. King Talon—Jeanine."

Jeanine shuffled into view just as her foot caught on the corner of the rug. She stumbled, nearly falling.

He eyed her with suspicion. This was the warrior they'd spoken of? Hmm...

She was dressed like one, forgoing the usual female attire. Dirtied clothes, worn boots, and a sword belted to her waist. His thoughts jumped to Claire. They'd get along, the two of them.

With very little grace, Jeanine dropped to one knee, bowed her head, and then muttered something unintelligible about how she was pleased to meet him.

The side of his mouth twitched. "You may rise." She did, keeping her eyes downturned. "I'm honored to meet you, Jeanine. Prince Feowen has told us of your bravery."

Her face flushed. "The...the honor is all mine, Your Majesty. I had not...I did not expect...that is to say..."

"Please, be at ease. Come, sit." He guided her to a nearby chair then turned to Prince Feowen. "I appreciate your assistance, Prince. Do not let us detain you."

Feowen's eyes narrowed. "I had planned to remain."

Jeanine's eyes bolted to Prince Feowen before darting away, settling on her hands folded in her lap.

"That will not be necessary. These are kingdom affairs."

Long seconds passed, in which they held each other's gaze, then the prince nodded at last. "Of course, as you wish. I will wait in the hall."

Jeanine's throat bobbed and she managed a nod.

Talon took a seat across from her, Bedelth beside him. He noticed the way her eyes flitted about. She looked everywhere but him. Others might have found it offensive, but he was all too used to it.

"This is Bedelth," he said, hoping to put her at ease. "One of my shields. He's served me faithfully for over a hundred years."

Jeanine's eyes widened.

"It's a pleasure to meet you," Bedelth said.

"Likewise," she croaked, then pursed her lips.

"No doubt you are wondering why I have requested an audience with you?"

"I…" Her face turned a darker shade of red.

"I certainly expected someone bolder," he said to Bedelth.

"Patience, my king. People fear you, remember?"

Jeanine cleared her throat. "I am surprised, was surprised, when Feowen, I mean, the prince, told me that you wished to speak with me." She glanced up at him for the first time. Her eyes lingered over his scars. But she did not balk. Good.

"I would have called upon you sooner, had I been told you were here." He considered his next words carefully. "Queen Jade told me everything a few hours ago."

"Oh. Yes." Her hands fidgeted.

"You have been through a great deal. Goblins are no easy enemy, yet you stood against them. I am told that your bravery saved many lives."

"I…It was nothing, Your Majesty."

"I disagree."

Her gaze fell to her hands again. "Anyone would have done the same."

"I disagree again. It takes a good deal of courage to do what you did. I can only imagine the chaos in Kaljah. Fear cripples the best of us, but to act in spite of that fear? That is another matter entirely." Her throat bobbed; she dared another glance at him. "I am convinced that in this, you have shown true bravery. For that, I wanted to thank you personally. So…thank you."

Her face turned its deepest shade of red yet. "Jahl helped too," she blurted.

"Yes, we have already spoken to him. While I found his story compelling, it was your deeds that stirred my emotions." He glanced at Bedelth before continuing. "Your actions were heroic, unquestionably. Jahl also told me of your father. Is that his sword?" He glanced at the sword at her waist.

"It...it was."

He stood, hand outstretched. "May I?"

She blinked up at him. And blinked again. Not quite comprehending.

"His Majesty wishes to see your sword, Jeanine." Bedelth's voice was a smooth rumble.

"Oh...of course." She awkwardly rose and handed it over. Her movements were surer now. Perhaps it took a weapon to rally her confidence.

He took the sword and held it against the light. It was like looking at something for the thousandth time. There were hundreds of thousands of weapons just like it in the kingdom. A soldier's sword.

Stepping away to give himself room, he swung the blade several times, cutting through the air with ease, trying it out for balance before he returned it. "A fine blade that—I am glad it has served you well."

"I had hoped it would do more."

He bowed his head. "I am sorry for your loss. War has a way of taking the people closest to us, those we love the most." His mind jumped to his parents, and he hated that.

Returning to his seat, he inquired into Kaljah's welfare, asking about the villagers, their journey through the forest, and future plans. Jeanine explained much of what he already knew, that they would remain in Esterpine until it was safe to return home. Though, he got the feeling she did not plan to return home with everyone else. He couldn't blame her for it.

When it was clear there was little else to discuss, he said, "It is my duty as king to reward bravery and valor. Is there anything you might want? I will grant you a boon of your choosing. You may request anything, so long as it is within my means to give."

This was not something he ever did.

"That is...you are too generous, Your Majesty. I couldn't possibly..."

"The king does not make such offers to *anyone*," Bedelth said, his manner frank.

"What is written on your heart?" he asked, trying to bring her from her shell. "Surely you have unspoken desires. A worthy match for a husband, perhaps? A home in the city of your choosing? A place to live in the capital? You need merely name it and it is yours." He paused, his eyes taking in her appearance once more. "On second thought, maybe some clean clothing? Did your hosts not offer you something when you arrived?"

She snorted and her stiff mannerisms crumbled. "Oh, they did. Some pretty feminine gowns. I'm afraid they don't know me at all."

He couldn't help his smile. "Very well then. Clothes it is. But I will not count that as your boon. Anything else?"

"It is a generous offer, to be sure. What...what if I am not yet certain? Would it be too much... May I have some time to think about it?"

"Very well." That she did not make demands spoke volumes to her character. Most females in her shoes would have requested a husband without hesitation. Or money. Or a lavish townhouse in Kastali Dun. "Do keep in mind that I depart in a few days' time."

She nodded.

They escorted her to the door. Bedelth hesitated, hand hovering over the knob. "It is rumored that you are skilled with the sword. How about a match or two before our departure?"

Surprised by the offer, he caught Bedelth's eye, lifting an eyebrow.

Bedelth shrugged, offering a toothy grin. "What? I always like a good challenge."

"But I am human," Jeanine said.

This earned a chuckle. "I am well aware of your...physicalities. Doesn't mean it cannot be fun. What say you? Care to match your kingdom sword against the sverak of a shield?"

A smile curled Jeanine's lips, showing more about her personality than the entire visit had. "Since you put it that way, yes. I accept. How about tomorrow?"

"Done!" Bedelth opened the door. Prince Feowen loitered in the hall, eyes burning a hole through the door where they'd been standing.

After a round of polite farewells, he was glad to have his privacy back. The day had been tedious—the entire visit to Esterpine tiresome. Assemblies in the queen's throne room, meetings with her advisors, conclaves with sprites from around the forest. It was more than he cared to endure, but it was necessary if he was to change a relationship that had persisted for tens of thousands of years. And gods above, Reyr had been right about the food.

"I think I will take a walk," he decided, glancing at Bedelth. "I need to clear my head."

Bedelth stepped forward. "You want company?"

"No. Not this time. Don't bother yourself—go do whatever you please. If I'm not back in a few hours, then you may worry."

Bedelth nodded.

He discarded his crown and descended through the belly of the palace. He wasn't one to fear heights, but the giant staircase circling the cavernous crystal chamber made his stomach lurch with each glance down.

The uneasiness dissipated once he was outside. With the news of his arrival no doubt spreading like dragon fire, he had no reservations about being seen. As suspected, few of Esterpine's Sprites showed any surprise.

The settlement grew sparse, the trees more densely packed. Only then did he find himself truly alone. He followed a worn dirt path and continued deeper into the foliage, careful not to stray. The forest pressed in around him. It felt so confining. He exhaled, long and slow, forcing his breaths to steady. What did the sprites see in such a place? Smothered beneath the canopy. Give him a wide open sky and empty space, never a cage.

He slowed and blinked, looking at the foliage around him. Vines twined around trunks and bushes. Mist swelled in hidden pockets between the trees. Bugs chirruped. Water trickled somewhere beyond. Flowers bloomed everywhere, their scent like a strong perfume wafting over him. He couldn't deny the beauty. The richness of color. Was this the reason Claire loved it here?

No, he shook his head, clearing his thoughts.

She liked it for other reasons—reasons he hated to admit. Reasons that had everything to do with the sprite marking he'd discovered on her skin. She had Sprite blood. Queen Jade had confirmed it, much to his dissatisfaction. He assumed the queen was happy to deliver the news. Her eyes had burned brighter, as if she sensed the blow. The woman who'd saved his kingdom wasn't a mere human, but rather, a rival of the drengr. Even if she wasn't entirely spriten.

But this wasn't what truly bothered him. A frown pulled at his lips. Claire was mystifying. After hundreds of years, shouldn't he understand females better? Their likes and dislikes. Their motivations and desires.

He snorted. The sound disturbed the forest. Was he completely wrong in his assumptions, or was Claire simply different? He ran a hand through his tangled mess of hair.

He parted a cluster of vines blocking his path. The drone of insects fell silent at his passing, continuing their song once he moved on. Claire would have loved it here, with him, walking beneath the trees. Exploring the path under his feet, discovering where it led. Like an adventure—just the two of them. She would have enjoyed that.

A heavy exhale left his lips.

He tried pushing Claire from his mind, instead thinking back to his meeting with Jeanine. She wasn't what he'd expected out of a warrior. Quiet. Timid. Fidgety. Was it because of his scars? No. She'd looked upon him without fear. No matter, Bedelth would free her from her shell.

A vined plant caught his attention. It had large, plate sized leaves with massive buds, some as large as his fist. They were all closed. He had seen something like this before—clinging to the fringes of his memory. He gravitated towards it.

"They are night flowers." He all but jumped out of his skin at the sound of the ethereal voice. He snatched his hand back and inwardly cursed at his lack of awareness.

Princess Taylynn wore a bemused expression. "They only open when night falls," she added.

"Right. I thought it looked familiar. We have one growing in the queen's garden atop my tower. Back at the keep."

"Would you like to see its petals?" Taylynn regarded him.

He frowned. "Doesn't it need to be night?"

"Here—" Before he could stop her, she went to the trunk of the tree and began to sing. He froze at the sound of her voice, no more than a whisper, growing surer with each word.

It wasn't the kind of song he was used to. More coaxing than anything. A beautiful invitation, full of reverence and longing. He blinked.

Gods above!

She was speaking to the plant. He nearly snorted.

Ana myrtah callohma, stalle edah hallodah luth.
Ana itzallia vahxah, stalle edah hallodah luahth.
Ana tunil kevjahi ana loah, stalle edah hallodah luth.
Ana realoah skina heiloh, agamaera Elduin, stalle!
Stalle hallodah ana myrtah, blathia myrtalla, stalle edah hallodah ana
myrtah.

HE TILTED HIS HEAD. The words were familiar, but not. She sang about the night. Of shadows and moonlight and stars. He gazed in disbelief, as one by one, the petals began to open, infected by the beauty of her song. He'd heard tales from fishermen of mermaids and sirens, females who could sing a man into enchantment. This felt much like that.

He couldn't so much as move.

Each flower was brilliant. A luminescent light purple interior that pulsed and glowed with dim recognition. He stared at them, his gaze transfixed. He hadn't spent time in his mother's garden after her death, but the sight before him transported him back to his childhood. To the times his mother took him into her private garden to scold or speak with him.

"I have heard tell that the sprites sing their magic, but I never truly believed it," he mused.

"Music is magic, King Talon. It is the ultimate path by which energy flows. What better way to conduct it than through one's voice in song?"

He fidgeted under her gaze, as if he were a child, young and inexperienced. Behind her, the flowers began to close up. He cleared his throat. "What do the words mean? They were beautiful."

"There is no way to translate them without destroying the true meaning, but let me see..." After a long pause, she began to sing again. This version was not nearly as ethereal as the last.

"The night begins to fall, come forth and greet it.
The shadows grow long, come forth and greet them.
The moon rises in the sky, come forth and greet it.
The stars twinkle bright, celebrating Elduin, come forth.
Come forth to greet the night, oh flowers of darkness, come forth and
greet the night."

Talon glanced back at the flowers. This time, they did not open.

She watched him. "You must find it strange that I encountered you here outside the city. I must apologize for my mother's behavior earlier today."

He huffed, looking away from the flowers to meet her gaze. "Any particular instance? Or all of it?"

She smiled. "She means well. My mother is... The sprites have long disdained the draconic races of this world. You know this. Dragons were created by our enemies. You cannot fault my people for their doubt, nor can you blame them for refusing the use of our warriors, should the need—"

"I never expected your warriors, Princess. Hoped for it, yes, but never expected it. I know enough to know you cannot live well or long outside of your forest. Your mother's confirmation today solidified my beliefs."

"Oh." Taylynn laughed, the sound like chimes hanging from the trees to catch the breeze. Even the night flowers twitched. "My mother deals in absolutes. But there are ways, yes. How do you think Queen Isabella managed?"

"She was mated to King Eymar. It was their bond that allowed—"

"No. That is a common misconception. Sprites can and do survive outside the walls of our forest. Quite well, if necessary. Even I have done so, on occasion." Something in her expression begged an explanation. "The secret is not well known, but it can be accomplished if the proper observances are followed."

"What do you mean? That there is a chance we might have your warriors after all?" A sense of hope bolstered his mood.

"That...among other things. Know this. While my mother may not support you in the ways you would like, I will."

His frown deepened. "You would go against your mother?"

"Move against her?" She gave a sarcastic chuckle. "How could you say such a thing? My mother and I both want the same thing. Just...in different ways. Our world is spiraling out of control, King Talon. Surely you have seen it? Look at the drengr—your people are a dying race. Balance is a precarious thing. One simple push could mean the ruin of all. Such has been the path since the Awakening. Some believed destroying the dragons would fix this. You know of whom I speak, and how wrong she was." The princess halted, looking around as if remembering herself. "It is getting dark. You had better be on your way."

Without another word, she faded into the gloaming. The mists swallowed her whole. He gazed after her, dumbfounded.

There were few things in this world that truly frightened him, but the forest came close. The idea of being lost within left his skin crawling. She was right, it really was getting dark.

He fled back the way he had come, careful to follow the path he had taken. All the while, Princess Taylynn's words echoed in his mind. What did she mean about balance? Yes, it was true that the Drengr's numbers were dwindling, but what did that have to do with anything? Most of all, how could she know such a path had been carved since the Awakening? What path? His? Dragonwall's? Or both?

He did not breathe easier until he saw twinkling lights appear between the trees. His heart did not slow until the city wrapped around him. And yet, Taylynn's words continued to follow him.

CHAPTER 7
THE WILDERNESS

Northern Coast, Galadhal

Claire unbuckled her harness, preparing to dismount the moment Koldis landed. The ground rose up to meet them. The air was thick with particulate matter, swirling up around her as other pairs touched down. She jumped, dragging her pack with her, leaving it beside Koldis to race away.

She followed after several others with the same idea in mind. She stumbled until her stiff muscles warmed up. It felt good after so many hours in one position.

They were making excellent time. Koldis was determined to utilize an unexpected tailwind, so he'd insisted they postpone their evening meal and keep flying well into the night. It would have been silly to waste such an opportunity. Hence, the reason her bladder was about to explode. Only once she'd threatened to pee on him, did he finally agree to stop.

The moon was still hidden below the horizon, giving rise to a brilliant starscape. Pinpricks of light splattered every inch of the inky sky. These stars were different than those she was familiar with—very different. She missed the big dipper, the north star, and many others like Sirius and Bellatrix. She missed a lot of things.

Despite the absence of civilization, the night air was rich with sounds. The incessant chirruping of insects permeated everything, reminding her of summer evenings spent on the porch with her boombox blaring Tim McGraw, book in hand, pages lit by the orange porch lights. She sighed. Those were good times...simpler times. No missions. No adventures. No kingdoms in need of saving. Just cornfields as far as the eye could see.

Now all she could see was the vast wide open. Along Galadhal's coast, a long swath of deserted beach lay less than a mile northeast of where they had stopped. Beyond the coastline, The Scattered Islands were invisible in the darkness. The southern coast of Celenore was just north of them.

That was their destination.

Finishing her business, she and the others returned. It was a flurry of activity and conversations. A makeshift camp had been erected, torches burning brightly, though they would not spend the night here. They would stay only long enough to rest and eat. Belwen, Celill, and Manir had already gone about constructing a massive bonfire, while Rhywyth, Til, and three other drengr had taken flight to hunt in search of game for their dinner.

Her stomach grumbled. She considered going for her reserves. Instead, she went to the bonfire, eager to chase away the chill. She rubbed her hands together and squinted against the blinding light.

"I found us a comfortable place to sit, if you would like to join me?" She jumped and turned, realizing a moment later the words were not meant for her.

There'd been a lot of that since landing. The drengr and their riders were more talkative on the ground. In such close proximity, it was nearly impossible to tune them out.

She crossed her arms, hugging herself. For someone with this ability, being able to hear multiple voices in her head all at once, these were the times she felt the most alone. She didn't have a special someone. It left her a little envious.

She glanced over their makeshift camp. Elaine was depositing a handful of wood beside the fire. She took a step forward. "I...I can help with that, if you need?"

"No need, my lady." Elaine offered her a warm smile. "I think we have enough for now."

She opened her mouth, but Elaine turned and busied herself with another task. She shut her mouth and turned away. Several smaller cooking fires had sprung up. She gravitated towards a group of drengr. They whittled away wood, lashing it together, working on spits for the fires. "Need help?"

Manir turned to her. "Thank you, my lady, but no need to trouble yourself." He walked off, positioning one of the spits into place. The others gave her smiles and nods before returning to their tasks.

She swallowed and moved away. Perhaps she wasn't needed anywhere. She sighed, returning to the fire, fixing her eyes on the blaze.

The day had passed in painstaking slowness, longer than any normal day ought to feel. Keeping busy in the sky had helped. Koldis and Jovari had spent time quizzing her on the names of their companions before moving on to words in the old language. Her existing vocabulary had impressed them, spurring small conversations between them.

"How are you tonight, my lady?"

"Oh. Hello, Faedrol. I'm doing well enough, thank you. My legs are a bit stiff, but not enough to complain about. And you?"

"Never better." His grin widened. "I am not sure if you know, but I am the drengr who heard your scream when you were kidnapped."

"You?!" Her eyes widened.

Faedrol's chin lifted. "Hannah and I were patrolling the area when we heard, well, your voice in my mind. Didn't think it was real. But then we heard you scream. I was able to tell everyone where you were."

A breath left her chest. "I...wow. I suppose I owe you my thanks. Thank you."

"I am honored, my lady, but your thanks aren't necessary. King Talon and his shields thanked me a hundred times over already. And besides, I was only doing my duty."

"Well, I'm grateful all the same." She studied him. Olive skin and dark, curly hair that reminded her of Cyrus. His eyes were a warm shade of brown. They danced in the firelight. His face was rounded, but it gave him a dimpled smile, which she immediately liked.

They fell silent, turning back to the fire. Its warmth, the way it crackled and popped, made her feel safe. She and Faedrol weren't the only ones basking in its glow. Several pairs had found comfortable places beside it.

Faedrol's rider, Hannah, was nearby, chatting animatedly with some of the others.

Claire smiled and said, "You know, I'm happy to have you here —all of you. Your protection means a great deal."

"It is our pleasure, Lady Claire. I am sure my kind would agree on that. Besides, adventures warm my blood, leave my heart bursting with excitement. I live for this sort of thing, if you can understand."

"Then...this isn't the first adventure you've been on?" She failed to hide the smile tugging at the corners of her lips.

He laughed. "Hardly, my lady! Perhaps if there is time, I will tell you about one or two of them—one involving Koldis in particular. They make good stories—adventures do."

"I'd like that."

Koldis and Jovari strolled up, cast in an orange glow. Her eyes narrowed. Koldis held two carved staves.

"Evening, Faedrol." Koldis turned to her. "We missed our practice this morning. Time to remedy that." He thrust one of the staves into her hand.

She gawked at him. "Like...now? How can you expect me to fight when I'm so stiff?" Faedrol chuckled, but watched on in amusement. "Besides, I can hardly see a thing."

"Lady Claire, our enemies will attack when they please, often when circumstances are not ideal. Stiff or not, darkness or not, your lessons must continue." He wore an expression of stern resolve.

She glanced down. Her makeshift weapon was well formed and

dense. She slapped one end into the palm of her hand, testing out the feel of it. "Where'd you get this, anyway?"

"Found them on the beach a few minutes ago." Koldis shrugged. "Had to use a bit of magic to fix their shape and make them sturdy, but they should do fine." He motioned with his head before walking away from the glare of the fire. Jovari flashed her a toothy grin and followed.

"Well, I guess that's that," she said, smiling at Faedrol.

"Good luck," he called in return, amusement coloring his voice.

It seemed Koldis and Jovari weren't the only ones with sparring in mind. In the glow of torchlight, six others had the same idea, forming pairs. Soon, the sound of clanging metal sang through the camp. These drengr held nothing back.

She faltered as she watched Belwin and Celill exchange a set of blows. Belwin brought down his sverak in heavy bursts, forcing Celill backwards, step by step. In a rapid show of skill, Belwin spun on his heel and swept his blade around, ripping into the flesh at Celill's side, tearing through skin and tissue, leaving a bloodied mess in his wake.

She flinched, gritting her teeth, imagining the kind of pain that would bring. It was barbaric, yet even in the mere seconds that followed, Celill was ready with a counter attack, his side fully healed. She shook her head, muttering about the unfairness of it all.

"Coming?" Koldis called. She turned away and trudged to where he now stood, allowing her eyes to adjust to the dim light. Jovari stood nearby, watching.

Koldis shook out his arms, rotating his neck, popping it. She did the same, stretching her stiff muscles.

"Ready?" he asked.

"Um. Ready as I'll ever be I guess." She eyed him suspiciously. Koldis, ever a dragon at heart, began to circle.

"This ought to be interesting." A drengr's voice cut through her mind. She faltered, glancing around.

Koldis took advantage and lunged, a dark shadow against a flame-colored backdrop. It was all she could do to lift her staff in defense. His crashed against it, the sound making a dull thud. Her muscles were slow at first, but they sprang to alertness at the jarring contact.

She swung around, disengaging. Her feet moved, shuffling backward. He came quickly then, lunging again and again. A feigned upper sweep from his left. A blow from above. A jab at her side. Each movement came in rapid succession. She barely had time to react. Her muscles struggled against the repetitive motions, but she dared not let her weakness show.

"She's got solid reflexes—"

Her feet faltered. She clamped her mind shut, trying not to think about the running commentary that came from those watching. She needed to get used to the sudden mental distractions if she was to hold her ground against Koldis.

They continued like this, Koldis attempting to get past her while she blocked and dodged. He left her no time for counterattacks, so she focused on each reaction to his movements.

A rapid series of blows left her panting. She danced away from him. He pursued her, sweeping around with his staff, right behind her knees. "Argh!" She was too slow. Sharp pain erupted where his staff landed.

"Too slow," someone said.

She spun around, trying not to be angered by the comment. Instead, she watched Koldis, keeping her focus entirely on him. It helped, and she was able to put up a good fight for several more minutes. Her movements grew sloppier. She found it more and more difficult to lift her feet, her arms.

Koldis sensed her fatigue and used it to his advantage. He dealt three rapid blows to her side, barely deflected. Then, he used his shoulder and rammed into her, sending her stumbling.

"Arghhh!" The world flashed by in a darkened blur as the ground came up to meet her. Stars danced in her vision. Time seemed to slow before speeding up again. And then her diaphragm opened and she dragged in as much air as possible, gasping.

Koldis threw himself at her, bringing his staff down hard. She rolled over in the grass, coughing, coming up to block, then rolling away again to regain her footing. He chased after her, trying to catch her by surprise as she danced away.

Another low sweep of his staff forced her to jump. He caught her as she landed, whacking her on her hip. She grunted, gritting her teeth. Now she was furious. A frustrated yell broke from her lips as she brought her staff around to meet him.

"Stop!" Jovari's voice broke the silence. "I think that's enough for one night."

She froze, chest heaving, holding her position as she gazed into Koldis's eyes. He was barely breathing at all. Hadn't even broken a sweat.

She gave her staff a none-to-gentle push against his and dropped it, sinking down onto her hands and knees, then rolled over onto her back, gazing up at the sky. Her muscles were jelly. Everything hurt.

"Well played, Claire." Koldis plopped down beside her. The whites of his teeth showed in the darkness. A smile.

"I'll get you next time," she breathed. "You can be sure of that."

"I'm sure." He chuckled and stood, holding out a hand.

They returned to the fire. A sheen of sweat coated her skin. A bath would have been great right about now. The hunting party had already returned and prepared their dinner. The meat roasted over the cooking fires, giving off a glorious smell.

They joined the circle that had formed, taking a seat with her legs crossed. Jovari passed her a wineskin and she gratefully accepted, taking several sips, letting the vintage roll over her tongue before passing it on. Her insides warmed as the liquid raced down her throat. An immediate calm settled over her, helping her relax. Her bruises hurt like hell. But she didn't need to look at them to know they'd already started healing. Tomorrow, they would be gone.

"We will reach the southern shore of Celenore tomorrow, mid-day," Koldis informed them. "From there, we will go inland and make camp. The attacks happen in the early hours of the morning, usually before dawn." The firelight danced on his skin, flickering in his eyes. Like all drengr, Koldis was handsome, even more so than most, if that was possible. Narrow nose, pointed chin, and nearly feline cheekbones. "Everyone will need—what?" His eyes narrowed.

"Oh." Her cheeks flushed. "Nothing."

He watched her a moment longer before clearing his throat. "Everyone will need a few hours of rest before we carry out our plans. We should be in the sky well before dawn. The villagers must be informed and organized. We want them at the ready. The constables will help with that."

"Constables?" Her brow furrowed. "The village heads?"

"Aye."

"But how will they know we're coming?"

"Messengers, disguised as travelers on foot," he said. "I suggest they depart as soon as possible."

She glanced around the camp before nodding.

"We ought to send four to each village. Two pairs," Kedan said. He'd taken a seat beside them to listen.

"Aye, a good number." Koldis nodded. Several others murmured in agreement.

"That would mean the loss of six pairs to our party," Verider pointed out. Claire didn't miss his hesitance. Verider was one of the older ones. "We must keep Lady Claire well protected."

"Fourteen pairs is still a strong number." Koldis looked at her. "What say you, Lady Claire?"

"Six pairs," she decided. "Our fastest. They should leave as soon as they've eaten."

Koldis stood, glancing about. "Odrick, Til, you and your riders take Swinston. Gradyr, Jorsid, Lormont. Nokin, Hiondel, Osbourne." His orders were met with verbal confirmations as the selected pairs set about their final preparations for their departure.

Dinner was distributed among those who wished to eat—some of the drengr had gone hunting on their own and were no longer hungry. She ate her meat with some of the bread Desaree had packed. It was a meager dinner, but when she finished it with a toffee, it didn't seem so bad.

The pairs made to depart. She went to each, bidding them farewell.

"We will not let you down," Odrick said. The others echoed his sentiment.

"Good," she said. "Fly quickly."

They crept away into the shadowed night, transforming. Minutes later, their riders were settled. She watched their shapes rise into the darkness and fly north.

She returned to the fire to join the others, enjoying what was left of their repast. Several riders had made themselves quite comfortable, stretching out on the ground to gaze at the stars. Her body ached for sleep. She thought of her feathered bed back in the capital and shook her head. This mission was far more important.

"You should get a few minutes before we depart," Jovari said, sidling up to her. "You'll be flying with me when we go."

She nodded, wrapping her cloak around her body before curling up on her side. It was unlikely that she would sleep at all, knowing they would wake her the moment she nodded off. But she tried anyway. As she lay there, she tried not to think about what was at stake, what would happen if she failed, or if Talon found out.

"It's time." A nudge at her shoulder told her she must have drifted off. Jovari's voice was low, urgent. "We've lingered long enough."

She furtively wiped a trail of drool from the corner of her mouth. Yep, she'd definitely slept some. The camp was dark. Someone had put out the fire. Shadows moved about, voices low.

"How...how long was I asleep?" She sat up, her body aching worse than before. Soreness setting in.

"Not long. An hour, perhaps."

"Where's Koldis?" She glanced around. The drengr were already transforming, their riders mounting up. She stretched and stood, the exhilaration of adventure taking hold.

"He helped the others take watch. He'll be along shortly." Jovari stepped away, lifting his voice to the camp. "Mount up and move out!"

She shivered, wrapping her cloak more tightly about her.

The moon was late to rise, just visible now, peeping up above the horizon. Jovari transformed, his dark blue scales mirroring the sky above, glittering with the sparkle of thousands of stars. Grabbing her pack, she scrambled up his back, securing it to the harness.

In a matter of minutes, the evidence of their camp was all but gone. Formations took form around her. She spotted Koldis, taking his position. Jovari roared, giving the signal. As one, sixteen dragons launched into the sky, swallowed up by the night.

CHAPTER 8
A CEREMONY GOWN

Fort Squall

Tamara yelped as another pin caught her shoulder.

"Begging your pardon, Lady Tamara," Mistress Anna removed the pins from her mouth to speak. Her face had turned an embarrassed shade of red.

She gave the woman a small smile. "It's fine, Anna. Please continue."

Anna fingers were deft, but not as deft as Master Phillip's. She missed her old dressmaker in Redport.

Anna hummed as she worked. She was a sight to see—pins sticking from between her pursed lips, several at a time, as she folded and tucked, folded and tucked, grabbing only as needed. When she ran out, she returned to her pincushion to refill, keeping her lips tight, holding the pins in place. Anna was perhaps ten years older, with dirty blonde hair, hazel eyes, and a dimpled smile. She was easy to be around, absolutely likable. Even if she did repeatedly stab her charge.

One week to go before her bonding ceremony. Her heart gave a nervous thump at the thought. Nearly all the necessary arrangements had been made, except for the finishing touches on her gown. She'd already acquired the pommel stone for Byron's sverak. Everything was in order with the cooks, already planning the feast to follow. Even Tamara's parents had agreed to attend at Lord Davi's invitation. Her father probably wasn't happy about *that*, but Lord Redwynn was not fool enough to refuse. Bonding ceremonies were a cause for celebration. Given Byron's parents and popularity, this was sure to be a memorable party.

The click of a latch announced Lady Emmy as she swept into the room, coming to stand beside Tamara. "Oh, my!" Her face glowed. "That color! With those eyes! Gods, it's perfect."

"The gown is nearly finished, my lady." Mistress Anna removed the pins from her mouth to speak. "Just a few more tucks here and there, a few more embellishments, and we should be ready for our final fitting."

"You have done splendidly, Anna. Thank you." Emmy took Anna's cheeks in both hands and planted a kiss right on her nose. "In such a gown, Tamara will shine like the stars." Lady Emmy caught her eye in the mirror and they both smiled.

The gown was the same color as Byron's scales, which directly matched her eyes. Like all bonding ceremony gowns, its extravagance was indescribable. Few expenses had been spared.

The bodice was rigid and laced up the back. The front showed off a conservative square neckline, which was a blessing. Her sixteenth birthday had only just passed, and yet, her breasts had not quite developed into the womanly curves she wished them to be. Across the bodice, crystalline beads were sewn onto the fabric, swirling in a snowstorm of patterns. The bottom of the bodice came to a sharp point just below her waist. From there, cascades of satin and lace flowed out like a frozen waterfall, making up the voluminous skirt.

"A gown fit for an ice queen," she found herself murmuring. Byron wouldn't be able to take his eyes off her. The selfish thought left her heart pounding.

"You know," Lady Emmy said, taking Tamara's shoulders, "despite Queen Isabella's price, I selfishly longed for a daughter. I love Byron, as I would have loved a daughter. I merely thank the gods he found you." In Emmy's face, she found love equal to any mother's.

"Thank you," she whispered.

"Now, hopefully we are nearly done?" Lady Emmy turned to Anna. "Tamara is to meet Byron for lunch. Lord Reyr has requested their company."

"Lord...Lord Reyr?" Tamara's stomach dropped. Lord Reyr the Gold had arrived at the fort a week prior. He'd been so tied up with duties that Tamara had scarcely spoken a few words to him. Like the other kingdom's shields, Reyr was something of a legend, especially since his family came from a long line of fort leaders.

"Indeed, Lord Reyr."

"I'm nearly done, my lady. Give me a moment more." Anna adjusted several folds before stepping away. She eyed the gown, her gaze traveling its length, before nodding. "There. Finished. Let's get you out of it."

They helped her break free. The gown, fabric and all, was then gathered up and gently folded into a cloth sack. It was bad luck for anyone to see a rider's ceremony gown, except for those closest to her. Anna could not risk outsiders laying eyes upon it.

When she departed, Lady Emmy helped Tamara back into her clothes, which were far too formal for other Riders in the fort. Tamara only wore a rider's attire when training. Otherwise she followed Lady Emmy's example. Emmy was a woman of titles and presented herself as such. It was a difficult balance, but the fort leader walked the line with ease. Something to be admired.

A knock came and Byron entered. Despite his mother's presence, he swept Tamara into a hug, lifting her off the ground. "It's been a brute of a day," he growled, his face glowing. "Yours is a welcome sight."

Emmy chuckled, shuffling into the other room to give them privacy. "Your gown?" he asked, his eyes searching. "Are you pleased with it?"

"Beyond pleased! Wait until you see."

"Is it the color of my scales?" A smile pulled at the corner of his lips.

"I think that should be obvious. But if you're asking for hints, don't bother."

"Not even a single detail?" He arched an eyebrow, teasing.

"My lips are sealed." She crossed her arms. "And if you think for one second you might try prying the details from my mind when we are in the sky together, you've got another thing coming."

"And how shall you stop me if I do?" he asked. She barked a laugh, pinching his arm. Hard. "I yield! I yield." He lifted his hands in submission. They eyed each other for a moment. "Not even something small?" he baited, giving her a pout.

Gods! He did look rather adorable like this. "Oh, very well. There are beads, lots of beads."

He lifted his eyebrows. "What color? The same as your gown?"

"Byron! I cannot tell you *that*, now can I?" She pushed at his chest and tried to step around him. It was no use. He swept her up and placed a gentle kiss on her lips. Her skin tingled everywhere he touched her. She wanted to keep kissing him. Just the thought had warmth pooling in her belly.

"Ready for our meal?"

She stepped free of him. "Are we really eating with your uncle?"

"Aye. He cannot escape me forever. But let's hurry. We have training this afternoon."

She rushed around to tidy up, placing her teacup on its tray and gathering up the books Emmy had lent her. They called a hasty farewell to the fort leader, who popped her head out of the other room to grin at them.

***

Lord Reyr was the spitting image of Lord Davi. She'd seen him a few times, but the surprise of it never got old.

"There you are!" He offered them a brilliant smile. "Come in, come in!"

His quarters were smaller than Lord Davi's, but adequate. A table for three was set near the window. They took their seats and dug into the small feast laid out.

"So, tell me of your training," Reyr demanded before she had the chance to take a bite. He had not yet bothered to dish up a single thing. When he saw her eying his empty plate, he lifted a shoulder. "I went hunting earlier."

Byron spoke through a mouthful, leaving her to eat. She'd skipped breakfast, again, and was starving. Being in Reyr's presence left her even more light headed.

Gods above! If she could have seen herself a year ago, dining with someone from the king's inner circle, she wouldn't have believed it.

"We spend most of our afternoons together now," Byron was saying. "And we have successfully completed our trust falls."

"Ah! Of course! I heard all about that. He's very proud, you know. So am I. To live to see the day…" Reyr trailed off, still smiling.

Twin siblings were rare among the drengr. Few throughout history had the luxury of nieces or nephews—mostly nephews. For Reyr to see Byron happily mated was something he had probably not planned on. "Anyway, I count myself lucky. That I might be here to witness your ceremony next week. Which brings me to my next matter."

Byron set down his fork.

"While it is customary for the fort leader to perform the ceremony, I thought perhaps you would prefer to have your father stand beside you. That I might perform the rite instead. I have spoken with Davi. He likes the idea. It is up to you, though—both of you."

"Done!" Byron blurted without hesitation, then glanced at her. "That is, if you are okay with this?"

She shifted in her seat. "I…we would be honored, Lord Reyr."

"Excellent! And please, Reyr, or Uncle, or even Uncle Reyr. No need for titles. We are family."

"Of course." Her gaze dropped to her plate. She used the opportunity to spoon a few more bites into her mouth.

"Now, what else is new?" Reyr looked between them, grinning.

Byron launched into an epic explanation of all the things keeping him busy. She was more than happy to eat and let him do the talking. He talked about the night they first met in Report. His efforts with Fort Squall's patrols. And even some of the discussions his father let him join. Soon the three of them were on to politics, talking about the condition of the kingdom and the war to come. She couldn't help but listen eagerly to everything Reyr said.

Getting news straight from the source was rare.

When mention of the mysterious Lady Claire crept into the conversation, an accidental squeal escaped her lips. She covered her mouth with her hands, face flushing. "Sorry," she blurted. "It's just...can you tell us about her? Surely you were around her during your time in the capital? I heard some of the volunteers talking..."

Reyr huffed, his eyes dancing.

"I knew it! So you *do* know her. Then you must put matters straight. Is it true that she can turn into a dragon, like the other drengr?"

Both males erupted into roars of laughter.

Byron turned his affectionate gaze on her. "Wherever did you hear such a story?"

She shrugged. "Sophie said something about it. Her grandmother was born to a drengr-rider pair, you know. She swears that women cannot fledge, but the rumors..."

"Rumors have a way of growing out of control, don't they?" Reyr's eyes danced. "But no, Claire cannot transform into a dragon. I will tell you a secret, though. If you wish to know? Yes? Good." He hesitated. "Lady Claire is special. She has a special ability, if you will. Something that was given to her. Lord Cyrus's soul. She can actually speak with him in her mind. And that stays between us," he added. "Although, that hardly means she can suddenly turn into a dragon. It would be most entertaining if she could." He fell silent for a span. "Anyway, try not to believe everything you hear. She *is* seemingly normal...for the most part. You won't find her breathing fire."

"Well, that's almost disappointing." Tamara grinned.

Reyr chuckled. "*Nothing* about that woman is disappointing. Believe me. You won't find anyone quite like her. She's brave and strong and adventurous. She never shies away from a challenge."

He went on to tell them about several of her escapades.

Tamara was almost jealous. "You're right. She does sound like quite a woman."

"Aye." Reyr nodded. "Few have her courage."

"I wish I could meet her," she sighed.

"Perhaps someday you will." Reyr winked.

After their meal, Byron led her to the fields beyond the fort where they met their trainers, Gavin and Tella. Other pairs were also waiting with them. "Today we will practice evading," Gavin said by way of explanation. Apparently it was to be a group exercise. "You never know when you will meet an enemy in the sky...a wild dragon, for instance." The mere thought left her skin crawling. "We must always be prepared for what may come."

After a bit more instruction, riders mounted up, and Byron launched them into the sky. She braced herself for the familiar heavy sensation that left her stomach plummeting towards the ground. But once he was airborne, she smiled wide and closed her eyes, relishing the sensations.

"Ready?" Byron's voice was in her mind. She gave him her confirmation and the drills began.

Her heart pounded as they flew in and out of the paths of swooping pairs. Each tried to cut them off, and even snatch her from Byron's back. All she could hear was her pulse in her ears, louder than the wind whistling by.

"Watch your back!" Byron shouted, swooping low.

She felt Raycor's talons graze her back. The light green drengr narrowly missed her, almost ripping her from her harness. Raycor's talons tore slits across the fabric of her vest. She cursed, ducking low. It was a close call. Too close. She hated to think what the chaos of a real attack might be like.

They evaded another pair. Her stomach lifted into her throat as Byron did a barrel roll. For a brief moment, she was upside down, blood rushing to her face. Then they were swooping to avoid the talons of another drengr. Blurs of colors rushed before her eyes.

She felt the painful scrape of a talon against her arm as the fabric on her tunic ripped. Blood sprayed, surging from the wound.

She hissed in pain. Her eyes watered, but she blinked away the tears.

"Tamara?"

"I'm okay. It's just a scratch." She covered it with her bare hand to staunch the bleeding. This wasn't the first time she'd suffered a wound like this. It was unavoidable. The only difference was, unlike the other riders, she wasn't yet mated, which meant she didn't have Byron's magic to immediately heal.

"Let's land and get you patched up."

"I'm sorry about that," Raycor's voice sounded in Byron's mind. She heard it as if it was in her own. When they were in the sky like this, their minds were connected, as long as her skin made contact with his scales. It was why she chose not to wear gloves, like the other riders.

"All part of the drill," Byron said. *"No hard feelings."*

Despite his claim, she could hear the tension in Byron's voice. She could feel his anger as he leashed it. He didn't like that someone had hurt her, accident or not. Even if he knew his anger was inappropriate in a situation like this.

After a short break patching her wounds with magic, she was good as new. They began again. The afternoon flew by. When the sun finally began to set, she breathed a heavy sigh of relief. This was her favorite part of each day. Seeing the sun over the water, and enjoying Byron's company as they leisurely made their way back to the fort.

CHAPTER 9

DEPTHS OF SHADOWKEEP

Northern Barrier Range

Mikkin crawled over the ridge that separated him from the dragons and Ice Lake. He was careful to watch where he placed his hands and feet, careful not to make a sound. The day had dawned especially cold. He clutched his cloak tightly around him, shivering against it. A light snow had fallen the night before, making it harder to go unnoticed. He would need to wipe his tracks when he retreated back to the camp he shared with Jamie in a nearby cave.

His current hideout was disguised by a dense pile of brush. He made himself comfortable and began to observe. His routine had been the same for nearly two weeks. He'd learned many of the patterns dragons were prone to, like when they fed and slept, when they came and went, and even a few spats. Though often harmless, they occasionally grew into deeper acts of violence towards each other. A deep sense of restlessness had settled over them.

Today, they appeared especially restless. "Something is different," he muttered, a frown pulling at his lips.

There was no flitting and flying about. The dragons had assembled on the far side of the lake, clinging to the rocky crests near their lair. Their sharp talons, sharp enough to slice through flesh and sinew, made deep gouges in the cliff. Their wings were held open, kept in constant motion to maintain balance. Some gnashed their heads about, snapping at air with their jaws.

A bone-rattling roar split the air. He shuddered, watching as the clan of dragons moved as one. They jumped, massive bodies vaulting into the air. A flash of blood-red scales caught his gaze. The clan's leader.

His grip tightened on his bow. Instinct had him moving, loading an arrow, pulling. He paused, shaking his head, releasing the tension in the string. There was no way he'd hit a single dragon at this distance. It would only betray his location. Growling, he sank back to the ground, hiding himself again.

He watched the creatures responsible for murdering his family —for taking Mardra from him. Watched them depart, moving farther and farther away. A new hollow formed in his chest. Growing. Engulfing his heart as the dragons disappeared over the ridge.

And then they were gone.

Silence pressed in around him. Gods, he was foolish! What had he expected, coming here? That he might have vengeance from a poorly crafted plan? A plan with no chance of success? He stood and kicked the nearest tree, howling as pain shot up his cold toes and into his leg.

The dragons had departed, and who could say when they would return? Scrambling away, he raced through the forest, caring little for the noise he made. Not bothering to wipe his tracks. The dragons were gone, weren't they? So they wouldn't see his trail.

He all but crashed into the cave he and Jamie shared.

Jamie gave a little shout, jumping to his feet, goblin sword at the ready. He'd been sharpening it near the small fire. "Gods above!" Jamie breathed, eyes wide. "Be quiet! Or someone will find us."

He stared at the lad, his chest heaving. "The dragons. They've all gone."

Jamie's sword arm fell. "You…you're sure? But if they've left, that would mean—"

"Yes, exactly."

He shook his head and began pacing. His innards squirmed. He had done nothing in his time here—no good whatsoever—to help future victims who might suffer the clan's wrath.

"But—" Jamie glanced around, looking at all the weapons they had laid out to inventory, weapons they had taken from the goblins they'd killed during their journey. "But we are so close. I've got everything sharpened and…and we…"

"We'll have to wait." His shoulders fell. "Wait until they return."

"No! I'm done waiting," Jamie hissed. "Mikkin, we've been here nearly two weeks. If we cannot deal them a blow, if we cannot weaken them in any way, then what's the point? We're going to freeze to death before we do a single thing. It may be autumn for the rest of the kingdom, but here in the mountains, winter is upon us."

"I…I know." He ran a hand through his matted hair, long overdue for a haircut. They didn't have adequate clothing to survive once the heavy snows came.

"Think, Mikkin. Think of all the damage they will do, all the damage they are about to do now that they've gone. Had we acted sooner—"

"Listen to yourself," he cried, his temper getting the better of him. "We could *not* have acted sooner. All my observations, all my—"

"We could have! If you would've let me help! I get it, you promised my father you would protect me." Jamie tossed the sword aside in his anger. It clattered, the sound reverberating through the small cave. "What about all the other fathers out there? All the other fathers who are about to lose *their* sons when the dragons attack? Gods! We don't even know where they're headed. Who's next? It could be anyone."

Mikkin's shoulders slumped. "We don't. You're right. But that's all the more reason we shouldn't jump to conclusions. Perhaps they've simply gone hunting, or to explore, or—"

"You don't believe that, do you?"

Mikkin sighed. Somewhere in the past few weeks, Jamie had grown up. "You're right. I don't. But they will be back. And yes, your life, as much as I wish to preserve it, is not worth hundreds more that might be taken."

Jamie stood a little straighter. "Then let me help you."

"Fine...fine." The words came reluctantly, but they came. If they managed, he and Jamie could use this time to prepare for the clan's return. They needed to be ready to strike.

THE DAYS PASSED in aching slowness. Jamie was thrilled over his newfound freedom, and Mikkin was forced to trust that the lad wouldn't do anything stupid. He was careful not to hover. Jamie would see that as a lack of confidence in his abilities.

They took regular watches at their hideout, waiting for the clan's return. In their off time, they either hunted or sparred with each other in the cave, building muscle. They'd be little use against dragons, otherwise.

At dawn on the third day, Mikkin found himself particularly restless. "I'll be back," he said after a meager breakfast. Jamie was getting better at hunting. He'd bagged them a couple of squirrels and a rat, as one could not survive on rabbits alone. It wasn't much, but it was enough to hold them.

"Don't stay out too long," Jamie murmured as Mikkin passed out into the daylight, squinting against the glare of the sun.

Another light snowfall dusted the ground. He grimaced when he saw the path left by his tracks. He did his best to cover them with a branch, but that only made a sweeping mess that looked nearly as obvious. There wasn't much for it, and he could only hope there would be no more goblins like Unka prowling about.

At the hideout beside the lake, he made himself comfortable. As he had guessed, the dragons still had not returned. The day prior, he had promised to remain calm. Two days was barely time for an excursion into Dragonwall. But now he was beginning to have his doubts. His worry was two-fold. Some of it was selfishness. If the dragons did not return, how would he seek revenge? That was his biggest concern, though his real concern should have been the people of Dragonwall, for what might befall them.

He sat watching, rubbing his tired eyes every so often. They closed for longer and longer periods as he waited, bored out of his wits. Until he heard a snap.

He must have dozed off. Probably Jamie coming to scold him for staying away so long. The lad was never as quiet as he should have been. He turned.

His eyes widened. A thunk and a sharp pain at the back of his head was all he knew before darkness took him.

MARDRA GREETED him at the door, rushing to him. Her hug was warm, her kiss, sweet like honey. He took her in his arms, burying his face in her hair. Thomas and Devden rushed to him, squealing with glee. He loved returning home, returning to them—

HIS EYES FLUTTERED, slowly opening. His mind turned over, mulling over the images in his dreams. He groaned. Pain split the back of his head. He twitched his fingers, attempting to rub the hurt. His arms didn't feel like moving. Neither did his feet. He twitched his toes, then his legs. At last, he hauled himself up.

His mind was fuzzy. Too much wine with Mardra the night before? Where was he? Was it morning?

He rubbed his eyes with his fists, blinking and squinting, trying to see in the muted light. His hand went to the back of his throbbing head and he winced against his headache. What the hell had he done?

Memories began returning. There was no Mardra. She was dead. No drinking either. He was in the mountains hunting dragons. Was he back in the cave? His eyes went in and out of focus.

No. Definitely not the cave.

A loud clang forced him to his feet. Several more followed. Sounds that were suspiciously like the opening and closing of iron bars. Still groggy, he backed away until his back came against a rocky wall. In front of him—bars.

He was in a cell.

"Gods damn it all to hell!" he snarled.

Iron bars ran floor to ceiling. The other three walls were made of rock. He glanced about. Trapped. His heart raced, splitting his headache wide open. He gripped his head and keeled over, attempting to get his breathing under control.

In. Out. In. Out.

His nerves calmed, easing some of his headache, allowing him to stand again. Perhaps losing his family, his home, made him less of a victim to fear. Fear was for those who had something to hold on to, but he had nothing, and that made him stronger. Or so he hoped.

Muted words drifted toward him. He stepped up to the bars and listened. There was the sound of boots against rock. Someone was coming. Somehow, he already understood where he was— deep within the bowels of Shadowkeep. His heart rate spiked again. His hunting knife was gone. So was the goblin blade he wore at his hip.

He blinked. Remembering. Mountain men, dressed in furs, ratted hair, browned teeth, dirtied faces. Cave dwellers. He'd heard of them before. Hadn't expected to see them so close to the sorcer-er's lair, though.

A figure came into view, cloaked, his face hidden. Time seemed to slow. His skin erupted into gooseflesh. Then the man spoke, and he knew immediately who it was.

"Good evening." The voice was unnatural, grating. "My men found you camped by my lake. As was their command, they have brought you to me."

Mikkin swallowed against his suddenly dry throat.

"At first, I thought nothing of it, you see. A lone man, gruff as you appear to be, camped out in my territory. Surely you are no more than a stranger, traveling through the mountains, no doubt captivated by what you have seen here." The sorcerer stepped closer to the bars. Two white hands wrapped around them. The hooded face leaned forward. "But after some thinking, I have decided that you are not here by mere chance."

Was this Unka's doing? Had the little urchin gone straight to Kane? He should have killed the damn creature. Jamie was right.

"Tell me your name and I will tell you mine."

"I already know yours." His rough voice surprised him.

"Then you have me at a disadvantage."

"Why would I tell you my name?" Something of boldness crept into his chest. A desire to fight against the puppet master pulling the strings. "You, being who you are, you'll probably find some way to use it against me."

"Tsk-tsk. Then I shall cut to the point. Why are you here, snooping about my lands? Speak carefully. If you give me the truth and I judge your reasons benign, I might just release you."

He snorted. "Right. And these mountains are full of fairies. Coins grow on trees. And horses fart rainbows. You really expect me to believe that?"

"Hardly. A smart man would not. But I'm not certain. Tell me, are you a smart man? If you were, you would not be here."

He shrugged. "It's like you said. I am traveling through the range to Kalderland and happened upon this...this place. I saw...I saw..."

"You saw the dragons?" Kane's voice was a pleased purr.

"Yes."

"And what did you think of my magnificent beasts?"

"I..." He cleared his throat. "Magnificent, my lord. Something I could not have imagined in my wildest dreams."

"Yes. Truly magnificent." Kane inhaled deeply. "Too bad you smell of lies. Why are you here, traveler?"

"Because your men captured me...obviously."

"Feast on your defiance all you like. Your words will change when you meet my bats. They are growing into something even the dragons will fear." The sorcerer's words left his skin crawling. "It is a shame really. I am in such a hurry, else I would get the truth from you through other means. You ought to see my library. It is something even the most creative mind cannot imagine. But never mind. I must be away. Important tasks await. Particularly with Fort Squall. I ought not to be late."

A chill ran down his spine. Fort Squall? Flashes of Belnesse, his beautiful city engulfed in dragon fire, wormed into his mind. Would the drengr at the fort be enough? Would their defenses save the city?

"Think about the truth while I am away. Consider wisely. When I return, I might still feed you to my bats. Nothing would make me happier."

The sorcerer vanished. He blinked several times. All fell silent... for a time. And then he heard something entirely new. It started as a coughing laugh. A voice from the shadows said, "You are wise not to trust him." A raspy voice, as if it had not been used in a long, long time. "Kane will never free you, even if you do give him what he wants."

"Who... Who's there? Who are you? Show yourself." He moved forward, close to the bars. His wasn't the only cell in the dungeon. There were others along the corridor beside and opposite him, though he couldn't see the occupants, if there were any.

There was a shuffling from across the corridor. A shape appeared in the gloom. "I was known as Berbik...once. That was my name...a long time ago."

Torchlight fell upon a small figure, stooped, and...hairy. He blinked. A fur-monster? The creature was heavily bearded, with hair that fell into its face, all the way down to the floor. Then the shadowed face lifted and Mikkin's jaw dropped. "You...you're..."

"A dwarg...yes."

It was the first Dwarg he had ever seen in all his life.

CHAPTER 10
BEFORE THE ATTACK

Celenore

Claire was not enjoying her adventure by the second day. Losing a night of sleep didn't help. She tried to sleep in the sky, resting her cheek against the warm scales of Jovari's muscular neck. At times she had dozed off, only to have strange dreams about Kane. She saw him on the back of a red dragon, flying into battle with the Ice Clan. The scent of fear thick in the air. Not coming from the dragons, but from whomever they were planning to attack. It felt like watching a catastrophic disaster unfold before her. Like a bad dream, but bigger. She found herself jerking awake to the unnerving feeling of being in the sky. It was disorienting and disconcerting.

They had crossed into Celenore hours ago, flying over the bay where it narrowed to meet the mouth of Flat River. Her nerves were frayed. Their mission loomed closer with each beat of Jovari's wings. The lower the sun sank on the horizon, the more her heart stuttered. The more her breathing heightened.

They made camp. A place to rest and eat. After having a slice of dried meat and some bread, it was time to check on the pairs she'd sent ahead. Had they reached the villages safely? Had they informed the constables?

She closed her eyes, contacting each of them. She found Odrick and Til first. It wasn't difficult to reach them over a short distance. She took a deep breath as her mind touched theirs. It was a strange sensation, reaching for them all at once. She gave them a mental prod, like a finger poke, getting their attention.

"Lady Claire? Gods above!" Odrick made his surprise quite clear. *"Forgive me."*

Til felt her too. *"So you really can speak to us over a distance? It wasn't simply a trick."*

"It wasn't a trick."

Talking to more than one drengr wasn't as hard as she'd expected. She merely treated it as if they were right in front of her, holding a group conversation. She also felt Rachel and Darcie's minds linked through their mates. Their presence was subtle, like a feather brushing against skin.

"Has everything gone according to plan?" she asked. *"Is Swinston ready?"*

"Aye." Odrick answered for them. *"We flew most of the way then transformed and snuck in as travelers. They were surprised to see us— surprised and relieved."*

"And they're cooperating?"

"Yes, so far. They didn't give us much trouble once we began working with the constable. His name's Rodney."

She exhaled, relieved. *"It sounds like everything is going according to plan. You will be ready by midnight?"*

"We will be ready, my lady. The villagers are hard at work as we speak, building trenches and collecting firewood in the dark. We are helping with our magic where we can."

"Well done." She forced her shoulders to relax. *"You've made great progress. Report anything that changes."*

"Aye, my lady. We will be in touch."

She cut the contact and relayed the conversation to Jovari and Koldis. Those gathered around her listened too.

Next she contacted Gradyr and Jorsid in Lormont. They had

utilized the assistance of Lormont's mage, combining her magic with theirs to build the trench that would circle the village. Lormont was the biggest of the three villages, so they needed all the help they could get. Finally, she contacted Nokin and Hiondel in Osbourne. They too were well underway with preparations and promised to be ready.

Satisfied, she tried to get some sleep. She wasn't sure how sprite magic worked, but she had an inkling that being rested would go a long way in helping. She made an honest effort of it, but the ground was too hard, the night too cold, and her nerves too frantic to drift off. She lay awake for what felt like ages, tense. Her anxiety left her shivering. Her tense jaw gave her a headache.

People were counting on her. Lives depended on her. But it was more than that—more than the pressure of it. Very soon she would have the opportunity to defeat the vodar once and for all. To deal Kane a heavy setback.

Vengeance might not be as sweet as you think...

Cyrus intruded on her thoughts. He was still with her, as always, hovering in the back of her mind. Showing himself at the oddest times. Often with bouts of wisdom, though she didn't always agree with him. Like now.

Vengeance would be sweet—she was certain of it. This was her chance to avenge his death, to get his killers for what they'd done to him. For taking him from her. He'd been hers to protect. They'd come to *her* home and killed him.

Nothing could be sweeter.

You should do this for the people, for Dragonwall, not for me, Cyrus said.

She grunted under her breath. For the people. As if the people were her burden to bear.

What if I can't keep them safe? she asked. *What if I fail?* The idea of it left her stomach in knots. Worse still, if they died because of her, because of her failed plan, how could she possibly forgive herself?

Cyrus snorted. A mental snort, but a snort nonetheless. *In all your time here, when have you ever failed? You always fear failure, yet you meet success.*

She opened her mouth to disagree, then closed it. What was the point in arguing? She wanted to believe him, but the feeling in her gut said otherwise. Said that this wasn't going to go as smoothly as she hoped.

Instead, she thought over her plan. They'd gone through it more than once. But there was plenty to go wrong. What if they failed to get the firelines ignited? What if it took her too long to do what she needed to do? What if her sprite fire didn't work? The vodar would be trapped in the villages *with* the villagers. Even with the assisting pairs, the villagers would be in danger before any reinforcements arrived. What if the vodar found ways to harm the villagers during that time?

These doubts will do you no good. You need to sleep.

She heard Cyrus's words like a command. He must have worked some magic because she dozed off almost immediately.

Dark blue water slid by beneath her, lit by the moon overhead. She could just barely discern little white crests of waves sparkling below. Beneath her, powerful muscles expanded and contracted as Wrath the Red beat his wings against the cold air. Their coming would be like the gathering of a great storm. Her body shuddered with longing. The thrill of battle lust. She couldn't wait for it. Death. Destruction. All the things she'd missed for so many years. Since the day the Kalds had invaded Dragonwall. She could almost hear their cries in her ears now. A smile split her lips open. Yes...they would cry, scream, beg for mercy—

"Claire." There was a firm pressure on her shoulder. "Claire!" She opened her eyes. Koldis hovered over her. "It's time." She blinked and her nightmare crumbled away like a cliff face breaking off into the sea. "Hurry."

"I think I'm going to be sick," she muttered, taking a deep breath. She trembled beneath her cloak.

"Just keep breathing." Koldis kept his hand on her shoulder, crouched beside her. "Here—" He uncorked his waterskin and passed it over. "Little sips."

She nodded, taking one and then another, letting the cool liquid fall down her throat. She took deep, slow breaths until her nerves felt steadier. "Everyone is counting on me, Koldis. What if I can't—?"

"You'll be fine." He gave her shoulder a final squeeze and stood. "Now, hurry up. You're flying with me for this."

She nodded into the darkness, mustering enough fortitude to stand and face the challenge set before her. The confidence that Koldis had in her—Cyrus too—only increased the pressure. She couldn't afford to fail, she just couldn't. If she failed...

Her mind drifted to Talon. She rubbed the back of her neck, trying to massage away the tension. He wasn't going to be happy when he discovered what she'd done—success or not. He'd gone to a lot of trouble to rescue her from Kane's kidnappers, only for her to throw herself into another fire.

She blinked, looking at the dark landscape around her, then she closed her eyes and pictured the words of the sprite song in her mind, saying them over and over again without thinking too hard. The skin around her mark prickled, as if encouraging her to let free the magic that had been hiding. She pictured the green flames that would erupt once she started to sing, imagining the emerald hues and the calm warmth her fire created.

"Come on. Let's go," Koldis said, snapping her out of it. "Leave everything here. We won't need it until we return." She gave a final sigh, looking around. Then she took her first steps forward, allowing Koldis to lead her away from their camp. Her last thought as she looked over their belongings, was that she hoped everyone would make it back alive.

CHAPTER II

FIGHTING THE VODAR

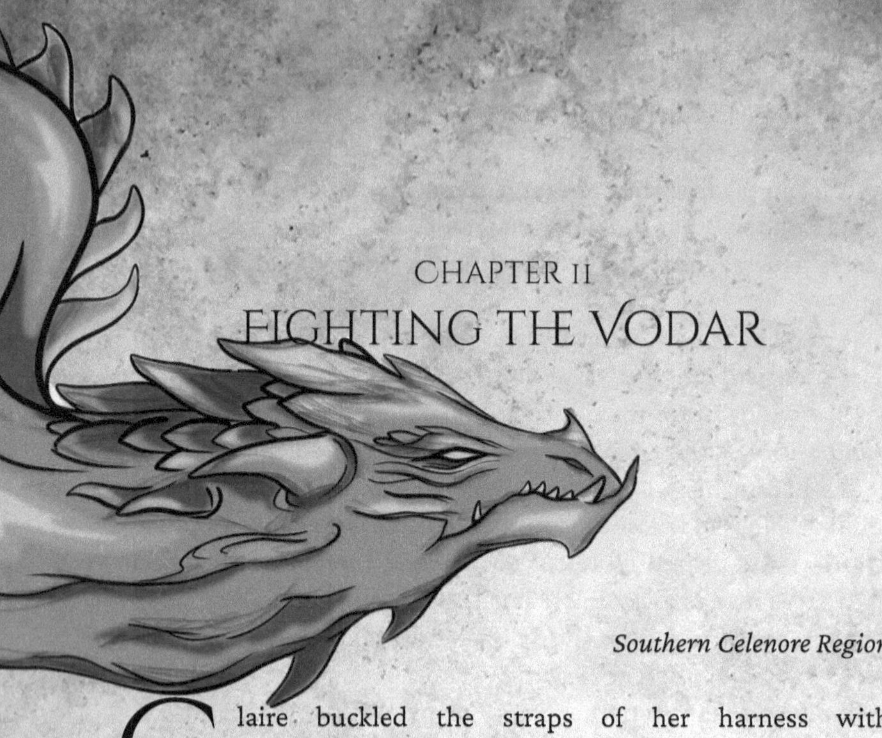

Southern Celenore Region

Claire buckled the straps of her harness with absentminded ease. The moon gave a soft glow to an otherwise dark sky. Koldis took flight, the others in formation around him.

She closed her eyes, repeating the spriten words that now came so easily, weaving them together in her mind. She didn't understand their meaning, but she did understand the way they felt. Like death and flames and justice.

"*We're here,*" Koldis said. His voice was a whisper against her thoughts.

She opened her eyes. Her stomach lurched as he turned on his wing tip, making a wide arc. Jovari led a second wing behind them.

They were positioned high above the villages nestled in the wilderness below. The world was black beneath them, as if they were suspended in nothingness. It was impossible to see where each village was, how far one was from the other, the miles between them. That didn't stop her imagination. She thought of what it might be like to call such a place home. How frightened the villagers must be, laying in wait for the inevitable appearance of Kane's wraiths. Terrified.

Her stomach squirmed. She was afraid *for* them. Afraid of what might happen if she failed.

Your magic is growing, Cyrus said. *You are getting stronger.* She frowned. She wanted to ask him what he meant, but now was not the time.

Multiple awarenesses brushed against her consciousness, feather soft, each a unique fingerprint, each ready to send thoughts at a moment's notice. She buzzed with anticipation. Theirs added to it.

She pulled her cloak more tightly around her shoulders.

There were six pairs in the villages and fourteen in the sky. Each was assigned to one of three groups. Jovari had opted to join Kilian's group in Lormont.

As soon as the signal was given, each group would depart to protect the villagers and distract the vodar. This would buy her time to work her magic. She and Koldis would remain safely above, unseen to everyone below.

"Lady Claire." Odrick was the first to contact her. She felt Til's presence piggybacking his. *"The trench is complete. Villagers are in position. Watch for our signal."*

"Thank you." She paused before adding, *"Be careful."* A plea more than anything.

"Aye, my lady. We will."

The others checked in after that. Koldis circled overhead. The others maintained their tight formation...waiting.

She ground her teeth together, frustrated that she didn't have a dragon's eyesight.

"We can't go any lower yet," Koldis explained. *"If they smell us on the wind, they may be alerted to our presence."*

She took a deep breath. No risks. They'd only get one shot at this.

"Know what you need to do?" Koldis asked. *"Are you ready to do it?"*

"I...yes. When it is time, I'll be ready." Her palms were sticky. She wiped them on her pants. *"Koldis?"*

"Yes?"

"Are you sure they won't be suspicious when they see the trenches?"

"I'm not certain," he said. *"They might assume the villagers have taken matters into their own hands."*

"And once the fire is going? They won't simply flee?"

"No. A ring of fire for the vodar is binding, remember?"

"I guess...I'm just nervous is all."

"I understand."

Each minute was agonizing as they circled. She wasn't aware of her trembling until Koldis told her to relax. He felt it through the harness. She took deep breaths, willing herself to be calm, but her body was like a bowstring stretched tight.

Hiondel's voice sounded in her mind. *"Something stirs in the darkness..."* Her skin prickled. Hiondel was in Osbourne. *"There are shadows. They are coming."*

She sucked in a breath. There was a flash of motion in her mind, piercing like a sharp pain. She saw moonlit fields, black shapes moving directly towards her. Another flash of images and the shapes were gliding into the village. A flicker of flames. Then a surge of blinding fire, saturating her sensitive eyes.

She gasped, eyelids fluttering. Everything turned black again. She was in the sky. She shook her head, trying to rid herself of the confusion. The images were definitely *not* hers.

She clenched her fists making her hands ache. *Cyrus?* He gave no reply.

"There!" Koldis shouted in her mind. *"Osbourne!"* A flicker of gold far, far below, shining through the darkness. Within seconds a blazing ring took form surrounding the entire village.

"Gristas, Bianca! It's time!" she called, sending her first command. Gristas and his mate Bianca were in charge of the Osbourne group.

"We follow." His voice resounded in her mind. A brief mental flash flooded her senses, similar to the one before. This one came from a different vantage point. She found herself plummeting

toward the earth, nosediving toward Osbourne. She blinked and the image was gone. Gristas, Bianca, and their small group of pairs took off into the darkness to reinforce Hiondel, Lily, Nokin, and Madeleine. The riders had their bows drawn.

"We will hold them as long as we can." Hiondel's voice again. Another image came with it. A brief flash of a blade near the fire line. She blinked and looked away. The image vanished.

Things descended into chaos. A second and third fire blazed into life. Thin, golden rings against the black landscape below. A cage for the vodar, trapped in the villages with their human prey.

"Kilian, Heidi, you're up!" She all but screamed the order. *"Get your team to Lormont! Faedrol, Hannah, to Swinston! And remember, distractions only. No killing blows. That's my job."*

The last thing she needed was a rogue vodar popping back into existence a few days later because someone's blade slipped too far and beheaded them.

"We follow," came their responses.

The sky was aflutter with wings, leaving her alone with Koldis. More images bombarded her mind as drengr reinforcements arrived in their respective villages. She shook her head, trying to clear them away.

What was happening to her? Why now, of all times, when she needed to focus? Was her magic going haywire?

I told you, Cyrus said, *you are growing stronger.*

She blinked, but the images kept coming. Blades. Black shapes. Screams. Fire. Fear.

She wanted to ignore it, to sever ties with the drengr, but they needed her. She put her head in her hands and squeezed her eyes shut, drawing deep breaths, bracing herself against the rising pressure beating against her temples. The skin around her spriten mark tingled, itching. It was a reminder.

She opened her eyes, dragging in air, filling her lungs.

You can do this. Cyrus's confidence radiated deep in her chest.

Turning her gaze below, she began to sing. Her voice wobbled. She struggled to keep it steady, to control her fear, to battle the wind as it fought against her. *"Fallam nemaloh sasilo valandur ellohdar.*" But knowing the words of a song was not enough.

She pictured the vodar within the glowing boundaries. Imagined the evil that seeped out of them. Imagined the way she wanted to see their bodies consumed by flames.

Her voice cracked as a series of panicked images bombarded her mind, flashing across her consciousness like the flipping of channels on a television screen. She faltered. Each came from a different point of view, from a different drengr.

In Lormont, reinforcements were forcing the vodar back into a concentrated group, keeping them away from the villagers. Jovari was there, his sverak in one hand and magic in the other.

Osbourne was more chaotic. Villagers ran about screaming and scurrying as wraiths stormed through their homes, dragging them out, using them as leverage against the drengr and their riders. Nothing about this situation was contained. Bianca, Lily, and Madeleine stood on a nearby rooftop, arrows whizzing as they shouted orders to those below.

In Swinston, Faedrol, Odrick and Til had driven the vodar into two separate groups, keeping them away from cottages. Their blades flashed in the firelight, accompanied by bursts of magic.

"*Claire!*" Koldis broke through her mind. Her voice had gone silent. "*Pull yourself together!*" he shouted. There was a panicked edge to his words.

Her pulse raced.

"*Claire, what's going on?*" Jovari all but yelled from where he fought down below. "*We can't hold them for much longer!*"

Other voices followed his, pressing in around her, begging her to hurry.

"*I'm trying, Koldis. I...It's...*" She trembled. She opened her mouth, but the only sound that emerged was a croak. It was happening. She was failing, just like she'd feared. "*I was wrong. I can't...*" She knew the words of the song but there were too many thoughts, too many images, too many feelings.

Too much fear.

A flicker from Hiondel flashed before her eyes. A wraith had a woman by the hair, dragging her from her cottage kicking and screaming. Hiondel raced forward to protect her, sverak drawn. He met the vodar's short sword.

"*Claire!*" She hardly heard Koldis screaming at her.

The vodar released its hold on the woman, turning its full attention to Hiondel, dealing several successive blows meant to cripple. Hiondel was tired, his magic all but depleted. The vodar lunged, thrusting its blade forward. A sick laugh hissed from its lips. White-hot pain seared her abdomen. She screamed, clutching her stomach as she doubled over in her harness. She looked directly beneath the vodar's hood, eyes locked on the dark shadows beneath as she clutched her wound. It was the last thing she saw, that awful hooded face, seared into her mind, and then nothing. Lily's cry was a dying echo in her mind.

"No!" she screamed. Her eyes snapped open and the pain vanished. "No! Hiondel!" Her breathing came in ragged gasps, faster and faster, until her head began to swim. Her vision blurred. She clutched her stomach and looked down, expecting to see blood. There was nothing. No pain. No wound. She was fine.

A shudder wracked her body. Failure clutched her, draining her strength like a monster that delighted in hopelessness. In the snap of a moment, Hiondel was gone, and it was entirely her fault. This was all her fault. They'd trusted her, and already she'd failed.

Do not give in! Cyrus pounded against her mind with invisible fists. *You can do this! Fight it! Fight your fear.*

"But...he's gone," she whispered aloud, as if the sky would hear her and do something about it. "I...I can't."

You can. You must *see* them. *You must truly see them in your mind, and then you sing your—*

A sharp cry cut through Cyrus's words. It was her own. Points of pain erupted in various places across her body. A slice along her arm. A gash in her leg. She screamed again as each misplaced parry, each misstep, each blow struck her down. The drengr were radiating their injuries along the connection, and she was helpless to stop the painful sensations assaulting her.

"*We can't hold them any longer!*" came their cries.

She was lost to pain.

Hiondel's killer filled her vision again. Rotting skin. Toothless snarl. Black eyes, glittering with disdain. The face of a demon. Even the stench of death reached her nostrils.

"*Claire!*" Koldis shouted at her. "*Damn it, Claire! Get yourself under control before everyone dies!*"

She blinked, dragging in a breath.

He was right. They needed her. Every injury. Every death. It was her fault. If she didn't do something now, it would all be for nothing. She had no other choice—she was their only hope.

She unclenched her hands from around Koldis's harness, and brought them to rest against his warm scales, hoping the heat would steady her frantic heart.

"I can do this," she whispered to herself, a lie she hardly believed. But she whispered it, nonetheless. "No, I *must* do this."

Using strength from the gods only knew where, she opened her mouth, picturing the Vodar's face in her mind, and began to sing again. The words were shaky at first. After a few lines, they became surer than before, steadier than before. There was still chaos. There was still fear. There was still pain. But there was also a deep need to make everything right—to fix her failure before it spiraled out of control.

Each phrase tumbled from her like a promise. A renewed pledge to protect. And this time, she felt the magic deep in her chest, accompanied by a burning sensation where her sprite mark tingled. Her voice fell upon the world below, words flowing like droplets of water, like rain, mixed with every emotion she felt, down a well carved path laced with intent and purpose.

This time, the wind did not swallow up her words. Instead it greeted her like a friend. It recognized her and rejoiced, carrying her, magnifying her magic for the world.

"*It's working!*" someone shouted. "*Gods above! It's working.*"

She was so focused, she almost didn't hear the roar of satisfaction.

Koldis went lower, sweeping around in a wide arc. Her eyes watered. Tears poured down her cheeks, whether from fear, sadness, or relief, she did not know. But she kept singing. Her mark burned, searing white-hot like a fire poker branding her skin. It radiated with brilliant luminescence beneath her clothing. And then she too began to glow with it. She knew then, surer than ever, that her efforts were working.

Koldis was low enough now, gliding over one of the villages. Flashes of green flame erupted beneath her, just discernible. Images flooded her mind, brief glimpses of the vodar as they burned and writhed, hissing in agony as her sprite fire took them. One by one they disappeared, leaving behind nothing more than a pile of ash.

Her hoarse voice faded to a whisper. It was finally over. They were dead, gone. But it was a hollow victory. An empty victory. Because all she could think about was the loss of Hiondel's life and those she had failed to protect.

CHAPTER 12

LOOKING FOR ANSWERS

Kastali Dun

Verath lifted the bolt on the cell door. It groaned open. He strode in, his nose twitching with disgust. The cell's innards were dark. With a muttered cantrip, he went about lighting the wall sconces, making quick work of the task.

Eagle was curled up in the corner. He didn't move. It was said that torture could turn any man's mind insane. He believed it. Fortunately for Eagle's sake, he appeared fairly sane, considering all things.

He unwrapped the cheese cloth from a warm round he'd pilfered from the cooling rack in the cookery and crouched in front of Eagle. "You've seen better days." He noted the signs of rapid weight loss.

Eagle grunted, pushing himself into a sitting position. "Is that supposed to be funny? Ha ha." He paused. "Has my *protectoress* decided what to do with me?"

"You're lucky you *have* a protectoress, otherwise I'd throttle you." Verath hesitated. "Every attempt to capture Collier has failed.

Either you have been lying or he's smarter than the lot of us combined." He smoothed the scowl from his face.

Eagle snatched the round, tearing a large chunk away with his teeth. "I told you all I know," he said, mouth full. "I wasn't exactly in a position to lie through my teeth, was I? Too busy screaming." He swallowed. "What? I told you how to do it. Go alone. Ring the bell. Wait ten minutes. Your people didn't follow a single instruction, did they? What did you expect?"

He ground his teeth together. The plan *had* gone awry, and every attempt to recover Collier since, had failed. The poison maker was a tricky little shit, but he hadn't left the city. Why would he? After living here for so long, getting away with so much. He didn't expect to get caught.

"Where do you think he is now? I'm sure he's got multiple places in the city."

"Listen, man." Eagle held up his hands, bread in one. "I'm from the north. I was given an address on a scrap of parchment. A single address. Not three. Not five."

Verath swore and set about pacing. Weeks had passed without success. Not a word. Not an inkling that would allow him to track Collier. He stopped and turned. "You're a criminal, Eagle. You know how criminals think, what they do, how they act. Where would he go? If you were him, where would you go if business was still too good to leave?"

Eagle regarded him. "En't it obvious? I'd go where you wouldn't be looking for me."

"Hmm...I *had* thought of that."

"Good. Then whaddya need me for, eh?"

"Quiet." He thought for a moment. Where was the king most likely to search? Places like the Pauper's District or Ambush Alley. Overcrowding made for the perfect conditions. They had searched both.

He let out a long breath. "He'd go to Oldham Road. Or perhaps the Merchant's District. Both are close to the keep."

"Glad you figured it out." Eagle tore at the rest of the bread, devouring it in a matter of seconds. "If you happen to find him this time, tell him I want my money back."

"Right." Verath turned on his heel and swept from the room, leaving the sconces lit. He had four weeks until the trial. Four weeks to prove that Lady Caterina was guilty.

"Imeir, you free?" Imeir was his oldest friend. He had agreed to help in whatever capacity necessary.

"Yes, why?"

"Got a fresh lead on Collier. Meet me in the courtyard—first level. We can walk. I'll explain on the way."

The dungeons spat him out near their meeting place, so he slowed his pace to allow Imeir time to fly over from Fort Kastali. In his younger years, Imeir had been like a younger brother to him. Without real siblings, older drengr often took younger ones under their wings. That was exactly what Imeir had been. They were both descended from the Desert Clan, and their fathers had been like brothers too. It only made sense that the tradition should continue.

As soon as he'd become a shield for King Tallek, Imeir had put in for the transfer from Fort Lin. Isobel protested at first, until she realized that the capital held more life than Lincastle had. His chest tightened thinking about her. Isobel had died in the Goblin Wars, one of a small handful of riders to be killed at that time. Imeir wasn't the same afterward, and the last ten years had been a trial because of it. But he did what he could for the male.

He stopped short of his destination, muttering a curse under his breath. A young drengr stepped out in front of him, blocking his path. He looked him over and frowned. There was something familiar about the set of his eyes.

"My lord." The young drengr bowed deeply—an odd gesture. Then he held his arm out in a more familiar greeting, reaching for Verath's forearm.

Verath took his in return, still frowning. "I know the face of every drengr in Fort Kastali and Fort Lin. You are from neither. Am I correct?"

The young drengr looked as if he'd been caught doing something wrong. "For...forgive me, my lord." He swallowed, opened his mouth to say something more, then closed it. He looked no older than fifteen, perhaps twenty. "Gods, boy, how old are you?" It had been some time since he had seen one this young.

The lad's shoulders straightened. "Twenty-four, Lord Verath."

"Then you're fledged?"

"Of—of course." His cheeks tinged with pink. "I wouldn't have come here if I weren't."

Verath's eyebrows pulled together. "And why exactly *are* you here? You haven't answered my first question."

"I am from Fort Edge, Lord Verath." He looked about, glancing into the corridor before speaking. "Might we speak in private? There is something...something I would like to discuss."

Verath's gaze darted into the courtyard. Imeir had just landed and was heading their way. He turned back to the young Drengr. "What's your name, lad?"

"Oh. I'm..."

"Don't lie to me," he warned.

"Dallin the Violet, Lord Verath." At this, Dallin's face turned redder. Shyness. An obvious symptom of a drengr so green he hadn't found his confidence yet, even at twenty-four.

"Dallin the Violet..." He frowned. "You're Lord Averaen's son, aren't you?"

Lord Averaen had been a King's Shield for King Tallek. Though Averaen was significantly older than Verath, they'd served together for a short period before Tallek's death. It shocked the world when Lord Averaen moved north to take over the fort and then found Evelyn. He claimed she was his mate. Most had doubted the truth of it, Verath included.

To find a mate at such an old age, at nearly eight hundred, seemed impossible. In fact, it was impossible, as far as most knew. There'd been no record of a drengr that old ever doing so. Some claimed he was merely lonely. That he'd found a way to trick the world so he could keep Evelyn close. But after their bonding cere-mony she stopped aging. Magic, some argued. She must have been a mage. These arguments continued. Until the pair bore a child nearly fifty years later. Dallin.

Unless that was magic too, somehow, the evidence could not be refuted.

"What have we here?" Imeir stepped up beside them, taking in the presence of the unfamiliar Dallin.

Verath smiled. "This is Lord Averaen's son."

"You don't say..." Imeir looked genuinely interested. The world had heard plenty of the miracle. Imeir was no exception. Dallin's eyes darted to the ground under the drengr's intense scrutiny.

"I served as shield with your father for a few years before King Tallek died," Verath found himself saying. "A true honor. He's a good male. I had my doubts, admittedly. But he deserved to find Evelyn. Especially after..." He cleared his throat. "Well, never mind that. What brings you here, Dallin?"

Dallin hesitated. "As I said, Lord Verath. A word in private?"

He sighed, glancing at Imeir. "Look, Dallin, the truth is, we're on our way into the city for business. Matter of fact, why don't you tag along? We could use an extra set of eyes."

Imeir's eyebrows pulled together as he glanced between them. Dallin's surprise was more evident. His whole face changed, radiating eager excitement. "Really, sir? I mean, Lord Verath. You—you're sure?"

"Call me Verath, please." He grew tired of the ever-present pretenses others insisted upon. Propriety be damned. "And yes. Why not?"

"Is this wise?" Imeir asked. *"He's a bit young and—"*

Verath placed a hand on Imeir's shoulder, silencing him. He gave a reassuring squeeze. "It will be fine, old friend. Let's go."

THEY WENT to Oldham Road first, splitting up. Imeir went on alone to scope out neighboring streets while Dallin stayed with him. Oldham Road was the most prestigious road in Kastali Dun. Townhouses sat just outside of the keep's lowest wall.

They walked the length of the street, from one end to the other, politely greeting passersby here and there. Nothing looked amiss. He didn't expect anything to.

A footman dressed in dark green livery emerged from a servant's entrance of a nearby townhouse. "You there!" he called.

The man faltered and turned. His eyes widened. He quickly bowed. "How—how can I be of service, my lord?"

"Good afternoon. Do you work on this street?" He motioned toward the townhouse.

The man smiled. "I do. Of course. For the Lowell's." He pointed to the same house.

"Excellent." A gold dragon materialized in Verath's fingers. "Might you know of any newcomers who have arrived in the neighborhood? I am looking for a friend of mine."

The servant looked at the gold dragon. His eyes widened. "Not...not sure I can help you, my lord," he said. "I'd take the money, gladly, but I can't say I've heard of anyone new to Oldham Road. All the servants would be talking."

He pushed the coin into the man's hand anyway. "Take it. Please. I knew it was a stretch, but you were kind enough to stop."

The servant closed his hand around the coin and nodded. He took a step, then looked as if he wanted to say more. "Listen, there's a friend of mine, knows everything there is about everyone in these parts. Great gossip. Works for the Kellys. If you can meet me back here in...say, two hours, I might be able to find out for certain."

Verath smiled. "That's more like it. Two hours. We'll be here. And your name?"

"Call me Alan." The servant bowed and departed.

Verath turned to Dallin. "Well," he said, flashing the lad a smile. "I suppose we have two hours to kill. I don't see Imeir. Maybe he is having better luck than us." He peered down Oldham Road and shrugged.

They began walking the length of the road again. "Who is this man you are searching for?" Dallin asked, genuinely curious.

"A poison maker."

Dallin faltered. "Truly?"

"I would not lie." He grinned. The lad definitely had some growing to do. "That being said, we have time to kill. You wanted to speak to me in private, yes?" Aside from a few passersby, the road was mostly empty.

Dallin swallowed, glancing about. While twenty-four was considered adult by human standards, it certainly wasn't as far as a drengr was concerned. In fact, most Drengr weren't fully mature until they reached fifty or more. Case in point, he couldn't help but notice Dallin's obvious youth.

"I had hoped...well..." Dallin rubbed the back of his neck. "This is rather more difficult than I thought it would be."

They continued walking, leaving Oldham Road behind and continuing on towards the Merchant District. Their pace was brisk enough to hide suspicion. "How about you start with why you left Fort Edge? Does Lord Averaen know you're here? Did he send you? I certainly hope everything is all right."

"Things are...fine. He does not know I left. He was gone when I snuck away."

"Then no one knows you are here?" His brow furrowed. "That's hardly responsible. I think you owe me an explanation."

"Right. I'm sorry, Lord Verath, I did not mean...that is to say...I came here in secret because..." He cleared his throat. "I am aware that there is an open position among the king's shields and I had thought perhaps since I am fledged now...and there should always be six—"

Verath stopped cold in his tracks and fixed Dallin with a deadpan stare. "*You?*"

Dallin's face turned its deepest shade of red yet. He stepped back a step. "You—you're right. It was stupid. I mean, how could I possibly—"

"Measure up?"

"...Yeah." Dallin shook his head.

Verath's chest tightened. He felt instantly guilty about the insult. Perhaps he thought this day would never come. Cyrus's death was still too fresh. Yet, every drengr was entitled to solicit consideration for the position.

He sighed. "The charter states that any drengr who wishes to be considered for the position of king's shield must be given due consideration. Forgive me, Dallin. I did not mean offense. I just— you were not what I would have expected out of an interested applicant."

"That's what *they* said too," he scoffed, kicking his booted foot against a small rock in the dirt.

"They, who?"

"Martel and Ashton—two of the others my age."

"Ah." Every generation created a cohort.

"They said I was too weak, too young, too...whatever. That I should be out looking for my mate, not daydreaming about..."

"Glory? Adventure?" He *almost* smiled. After all, those were the things *he* had thought about at Dallin's age. In that sense, he couldn't help but see a little of himself.

"Yes," Dallin muttered. "Does that mean you—you'll consider me?"

He had to fight the chuckle rising in his chest. Even still, he was sure his dancing eyes would give him away. "Listen, Dallin. It is not for me to make the decision. The king chooses his shields."

"But you...you're...can't you put in a good word for me? You served with my father. Surely that counts for something."

Verath's lips twitched again. "You're right. I'm sure it does. I'll speak to King Talon about the matter when he returns. It could take some time, this process. Perhaps it would be a good idea for you to inform the fort of your whereabouts, so that they do not worry. In the meantime, you're welcome to stay here in the keep, if that is to your liking."

"Absolutely, my lor—" He stopped himself. "Absolutely, Verath. I...thank you." A smile plastered itself to Dallin's face after that.

Verath sighed, nodded, and then continued down the street. He was tempted to tell the young Drengr to kick rocks, but the law was the law. Besides, there was plenty of time to dissuade him, to help him understand what he would be giving up as a shield. Once most made the realization, they went running in the opposite direction.

His stomach dropped at the memory. If only it had been the same for him. If only he would have known.

THEY MET up with Imeir not long after and returned to Oldham Road to meet Alan. By this time, Verath had filled Imeir in, and vice versa. Unlike them, Imeir had less luck, even after speaking to numerous servants.

They strolled up and down the street until Alan walked up, a bounce in his step. "Afternoon, *sirs*." Alan's eyes lingered over Imeir. "I bring good news."

"I like good news," he found himself saying.

Alan nodded. "Friend says there is indeed a few whispers of a new presence in Oldham Road. Says the servants can't say which house, but they believe one of the nobles here is housing someone in secret."

Verath and Imeir exchanged glances. Alan's news was better than expected. It sounded a lot like Collier but there was no way to be certain. "Do you think you can do me a favor?" Verath asked, producing another gold dragon. "Not right this moment, of course. But I can pay well."

Alan's eyes widened. "I hope I can help, sir." He took the coin. "What will you have me do?"

"I would like you and this *friend* of yours to do a bit more digging. See if you can find out more. I need to know which house."

Alan nodded. "I can try, of course."

"Meet me here at the same time, say, two days from now? And tell no one of my inquiry. I'd like it to be a surprise."

"As my lord wishes." Alan bowed and then departed.

Verath turned to Imeir, a smile on his face. "Looks like that is as good as we're going to get for today. Can't say I'm disappointed. I've learned more than one *interesting* tidbit already." He winked at Dallin, whose gaze dropped to the ground.

The young Drengr was going to have to shed more than shyness if he wanted to fill Cyrus's boots. But perhaps Dallin would surprise him. The underestimated ones often had the most to prove. But there was still one thing that bothered him. He didn't want Dallin to make the same mistakes that he had. Everyone had their own lessons to learn, their own choices to make. Only, this wasn't a lesson someone could come back from. He understood too well. He had made his own choice long ago, and now he was forced to live with it for the rest of his life.

CHAPTER 13
BENEATH THE KEEP

Kastali Dun

Saffra descended into the depths of the keep, making her way down to the mysterious cave beneath. Desaree and Jocelyn followed behind her. Orbs illuminated their way, creating pools of light and shadow.

Nearly three days had passed since Claire's departure north. They were determined to find answers while she was away. Saffra had wanted to come sooner, but it was a challenge getting Desaree away from Verath these days, especially in the evening. The two of them spent an increasing amount of time together.

"Tell me again about your dreams?" Desaree asked as they walked. They followed their original dusty footprints. Because of the dim light, they were often forced to stop and backtrack.

"I've told you all I know." Saffra paused to glance down a dark corridor.

"Well, perhaps you missed something."

"Perhaps. Dreams are not as straightforward as visions. Even now, everything feels so vague."

"But aren't they the same thing?" Desaree asked. "A telling of the future?"

Saffra opened her mouth to explain, but Jocelyn beat her to it. "Not necessarily, Des. Both can tell the future, the past, and the present, but Saffra's visions take her at any time. They are fully fleshed out scenes. Dreams, which come while she sleeps, and are usually difficult to comprehend, especially come the morning."

"Which is why these have been particularly frustrating," Saffra muttered, glancing down another darkened corridor.

"Well, what do you remember?" Desaree pressed.

"Just...dragons. Lots of them. A battle. The drengr. Fear. Death. Loss. I..." Saffra shook her head. "It's hard to say."

They descended a narrow flight of stairs single file, which took them deeper underground.

"Hmm... Dragons." Desaree sounded thoughtful. "What if there is going to be a great battle between the dragons and the drengr?"

"Gods, I hope not. But if current events are anything to go from, it seems inevitable." Saffra shuddered at the thought. "And if that's what I'm seeing, then it will likely happen sooner than later. But when? And where?"

"Perhaps in the north?" Desaree ventured. "Surely we're safe here."

"Safe indeed!" Saffra snorted. "For how long? Here—I think it's down this hallway. These are our old footprints, and I remember the roughness of the walls."

"So there really *is* a cave?" Jocelyn wondered.

"We wouldn't lie to you, dear Jocelyn," Saffra said. The narrow walls widened, spilling out into a vast space. "See? We're here." She sent her orbs soaring high into the center of the cavern, casting the entire chamber with a soft glow.

Jocelyn and Desaree crowded close, trying to get a better look.

"Incredible!" Jocelyn whispered. "To think, it's right under the city and no one knows about it."

"That was my reaction too," Desaree said.

"There—" Saffra pointed. "There's the gate, and the monument building beside it." Everything looked exactly as it had when she and Des had first discovered it. Untouched.

"Let's get a closer look!" Jocelyn shimmied past them into the cave, clearly more adventurous than Saffra might have expected.

They made their way into the open, treading carefully around the gnarled formations growing up from the bottom. The air tasted of salt and sea, and if you listened, you could hear waves crashing against the walls in the distance.

Shadows danced about them, as if the cave had come alive with monsters. "*Dagar*," Saffra muttered, creating yet another orb that followed them closely. Each pulled a little at her energy; if she made too many, she would grow quickly fatigued.

They circled the little building at the cave's center. "It looks like a large mausoleum," Desaree said, breaking the silence. "You know...for dead people. Maybe someone important is buried here. Ugh. I hope we don't find a bunch of bodies inside."

Saffra huffed. "I should hope not. But we cannot know until we open it."

"What if this is where Queen Isabella was laid to rest?" Desaree asked.

"I suppose anything is possible." Saffra slowed, studying the walls. "*Hopefully* we find something more useful—something that might bring Claire answers about who she is and how she's tied to Princess Irelia. Something about how she might defeat Kane."

The structure was more than twice their height. It was a perfect square with a triangular roof held up by pillars that spanned its front. The outline of a door at the front drew them to it. "How do we get in?" Jocelyn asked. "There aren't any handles. It's just a smooth surface."

Saffra frowned. "Magic, probably. But for some reason, I'm hesitant to touch it. We have no idea what kind of spells could be protecting it, defensive mechanisms, or what might happen if we try to open it." She stood before it and held out her hand, careful not to make contact as she began muttering words of magic. Nothing happened. She tried a few more cantrips. Still, nothing.

"Oh come now, why don't you give it a push?" Desaree stepped forward.

"I...don't think that's a good idea, Des."

"What? You think it will zap you? Turn you into a frog? I'm sure it's fine." Before they could protest, Desaree stepped forward and laid her hand on the smooth surface.

"Des—" Saffra stopped herself, watching with wide eyes. Nothing happened. She exhaled.

Desaree's smile turned triumphant. "See? All safe."

A scratching sound made them shriek and jump back in unison.

"Gods above!" Jocelyn cried. "Des, what did you do?!"

Something scratched against the stone. They backed away.

"It's the dead," Jocelyn hissed. "You've disturbed the dead, Des. Now *we're* going to die."

"Oh hush, both of you." Saffra glanced up, immediately relaxing. "It's writing. Look. There." She pointed above the door frame. Symbols had appeared. She studied them, frowning. There was absolutely nothing familiar about them. "Not sure it's any help to us."

"They must mean *something*," Jocelyn said. "But what? They aren't our language."

"Maybe it's instructions for how to open the door?" Desaree asked.

"It very well could be." Saffra sighed. It was a dead end.

A minute later, the symbols disappeared. "Well, that's no help!" Jocelyn threw up her hands. Desaree rushed forward and placed her hand on the door again. The symbols reappeared.

"It's like someone invisible is standing there, writing them in by hand," Saffra mused. Her mind turned over, thinking through the various types of magic she knew of. "In all my training, I've never seen symbols like these."

"It must be sprite language," Desaree said. "You know, for Queen Isabella."

"I'm not so sure, Des. I've seen spriten writing. It doesn't look quite like this. No...this is different."

"But...what are we supposed to do, then?" Jocelyn asked.

"We write it down," Saffra said. "And then we take it to the library to see if we can find the language it represents. Crack the code."

"And you think *that* will tell us how to open it?" Desaree chewed on the skin of her lower lip.

"Let's hope so. I'd like to have *something* to tell Claire when she returns. She's counting on us."

"Come, look at this," Jocelyn said, moving away from them. "The symbols look a lot like the ones on the gate, don't they?"

Saffra rushed over. "You're right. I hadn't even considered it, but you're right. We should write some of them down too."

THEY ATE their evening meal before heading to the library. Candles in hand, they split up and searched through aisles of texts. Jocelyn wasn't great at her letters, so she stuck by Saffra's side, occasionally wandering off, while Desaree took off to the opposite end.

Saffra went from book to book, pulling anything that mentioned ancient history or language. Jocelyn acted as her runner, carrying the books to a nearby table where they had set up. Once they had a stack that would take them months to work through, they sat down and began the odious task of flipping. Page after page.

"Let me see the parchment again," Desaree asked every so often. Each time she looked at it, her frown deepened. "No...no. That won't do." A frustrated sigh escaped her lips.

"Just keep trying," Saffra murmured without looking up from the book she held. She had already flipped through several texts herself with no luck.

Someone shuffled over to them. "My dears, it is awfully late. Can I help you find something?" Master Roland, the resident librarian, had appeared. He eyed their stack with a frightful glare. No doubt imagining all the work he had ahead of him if they snuck away without cleaning up.

His gaze fell upon the parchment. "Interesting. May I?" It was too late to tuck it away. The three of them stared back at him with open mouths, too surprised to reply before he snatched it up. "Hm…" He stooped, hands clasped behind his back, figure bowed at the waist, for a closer look. "Strange. I feel as if I have seen it before…but no. I cannot remember. Who wrote this? What is it?" He glanced between them. "What does it mean?"

"Well," Saffra said, "that's what we're trying to find out. It's copied. From…well, I can't say. But we're trying to figure out what it means. We think it's a language of some sort. We are searching for a source that might tell which one. You think you've seen it before? In this library, perhaps?"

"Bah! No. But perhaps on my travels. I have been to many libraries around the world before coming here."

"But this is the capital's biggest and only library. We're more likely to find what we need here, aren't we?" Saffra hadn't meant to sound so desperate.

"Not necessarily, my lady. I know every book in my library…" He frowned. "You won't find that language in any of them. It's… old. Very old."

"You…you're sure?" Desaree snatched the parchment from the table, looking at it again, so closely it nearly kissed her nose.

Roland shrugged. "You're better off looking in the library at Northedge. It is the oldest in the kingdom…Well, the sprites probably have one that's older, but don't let me stop you from trying." He turned to leave. "And make sure you put those back where you found them before you go!"

They waited until his shuffling faded away, exchanging silent glances.

"Do you think he was lying?" Desaree asked at last.

Saffra sighed. "Roland is quite knowledgeable. But he is old, and his memory… Well, he did seem to recognize it at first." She scowled.

"Don't you think it's strange? The writing on the mausoleum matches that on the gate. It cannot be a coincidence."

"We don't know for certain that it is a mausoleum, Jocelyn. I know you want to believe there are dead bodies in there, but I'm not so sure. And after all the work we're going to, there had better not be!"

Jocelyn shrugged. "Until we know otherwise..."

"But yes," Saffra added. "It certainly is interesting."

"If the two writings are the same, doesn't that mean it was made by the same people?" Desaree cut in.

Saffra opened and closed her mouth several times. "I..." She frowned. "I guess you're right. Gods! I've been so consumed with Queen Isabella, I've almost tricked myself into thinking it was her doing. After all, she built this keep. But you're right. Each gate was made by the asarlaí."

"So *that* means the writing is from the asarlaí time too," Desaree said, sitting up straighter. "We should have realized that before."

Saffra groaned, sinking low on the bench. "Which *means* we just wasted so much time. Why didn't I think of it sooner? And perhaps that is why Roland thought he recognized it. He must have encountered some writing similar to it during his travels."

Desaree sighed. "I think we've been so caught up, we merely forgot to use simple logic."

"Happens to the best of us, I suppose." Saffra tried to hide her scowl as she eyed the stack of books they now needed to return, nearly groaning at the prospect.

"What about Marcel?" Jocelyn asked. "He has an extensive knowledge of magic. Perhaps he might know?"

"Joce, that's brilliant!" Saffra threw her arms around Jocelyn and kissed her cheek. "I'm so tired I'm not even thinking clearly."

"Or maybe your dreams are simply taking a bigger toll than you realize," Jocelyn muttered, scowling.

It wasn't the first time her handmaiden had pointed it out. Jocelyn insisted that she ought to be taking aegan to help her sleep better. But she didn't like how disconnected it made her.

"I...I'll go and ask him tomorrow."

They returned their books—a tedious task, as always—and retreated to their rooms to sleep. That night, she dreamt of more dragons. This time, she was forced to watch as they bathed sections of a large port city in flames. She tried to remember specific details before they slipped away. But it was almost impossible, especially once she was up and about the following morning.

After hurrying through her daily routine, she visited Marcel in his study, eager to solve their mystery but also excited for other reasons. "Any news on Dax?" she asked the moment she entered. Ever since the loss of his memories, she had been checking on him daily, but the answer was always the same.

"I'm afraid not, my dear." Marcel's eyes were sad. "I believe it is time to send him on his way."

"His...his way?"

"Yes...I have sent him away."

"Away?"

"Dax believes that if he goes back to his old routine, he might remember some of what he used to know. He knows you've been checking on him and he requested that I not tell you immediately—that he be left to his own devices without interference. He has taken the loss of his mind very...personally."

"Oh." She faked a smile, trying to ignore the sinking feeling in her chest. Dax had wanted very little to do with her now that he no longer remembered her. That hurt the most. Guilt, perhaps, for not remembering who she was. It was hard to be certain.

"Well," she said, trying to sound cheery, "I'm sure retracing his footsteps will help. As long as you feel certain that we can trust him?"

Marcel shrugged. "You knew him better than most. Do you feel that his mind was manipulated by Kane?"

She opened her mouth, then hesitated. "I suppose not, but Kane can fool even the king."

Marcel hesitated. "Yes, that was my concern too. But I cannot keep him here any longer."

"So, he is back in the barracks?" Her heart quickened. Perhaps she would go and see him. No. No, that wouldn't be a good idea. Not if he didn't want to see her.

"Yes. And I know what you are thinking, Saffra. Give him space."

Her heart felt pained. "It...hurts. His avoidance."

Marcel put a hand on her shoulder, giving it an affectionate squeeze. "Love always hurts. Now, what brings you in today? I can tell there is something else on your mind."

"Oh...yes. Right." She fumbled in her pocket for her parchment and held it out to him, explaining her quest to find out more about the asarlaí's language. "Might you have any books that depict their writing?"

"Hm..." He looked over the parchment before handing it back. "Let me see..." He moved over to his bookcases. "I'm afraid I haven't much on the asarlaí language as a whole. But I do have some of their script. However—" He removed a small stack of old tomes from various locations and set them before her. "None of them come with interpretations." He eyed her for a moment. "Where did you get this, anyway?"

"The writing on the gates," she answered.

"How in the name...how did you manage that?" His eyes narrowed. "The closest gate to us is leagues away."

Her heart hammered in her chest. "Oh, well, when I was a little girl we had one near Brushbridge, remember? The Austar Gate."

"And you...you went and copied down its glyphs when you... eight? You've had them all this time? Gods, girl! Didn't anyone warn you to stay away from there?"

"Oh, come now, Marcel. The gates aren't *that* dangerous if you don't go through them. Besides, Claire came from one, did she not?"

"Yes...but..." Marcel sighed. "Oh, never mind. You have a mind for adventure. Very well. Look through those, but don't count on anything. Like I said, you won't find a dictionary that translates the writing." He gave her another peculiar look before moving away to his desk.

Marcel was not one to loan out books, except perhaps on the rarest occasion. She was forced to comb through each on her own. She worked for hours, skipping the midday meal. Marcel left her alone, but she noticed the quizzical looks he shot in her direction.

The work was time consuming and tedious. When she found a

set of glyphs in one, she nearly squealed, but her excitement was short lived. The symbols were copied down with only a loose interpretation about what they meant. Mostly as an example of the writing. "Why write it down if you are not going to say exactly what it means?" she muttered, snapping the book closed before moving on to the next.

It took her two days to flip through all the material Marcel had provided. Most of the content was historical, telling of deeds and events involving the Asarlaí. She did find one image of the Kengr Gate sketched out, its glyphs written in meticulous hand. Many of the symbols matched the ones she had copied, but none of it got her any closer.

She was forced to give up.

She admitted defeat to Desaree and Jocelyn during the evening meal. "Claire will be back in a few days, and we are no closer to solving it." Disappointment riddled her voice. One task. That's all Claire had given them. "I feel as if we have accomplished nothing."

"At least we know more though," Desaree said.

"Like what?" Saffra pushed her food around on her plate.

"We know that both the building and the gate were put there by the asarlaí. So we've got a lead."

Saffra snorted. "Well, the only living asarlaí is Kane, and unless you plan on asking him to decipher the script for us, we're no closer to answers."

Jocelyn remained silent, a frown pulling at her eyebrows.

Later that night, Saffra donned a cloak and snuck away, making her way to the barracks, hoping to find Dax. She didn't plan to confront him, not when he didn't want to see her. But she needed to know that he was okay.

She wasn't a soldier, so she was forced to sneak through and stick to the shadows. She used an incant to disguise the light around her and increase the shadow, making it easier to go unnoticed. She managed to get to the end of the main corridor undetected.

Rambunctious shouts of laughter drifted from open doors at the end, spilling light out into the corridor. She let go of her magic and peeked around the corner, holding her breath. It was the mess hall, and it was full. Dinner was long over, but the occupants were gathered around card tables. Her gaze darted over their faces until it settled on Dax. Her breath caught. He sat alone, drinking, watching the activities with a blank expression.

"Oh, gods," she whispered. A single tear rolled down her cheek. Seeing him brought a wealth of emotion to the surface, making it difficult to breathe.

"Hey! You're not allowed in here." A voice made her jump.

She pivoted, careful to keep her face shadowed. "I was just going." She fled, taking her heartbreak with her.

CHAPTER 14

BATTLE AFTERMATH

Celenore

Claire fled camp the moment Koldis landed. She took off into the wilderness hoping to leave everything behind. She ran, hand pressing against her shooting side ache. Her vision blurred, her breaths coming out half gasp half sob.

"Claire!" Koldis chased after her. "Claire, stop!" He caught her around the waist, gently spinning her to face him. "Claire..."

"It's my fault," she gasped. "It's all my fault." She slipped through his arms, onto her knees before curling in on herself. She couldn't be there when the others returned.

"Claire..." Koldis crouched before her, rubbing her back in calming circles. "It's not your fault. Everyone knew there were risks."

"But I—"

"No. I will not let you take the blame for this."

She sobbed harder. It didn't matter what he said. She blamed herself.

"I can't go back. I can't face them."

"We don't have to go back yet. Besides, they won't return for some time. Deep breaths. Come on. Breathe."

126

She nodded into her hands, trying to do as he said. Each breath was a painful gasp.

He took her by the wrists, gently pulling her hands from her face. She was forced to look at him through blurred eyes. There was genuine concern on his features and she hated it. Why couldn't he look at her the way he used to? Cold and unfeeling.

"What happened back there?" he finally asked. "Tell me what went wrong."

"I...I thought I had it under control but...the images. I couldn't focus through them. When I didn't get it right on the first try, I panicked."

"Images?"

"I don't know what they were," she cried. "Flashes. I saw things. Scenes of what was happening in the villages. From the drengr. I didn't know what it was, what was happening to me. I...I panicked."

He swore. "You saw projections."

"What?"

"Projections. When we go into battle, words are often too much, take too long. Drengr revert to a more primal form of communication. Emotions, images, feelings, bursts of thought. It's hard to explain. It's instinctual."

"I...but I'm not a..." She shook her head. What did it matter? It wouldn't bring Hiondel back.

"I did not think—" He stopped himself, studying her face. "You can hear our voices but I never imagined you'd be capable of projections. None of us would have guessed it. Not even King Talon. I should have warned you earlier, but the possibility didn't cross my mind." He sighed and sat back on his heels.

"It's not your fault," she muttered. "How were you supposed to know?"

"Because unlike you, *I'm* not new to all of this."

She swiped at her tears. It felt like she was a single crack away from shattering.

"You should get some sleep," he said at last. "Come on." He pulled her to her feet.

"I can't sleep like this, Koldis. Someone is dead! Don't you get it?! Hiondel is dead because of me!"

He growled then, the sound deep and primal. And when he opened his mouth, she took a faltering step backwards. "That's enough. I will not let you take the blame for this. Hiondel is dead because he had a misstep and got stabbed. You did not stab him, did you?"

"I...of course not. Why would you—?"

"If you did not stab him then—"

"I failed to work my magic in time!" she roared, angry with him for not understanding. "Had I burned them when I was supposed to, Hiondel wouldn't...wouldn't have...wouldn't..." Her breaths came out as gasps. It wasn't even just Hiondel. The villagers had suffered, too. She didn't know how many were harmed. How many had died, because of her.

"I cannot believe you expect this level of perfection from yourself, Claire. You're living under a delusion. Stop it. Wake up. Magic takes a great deal of practice. You're trying to do sprite magic with no training. Just because it worked once, does not mean you will get it on the first try, or every time thereafter. Gods!" He pinched the bridge of his nose, looking up. She stared at him, lips parted. "What you did tonight, I have never seen anything like it. It was nothing short of incredible. Our magic does not work that way. We couldn't have done anything on that scale. You destroyed them all! And you're standing here blaming yourself because you didn't get it perfectly right the first time? Just—stop."

She blinked at him, speechless. She wanted to fight back. To argue. To tell him how wrong he was. But she couldn't find the words.

"Now, come. You need sleep. Talon would kill me if he saw you in this state." He took her hand, leading her back to camp.

The moment she saw all their belongings scattered about. Bedrolls. Cooking pits. Packs. The tears started all over again. She was careful to keep her face averted in the muted glow of dawn. The sun was close to rising and she didn't want Koldis to see her. Not after his outburst.

"I'll just sleep, then," she muttered, dropping his hand. She went to her bedroll and buried herself beneath the blanket, blotting out the rest of the world. The cocoon was welcome. A sliver of safety while everything else around her went to shit.

The sound of Koldis's boots stopped beside her. His voice was close, like he was crouching over her. "Claire, I may not have said it, but thank you. For what you did. Not just for risking your safety, but for risking us too. I'm proud of you, even if I haven't been the best at showing it. I'm proud of what you have accomplished. And King Talon would be too. Please...please do not let your grief overshadow your success."

Something deep inside of her cracked. Fresh tears seeped from her closed eyes. When she didn't answer, he stomped away. She wanted to take his advice, but something held her back. So she cried and cried, letting everything out until it seemed there was nothing left to give.

Eventually, her exhaustion was deeper than her grief. She drifted into a deep slumber. When she woke, the pressure was still there, deep in her chest. She couldn't fight past it. The sadness. The disappointment.

Her ears pricked. There were noises around the camp, but she didn't have the courage to emerge from beneath her blanket. Groans of pain broke the silence. She knew what it meant. The wounded had returned. And she knew what kind of wounds they had suffered.

At this very moment, vodar poison was threatening their bodies. Turning skin black as they used their magic to fight it, to keep it at bay. She knew what that felt like. Knew exactly what kind of pain it was.

She huddled deeper beneath her bedroll. It wasn't simply Hiondel's death she'd have to face when she saw them. And because of that, she wanted nothing more than to disappear and never be seen again. Better she had died in Hiondel's place than face them now.

At some point, she drifted off again. It was nearly dusk when she next woke. The camp was louder, signaling the return of the remainder of their party, back from the villages where they'd spent the day helping rebuild.

"Claire..." It was Jovari's voice, this time. He stood near her. "Claire, surely you'd like to eat. You should come out from there." She felt a gentle tug on her blanket. "No one blames you."

"Go away," she grumbled.

"We're going to heal the others," he explained. "Their magic is barely strong enough to hold back the poison. If we don't, they could die overnight. It's spreading." She winced, thinking about it. "One of us isn't enough to heal them. Not even Koldis, with his affinity. But together, we can combine our strength."

At that, she sat up, pulling the blanket away to look at him. "You mean, they aren't going to have to suffer with it, like...like..."

"Like you and Cyrus? No." He looked her over in the fading sunlight. "Gods, you look like hell." She grunted, rolling her eyes. He grinned. "I thought that would work. You going to help or not?"

"Yes. I will do everything I can, just tell me what is needed."

He helped her to her feet. She wrapped her cloak around her shoulders. It took all her self control to keep from pulling the hood up to hide her face.

She followed him through camp, keeping her eyes averted. The others mutely watched as she passed. She expected a train of telepathic thoughts in her wake, but there was nothing, like they were all too numb to speak.

She stole a glance at one face, and then another. Instead of narrowed eyes and anger, she saw the opposite. Until she spotted Lily, not five paces from her. She stopped dead in her tracks. "Lily..." she whispered. "I...I'm so sorry." Lily gazed back at her with a blank expression, then turned and walked away.

She covered her mouth, stifling a sob.

Faedrol strolled up, placing a hand on her shoulder. "What you did, Claire. We have never..." He shook his head, glancing over to where Lily had retreated. "She lost her mate today. Her hurt isn't directed towards you. Do not take it personally, all right?" He searched her face. All she could do was nod and pretend that she wouldn't. She couldn't tell him what she really thought. What she really felt.

Jovari stood silently, waiting.

"What...what will happen to her now?" she croaked. "Now that Hiondel is..." She couldn't even say the word.

"Probably best not to discuss that right now," Jovari answered, crossing his arms.

"No. Tell me. I need to know."

Jovari exhaled. "She will die."

"What?" The word came out choked. She swayed on her feet. Faedrol's grip on her shoulder tightened.

"Not immediately, but Hiondel's magic is fading from her. The years of her long life will catch up rapidly. A rider cannot exist without their dragon. She will quickly age and..." He sighed. "Come, we should heal the others."

"You mean, I didn't just kill Hiondel? I also killed her?"

Faedrol swore, looking over at Jovari. "She blames herself?" Jovari nodded. He turned back to her. "Lady Claire, that is not the way of it. And Hiondel would be dishonored if he knew that you took the blame for his actions and his death. You must allow his soul to rest in peace. Taking this burden will not bode well for him in the afterlife."

"I..." She blinked back at him. "You mean—"

An anguished cry split the air. Koldis rushed over, his face etched with worry. "Some of them are in bad shape," he said, breathless. "We don't have long. We must act now if we are to save them. Come." He motioned to the others and they all gathered around the injured.

Drengr and rider alike had suffered at the hands of the vodar. She tried not to think of the villagers who had been killed instantly by their poisonous wounds. At least the drengr and their riders had magic to hold the poison in check.

Some of the injured were worse than others. Jorsid had a massive gash on his leg. Darcie had been stabbed in the gut. Rhywyth was curled into a ball, groaning. Edith had a gash on her arm.

Her stomach lurched. Memories of Cyrus's suffering came racing back to her. Her leg gave a twinge. She felt the phantom pain of her old wound. She squeezed her eyes shut before turning to Koldis for direction.

"We will link up," he said. "I will lead the incantation."

Those uninjured crouched together, gathering around the wounded. They placed their hands on shoulders and arms, until they were all linked through physical contact. She hadn't realized it would strengthen the magic. She did the same, sitting on her heels as she placed her hand against Koldis's shoulder. She gave it a reassuring squeeze. He glanced at her and nodded before turning back to Rhywyth. Jovari placed his hand over hers. She sighed at the warmth of his familiar contact.

"Let us begin." Koldis began to speak, filling the air with his incantation, words of the old language. She felt a surge, like a powerful wave sweeping her up, from all the minds linked to hers. Her eyes blurred with tears, overcome with emotion, with exhaustion. She wanted nothing more than to fix them, to heal them, to undo her panicked mistake.

Koldis continued to chant. The sound of his voice wrapped around her, his words melding together. She started humming along with him, a painful keening at first, creating a musical backdrop to his words. Jovari's hand squeezed hers again and he whispered, "Don't stop. Whatever you're doing, it's working."

The wounds on the injured began to glow as the air was filled with the magic of healing. It twisted together into shades of blues and greens, until she realized what was happening. Something in her voice was lending assistance to Koldis's words.

She shut her eyes and continued humming, until her voice turned to soft singing. They were words she did not know, words she'd never heard before, of a language that simply seemed...right. A language filled with the emotion of everything she felt. Everything that hurt within her. She weaved her words together with Koldis, like adding threads of fortification to his incantation, tightening it with ties and knots. Fixing it into place. Making sure it held fast.

Their words lifting up to a crescendo before dying down into softness.

When they finished, she opened her eyes, removing her hand from Jovari's grip and Koldis's shoulder. A weariness flowed through her, but it was different from what usually came after performing mage magic. This exhaustion was filled with the satisfaction of having done something good.

Her left shoulder burned. On her back, just below her neck. She resisted the urge to claw at her skin, almost certain that if she looked, she would find a new sprite mark glowing there. Instead, she turned her attention outward, glancing around. No one was looking at the wounded. They were all staring at her, some wide-eyed, others with open mouths. She scowled, not quite understanding their expressions.

"Is it...did we do it?" she asked. "Are they healed?"

Koldis grunted. "Unbelievable. Absolutely unbelievable." She opened her mouth, then closed it. "Yes, Claire. They are healed, no thanks to whatever you just did."

"I...I think I need to lay down."

She tried to stand and stumbled.

"I've got you." Jovari's hands wrapped around her, lifting her, guiding her away from the others. "Sleep for a bit. Unless you'd like to eat first?" On cue, her stomach gurgled. He laughed. "I'll get you something to eat."

She took a seat on her bedroll, groaning. No one bothered her. They were still huddled around the recovering wounded, who were now getting to their feet. Darkness had fallen. She had to squint to make out their shapes.

"Someone get a fire going," one of them called.

Not long after, a blaze of flames lit the camp.

It all felt like a disjointed dream.

Jovari returned with some dried meat, cheese, and bread, passing her a water skin after she'd had a chance to devour some of it. "What you did back there, was that more sprite magic?"

She licked her fingers clean before wiping them on her pants. "I think so." As if to answer, the burning on the back of her shoulder flared and then disappeared.

"How did you know how to do it?"

"I..." She shook her head, too exhausted to think. "I don't know. Instinct, I suppose. It just felt like the right thing to do."

"Well, whatever it was, it worked. Remember your leg?"

"How could I forget?"

"It took Koldis nearly an hour of incantations to stop the poison from spreading to the rest of your body. You were passed out for most of it, if I recall."

"Your point?"

"It took minutes to heal them, Claire. Minutes. For what should have taken an hour or more with all of us linked like that. I don't know what you did, but it worked." He shook his head, taking the water skin from her hands and having a drink. He cleared his throat. "You need to sleep. Go on."

She nodded, getting situated beneath the blanket of her bedroll. Jovari knelt and adjusted it, tucking her in. She almost laughed at his fussing. Her eyes fluttered closed.

"Sleep well, Lady Claire..." She felt his fingers brush her forehead, and then she felt nothing at all, drifting off into an exhausted slumber.

CHAPTER 15

A STORY

Celenore

Claire woke to hushed voices. Her body hurt. She was sore from flying and exhausted from magic. She almost curled up and went back to sleep, but the previous events rushed back. Hiondel was dead. Lily, as good as.

She got up, immediately struck by the cold. Shadows moved around the campfire. "Lady Claire!" Faedrol whispered, beckoning her over. "Come, join us."

She swallowed, hesitated briefly, then claimed a seat beside him. The others gave nods of greeting. Warmth radiated through her, both from relief and the dancing flames. "What time is it?"

Faedrol glanced up at the sky. "Just about midnight, I think. Did you get any sleep?"

"A little bit." Her muscles clenched. She waited for him to say something about the attack, about the green flames that had enveloped the vodar, or about what she'd done to help Koldis heal the injured. Instead, Faedrol was quiet.

Jovari and Koldis appeared, taking seats beside her while greeting the others. Her shoulders relaxed.

Faedrol nudged her. "I promised you a story, didn't I?"

"A story? Oh!" She could have hugged him. "About Koldis. It's something funny, I hope?"

"What's this now?" Koldis lifted his brows.

"Is this the one about the bandits?" Jovari asked.

"Of course." Faedrol chuckled. Koldis groaned.

"Now you've got me interested," she said, grinning.

From Faedrol's other side, Hannah said, "I think *I'll* do a better job of it than you, darling."

"As you wish." Faedrol shrugged.

"It was nearly fifty years ago, now," Hannah said. "Rumors of bandits reached the capital. We generally don't concern ourselves with bandits. They're mostly harmless, and most local villages have militias to address things like this. Anyway, this particular bunch of brigands began patrolling the roads in Galadhal. The Royal Road."

"The Royal Road?" She looked at Koldis.

"The road that leads from the Gable Forest directly to Kastali Dun. The main thoroughfare."

"The bandits were brutal," Hannah continued. "They believed it was their gods' given right to exact an impossible tax on those who wished to travel. A tax few could pay. They didn't simply rob their victims, they found places to string them up, hang them from trees, and where there weren't trees, they simply mounted their heads on spikes. It got so bad that travelers refused to use the road. There weren't exactly a lot of alternatives. Traveling over open country doesn't offer much cover."

"So...what did you guys do?" Claire shifted her position to get a better look at Hannah. Hannah was tall, and quite pretty, with chestnut skin and a feline face. Her dark eyes danced in the firelight.

"Well," Hannah said, "Koldis can correct me if I've remembered wrong, but as I understand it, the king sent him to gather a team—Faedrol and myself included—to put a stop to the problem. Matters as great as this, matters of the law, are taken directly to the king. Usually. But these men were fairly far from justice. As such, King Talon would have been plenty fine with us ending their pathetic lives." Hanna paused, arching an eyebrow at Koldis. There was some kind of hidden message in her expression.

Koldis snorted. "Death is too easy for people like that. Debts should be paid where warranted."

"So, you made them suffer?" Claire turned to him, more curious than ever.

A wicked smile twisted the corners of his mouth. "Something like that." He nodded at Hannah to continue.

"Koldis took advantage of the king's vagueness. He followed what *he* felt was the best course of action." Several low chuckles sounded. "When we found them, which wasn't too difficult—"

"Not when you leave a trail of trash and bodies," Koldis interrupted.

Hannah cleared her throat. "Koldis decided to take a more frightening approach. And what could be more frightening than facing King Talon? Everyone fears him. These bandits needed to be reminded of their king's power. So he decided to transport them directly."

"You didn't!" Claire turned to Koldis, trying to guess the rest of the story from his expression.

"We couldn't exactly chain them up and walk them to the capital," Hannah explained. "Besides, Koldis wanted to have some fun. He gets bored so easily, Koldis does." A snort fell from Claire's lips; she covered her mouth with her hand to stifle it. "He appeared in his drengr form and gave them quite a fright."

"Oh no..." She turned to Koldis. "What did you do?"

He shrugged his shoulders. " Nothing much. Chased them about for a bit, roaring and spewing flames."

"He nearly frightened them to death, that's for sure. The rest of us had a right time rounding them up," Hannah said. "Once *that* was done, we took the nets they used to haul their goods. Faedrol managed to tie them together to make a basket."

"Tell me you didn't!"

"We tossed the lot of them into the net," Hannah said. "Faedrol and Koldis carried them all the way back to the capital to receive the king's justice in person."

Claire laughed. "They must have been terrified."

"You have no idea," Koldis said, smirking. "A few of them may have shit their pants, but it was nothing they didn't deserve. We never got the exact count from them, but they were responsible for nearly two hundred deaths."

"Two hundred?! And how many bandits were there?" she asked.

"Only twelve."

"Gods! Well." She huffed. "That's a unique way to take care of business, especially when the king gave you leave to kill them."

Koldis shrugged. "I admit, I had other motives."

"Oh?" She arched an eyebrow at him.

"Let's just say I was a little annoyed with King Talon for treating me like a local sheriff, to exact justice. The last thing I wanted was to leave the capital like an errand boy. There was a bit of spite involved, on my part. I figured if I brought the bandits to him, it might annoy him a little, if not surprise him."

"And did it?"

"Oh, he was annoyed all right. But amused more than anything."

"Sounds like you don't always follow orders as a *good little shield* ought to?"

He laughed. "Not always. But when it matters, yes. Emotions can, at times, get the better of me."

"I get that," she said. Their quiet mirth died down. "Thank you for the story," she said to Hannah and Faedrol. "I needed a good laugh."

Adventures did have their moments. Hers had turned out quite differently. There would be nothing to laugh about when this one ended.

"You should try to get some sleep," Jovari said, standing. He held out his hand. "We depart in the morning, to beat King Talon back to the capital."

She stiffened at the reminder. With everything that had happened, she hadn't given Talon much thought. Now all she could think of was having to tell him she hadn't been fast enough —that one of his drengr had died.

~

SHE FELL BACK into the same pattern of dreams that had plagued her before. She dreamt of wild dragons flying into battle. Of Kane. Of death. She woke several times in the dark with a restless stomach. When she was sure dawn was only an hour or two away, she abandoned sleep and went to stand watch with whoever was on duty.

It was a relief to find Koldis, turned eastward, as if waiting for the sun to rise. She came up beside him, her cloak pulled tightly around her. They stood silently.

"How are you holding up?" he asked at last.

She sighed. "Hiondel's death aside, I thought once we destroyed the vodar I would feel better. Instead, I feel...I feel more terrible today than I did yesterday."

He turned to her, frowning. "Something does not sit well with you?"

"I..." She opened and closed her mouth several times. How much did Koldis know? How much had Reyr told him, told the rest of them? "I've been having these dreams..."

"Dreams about Kane?"

"You know about those?" That answered her question.

"Just a bit." He spared her a quick glance. "Reyr mentioned it to King Talon the night before he left—that you'd been having dreams about Kane." He cleared his throat. "It's concerning, to say the least."

She chewed at the chapped skin of her bottom lip until she tasted blood and forced herself to stop. "These are different from the ones from before," she admitted. "They almost seem like...like a vision."

"What have you seen?"

"Dragons," she whispered. "Lots of dragons." She recounted as many details as she could, how she had *been* Kane, riding on the back of a red dragon, flying over the ocean towards...something.

She shook her head. "All I could feel was fear, as if I could smell it soaking through the very air I breathed. I—he, I mean—liked it. There was a city in the distance, I think. He was preparing for battle."

Koldis faced her, frowning. "What did the city look like?"

"I..." She closed her eyes, trying to picture it. "Coastal. There was a shoreline. It was sitting in a bay, I think? It's hard to tell. I saw docks. And flags flying everywhere. A big castle? I'm not..."

"I do not like the sound of this," he said, mirroring her concern. "How far can you reach—with your mind, I mean?"

"Um. I...pretty far, I think. I don't know."

"Can you reach Reyr? Listen in on what's happening there?"

"Reyr?" Her eyes widened. "You don't think that's where...? Oh gods!" Her hand flew to her mouth.

"Your descriptions sound a lot like Squall's End. But I don't think they have been attacked. Not yet, anyway. We would know. At this distance, we would feel it." They were halfway between Kastali Dun and Squall's End. He turned to face the north. "We would know," he repeated.

"So, you think I wasn't seeing Kane in the present? I've always assumed it was the present. When I've seen him before, hiding the dragonstones, it felt like the present." She frowned, trying to piece things together.

"I can't say whether you were seeing him in the past, present, or future. I only know that you have seen Kane flying towards Squall's End with battle written on his heart. The rest is guesswork."

She nodded. "I've got an uneasy feeling, like I'm going to be sick. Ever since..."

"Since you woke up this morning," he finished for her. "That's why you came to keep watch." His gaze darted over her face, searching, as if he'd find all the answers he needed written in her expression.

"I feel it here." She put a hand over her gut. "Like something ominous. Something's going to happen, Koldis. Something bad."

"We need to contact Reyr," he said. She looked at the horizon, still dark. A breeze picked up, rustling her hair, giving her goosebumps.

"In my dreams," she whispered, "it happened just after dawn."

"Give me a minute. I'll get Jovari. The three of us can join our minds and reach out to him. It should be enough."

She tried to nod, but her head was spinning, the ground was spinning.

"You don't look well." His words came out rough and worried. He hesitated, reaching out a hand to steady her.

"Something's wrong," she whispered, not quite hearing her own voice. Her legs trembled. Her consciousness slipped. Her knees gave way. The last thing she saw was the ground rushing up to meet her as hands gently caught her.

CHAPTER 16
A SPRITEN WARNING

Esterpine

Talon's final days in Esterpine were a blur of meetings, but he successfully convinced Jade to put the stones back where they belonged, a victory he couldn't wait to share with Claire. Would she be proud of him?

He wandered the streets of Esterpine, eager for his impending departure. The sprites generally avoided him. Some regarded him with hooded gazes, while others slipped away into the mist. A few offered friendly smiles, but overall, they were a hard bunch to get on with.

Would their dislike of the drengr ever change?

Gods, he couldn't wait to leave. To go hunting. To eat the meat his body craved. To go flying. To exist under open sky.

To reunite with Claire.

Dragons were greedy creatures by nature. The drengr, less so. But if ever there was a thing he craved, it wasn't gold or jewels. No, it was the way she looked at him. The way it made him burn inside.

The clang of metal drew him to the sparring grounds. Several of his drengr were occupied, a few partnered with sprites. Now *that* was a sight he thought he'd never see. Was this how they'd been occupying themselves while he went from one meeting to another? He envied them, naturally. Riders had taken up positions along the perimeter to observe their mates. He offered them a polite nod. "Glad to see you, my king," a familiar voice drawled. Bedelth strode over, gripping his shoulder in greeting. "Jeanine and I are sparring over there, but I would be glad to cross blades if it suits you. She's ready to drop anyway." This last, he delivered with a chuckle.

Jeanine stood all but sagging and red-faced, taking in gasps of air.

"Looks like you've given her a good run." Talon found his mouth twitching, though he didn't smile.

"I'm going easy on her, whether she knows it or not."

"Is she any good?"

"Decent enough—for a *human*. Care to observe?"

"Lead the way."

They passed by Raynor and Sellel. Their sveraks flashed back and forth in a blur. Both glanced briefly at their king, bowing their heads in respect.

Talon returned the gesture before continuing on.

Bedelth strode to Jeanine's side, speaking in a low voice. She nodded at whatever he said.

Talon came to a stop at the edge of their sparring ring to see Jeanine's wide eyes fixed on him. She offered a sloppy curtsy that made him chuckle. "Extra points if you can make my shield bleed."

Her lips parted in surprise.

"Ready?" Bedelth asked.

She took up a fighting stance. Bedelth drew his blade. It glowed blue, imbued with magic that made it safe against her. She was human, after all. Jeanine's blade, however, carried no such protection.

They circled before Bedelth lunged, bearing down on her. She met his sverak as the clang of metal broke the silence. They danced back and forth. Talon watched her footwork, noting the way she placed each step and how she held her weight. Impressive. She wasn't a novice. His eyes narrowed. Her style was almost like the sprites, with fluid movements and calculated intent. Had they trained her?

Jeanine whirled in a circle. Her blade sliced Bedelth's thigh, drawing a spray of blood. "Ah!" Bedelth gave a half-hearted yelp, probably for her benefit, and jumped backwards. The wound disappeared, but Jeanine's victorious smile did not.

"He does her no favors—going easy on her like that."

Talon tensed at the voice, turning. "Prince Feowen."

"I don't go easy on her." Feowen shrugged. "Her request, not mine."

Talon disguised his surprise as he said, "*You're* the one training her?"

"Guilty as charged. But what of you, King Talon? Care to cross blades with a sprite?"

He eyed the prince. It was unsettling to think that the creature before him was thousands of years older. As a drengr, he was used to being the best—the top of the food chain, the top of Dragonwall's hierarchy. But not here. With a blade in hand, this pretty little prince would shred his skin into ribbons.

"Tempting," he answered. "Perhaps another time."

Feowen arched an eyebrow. "Very well."

He gave the prince a nod before slipping away into the shadows, leaving Bedelth and Jeanine to their sparring. When he got far enough from Esterpine, he found an isolated tree stump and sank down onto it.

Finally. A moment of peace. He removed Claire's latest letter. It was longer than he expected. From anyone else, that would annoy him. Instead, he only felt eager.

Dear T,

Thank you for your letter. It was a pleasant surprise. I am glad to hear that you reached the forest's edge safely. By the time this reaches you, you will be happily settled.

I wish I were there, too. I long for the forest. Especially for the way it makes me feel. Please don't forget to speak with you-know-who on the other matter we discussed. It has frequently been on my mind since your departure.

I am sorry that your journey was difficult. The burden you carry, as you say, was my own for a time. I know what it is like. Soon, it will be behind you.

Please do ensure that you return in time for the tournament. I would hate to attend the ball without a partner, now that we have decided to go together. My gown is nearly finished. Madame Rosanne fitted it yesterday. I am afraid to gush on the matter. Do kings care about silly things as beautiful gowns? Or shall I save that for my handmaiden. Oh, drat, but I must say something at least. So here: this is Rosanne's finest creation and I was breathless to behold it. I think even you will be impressed.

My lessons with Koldis and Jovari are progressing slowly. Perhaps I am inept, but I find myself frustrated with my improvement. Yes, yes, you are probably thinking, these things take time. I understand that. But time, we do not have. Fortunately, I am a much better archer than swordswoman, except for the times Cyrus decides to show himself.

On that matter, I still haven't the courage to open the box you gave me.

My magic lessons are progressing slowly, too. Marcel and I haven't had luck with our research. I will forgo details, as you have requested, in case this letter is intercepted. It nearly brings me to tears when I think about all those suffering. I hope a solution presents itself soon, before more die.

As for behaving myself, I suppose that is up for debate. I haven't gotten into trouble yet, if that is what you're wondering! But I have done a bit of... exploring. In fact, just this morning I stumbled upon a storeroom in the keep with a very interesting painting. Can you guess what it was? No! Then I shall tell you. It was a painting of you—Your Majesty. Of the younger version, of course. I had always wondered what you looked like in your early days, and now I know.

It almost felt wrong, to view you as you once were. Like I needed your permission first. I hope you will not be angry with me. Seeing your younger self has helped me to understand you better, if that makes sense?

That's all for now. I look forward to your response and your return.

Yours Truly,
Claire

Ps. I hope you are enjoying their food.

.   .   .

HE LAUGHED OUTRIGHT, then read the letter again, slower this time, before returning to the Crystal Palace. He considered drafting a letter in response, but he was so close to returning home, that he would rather say it all in person. The sooner he was back, the better.

He was in the process of packing when a knock sounded. He glanced over the items littering his bed. Trinkets, mostly. Things he had received in honor of his visit, like silken tunics and a new spriten dagger. Not everything was for him.

The knock sounded again, this time more insistent. "Expecting a visitor?" he asked Bedelth.

"Perhaps Jeanine, come to claim her boon?" Bedelth shrugged.

"You may enter," Talon called.

Prince Feowen appeared. He offered them a hurried bow. "Pardon the intrusion, King Talon, Lord Bedelth. My mother requests your presence at once."

"Has something gone wrong?" he frowned at the thought of spending another day here.

"I don't think so, King Talon. You... It is better if I let my mother tell you." Something in Feowen's abruptness held his attention. "Please. We should hurry."

"Of course. We will come at once." They followed after the prince making their way down the spiraling stairs. Far below—if he dared to look—Queen Jade occupied her throne. There was another figure beside her.

When they reached the floor, he moved forward and bowed politely to the queen. Princess Taylynn stood beside the dais and caught his eye. Her face was unreadable.

"Forgive me, King Talon, for summoning you so abruptly." Jade shifted on her throne. "I am sure you are busy with departure preparations."

"Not a problem. Should I be concerned?"

"I... Yes." The queen hesitated, glancing at Princess Taylynn. "Every Sprite within my kingdom is connected to this forest in ways we cannot always explain. It speaks to us, shows us things. Sometimes, these things are not always obvious. Today, there has been a change. A new danger. A warning that cannot be ignored."

The hairs on the back of his neck stood on end. "What warning? Is it Kane?"

"I cannot say. These things are not always straightforward."

He exhaled. "Please forgive me, but how is this supposed to help me?"

"You must take a different path than the one you intend."

"It *is* Kane." Princess Taylynn stepped forward. "You must go to Fort Squall, King Talon. Even then, it may be too late."

"Fort Squall?" He frowned, glancing between Jade and Taylynn.

Queen Jade shot her daughter a look. "You have seen something, child? Something more than I?"

Taylynn's shoulders tightened. He almost missed it. "I have seen enough, *Mother*."

"Then you felt it too? The warning? What did you see? Why did you not...? I thought..." Emotion flashed across Queen Jade's face.

"I saw Fort Squall fall to Kane and his dragons."

A chill burrowed into Talon's bones. "Survivors?"

"I cannot say," the princess said. "I only saw what is to come, not the manner in which it happens."

His jaw clenched with irritation. "How much time until this comes to pass? I will write to the other forts—seek aid."

"There will be no time for that," Taylynn said.

"No—?" He cut himself off, then asked, "When?"

"Tomorrow." Taylynn's voice was soft, but there was a finality to it. She had no reason to lie.

His heart raced; he thought of a million reasons this couldn't possibly be true.

Bedelth cursed under his breath.

"Can we not warn them?" Talon found himself asking. "They must be given time to prepare. Is there no way? Surely with your magic..."

"I am sorry, King Talon." For her part, Queen Jade *did* sound sorry. "The barrier is not as simplistic as you make it. It is not something that can be removed to suit our needs."

"You cannot simply open a hole?" he sputtered. "A small segment—just enough for our thoughts to get through?"

"I am not here to school you in the ways of spriten magic." This time, her voice was cold.

"Fine. Then we must go at once."

"I believe that is best," the queen said. "Even if you do not reach the fort in time. My envoys will take you along the western path. This will place you closest to Squall's End."

Hopeless. It was hopeless. He turned to Princess Taylynn. "Is there no other way?" he begged. "No way to prevent this?"

She was quiet far longer than he liked. A myriad of emotions crossed her features. An internal battle playing out on the canvas of her face. "I am afraid not, King Talon. This...this is how it must be. But do not give up hope. For your journey to Fort Squall holds great promise."

"How?" He all but choked. "How can it, if the fort will still fall?"

She closed her eyes, then opened them to gaze back at him. "You will see. Now go."

～

It took less than an hour to depart Esterpine. Jade saw them to the edge of the city, Prince Feowen with her. "I bid you a warm farewell, King Talon," she said. "I am glad that you have come, that we have reconciled, and that the stones are safe. They will remain so. On behalf of myself and my people, I bid you safe travels." She lifted a hand in farewell. "May the king of all trees watch over you."

With that, she bowed her head. Feowen mimicked her behavior, as did the nobility who'd tagged along. Then the sprites turned and departed, leaving their group alone with Jade's envoys.

Jade's envoys led them through the forest at a rapid pace. Their path was nearly indiscernable. The dirt was not worn from trampling feet. The foliage only separated when they neared, otherwise it looked no different than any other part of the forest. They wouldn't have found their way alone.

Every moment felt like a lifetime.

Six hours passed on foot before they stopped to rest. They had skipped dinner in favor of haste, so they quickly replenished their thirst and ate the travel rations they carried. While the others caught their breath, he felt a strange urge to wander away—not far, just beyond a nearby tree.

He could still hear the sounds of the others as he slipped into the foliage. The cadence of their voices fell into a low murmur, melding with the sounds of the forest. He found Taylynn standing beneath the shadow of an ivy veil. The vines had grown up around the tree and its lowest limbs.

She held a finger to her lips before backing deeper into the darkness. Her markings glowed brightly like a beacon. He frowned and stepped closer. Was this a trick of his mind? An illusion? It was said that those who entered the forest often vanished. His hand came to rest on the hilt of his sverak, following after Taylynn's figure until she came to a stop.

"How are you here?" he hissed. "Did you follow us?"

"There is something I must say to you, King Talon. I did not wish to say it in the presence of my mother. She and I do not always see eye to eye."

He exhaled. Was she about to offer reinforcements? Did she have a plan? A way to save Squall's End?

"I can see it on your face, even now," she said, her own was a tableau of sadness. She gave her head a brief shake. "The answer is no. I cannot save your fort. Events have a way of unfolding to nudge us back onto our rightful paths. There is a reason for everything, even this."

Anger surged, clawing at his skin. His hand tightened around the hilt of his sverak. "If you are not here to help," he said, teeth clenched, "then why have you come?"

"For something much bigger than the loss of Fort Squall." She took a single step towards him then stopped. Her eyes darted to a spot behind him before returning to his own. "I came here for Claire."

"Claire?" He froze. "I... Is she hurt? I would have you tell me—"

"She has come to no harm."

"Then, what?!"

Taylynn appeared to contemplate something. "I will make a deal with you, Your Majesty. A trade. I would like to know what my mother has shared about her. In exchange, I will tell you the truth of it—the genuine truth."

He stood, rooted in place. His mind stumbled over the conversations between himself and the spriten queen, over the queen's guarded words and vague explanations. Was Taylynn suggesting that Jade had manipulated him? Lied to him? Given him false advice?

"The choice is yours," Taylynn said.

He glanced over his shoulder. The murmurs from his party continued. Taylynn's scrutiny made him itch. Her eyes belonged to something far more ancient than the woman standing before him. The forest was in her, wild and unforgiving. "All right," he said at last. "I want the truth."

Something akin to victory flashed across her face, so brief that he found himself blinking. She nodded and said, "You have made the correct decision. Come."

He followed her deeper into the forest.

CHAPTER 17
CHANGING PLANS

Celenore

Claire was with her army again. They settled on an island, a rocky outcropping, more or less. Nearly one hundred dragons clotted the rock faces in the dark pre-dawn. Wrath gave a mighty roar. Opening his maw, snapping at the air. The sound echoed out over the water, but there was no one to hear it.

"How far to Squall's End?" she asked.

"Less than an hour east, my lord." Wrath's voice was rich, but there was something beneath it. A measure of condescension that made her want to rip his head from his neck. Wrath despised her. He only worked with her as the better of two poor options. But she would outwit him in the end. She would be the one standing victorious when the dust settled.

She gazed out over the hoard of beasts, hiding her distaste. "Let us go, then. And remember what we discussed. If they surrender the fort, we cease destruction of the city."

"And if they do not?"

"Then you burn the city to the ground."

Wrath was silent for several moments. "Surely you do not believe those abominations would surrender."

She hesitated. "For their people, they might. If they do, we will honor the bargain. Am I clear?"

"We are clear."

She was thrown forward in her harness. Wrath crouched and shot into the sky. The ground disappeared beneath her, and they were soaring above the sea. Victory was a sweet scent in her nostrils, she need only open her mouth and take a bite—

SHE OPENED HER EYES, chest heaving. The ground was firm beneath her. She took a handful of dirt into her fist, convincing herself that this was real. Above her, the stars were growing dimmer in the pre-dawn.

A dark shadow fell over her, settling into a crouch beside her.

"She's unwell." It was Koldis. "Get me some water and something to eat. Hurry."

"Koldis?" She tried to sit up. He supported her back, helping her. "I'm fine," she croaked, wincing. A dull headache pounded against her skull. "Really, I'm fine."

"You don't look it. You pushed yourself too hard yesterday. Your magic is taking its toll." He glanced up, accepting a waterskin and a chunk of bread, handing both to her. "Here. Drink, eat."

She shoved both away. "No, I..." She wiped her dirty palms on her pants then massaged her temples.

Jovari crouched down beside them, studying her. "What happened?"

"I..." Her eyes went wide "I saw him. Oh, gods! It's happening. The attack. It wasn't just a bad dream. It's..." Her breaths turned ragged.

"What is she talking about?" Jovari kept his voice low. The others in their group were only just stirring.

"She believes she saw an attack on Squall's End," Koldis explained.

"What?" Jovari hissed. "How? When?"

"We need to go to Squall's End," she said, a hint of desperation in her voice. " Right now. We need to help them. To help Reyr." She tried to stand up, wobbling.

Koldis pushed her back into a sitting position. "Stay," he demanded. "Take a deep breath. We don't have proof that this is really happening. Do we? Besides, Squall's End is at least a day's flight from here, and that's if we make good time."

"A day?" She all but choked, shaking her head. "And how can you even question it?! It's happening. Right now! It's happening." A frantic desperation took hold of her.

"Okay. Okay." Koldis held up his hands, attempting to calm her down.

"We have to help them," she cried. "To warn them."

"How long do they have before the attack?" Koldis asked, sharing a worried glance with Jovari.

Ice seeped into her gut. She began to tremble. "An hour? Less?"

Koldis swore. "You're sure?"

A hopeless laugh escaped her chest in answer.

Jovari said, "If there is an impending attack, then we need to warn Reyr. It's the least we can do—all we can do, really." Jovari took her hand in his. Her own skin was a cold contrast to the calming warm that seeped from his palm. "We will do it together, Claire. We're with you."

"But, I don't know how. Not for this kind of distance. When I worked with our pairs in the villages, they were nearby."

Koldis nodded and put a hand on her shoulder. "Close your eyes and reach for him the same way you would normally. Just... reach. We're right here, lending you our strength."

She felt them beside her, felt their physical contact, but also felt their minds brushing against hers. Mustering her strength, she fought past the pounding in her temples and called to him. *"Reyr?"* At first, there was nothing. *"Reyr?"*

And then a blast, as Reyr's mind sensed hers and pushed her back some of the distance, meeting her halfway. *"Claire?! How?"* His shock and confusion were both obvious, vibrating at different frequencies along the plucked threads linking their minds together.

"You...you can hear me?" A relieved breath escaped her lungs. He sounded okay. Unharmed. Safe. But that wasn't what rattled her. This was the first time she'd heard his voice since he'd left her. They'd parted on bad terms.

Koldis relaxed his hand on her shoulder.

"I can hear you just fine. But...I shouldn't be able to hear you at all. What's going on?"

"There's no time to explain, Reyr. You're in danger. There's going to be an attack on the fort. Kane is coming."

"Kane?" There was a pause. *"But, you're serious? How can you know this? Did Saffra have a vision?"*

"I'm certain." It was almost a whisper, a thin thread of a thought close to snapping. *"He's bringing the dragons, Reyr. They're coming from the sea. That's why there wasn't any warning. They're coming."*

"Gods!" A long silence followed, and then, *"How long do we have?"*

Her heart crumbled in on itself. *"Less than an hour."*

"No..." It was hard to believe Reyr could muster such disbelief and fear in a single word, but he did.

Jovari must have felt her trembling. He squeezed her hand. Her eyes danced and darted frantically beneath her eyelids. *"I...I'm sorry, Reyr. I'm so sorry."* The apology was out before she could stop it.

"For what?"

For hurting you, she wanted to say. For all the things we said before you left. For the way things ended between us. For being the reason you ran away. For being the reason you're in Fort Squall, putting your life at risk.

Instead, she said, *"I'm sorry that I cannot be there to help. That I cannot do more. That I—"*

"Claire..." His voice softened. *"You have done plenty. You have given us a fighting chance. I must go and warn the others."* A pause and then, *"Thank you."*

The contact broke like a snapped twig. She opened her eyes and stifled a cry, looking between Koldis and Jovari. "He's going to be okay, right? He's going to be okay?"

When they did not answer, she began to hyperventilate. Koldis stood, putting his hands behind his head, running his fingers through his hair, cursing under his breath. Jovari opted for pacing, striding back and forth across her field of vision. They didn't know what to do, either.

Their companions were awake now. Some even sensed the tension.

She stood, ignoring her trembling muscles. "We must go to them, Koldis." She raised her voice so everyone could hear. "We must fly to their aid."

The demand was stupid. Unless the battle lasted a full day, they would never make it in time. They would arrive after it ended. Everyone might be dead by then.

But, what else could they do? Turn around and go home? Hope things might work out? Hope that Fort Squall would be okay?

No. She refused to retreat.

"This is *Reyr* we're talking about, Koldis, your brother in all but blood! We cannot just leave him to face Kane alone. Remember what happened to Cyrus? We..."

Jovari stopped pacing. "She's right. We cannot lose Reyr, too. Even if we don't make it in time, he will need us for whatever comes after. They all will."

"We'll be too late," Koldis said. "We'll be too late." Silence followed, and then he exhaled. "But you're right. We cannot abandon him."

Her shoulders dropped with relief.

"Mount up and move out," Koldis called, his voice booming through their camp. "We fly north."

She hugged her arms around herself, but found little comfort in them. She hadn't expected to convince him this easily, but she was grateful nonetheless. Koldis turned to her. "We must do whatever we can. I already lost one brother. I'll not lose two. Even if it means suffering my king's wrath."

"I know." She reached out for him, then let her hand drop. "I know."

Their camp burst into a flurry of activity. Within minutes everyone had gathered their packs, no questions asked, and assembled.

"What about Lily?" she asked, glancing around. Koldis stood, arms crossed, watching the others shift and mount up. "Where is she?"

His face hardened. "Lily slipped into the wilderness just before dawn."

"What?" She all but choked. "What do you mean?"

Koldis hesitated. "The loss of a mate is a terrible thing, Claire. I cannot begin to understand..." He shook his head. "She will live out the rest of her days in isolation. It was her choice."

"But...no." She couldn't stop the strangling sensation clawing at her throat. Or the tears that blurred her vision. This was *her* fault. Her failure. And now she wouldn't be allowed the chance to reconcile her actions? To apologize? To show Lily how sorry she was for...everything?

"It was her choice, Claire."

"I...understand. How long until...?"

"A few days, at most. The magic that gave her a long life is gone. She isn't young by human standards. With Hiondel gone, her human years will catch up at a rapid rate."

"A few *days*?" Her voice cracked.

"Best not to think about it," Koldis said. His throat bobbed. "We've got bigger matters at hand." Even though he sounded unaffected, his mouth was set in a frown. "Come. We must make haste."

They were in the sky in less than ten minutes, flying north. With the ground far below, she allowed her tears to break free, grateful no one could see her. The droplets froze on her cheeks and she wiped them away.

A strong tailwind helped speed them along, thank the gods, but it wasn't enough to defy distance. The sky was soon bathed in hues of pink and orange as the sun reached the horizon, greeting the day. How could a sunrise feel so ominous? So catastrophic?

Fort Squall would meet Kane's dragons in battle and she could do nothing to stop it. Just as she could do nothing when Hiondel died. Just as she could do nothing for Lily.

With each passing minute, she felt sicker. "I think I'm going to throw up," she muttered.

"Try not to get it on my scales, won't you?" Koldis must have heard her.

Under different circumstances, she might have laughed. All she could do was clench her jaw.

The open sky had a way of sharpening everything into clarity. Today, it was cloudless. Empty. A wide space to be filled with the worst things a mind could conjure.

Since coming to Dragonwall, Kane had always been a distant threat, acting through others. His nasks. The vodar. Now he would deal his heaviest blow, and no one was ready for it.

"Any word from Reyr?" Koldis didn't bother disguising his hopeful tone.

"No." She kept her mind open, but there was nothing.

"The battle should start very soon," Koldis mused. *"I want to hear what happens. Jovari and I can link up with you. Your abilities will let you see and hear what's taking place."*

She considered this, even though it scared her. *"I don't think we have a choice, really. It's the only way to know what happens."*

Each minute in the sky felt like hours, but not knowing was far worse than what she might hear if she stretched her mind to Fort Squall. Even if whatever happened turned out to be much like the attack on the vodar. She feared the projections, the images, the emotions she would be forced to experience, but it would mean knowing that Reyr was alive.

Jovari and Koldis brushed against her mind, bolstering her. She wasn't sure how to extend herself when she had nothing to say, no target for her thoughts. It felt like wandering around in the dark with no destination in mind.

"Just relax and push," Koldis said.

With her eyes closed, she imagined her mind as a soap bubble, growing larger to encompass the world around her. Long moments passed in silence and darkness. Then everything hit her all at once.

She gasped, choking. Fear, pain, frantic words, violent images. It happened so quickly she had no time to react as she was dragged into the maelstrom. She couldn't even tell what side she was on.

"Approach them from behind!" "We cannot push them back!" "Fall back!" "We follow!" "Look to the city. It's burning!" "Fire! I will taste your flesh!" So many voices and no way to tell where one ended and another began. So many emotions. Images of wild dragons in formation, of drengr facing them, of riders with their bows drawn. All swooping and diving and clashing. Screams. Roars. Blood.

So much blood.

She caught a snippet of Reyr's voice mingled with the others. All she could do was sag with relief before another set of projections overcame her. A flash of Squall's End, burning. Dragons diving towards screaming bodies, hunger in their stomachs. Evil in their hearts. She wanted to taste bones crunching between her jaws, sweet flesh, warm blood.

Images of a plummeting pair. Pain. Fear. Her limbs burned. She cried out, uncertain if it was her own voice or another drengr's roar echoing in her ears. The screams. Oh gods, the screams. The same screams Kane's dragons longed for. Rejoiced in. Celebrated.

Chaos. Utter chaos.

"Claire!"

Another swath of Squall's End erupted into flames along its towering protective wall.

"Only the western block." She knew this voice and shuddered. It was Kane.

"Claire!" Someone called her name. And then everything disappeared.

Koldis and Jovari had pulled from her mind, leaving a deep and empty well behind.

"Oh gods!" she cried, covering her face with her hands, fingers digging into her skin. She hadn't merely seen things from the drengr, but also from the dragons. Her stomach roiled with nausea.

"Gods, gods, gods!" There was nothing she could do. She sagged against Koldis, resting her face against his neck, breathing hard.

"*It's an absolute nightmare,*" Koldis said to Jovari, his voice heavy. "*Worse than I expected. But we need get her back there, Jovari, to the battle. It is the only way to see what happens.*"

"*What?! No!*" She sat up straight, gripping the harness. "*No. I cannot go back.*"

Celenore's landscape slid by beneath them. All she could think about was the screaming. The pain. The death. The people in the city, running from dragon jaws.

Was this how Saffra had seen Belnesse? How she had felt after her vision? Tremors shook her. She squeezed her fists until her hands cramped. "*I can't go back, Koldis. I can't.*"

"*You must,*" he said. "*It is the only way to know.*"

"*No. It's...it's not right. You cannot ask this of me.*" Hadn't she done enough already? She could already feel pieces of herself crumbling away. If she went back...

"*Please, Claire. We cannot abandon Reyr.*" Jovari knew exactly what to say to convince her. For Reyr, she would do just about anything.

"*Fine,*" she hissed. "*I...I'll do it. But I hate you for asking this of me.*"

"*You'll forgive us, eventually.*"

Their minds were waiting. She braced herself, linking up once more. Taking a deep breath, she plunged herself back into the battle, losing herself and everything she had ever known in the heat of it, certain that she would burn to death with all those in the city below.

CHAPTER 18

PREPARING FOR BATTLE

Squall's End

Tamara's fingers paused on the fastenings of her gown. She heard shouting—probably a group of drengr returning from patrol. Today she dressed in a shade of deep green velvet with just enough stretch to make it more comfortable than other gowns. She preferred old fashioned styles that clasped in front, rather than those with corsets squeezing the life out of her. Corsets were better suited for women with chests anyway, and without a handmaiden to assist, it was a near impossible challenge.

Her current roommates were already out, tending to their chores. Kiviana, Lara, and Sophie had earlier mornings than she did. They hadn't been successful during the touching ceremony. Sophie didn't hold it against her. They'd become fast friends. Kiviana and Lara, on the other hand, who had hated her since the beginning, took every opportunity to shoot her simmering glares. Especially Kiviana with her beautiful face and perfect figure. Kiviana, whom everyone was certain would have found a mate.

Gods, she couldn't wait to move out of their quarters. But not until she bonded with Byron. They'd be sharing a room once that happened.

She quickly fixed her loose strands of hair into a tight braid, rushing through the motions. She was late already. Perhaps she ought to simply skip breakfast and head straight for Emmy's apartments. In hindsight, sleeping in had been a bad idea.

She and Byron had stayed up late, walking the length of the fort's battlements, discussing the possibilities of their future. Their bonding ceremony was two days away, which shouldn't have seemed like much, except each day moved slower than the last. She may as well have been wading through molasses.

Her gown was finished, as of yesterday, and locked away with the rest of her belongings. She wore the key around her neck, even though she knew Byron would never be so conniving as to sneak a peek. She glanced over at the wooden trunk and smiled.

Another cry outside made her frown. She glanced at the window and her frown deepened. A group of people rushed past. "You'd think we were under attack," she muttered, finishing with her hair.

The door to her chamber burst open, slamming against the wall.

"Good gods!" She clutched her chest and gasped. Sophie sprinted into the room straight for Tamara, grabbing her wrist, dragging her away from the mirror.

Tamara pulled free. "What...? Sophie! Stop it! What are you doing?"

"Gods, Tamara! Don't you know? We're under attack. You've been hiding out here all this time? Hurry up!"

She blinked. "That's impossible. We cannot be."

It was a drill, it had to be. The fort leaders feared an attack for weeks and promised drills would become a regular way of life. It didn't mean Sophie needed to drag her from her room so forcefully. On cue, bells began ringing in the distance.

"Tamara, you must believe me! The attack is real!"

She glanced outside, her brows drawing together. "But it cannot be."

"Please, we've got to go!" Sophie managed to drag her into the corridor.

The quadrangle was a rush of running bodies. People shouted and ran about. The frenzy was uncoordinated and chaotic. "But I don't understand," she said, almost dazed by the rush. She rubbed her wrist. "Byron would be here if we were in danger." She glanced up at the sky. There was no sight of the drengr. Wouldn't they be in flight already?

"Come." Sophie took her arm this time. In the light, she got a good look at her friend's face. It was bloodless, pale as parchment. "We've been ordered to shelter below the dining hall. It's the safest place in the fort."

Other fort dwellers were headed the same way.

"No. I...I can't go below. I will not. I'm a rider, Sophie. I need to find Byron."

She was meant to be by Byron's side, not cowering in the darkness. A flash of anger heated her face. This was why they should have been mated sooner, to function as a team. Instead, they were cut off from one another. She could not look into his mind, could not contact him, could not determine his whereabouts.

Sophie growled in frustration. "I will drag you if I have to, Tamara. Lord Davi has already given the ord—"

They froze. A distant roar silenced the chaos around them. A roar unlike any she had heard. Deeper, more guttural. Almost painful. Her eyes went wide. The sound was unmistakable, because somehow her body knew what it had come from by pure instinct alone. Wild dragons.

"*Now* do you believe me?" Sophie demanded. "Hurry! All of us are to go below."

Tamara took a step back, away from Sophie, shaking her head. This could not be happening. This wasn't real. It was some trick. Something to make their drill feel more realistic.

"Tamara!" Byron sprinted across the courtyard. At his expression, the rest of the blood drained from her face. But she knew the truth from his expression alone.

"No." she whispered, stepping back another pace. "No..."

Byron came to a stop beside her. "Sophie will take you below. You'll be safe there."

Her anger returned in full force, like a match struck. She offered him a withering glare. "I am your rider, Byron. I will *not* cower in fear. If we are not yet mated before we die, that travesty is on *you*. But I'll be damned if I cower beneath the dining hall simply because you needed your month to get to know me better." She'd never spoken to anyone like this, least of all her mate. But the words were out and there was no taking them back. Her chest heaved with each rapid breath. In a calmer tone, she said, "My place is by your side, upon your back, as it has always been. Go, Sophie. Get yourself to safety before it is too late."

Sophie nodded and rushed away, but she didn't watch her friend's retreat. She kept her gaze on Byron, eyes narrowed. If they died before she mated with him, she would never forgive him, not even from her grave. She ignored his stunned expression. "Well? What are you waiting for?" she demanded.

He closed his mouth at last. "There is no way to change your mind?"

She pulled her shoulders back. "I am unyielding."

Did he truly think she would let him fly into battle without her? That she would simply cower in the dark, waiting, wondering what was to become of him? She? The woman who would someday take over Emmy's place as fort leader? Did he even know her at all? Perhaps not. Perhaps he had no idea. "I would rather die with you than live the rest of my existence wondering what I might have done differently."

His face softened. He exhaled. "Very well. There is little time. Grab your flying things and let's go."

She sprinted back into her room and retrieved her practice bow and quiver, slinging one over her shoulder and strapping the other to her waist. There was no time for anything else, not even enough time to change into flying gear.

Byron took her hand and they sprinted through the fort. They reached the assembly field in minutes. She faltered when she saw the scene before her. Every available drengr and rider had assembled. It was a hoard of colors. Blues, greens, hues of red and orange, some purples, golds, whites, and all shades in between. She squinted against the rising sun's glare to see it all. If she weren't so terrified, she would be awed.

It hit her then, like someone had barreled right into her chest, nearly knocking her off her feet. This really wasn't a drill. This was very, *very* real. They were under attack, and by the end of it, some of the people before her would not live. Perhaps even she might be among them. She pushed the thought aside, squashing her fear.

Better to think of it like the stories she had grown up reading about, of great battles in history, like those against the ice giants and goblins. The stories never mentioned how scared the heroes were. Maybe the heroes weren't scared. But if that was the case, what did that make her? Tremors spread through her muscles. She tensed up to keep from shaking, to keep her nerves from showing.

Byron dropped her hand and jogged away from her, transforming as he ran, coming down on sharp talons that left deep furrows in the ground. She lifted her skirts and ran too, until she caught up to his hulking icy blue form. He was wearing his harness, ready for battle. She vaulted up his forearm and onto his back as if she'd been doing it all her life.

Her clothing made things difficult in the harness. Her gown wasn't intended for battle, but she would make do. She fastened the buckles around her legs. The fabric bunched up uncomfortably around her thighs but she ignored it. The other riders on the field were in thigh-length tunics, light protective padding, and leggings.

"There is naught to be done, about your gown. Do the best you can." Byron's voice was calm, but she sensed the anxious edge to his words.

He got them into position, flanking Lord Davi and Lady Emmy. She glanced about, realizing that he'd taken the position as Davi's wing-second. A position of honor and huge responsibility.

Davi's voice sounded in Byron's mind. *"Stay close, Byron. No matter what happens. Stay with me."*

"I've got your back, Father, Mother. I'm with you all the way."

Her chest tightened at the love and reassurance in his words.

She took a deep, calming breath, then another, listening to the air pass into and out of her chest. Better than focusing on the blood pounding in her ears. The bells of Squall's End continued to ring, increasing the cacophony of noise filling the air. If she strained her ears, she could hear the cries from the city in the distance.

Her gaze swept the field, taking note of each battle formation. They were different from the smaller formations of the patrols. Each battle wing held between ten and fifteen drengr. A glimmer of gold caught her eye. Reyr was one wing over, leading a group with Byron's friend, Fierran, as wing-second.

Emmy turned, capturing her gaze, her face one of stone. Was she afraid? She gave Tamara a solemn bow of her head. Tamara bowed her head in return, grateful that Emmy didn't shoo her away, or treat her like a child and demand she cower with the others.

Emmy took her bow in hand and prepared herself. Tamara followed her actions, stringing her bow, getting it ready for battle. Her fingers trembled. She had to fuss with the loops more than usual to get them fitted into the notches on each bow arm. She took another calming breath. With every passing moment, her anxiety increased.

They faced Stormy Bay, watching the sky, waiting for the inevitable, waiting to fight the very beasts they had once been created to destroy. And then she saw them, speckled across the horizon in a rainbow of colors. The dragons were here. Battle was upon them. She only hoped the cost wouldn't be too great.

CHAPTER 19

UNTIL THE VERY END

Fort Squall

Davi looked out over the pairs assembled across the field. Nearly half their forces were patrolling the wilderness, scattered over the extensive territory of Vestur. His chest reverberated with a growl. A plume of smoke seeped from his nostrils. Only one hundred and fifty-two drengr today. *One hundred and fifty-two!* Gods! Some were so old they would tire quickly, while others were too green to have any business taking part in this attack. Like Byron.

His lids closed over his eyes for the span of a breath. A dark calm in the chaos of his mind. A moment of peace.

"I am with you," Reyr said. *"We are in this together. We will see it through."*

"Aye. We have no choice."

He had always wondered if something in their twin bond allowed them to sense the other's emotions. That theory held true today. He swung his head to the right, looking over at Reyr. Thank the gods Reyr was even here. The king's own drengr fairtheoir, flying beside them into battle. Still, it did not guarantee victory. Far from it.

He turned back to the bay, back to the enemy dotting the horizon. He mastered his fear and spoke, *"Fort Squall, I call upon you! The day has come to meet our enemies in battle!"* All around him, the drengr clawed the ground with their talons, anxious but eager. *"We will not allow these beasts, these kingdom destroyers, to harm the innocents we are sworn to protect. We have a pact with humanity, a pact as old as an age. We were created to destroy this clan. To bring peace to Dragonwall. And destroy them we will!"* Roars shook the ground beneath him. He thrashed his head, letting his agitation show. *"They must not reach the city. We will meet our foes over the bay. Are you with me?!"*

Increased bellows from his kin pierced the morning air. *"We are with you!"* came their words.

"I am with you, my love, until the very end." Emmy's voice wrapped around his mind, warm, enduring.

"And I with you," he returned. *"Until the very end."*

The bells in Squall's End continued to toll, to sing the song of impending battle, to cry out in fear, in warning. So many people within its high walls. So many refugees from all over the territory who had fled south from the dragons' pillaging and burning. All helpless.

He hoped they were shut away behind closed doors, their windows shuttered. Those of higher birth would be deep within the bowels of the city's keep. As if the deep places would offer solace from dragon fire. Opening his jaws, he let out a battle cry.

It was time.

He'd made good use of their share of the ice metal. It had been melted down with the help of Lord Averaen's skilled smiths. It now graced the heads of the dragon lances along the city and fort's walls. It also kissed the shafts of the arrows nestled in the quivers of every rider.

Crouching low, he mustered his energy and sprang from the earth. His body catapulted upward, heavy but powerful. Around him, the others followed, moving as one. Hundreds of years of practice, of drills, of growth, for this moment.

He was overly aware of Byron, flanking him on the right in

third position. His heart tightened. He couldn't keep his son from this fight no matter how much he wanted to. But he was proud to have him here.

"Byron's fierce heart makes up for what he and Tamara lack in training," Emmy said. *"They will fight well."*

The fort's drengr were airborne now. They maintained their formations, advancing. Each set of wings beat steadily against the morning chill. The sun climbed from the horizon, bathing the world in a fierce golden glow each time it peeked from a distant cloud.

The clouds.

That would complicate things. The wild dragons would use the cloud cover to their advantage. His pairs would need to do the same.

Their enemy advanced, the blur becoming distinct individual shapes.

A frenzy gripped him. Ancient. Instinctual. He wanted to taste blood. He wanted to rip their bodies to shreds with tooth and claw. Hatred pounded against his chest. These were beasts he despised more than all else, even more than he had hated the Kalds responsible for killing his parents and Reyr's Gemma.

The wild dragons offered them challenging roars across the sky, guttural and raw. The same hunger he felt was echoed in their cries. His forces answered. He answered. And then he faltered, blinking, blinking again. A deeper sense of dread took form in the pit of his stomach.

These dragons carried weapons in their forearms, tightly tucked against their scaly bodies.

"Ice metal," Emmy said, reading his thoughts.

Ice metal in its virgin form was blueish grey. Often with swirling lines, giving it the appearance of marble. Virtually indestructible. Perfect for breaking through the hardest materials, like dragon scales.

Mixed with steel for sveraks, ice metal lightened up in color turning a cool gray, able to be shined and polished. Less crude.

He had expected weapons but hoped against it. These were half spear, half sword, sharp on both ends, with a large arrowhead on the tip for carving an easy passage into bone and sinew.

"*Be wary of their weapons!*" The warning was sent to everyone.

"*Focus, my love.*" Emmy brought his mind into clarity, and then there was no more time.

Their lines met with full force. Both sides powerful. Both struggling to push the other back. Cries erupted all around him and the world descended into chaos.

A dragon flew for him, its weapon extended for a deadly strike. He reacted, rolling left. The roll put him in the path of a second dragon. He was forced to drop in altitude. Emmy took aim and fired, striking the dragon's underbelly. The arrowhead sank into its scales. It screamed from above, writhing around. Hot droplets of blood sprayed him.

He changed direction, aware that Byron and the rest of his wing were still with him. Their minds were connected to his, ready to project as the need arose. Already, a trickle of images were pouring in. He sifted through them quickly.

They circled around. Another wing of dragons dropped from overhead, obscured by clouds. The collision was jarring. Water droplets scattered everywhere, sparkling in the sunlight as they evaporated.

His wing engaged. They fought with tooth and claw, using their powerful hind legs to kick at their enemies. As quickly as possible, they disengaged, regaining formation. Roars echoed in his head, some of pain, some of anger. The noise left his ears ringing painfully.

He didn't need to glance behind him to know Emmy's actions. She fired arrow after arrow at any dragon within range. Battle cries were commonplace now, sounding at random as other wings collided and engaged.

The other riders followed Emmy's example. They nocked, pulled, fired, nocked, pulled, fired. Their movements blurred. Each arrow sank deeply into the scales of their enemy, but they were little more than hindrances. He prayed to every god he knew that the poisoned tips of the arrowheads would be enough to quickly wear the dragons down. As long as his drengr could keep them engaged, there wouldn't be time to remove the shafts.

"I need a clear shot at its head," Emmy cried, bringing his attention to an orange dragon. He swept upward, angling himself. She fired. The arrow sank into the dragon's skull. It thrashed, trying to dislodge it. She released another. The dragon gave one final roar before it spiraled down into the sea below.

He blinked, then roared, pride lacing his challenge. *"Well done, my love! Well done!"*

"Good work, Mother!" Byron's cry came seconds later. *"You did it!"*

Byron stayed close, Tamara letting loose a constant stream of arrows. She moved slowly, clumsily, nothing like a seasoned rider. But even now, he saw one of her arrows meet its mark. His chest swelled. She would make a fine rider someday—if such a day came.

"It will," Emmy said. *"You and I know it will. We will ensure that it does."*

Davi brought his wing around for another confrontation, hoping to keep the dragons from pushing closer to land. His breaths came in great gasps as he strained against his muscles, pushing his body to the limit. The air was already thick with smoke from dragon flames. Though fire was useless for both sides, most breathed it out of instinct.

The wind whistled over his scales. Projections flashed through his mind at a constant stream. He did his best to split his focus between the fort's progress and his own movements. Emmy was a huge help in that regard, helping him organize his thoughts.

"We've got trouble!" she cried, directing his gaze toward the city. Two wings of wild dragons had escaped their clutches. They worked their way around the edge of Davi's forces and raced unhindered towards Squall's End.

"Gods! Not the city!" A chill doused him. The wing leader of the second wing carried more than just a weapon. Sitting on its glittering red back was a lone figure. His stomach plummeted.

"Kane!" Emmy hissed. *"He's here—with them! We must protect the city, Davi."* Despair seeped into her voice. They hadn't noticed

the sorcerer amidst the chaos. With him here, how could they possibly hope to win?

"None of us is powerful enough to fight him."

"I'm on it!" Reyr cried, sensing his thoughts. Reyr's wing swept past Davi towards Squall's End and Kane.

"Be careful, Reyr!" he called. There was no way Reyr could take on Kane alone, king's shield or not. He needed Davi's help. *"With me!"* he cried, giving the order to his wing. They turned, moving into a sweeping arc to follow after.

A screech sounded above. Another cluster of wild dragons crashed down upon his wing from the clouds. He roared, infuriated by the thwart. They engaged, kicking and biting.

"I will eat you alive, fort leader." The feral voice was filled with hate, with promise, and heavily accented.

The taunt had come from the dragon before him, heading straight for him.

"Ignore its words, my love."

He tried to follow Emmy's advice, focusing instead on the task at hand. His body slammed against the dark blue of its scales.

"You may call me Terror!" it said, sending the words hissing into his mind.

"Terror?" He snorted. *"What a stupid name. Hope you don't think it makes you more terrifying."*

Terror let out a high-pitched scream. *"I will bring you down."* It bared its weapon, sweeping it around. Too slow.

Davi used his hind legs to push the dragon away, careful to score Terror's hide with his talons. He felt the scales rip apart beneath his claws and growled with satisfaction. Terror screamed and moved away to recover, but not before another dragon latched onto Davi's tail with its teeth. *"I am Panic. I will show you no mercy."*

Pain—hot, searing pain—erupted up his tail and into his body. His vision darkened before he bellowed into the sky, letting his agony be known. His lower body thrashed, writhing about as he tried to shake himself free of Panic. Emmy cried with him, feeling all that he felt. He twisted around and freed his tail. The end of it was missing. He would mourn it later.

Terror recovered, flying directly for him, roaring and bathing him in flame. Their shared magic would protect Emmy. She coughed and sputtered as the smoke filled her mouth, but the sound of her coughing was drowned out by something else. A scream he knew well. Something that turned his hot scales cold.

"Reyr!" He faltered.

His hesitation left him vulnerable. Terror collided with him, sending them both spiraling off course. His shoulder wailed in agony as something sharp pierced his scales. He didn't think about it. His eyes were turned upon Squall's End. Along the eastern wall, dragon fire erupted in the city clearing a path several blocks wide. Enough to kill hundreds.

"No!" Emmy's frantic voice echoed his fear.

All it took was a single dragon to burn the entire city to the ground. A single one. Yet, there were nearly one hundred. And if someone didn't stop them now, thousands upon thousands would die. He couldn't let Squall's End burn.

But...it was already happening. He caught a brief flash of gold over the city. Reyr.

"Focus, Davi!" Emmy's mental shout had him turning his attention back to Terror and Panic. The blue was grappling with him, clawing at him. He tried to gouge Terror's eyes out, thankful that its weapon had been knocked free. All they had now were their teeth and talons. A fair fight.

His anger made him bold. His fear for Reyr made him bolder. He snapped at Terror's neck, sinking his jaws into the dragon's scales. Hot blood, acidic on his tongue, gushed through his mouth. He shook his head back and forth with two forceful flicks. Terror was smaller than him—a much younger dragon—and couldn't take such a thrashing. He felt Terror's neck snap and the dragon went limp. He released him to the sea.

Panic attacked, sinking his own jaws into Davi's hind leg. His vision flashed from red to white and he howled.

"I will make you pay for that, drengr scum!"

He dived and rolled, dragging Panic with him. In his peripherals, he caught a glimpse of the green dragon. Emmy fired what was left of her arrows, forcing Panic to disengage. The pain receded somewhat, but blood could be felt dripping down his foot.

An ear splitting scream made him forget what he was feeling—the scream of a rider in peril. A projection that spoke of fear and death flashed before his vision. It was followed by a drengr roar, cut short. Pain seared his chest like the plunge of a knife into his heart. Selwin, his oldest drengr, was dead. Another set of roars followed these. He felt two more sharp pains. Two more deaths.

More wild cries from the city floated out over the water. Smoke billowed up into the sky over Squall's End. His drengr needed him, but the people needed him more. "*To the city!*" he cried, giving up their fight over the water. His wing roared in response, moving to follow orders. After that, there were too many death pains to count.

Time seemed to run together.

"*Davi!*" Emmy's scream distracted him. He felt an isolated pressure against his scales. A red-orange dragon had come up beside them. It tried to rip Emmy's harness from his body. He struggled against the beast. Emmy screamed again before trying to cast an incant that might help her. Pain erupted across his chest. Emmy's pain. She slid off the other side of his body with the harness still attached to her legs. "*No!*" His heart leapt in his chest. He tried to grab her, to snatch her from the air. A force sent him sideways and he missed. He missed!

"*Davi!*" she screamed, reaching up for him with her arms as she fell. They'd performed thousands of trust falls for this very moment.

But a single image flashed through his mind—a memory from a dream.

He was frozen in terror, in shock. He tried to go after her, but something held him back. At first, he thought it was simply his dread, but then he realized it was something much worse.

"*We will kill you, fort leader! She is lost to you!*"

A cluster of enemy dragons had converged upon him, isolating him, holding him in place. He was caged, helpless. Below, his vision was filled with Emmy. Her face was turned towards him as her body fell, eyes wide. Across her front, a large gash had opened her up, staining her tunic deep red. The wound was trying to close, to heal itself, but it was too slow. She was too tired. And he was too wounded. Their shared magic had been all but drained.

He screamed. With a mighty jerk he twisted in the air, working to kick free of his assailants. How had it come to this?

"Emmy!" he screamed.

The dragons were too strong. There were too many. He writhed within their grasp, scratching and biting.

The seconds ticked by in slow motion, drawing out his agony. There were others around him, helping him, fighting against the dragons, fighting to free him. He heard their voices in his mind. He saw their projections. None of it made sense. All he could think of was Emmy. She was far below now, nearly lost to the world.

A new bugle split the air. Byron's ice-blue scales plummeted past him, wings tucked tight as he dived to save his mother. Davi had but a moment to rejoice.

A pain unlike anything he ever felt erupted in his neck. Sharp teeth sank into his scales. He opened his mouth, but no sound came out. His last thought was of Emmy, of her face as she fell away from him.

"I love you, Davi." Her words were in his mind again, weak, faint, as if death was already taking her. *"Until the very end."*

His own vision was fading, growing dark at the edges. Was this the very end? If so, then he had failed her. He had failed them all. There was only darkness. And then...there was nothing at all.

CHAPTER 20
DEMANDS FOR SURRENDER

Fort Squall

Reyr disengaged, kicking a dragon away with his hind legs. The frenzy of battle sent him into a frenzy. He hardly recognized himself—who he was. He only knew one thing: defeat his enemy.

His thrust sent the dragon spiraling off course. Freed, he abruptly changed direction, looking, searching. There! He spotted what he wanted.

Below him, the eastern quarter of Squall's End erupted in flames. The smoke billowed up in black plumes, blotting out the sky. He flew through it and the world around him winked out. Moments later, the sunshine reappeared.

Sounds pierced the air like knives slicing through the world. Screams. So many screams. Everywhere. The scent of charred flesh drifted up into the sky. He followed the green dragon responsible for the flames, beating his wings to their breaking point, pushing against the strain to catch his prey. To kill it. And then he'd find Kane.

Closer, closer...

He could almost reach out with his snout and snap its spiked

176

tail. He flapped his wings harder, pushing. Nearly there now. His jaws opened, readying for the bite. His teeth—sharp enough to rip through dragon scales—clamped down! He latched onto the tip of the green's tail, jerking it back with a flick of his head.

Everything stopped.

His vision flashed white. Something was wrong. Blinding, immense pain pounded against his chest, stabbing, suffocating. He roared and forgot all about the the green dragon. It flapped away, putting distance between them. He didn't notice its retreat. He didn't notice anything. Only the death pain in his chest as it all but stopped his heart. His body seized. He forgot to flap his wings, forgot to breathe, to think.

"Davi!" His cry was panicked. *"Davi!"*

There was no answer. He cried out again, already knowing there would never be an answer. His body shuddered. His maw opened wide. His roar split his throat wide open, tearing through his vocal cords.

Davi was...gone.

Other roars followed his. He joined their cries. Each keening call, each choking screech turned pitiful, pathetic. He searched the sky, scanning the bay, the coastline. Davi had fallen, and Emmy with him. There one moment, gone the next.

How?! How could this have happened? What he saw broke him anew.

The city burned, dragons and drengr alike were dead, floating in the bloodied waters of the bay. Screams of loss and pain. And for what? Death? Destruction?

They had lost. It was all lost...

His breaths turned to sobs as memories of Gemma's death began to mingle with Davi's. His heart skipped. Convulsed. His lungs heaved, gasping for air as he tried to remind his wings to keep beating, to keep flying. He wanted to stop, to fall to the earth, to leave the fort to its fate. And why shouldn't he?

It was over...wasn't it?

Shock and denial gave way to burning anger. It replaced the clawing ache in his chest. Dragonwall had taken *everything* from him. Everything! This kingdom had taken the people he held dear. Taken them hungrily. His parents. Talon's parents. Gemma. His brother. Gone. All gone.

His chest deflated.

"*I couldn't save them, Uncle...*" Byron's voice was a distant thought, barely noticeable.

Byron. His nephew. He still had his nephew. There was still something left, *someone* left. Someone worth fighting for.

Images flashed through his mind. Byron sent a stream of explanations for what had happened. He saw Davi's neck snap. He saw Emmy's maimed form, her innards spilling out, cradled in Byron's arms.

"*Father and Mother, they are both... I couldn't... Reyr, what do we do now?*"

At the barrage of projections, he screamed again, loud enough to shatter glass. The gods were cruel. So cruel.

"*Uncle Reyr?*"

He hadn't the will to respond. What was he supposed to say?

He flapped his wings, laboring, fighting as the air became viscous and thick. He glanced around, frantic—

Everything seemed to freeze. He blinked as a voice filled the void. Kane's voice. "*Your leaders are dead!*" Kane hissed. His mind reeled. The telepathic thought permeated everything. "*Give up the fight. Surrender, and you will be spared. Surrender, and the city will be spared. Or I will burn the city to the ground and kill every last one of you. You have one hour.*"

As quickly as it had sounded, Kane's voice disappeared.

He blinked, coming to his senses, looking around. A fourth of the city was in flames, the rest was unharmed. The dragons disengaged. They retreated, giving the drengr room to recover.

Was this a trick?

He looked at their forces, still in shock. How many pairs had they lost? Ten? twenty? Thirty? And for what? So that Kane could prove a point?

Fury washed over him. Left him trembling with rage. His vision flashed red.

Kane could have flown in under a white flag. Could have negotiated the terms of surrender before needlessly killing so many. The sorcerer had done this on purpose. Had intended to kill the fort leaders on purpose. Kane had waited for that very moment, waited until they were dead, to offer his terms. To weaken the fort. To send it spiraling into grief. To break them.

Davi would have surrendered in a heartbeat. Davi would have handed the fort over if it meant keeping everyone safe. Davi would have done what was necessary to save the lives of thousands. His death was needless.

A roar built in Reyr's chest. It came barreling from his maw, mingled with flame. It was a rage he had never known. Not even when Gemma died. This was something deep. Something primal. Blinding. Engulfing.

Kane needed to die. Right here. Right now. There would be no surrender. No negotiating with that monster. He was going to rip the sorcerer to shreds. To ribbons of flesh. It ended today. He would kill every last dragon if he must, even if it was the last thing he lived to do.

Without another thought, he shot forward.

Kane was some distance away now, taking up a vantage point to witness their retreat. He took off in that direction, beating his wings against the air.

"*Uncle, no!*" Byron's voice filled his mind. "*We cannot engage! You will die! The entire city will burn!*"

"*I don't care if the whole world burns! I will tear him apart!*" His voice was unrecognizable.

He gained speed, flapping harder. He would reach Kane in minutes. The sorcerer would die.

"*Reyr! This is madness,*" Byron cried. "*We must retreat to Brezen! It is the only way to save them.*"

"*Who said anything about retreat? I never gave such an order.*"

Byron hesitated, and then, "*The order is not yours to give.*"

He blinked, faltered, pushed away Byron's words. With his father's death, the role of leadership passed directly to Davi's son until a vote was cast.

Kane was almost before him, his features discernible. He saw the sorcerer's red eyes, the twisted smile on his lips, daring him to attack. Daring him to give the sorcerer an excuse to burn the city.

"Uncle, disengage now! That is an order!"

He faltered again.

"Disengage! I repeat, disengage!" Byron's order, the same word over and over, echoed in his mind. Disengage. But he didn't *want* to disengage.

Kane was within his grasp. He might never get another chance. And...he wanted to die. Wanted Kane to kill him. Begged for it. To end here. Death was easier. Easier than facing his loss. Easier than facing the world without Davi and Emmy.

Kane watched as he approached, doing nothing to lift his hands, nothing to prepare a magical incantation or counter attack. He simply watched.

Reyr strained, heaving with each downward sweep of his wings. It was now or never.

"Please, Uncle. King Talon would never *forgive you."*

His mind jolted. King Talon. He swerved, turning on his wing tip at the last moment, just in time, sweeping up and over Kane. The sorcerer's mouth turned up at the corners. A victorious smirk.

The world pitched and heaved. Stormy Bay was before him, beckoning him. Calling to him.

"Thank you." Byron's voice was little more than a relieved whisper.

He said nothing in return. There was nothing to say. He wanted no more of this.

Flee, his instincts cried. *Flee.* Everything he was pushed him to get as far away from this as possible. To leave this kingdom behind. To be alone. To escape his hurt. His loss. To escape its cruel gods.

He hadn't fled when Gemma died, though he'd wanted to. Talon had convinced him to stay. This time, Talon wasn't here to stop him.

Each downward stroke took him towards the bay, and then out over the water. He felt the eyes of every drengr, every rider, following his retreat. Let them witness it. Let them think what they would. His brother had died this day. How could they ever know what that felt like?

"Uncle?"

"I'm done, Byron. The fort is yours. Do whatever you see fit."

"You...you're leaving?"

"Do not come looking for me." He closed his mind, silencing Byron's words. Silencing everything. The deepest wounds were best licked alone. And that was exactly what he intended to do.

CHAPTER 21
ARRIVING AT CAMP

Brezen

Claire extracted what was left of her mind from the battle at Squall's End. It was a slow and painful process. Her body trembled. Each breath was a painful gasp. She placed a hand over her churning stomach, willing it to calm.

Death keens filled the air around her. The drengr mourned their losses. But they didn't experience them as she had, as Jovari and Koldis had. Each pain a blade to the chest.

Bile rose in her throat. *"Koldis, I need to land. Now!"*

He dropped into a nosedive. Seconds later, she was on the ground, retching. The others landed, maintaining formation around her. Jovari rushed to her side, holding her hair back, whispering soothing words, rubbing her back. She hardly noticed him. Screams still echoed in her ears. Tears blurred her eyes, leaking down her cheeks.

She heaved until there was nothing left. Then she kept her hands braced on her knees. "Here—" Jovari handed her a handkerchief, summoned from gods-only-knew where. She wiped her mouth then crumpled it in her fist. Her head began to clear. She exhaled, standing upright, ignoring the gazes of everyone around her.

"Reyr lives," she told Jovari and Koldis, even though they'd been there in her mind. *"We will meet the fort's survivors in Brezen,"* she added. She couldn't summon an ounce of emotion to color her voice. She was too...broken. Like she had shattered over and over with every death, with every injury, every loss.

She climbed back into her harness, strapping herself in. They returned to the sky minutes later. A few sips of water eased the clawing rawness of her throat, but it did little else.

Anger soon stabbed through the hollowness in her chest, leaving her flushed. Talon's shields had asked too much of her. They'd taken advantage of her ability, using Reyr as a bargaining chip. They'd used her unfairly. Had she known the cost—

"You going to be okay?" Koldis asked.

"What do you think?" she snapped, glaring at his green scales. Muscles bulged beneath them every time he flapped his wings. *"No, Koldis. I am* not *going to be okay."*

"I...I am sorry. I did not know it would be—"

"Didn't you?!" She paused then said, *"You had no right to ask that of me. Especially after you saw what happened the first time. And especially after..."* She couldn't say Hiondel's name aloud. Or Lily's. She'd had enough. She was done. She never wanted to hear another telepathic voice, never wanted to see another projection ever, *ever* again.

"Claire, I really am sorry." Jovari this time. *"You are right. We shouldn't have—"*

"Stop talking!" she hissed. *"Both of you. Just...stop."*

She massaged her temples, trying to get rid of the ache. Jovari didn't say anything else, though he flew beside her, regarding her, his giant head turned in her direction.

She closed her eyes and placed her face against Koldis's neck, against his glassy scales. Sleep. All she wanted was sleep. To forget. To make everything disappear.

Plumes of fire and smoke raged behind the backs of her eyelids, stinging her nostrils. She groaned. Would she ever get away from it? The ringing screams in her ears? The smell of charred flesh? The feeling of talons ripping through her scales?

It was useless. How could she expect any semblance of peace after something like that?

"We need to inform King Talon of Fort Squall's demise," Koldis said to Jovari, cutting through her thoughts. She clenched her jaw, trying to ignore his voice.

"I was thinking the same," Jovari said. *"But how? We don't even know if he has left Esterpine yet. Even if we send a runner..."*

"It will be days," Koldis finished.

"This news will devastate him."

Her muscles tensed. Couldn't they just be quiet? Was it too much to ask for a bit of silence? A few minutes of peace? She thought about saying as much.

It is not their fault, Cyrus said.

Can't you make it go away? she asked, desperation seeping into her plea.

That was a very brave thing you did, Claire.

That's...great, she said. *But I don't care about being brave. I just want it to stop. Is there a way?*

Even after learning the mechanics of blocking, she had never successfully blocked anything within close proximity. In fact, she had accepted that it was something she would grapple with forever.

Proximity makes it difficult, yes. But even a drengr can block whilst side by side.

A feeble flame of hope ignited in her chest.

If it's possible, then why can't I do it?

Your ability is different. But I believe...there might be a way.

Then do it! Take it away. Take it all away.

There was a long silence, and then, *Shutting them out will not fix the way you feel.*

I don't care! I want it to stop! Please...make it stop. She was shouting now, shouting at him because she had no one else to shout at. In her head. Like a crazy person. *Can you help me or not?*

He gave a mental sigh. *Claire, your abilities are yours and yours alone to grapple with. My interference does not allow you to grow.*

Hot anger poured over her thoughts. *So, you would rather see me suffer? I know you want to see me figure things out, but we don't have time for that. If you have a way to help me, stop holding back. I need you. Isn't that why you planted yourself in my head in the first place? Why you gave me your soul?*

Planted. There was anger in his voice. She could almost picture plumes of smoke seeping from his pearlescent nostrils. *That's a rather rugged term for it, don't you think? I gifted you my soul. Being in your head is simply a result of that. Remember, it isn't all fun and games for me either.*

She knew it was unfair to lash out at him, but she couldn't leash her emotions. *Are you going to help me, or not?*

He was silent for longer than she appreciated. And then, *I will help you. Relax your mind. It will require a bit of control on my part.*

"Thank the gods," she muttered aloud, relaxing her mind as he advised. A few scattered conversations from the surrounding drengr broke through, and then...everything disappeared. Her mind went silent, as if Cyrus had flipped a mental switch. She sat motionless, listening, unsure if the fix would hold.

There was only silence. Blessed, blessed silence. She exhaled, long and slow. It had worked.

Thank you, she said.

He did not respond. At last, she closed her eyes. Sleep swept her away.

She woke to find Koldis descending beneath the clouds. The sun was high in the sky. Her muscles weren't shaking anymore, and she felt stronger, more alert.

Their break was short, just long enough to see to their needs. She was painfully hungry, but when she tried to choke down food, she couldn't work up the appetite. Instead, she paced back and forth, trying to loosen up.

Silence settled heavily around them, as if the world knew what had happened. Their group was quiet. Everyone wore their grief openly, mouths set in thin lines, eyes bloodshot.

"You've been ignoring us," Koldis murmured, coming to stand beside her. Jovari joined them.

"Blocking, not ignoring."

"I thought you couldn't turn us off like that."

"Apparently, I can now. So if you have something to say, then say it out loud."

"What about when we are in the sky?" Jovari crossed his arms, eying her warily, like she was a dragon that might bite his head off at any given moment.

"Guess we'll have to opt for silence."

Jovari sighed. "Look, Claire, I know what we asked was—" he stopped mid-sentence at the look in her eyes.

"Fine, we will let you be," Koldis said, lifting his hands, placating. "We depart in five minutes. If...if you want to fly with Jovari instead of me, that's fine."

"I'm mad at both of you equally," she snapped, but immediately regretted it when Koldis flinched.

He gave her a curt nod. "As you wish." They both left her standing there, staring after them, feeling absolutely horrible about how she was acting.

She walked from the group, taking advantage of the few remaining minutes she had to be alone. When it was time to depart, she went back to Koldis. He snorted when she climbed into the harness. Probably offended, but whatever.

They flew for the remainder of the day, only stopping once more for a quick break. She spent most of the time in a dreamless sleep, thanks to Cyrus. But after darkness fell, she could no longer keep her eyes closed. Her legs ached and her stomach grumbled. She just wanted a bed and silence. To be left alone.

All that was forgotten when she saw the glitter of lights on the horizon. A tiny cluster, about the size of her thumbnail.

"*Is that Brezen?*" she asked before remembering that Cyrus had barricaded her mind. There would be no answer.

Should I lift the barrier? Cyrus asked.

She snorted. *No, thank you. Save me from the misery of it.*

As you wish. He sounded resigned.

The cluster of lights grew larger. Stormy Bay yawned dark beyond it. She'd seen enough Dragonwall maps to know the geography here. Directly on the other side of the inlet was a small peninsula where Squall's End and Fort Squall were nestled. She tried not to think about what had happened there.

They changed direction, beginning their descent. The ground approached. A wooden settlement took form, sprawling comfortably across the landscape. It wasn't tightly constructed like Kastali Dun, with houses upon houses. Instead, there was plenty of space between the buildings to spread out. Cottages with gardens and small farms with barns. She wished it was daytime so she could better see.

Sitting beside Brezen was the extensive camp where the refugees from Fort Squall had settled. Here there were far more lights than in Brezen. The camp was complete with rows and rows of tents and torchlit aisles. Sentries stood guard around its perimeter, but otherwise all was quiet. She half expected to be greeted by excited drengr bugles.

The ground swept up before them. Both of their wings landed. She unbuckled her harness before Koldis had come to a full stop, and when he did, she bounded off his back, slinging her pack over her shoulder.

"Hey! Claire! Where are you going?" he shouted after her, then jogged to catch up, already in human form. Jovari caught up with them.

"To find Reyr," she said, as if that wasn't obvious enough.

"You really think you'll find him in this mess all by yourself? Besides, didn't he say something about leaving—"

"I don't care what he said." She rounded on them, glaring at Koldis. "I'm going to find him." He opened his mouth to speak, but she stormed off toward the camp. They followed, keeping a safe distance.

Guards intercepted her when she reached the camp. "Where can I find Lord Reyr?" she asked. "Well?"

"Lord Reyr?" They regarded her before glancing over her shoulder at Jovari and Koldis. "He...isn't here, miss."

"Isn't here?!" Her eyes fell over the rows of tents.

She didn't want to believe it. It hurt to think he'd left without a word to her about it. Without saying goodbye. Without letting her know that he was alive after the battle. He didn't know she had been listening in, that she had observed the battle's entirety.

She took a deep breath. "Who is in charge here? Where is the command tent?"

The soldiers glanced at Koldis and Jovari before answering. "At the center of camp, miss. Follow that main aisle there and you'll find it." They stepped aside.

She set off. In her wake, she heard Koldis and Jovari muttering apologies to the soldiers, informing them of the new arrivals before jogging to catch up to her.

"Claire..."

"Don't, Koldis. I don't need a lecture. I'm going to do all that I can to find him."

They passed into the camp, continuing down the main aisle toward the camp's center. Torches were evenly spaced, all burning brightly. A few tent flaps opened as she passed, heads popping out to gaze at her.

"What if Reyr doesn't want to be found?" Jovari asked.

"That's stupid. Why would you think that?" But she knew he was right. Something in the way Reyr had spoken to Byron during the battle had said as much. She didn't want to accept it, though. That he was gone. That he might never come back. That she might never apologize to him for what had happened between them.

When she reached the center of camp, she found the command tent. There were six guards outside. Their hands went to their weapons at the sight of her sudden appearance.

She walked right up to them. "I'm here to see the fort leaders."

They eyed her. "Forgive me, miss. They're in an important meeting. You'll have to come back later."

"A meeting in the middle of the night?" She moved forward, ignoring their recommendations. Two of the guards stepped in front of her, barring her way. Her gaze narrowed. "Let me pass."

Behind her, Koldis sighed. "You had better let her pass."

"Begging your pardon, drengr sir, but we have our orders."

"Right. Orders. I really didn't want to play this card. Whatever your orders, I override them in the name of the king. I'm Lord Koldis, this is Lord Jovari, and this feisty female is Lady Claire. We're seizing control of this camp. Now, step aside."

The guards went rigid. Their eyes darted between the three of them. "Forgive us, my lords, my lady. We did not know." They moved aside and pulled the tent flaps open, permitting her to pass. She stepped through, ready to confront whatever she was about to find on the other side.

CHAPTER 22

LOVE IS ENDURING

Brezen

Claire gave her eyes a moment to adjust to the tent's dim interior before looking around. It was sparsely decorated. A few fabric inserts shielded private areas from view, but the rest of it was open and housed a large makeshift table, around which nearly thirty chairs were occupied by drengr and their riders.

The group fell silent, gazing at her with a mutual lack of recognition. She took in their bleak expressions, their slumped posture, and her skin flushed with heat. She'd spent the entire day playing the victim, when *their* pain was real. She was ashamed of herself.

She locked eyes with a male standing at the head of the table. Her heart jolted, then relaxed. It wasn't Reyr, but he looked a hell of a lot like him.

She cleared her throat. "Forgive the intrusion. I am looking for the fort leader."

"You're looking at him." Behind her, the tent flaps rustled. The male's eyes widened, and she couldn't take her eyes off him, drinking in his features, the similarities to Reyr, which only made her miss her friend more. "Lord Jovari? Lord Koldis?"

She felt their presence at her back.

"I did not expect to see your welcome faces, but I am glad of it. How are you even here?"

"Byron." Koldis said. "We were in the neighborhood. Thought you might need some help. Got here as quickly as we could."

"You are most welcome!" Byron's relief was palpable.

"Allow me to introduce Lady Claire. The king's ward."

Byron strode over, frowning. His gaze assessed her, taking in her journey-worn tunic and leggings, her pack with Cyrus's Sverak strapped to her back, and her disheveled hair that had long since come undone. Mutters erupted around the council table, followed by the sound of scraping chairs. Everyone in the tent stood and bowed.

She frowned, half expecting her mind to erupt into speculative voices. But it didn't. Not with Cyrus maintaining his protective barricade. Thank the gods for that.

"Claire," said Koldis, "this is Byron, Reyr's nephew."

"Oh..." Her chest instantly tightened.

Byron straightened. "Well met, Lady Claire. We have heard much about you." He turned back to Koldis. "As you can imagine, your appearance is a surprise. We did not expect reinforcements, but we are glad to have you. We will take every drengr we can get. I must thank the king personally for sending you."

"The king did not send us." Koldis pointed a thumb at her. "She did."

Her muscles went rigid.

Byron bowed to her. "We are forever grateful, my lady. Were you...Uncle Reyr said something about a warning. Was that you? Is that what he meant?"

"I..." She licked her lips. "It was. I'm sorry it didn't make a difference."

Byron's brows pulled together. "It made all the difference in the world."

The tight knot in her chest loosened. "You really mean that?"

"I do. We lost the fort, yes, and many lives. But they would have attacked us with our pants around our ankles. You saved us our dignity."

She exhaled. "And...Kane?"

Byron's eyes darkened. "He's with his hoarde now, lording over the fort like he owns the place." He spit on the ground beside his boot.

She looked around the tent again. "Where's Reyr? He should be here. I... I need to speak with him."

Byron hesitated. "He has left us—for now. I am sure he will return when he is ready. He took the loss of..." His shoulders dropped. "It was a heavy blow for him—for all of us."

A fresh wave of nausea poured into her stomach. A projection flooded her mind of a woman falling to her death, her insides spilling out, and the drengr whose neck was snapped trying to save her. Somehow, in the chaos, she'd failed to make the connection. "I'm so sorry for your loss," she choked. "I cannot even imagine what it's like to lose...to lose..."

"You have nothing to apologize for." Byron reached for her arm and squeezed.

A dull ache filled her chest. Gods, she regretted her parting words with Reyr. If she could see him now, she would tell him how sorry she was for her anger, for the way they'd shouted at each other. She'd told him that he would lose her friendship if he left, and at the time, she'd believed it, but she was so, so wrong, and he'd already lost so much.

Koldis stepped forward. "This loss is a heavy blow to the kingdom, Byron. You have our sincerest condolences. We have nineteen pairs. It's not much, but it's something. Do you have a plan?"

"Nineteen?" Byron looked disappointed but he quickly recovered. "Nineteen is fine. We'll take whatever we can get. No plan as of yet. But come, you must be exhausted." He turned to the table. The tent's occupants watched them. "We're done here for tonight. Go and get some rest. The gods only know we all need it."

"Aye," they said, nodding in agreement. The tent erupted into activity as everyone departed. Many of them nodded and bowed in passing, offering respect she didn't feel she deserved. And then they were gone, and everything fell quiet.

She didn't notice that someone had come up beside her. "It is a pleasure to meet you, Lady Claire. I can hardly believe...well...I never thought I would actually get to meet you. You must be exhausted."

She frowned, studying the young woman. Her hair as black as midnight and her eyes an unsettling shade of blue. She was young. Sixteen or seventeen at most. "I'm sorry... but who are you?"

"Oh!" The young female curtsied flawlessly. "I'm Tamara. Well technically, *Lady* Tamara, but that's too formal for my tastes. It looks like you've been to hell and back, just like the rest of us."

A bark of crazed laughter escaped her lips. "Something like that, though, not nearly what you've been through."

"Yes. I suppose." Tamara blinked several times. Whatever sorrow she'd felt was quickly hidden. "How rude of me to keep you standing here like this. Come on. Let's get you cleaned up and resting."

Claire opened her mouth to protest, then shut it.

"Bring them some food, too, dear heart," Byron said, coming up beside them. "Our guests must be starving. Sir Wentworth was particularly generous. Most of this is because of him."

"Food. Of course," Tamara said. "I will see to her every need."

"Thank you." Byron's gaze was gentle. He ran a hand down her arm with obvious affection.

"Food would be welcome," Jovari called from across the tent. "Thank you."

"Of course," Byron said. "My guards tell me they have already seen to the rest of your companions with proper accommodations."

"Good," Koldis said. "Thank you."

Tamara took hold of Claire's arm, pulling her towards the back corner of the tent, to a small wash basin filled with water. It was cold but clean. "Here, I'll take your pack." She disappeared behind one of the cloth dividers and reappeared a moment later with a washcloth.

Claire took the cloth from Tamara and dipped it into the bowl, all but groaning as she washed her face, neck, and hands. She could have magicked herself clean, her clothes too, but she refrained from performing that kind of magic as much as possible. Besides, magic didn't offer the same feeling of clean water on skin.

"Perhaps tomorrow we can visit Sir Wentworth," Tamara suggested, watching her. "His lady promised me a bath in his manor. I can't imagine what a tizzy seeing you would put everyone in."

She nodded, too exhausted to say more, too exhausted to be flattered. Once she had washed up, Tamara showed her where she would be sleeping. It was a small space with two cots and a large wooden trunk. She was tempted—more than tempted—to crawl under the blankets and escape from the world. She craved a moment alone.

Instead, she joined the others at the table, taking a seat beside Tamara. Bread, cheese, honey, and ale were set out before them. She was starving, but the food tasted like sawdust in her mouth. She didn't want to appear rude, so she choked it down as best she could. Tamara's eyes were frequently upon her, but she remained silent and unquestioning.

"Now that we are fed," Koldis said, "I would like to hear what happened. Beginning to end."

Her body went rigid. The last thing she needed was to relive the battle. She downed half of her mug of ale in several big gulps, bracing herself for the conversation. A huge belch crawled up her chest. She glanced at Tamara before silently expelling it so that no one noticed.

Byron and Tamara took turns recounting everything that had taken place from the moment they'd received Claire's warning. Their details filled in what she had seen and heard.

When Byron retold the part about his mother's death, fresh tears slid down her cheeks. She brushed them away, hoping no one noticed. "I thought riders were immortal?" she said, trying to understand. "I thought they healed like the drengr."

"They do," Koldis said. "To an extent. Riders inherit the same magic as their drengr mates—a shared magic. But no one can heal from a lethal wound. You know enough about magic now, about how it exhausts you. How it wears you down over time."

She swallowed and nodded.

"After their deaths," Byron continued, "we had no choice but to retreat. Reyr wasn't himself though. He tried to go after Kane, and I understand why, though not at the extent of our people. Truthfully, I wasn't sure if he would back down. I thank the gods that he did. Kane would have burned the entire city to the ground."

"And the fort?" Koldis asked, shifting in his chair.

"We did all we could in the hour we were given. We got everyone out, everything that we could carry. Our fort boasts some sixty staff, hundreds of foot soldiers, guards, the like, so we took boats from the docks. I'm not proud of my actions—commandeering vessels that weren't mine to take—but it was the best I could do." He shrugged. "I'm sure the city folk will forgive us."

"You did the right thing," Koldis assured him. "I had wondered how you managed it, getting everyone out without flying them over."

"Oh, we flew plenty of goods over, whatever we could carry. I wasn't about to leave anything for Kane. We purged the fort of valuables. I've never seen our people move so quickly. We gutted the whole damn place. Should have burned it to the ground, too. My scales crawl when I think of that worm living in our home."

Claire felt her own skin crawl, too.

"How is it that you were able to be here so quickly?" Bryon asked, as if the question had been eating at him.

"We had business in Celenore," Jovari explained. "We had planned to fly directly back—" He stopped, gasping mid-sentence, then shot to his feet. Koldis did the same.

Her hand jerked from her chin. "What is it?" she hissed, taking in their shocked expressions, their wide, unseeing eyes. They did not answer. Her senses tingled. There was only one thing—*one person*—that could make them react like this.

Her stomach fluttered restlessly. She watched the king's

shields, watched their faces move through various expressions. When it was over, they sank back into their chairs.

She swallowed. "He contacted you, didn't he?"

Silence.

"Tell me."

Koldis exhaled, running a hand through his hair. "He is out of the forest. A day's flight from here. He will arrive around dusk tomorrow."

"What?!" she cried. Her blood turned cold. "Does he...does he know I'm here?"

They both nodded. Oh, gods.

"And?! Was he angry? What did he say?"

"He's furious," Koldis said.

"But restrained," Jovari finished. "He didn't yell. Usually he yells."

The knot in her stomach tightened. Bad—this was so bad. "I'm going to be in so much trouble," she whispered. "You know how he gets, especially if he wasn't yelling.."

Koldis and Jovari shared a look but said nothing.

She lurched to her feet. "I've had enough for one day. I'm going to bed."

"Claire?" She froze mid step at the sound of Koldis's voice. He'd come to his feet. "Are you going to be okay?"

She exhaled. "I don't have a choice, do I? I'll be fine."

He nodded, his throat bobbing.

The sun wasn't up yet. Hopefully she could manage a few hours of sleep. Tamara followed her into their shared space but kept quiet. She didn't ask why she wasn't sleeping with Byron when they appeared to be mates. She was too tired to care.

When she curled up in her cot, she couldn't sleep. She was too distracted by what Talon would do once he arrived. By how angry he would be at her having broken her promise to him. Gods, she was in so much trouble.

After tossing and turning, she began to play through the projections she had tucked away. *Are you sure you want to do that?* Cyrus asked. She exhaled and considered his question. Yes, she was sure. She owed it to herself. Otherwise like any wound, the projections would fester and rot, and her mind wouldn't thank her for it. So, she closed her eyes tightly, and braced herself.

After a bit of coaxing, they began to trickle through her thoughts. The first few were meaningless, quick flashes of what had taken place during the onset of battle. Then the first death was upon her. An orange dragon. She felt the arrow through her skull, a poisoned arrow, and her anger turned to rage. Then the second arrow struck and she gasped, feeling the brief flash of pain accompanying the projection. In that moment, she knew she was going to die. Then there was nothing.

She was on to the next. And then the next. And the next.

Dragon, drengr, rider. It didn't matter which death she felt. They were equally difficult to bear. After four or five of them, tears soaked her pillow.

"Claire?" A whispered voice in the dark called out to her. The projections came to a brief halt. "Are...are you okay?"

Wiping her eyes, she flopped over onto her back. "I...I'm fine." The white tent ceiling loomed above her.

There was a noise. A shadow passed over her as Tamara came to her cot and squeezed in beneath the blankets beside her, uninvited.

"It's okay to cry," Tamara whispered, then put an arm over her shoulders and nuzzled her head down beside her the way a loving sister might, the way her best friend often did when she needed it. It didn't matter that they hardly knew each other, that Tamara was a stranger. They shared something deeper. A common grief.

"I saw them, you know," she managed to croak. Her throat was scratchy. Tamara remained quiet, almost as if she knew these words needed to be spoken. "I saw each death as it happened. Dragon. Drengr. Rider. I felt them, too. Not just the pain. The raw emotion of it all. Emotions that my human years can hardly fathom. With each life taken, I felt things I've never felt before. Anger that redefines what I ever thought it meant to be angry. Hatred I never imagined could be so powerful. Love...love that makes my knees weak." She swallowed, stifling another sob.

Several more projections flashed through her mind. Tamara's presence seemed to encourage the onslaught. She wasn't sure if she could handle it all in one night. But maybe it was like a Band-Aid—better to peel it off quickly.

"You don't have to bear it alone," Tamara whispered.

A dam broke and the remainder of the projections broke free. This time, she didn't fight them. She stumbled through them. The worst, she saved for last, even though she was trembling beneath Tamara's arms. Even though she had to gasp for each breath.

The projection of Lady Emmy's death played out. This time, she watched Emmy's falling body and didn't fight it. She let the small details seep into her. That's when she noticed something greater than fear and disappointment. There was something much, much deeper. Something worth remembering. Another quiet sob escaped her chest.

On the surface, Davi's failure appeared to have broken him, as if Kane had won. Up until now, she was certain that he had. But the truth was, Kane had won nothing. Beneath all of the obvious emotions, there was something stronger, more enduring. Something Kane could never take.

"*Until the very end,*" Emmy said as she fell to her death. And it was true. Davi had failed to save her, failed to protect her, failed to save his people. Emmy knew she was going to die just as she knew of his other failures. Yet, she loved him anyway. Her love rose above everything.

She thought about the other mate deaths and noticed the same thing with each of them, the same kind of love. It wasn't just the fort leaders. It was all of them. It had taken Emmy's words to make it clear, but she finally understood what Cyrus and Reyr had truly lost when they'd lost their mates. What Lily had lost when Hiondel died and why she wanted to disappear into the wilderness to be alone. She also understood why Reyr sometimes wished he had died with Gemma, the way Davi and Emmy had died—together.

Her heart broke a little more.

When she finally had the nerve to speak, her voice was a strangled whisper. "I just realized something."

"What is it?"

"Love is enduring," she managed to say. "Beyond death. I'd like to think the love shared between mates transcends time and space. That's how I plan to remember them, all of them."

Tamara must have understood her well enough, because her body began to shake, too. She shifted until she had an arm around Tamara. They cried together, arm in arm, for all they had lost. For all that their friends had lost. For everything that Dragonwall had lost, until sleep took them at last.

CHAPTER 23
SECRETS COME TO LIGHT

Kastali Dun

Verath gave Imeir a silent signal, motioning him forward. They crept down an alley that ran along the back of Oldham Road. Imeir's wing mates were positioned along Oldham. Some were perched inconspicuously on rooftops in their human forms. Others had taken up their drengr form to circle high above.

Dallin was with them too, strolling down the street as a bystander in case they needed backup. Mostly because he wanted to give the young drengr a taste of life in the city. A taste of what it was like working for the king.

"*Have your team maintain position,*" Verath said, glancing at Imeir. Then, to the entire team, "*Collier is short and stocky, black hair, a scar on his left temple. If he tries to run, I want him taken alive.*"

They closed in on the suspected house—a whitewashed four story building with large windows and a servant's entrance in the back. Their informant, Alan, had been most helpful, narrowing Collier's location. He'd been paid handsomely.

They reached the servant's entrance and paused, waiting for

the signal. On the other side of the house, Nellisk knocked at the front door, posing as a visitor to draw attention away.

"*It's time,*" Imeir said.

Verath moved, descending the stairs leading to the servant's entrance. "*Hinga,*" he muttered. The latch clicked and the door swung wide. He glanced over his shoulder. Selith and Emmin waited behind them, ready to take anyone who tried to flee through the back.

The servant's entrance took them into a cookery. Servants looked up, wide eyed.

He grinned, flashing his teeth. "Well, hello there. Wouldn't happen to know where we can find the poison maker, would you? His name's Collier." He was met with shocked silence. "All right then. We'll do this the hard way."

He lunged as Imeir added, "None of you scream, or we'll kill you all."

Bounding around the large work table, laden with vegetables, Verath pulled a dagger from his belt. He grabbed the head cook, holding the blade to his neck. "I will kill you if I have to. Now, are there any underground tunnels leading out of this place? Ways to escape in secret? Tell me. Where?"

The cook trembled. He lifted a hand and pointed. "Th-there, sir. The root cellar."

"Any others?" He applied pressure to the blade.

"No. No, sir. I swear."

"Good." He released the cook, who stumbled away and gathered with the others. He sent out a silent command. "*Selith, send Emmin to guard the root cellar. I don't want anyone getting out.*" A moment later Emmin entered and was directed forward.

"Now..." Verath looked back at the group. "I'll only ask once more. Where can I find Collier?"

"*I'm in position in the parlor,*" Nellisk said. "*The front is heavily guarded. No one is getting out this way.*"

"*Excellent. Stand by.*"

"Please, sir." One of the women in the group took two steps forward. She was on the younger side, in her mid-thirties perhaps, with dark hair twisted in a tight bun, and a crisp apron. "If you take the servant stairs there, he's in the attic. All the way at the top."

"Good. Thank you, miss. The rest of you—wait outside. Now, you miss, you are coming with me." He sent the gaggle of servants to be guarded by the rest of their team. He didn't want them trying anything while Emmin stood guard at the cellar.

They followed orders, looking none too happy about it.

"What's your name?" he asked his guide.

Her eyes darted back and forth. "Hepsa, sir. If it please you."

"Thank you, Hepsa. Lead the way. And keep quiet. One peep out of you and you'll wish you hadn't." He wasn't fond of making threats, but Collier had evaded them long enough. He wasn't taking any chances. Desaree's livelihood was at stake.

They ascended, emerging on a landing in the attic. All was quiet. He waited for several minutes, breathing, listening. Nothing appeared amiss.

He hesitated. *"Nellisk? Any issues?"*

"None, Lord Verath. I've got the family here, sir. Their children don't quite understand, but Sir Andrew Eddie and his wife do. Their eyes keep darting up at the ceiling. Their butler's here too."

"Good. Sounds like they know what we're about. Question is, does Collier?"

He took a rough hold of Hepsa's arm. "No games now, Hepsa. This man isn't worth your life. Which door is it? Tell me wrong and Imeir will slit your throat. Tell me correctly, and you will be paid handsomely. Handsomely enough to leave the life of a servant behind. You will be well protected from any retaliation from your masters."

Her eyes grew round. "Thank...thank you, sir. The door at the end," she whispered and pointed, expression anguished despite his generous offer.

He handed her off to Imeir and proceeded down the hall. Imeir kept a safe distance, keeping hold of Hepsa. They moved into position before the door. There were sounds from within, but nothing to raise concern. A quiet female giggle. The growl of a male's voice.

"It's Tilly, sir," Hepsa whispered, her cheeks reddening in the dim light. "He...he favors her. Please, this ain't no doin' of hers. He... he insists."

"I see." Verath glanced between Hepsa and Imeir, then nodded. "No harm will come to her so long as she complies. Now..." He hesitated. "Announce yourself and say something to distract him." Hepsa's mouth opened in protest. "Go on," he whispered. "Something convincing."

She nodded, stepping forward. She knocked. It was a timid knock. "Begging your pardon, Collier, sir. I got more water for your pitcher."

"Go away!" came the gruff reply. "Didn't I say I was not to be bothered?"

"But...but please sir, if you would..."

There was some shuffling and swearing from behind the door. The sound of furniture creaking. Footsteps. The door flew open. Imeir pulled Hepsa away just in time. The round face of a squat man peered out onto the landing. His hair was black, as Eagle had described. And a scar ran the length of his temple from his hairline. His eyes widened. He cursed and stumbled backwards, trying to close the door, only to be blocked.

"I don't think so." Verath slipped his hand into the opening and forced it back, pushing it hard enough to send Collier scrambling away like a crab on his back.

"Gods damn you, bitch!" Collier spat at Hepsa, who was just visible behind Verath in the shadowy doorway. Collier jumped to his feet and retreated farther across the room. "You led them right to me!"

Verath remained motionless. The girl on the bed, Tilly, had gathered up the sheets around her naked body. She sat blinking, stunned.

Collier tore the window curtains back and cursed. He raced across the room and threw open the lid of a trunk—a trunk full of tiny glass vials.

"Oh no! I don't think so." Verath bounded across the room in a single breath. Collier tried to stumble away, ripping the cork from a vial in his hands. "No quick death for you, Collier." He swatted the vial away. Glass shattered across the floor. Grabbing Collier by the hair, he placed his blade against his jugular. "I won't kill you, because I know that's what you'd prefer. But I'll make you hurt if you struggle."

Imeir had the sense to gather Hepsa and Tilly and send them away. Hepsa ushered Tilly from the room, whispering words of comfort.

"Quite the little squirrel, aren't you?" Verath said. Collier went limp in his grasp. "That's right. No more hiding. I've had enough of your games. In the name of the king, you are under arrest for high treason...among other things." He glanced at Imeir. "Bind his hands and gag him. Don't need more of a scene than necessary."

They were out of the house in record time. It had all gone well—too well. Then again, with the number of failures previously faced and the amount of planning that went into this, success was inevitable. He glanced at the crowd gathered on the street, then towards the group of servants and noble family under guard.

To Nellisk, he said, "Take them to the keep, children included. I've got some questions for them."

He led Collier away by the collar. He wouldn't be harsh on the family or servants if it wasn't needed. But harboring a fugitive was no small matter.

Collier was deposited in the dungeons along with his chest of concoctions. Imeir set it down with a loud thump near the door. Wall sconces were lit, and the chamber flared into life. "Get him settled there, Imeir," he said, wrinkling his nose against the pervading scent of death. "I'll be back in just a moment."

He left and went next door. Eagle was sitting, still chained, his head lolling on his chest. "Sounds like there's some commotion," Eagle slurred, looking up. "Caught 'im yet?"

"We have, thanks to you. Though I can't say you did much."

"Well, if you ain't here to thank me, why you here?"

"Ah. For you to give us visual confirmation that we caught the right person." He unlocked Eagle's chains and led him next door.

Eagle took a look at the man in the middle of the room. "That's him. Collier. Well done, Drengr. Perhaps my protectoress will smile upon me for my assistance. Can't say it will earn me a ticket out of here, though."

"Ticket out of here? What for? So you can go back to killing in Misport, or whatever rathole you come from?"

Eagle shrugged. "Pretty much. It's what I do."

"Well, you're not very good at it," he said, leading Eagle back to his cell.

"Tcha! Kidnapping, no. I told that damned sorcerer I don't do kidnapping. Only killing."

"Right, I'll remember that next time I need someone dead." He refrained from rolling his eyes. "In you go. No chains this time. I'll have some food brought down." He shoved Eagle through the door and slammed it before the man could respond.

Back in Collier's cell, he began going through the box of vials. Each was slightly different. Some were clear, others tinted with color. Some of the liquids were shades of red, or brown, or yellow. Most were labeled. Some were not. He was especially curious about those left unidentified.

Dragging the box over to Collier, he took a seat on top. "Welcome to the keep, Collier. Let's play a little game, you and I." Imeir lurked in the corner, observing. "I'm going to remove a vial from your nice collection here,"—he patted the chest beneath him—"and you're going to name it for me. If you lie, I might just test it out on you. Best that you be truthful."

Collier said nothing.

This sort of thing was easier in the old days with Cyrus around. There was no need to coax the truth from traitors. Cyrus simply pried into their minds. Ah well, those days were behind them.

He stood and began removing unlabeled vials. "This one?" he asked, listening to Collier's mumbled answer before moving on. "What about this?"

Most were unremarkable. But he did perk up when he heard names like curare and hemlock. They were making good progress, working their way through many he suspected might have been used on Desaree's mother.

He knew a little about what it took to craft the concoctions in

Collier's collection. He had learned a little of the art during his training in his younger years, but was never one for the patience it took to make them. He had the Magoi for that.

He pulled another from the chest. "Ah, this is a curious one. Clear, unlabeled." He broke the seal and removed the stopper, sniffing it. The putrid smell was jarring, disorienting, giving him an instant headache. "Mmm. I know *this* one. Dragon's bane. The same used on Claire, no doubt."

Collier said nothing. He didn't need to.

He sealed the vial and returned it. Working his way through a couple more. "What about this one? Curious. Red liquid?" He was tempted to open it but decided against it. Instead, he turned to Collier and arched an eyebrow. Collier hesitated. "Well?"

"It's…it's *fever ice.*"

"Is that so?" He turned the vial over, studying it. "No, I think not. You would have labeled a simple fever reducer as you did the others. In fact—" He rustled around in the chest, pulling a few different vials from their cubbies. "Here, this one is labeled as *fever ice* and it's blue, not red." He glanced at Collier. Beads of sweat dripped down the man's brow as his shifty eyes darted about the cell. "No, indeed, I don't think this one is *fever ice.* You're going to have to lie better. How about we try it out, eh?" It was a risk. If it was a swift poison, Collier would die before giving up the answers needed. Which was likely exactly what Collier wanted. "Last chance…I might even pair it with this one." He removed a vial of Night's Scream. "I wonder how the two would work together? Hmm? I'll have you begging for death in no time."

Collier's eyes widened. Clearly he didn't like the idea of torture by poison. "No. Please. It's…it's truth…truth serum…*sanidi.*" He appeared to struggle as he attempted to get the words out.

"Ah-ha! Even better. Bottoms up then." In a flourish, he removed the cork and tipped the serum down Collier's throat. Collier gagged but could do little more as the liquid went down.

"There now." Verath replaced the emptied vial and closed the lid of the chest, sitting down atop it to watch the potion work its magic. "Things should get easier now, I hope," he said to Imeir, who continued to watch.

He plucked a few specks of lint from his tunic sleeves, waiting. "You're lucky it's just me, you know," he said, looking up at Collier. "If my king were here, he would torture you. He has a stomach for such things. I, however, prefer more elegant solutions when I can afford it. Even better that you possess the means for truth, else you might be on the rack over there." He motioned with his gaze. "We'll see how you do, though." He took a deep breath and started simple. "You were involved in Lady Claire's kidnapping, yes? The king's ward? She's got long, blond hair. Green eyes. Stands about yay-tall. Ring any bells?"

"Y-yes." Collier's eyes widened, as if he couldn't believe he had answered.

"Good. You provided dragon's bane to weaken her abilities. Correct?"

"*Yes.*" The word was a hiss.

"Anything else?"

"N-no, my lord. I was only hired to ensure her magic did not interfere with Eagle's plans. I was told that dragon's bane should do the trick. Weakening her mind to make her easily controllable. I found it funny, since she ain't no drengr. But I didn't question it."

"Not a drengr, indeed." Verath nodded. Some of Claire's power belonged to Cyrus, who was very much a drengr. But few knew about the gift. Did that mean Kane knew?

"You're doing well so far, Collier, so stop fretting. I received the same story from Eagle too." He paused, thinking of how best to proceed. "Does the surname Kendall mean anything to you?"

"N-no, my lord." Collier grimaced, as if pained. "Yes," he hissed. "Yes."

"I thought it might. Tell me all you know about the surname and those who bear it."

"None bear it now. They are dead, far as I know. I killed them... poison—"

"You're wrong. They are not all dead. There was a girl. Lady Desaree Kendall."

"I...I didn't know."

"Right. Do go on."

"The...the Kendalls were a wealthy family living in the Merchant District. I was instructed by my contractor to interfere on their behalf. Lord and Lady Kendall were direct targets, but each was to be treated differently. It was Sir Kendall I was charged to target first. Once he was out of the way, my contractor could move his Nask into place. From there, I was to act again, but in a less direct manner."

"Less direct, hmm?" Verath sat up straighter, already forming his own suspicions. "So...you did not poison her yourself?"

"No, my lord. I was instructed to give the poison to another...a young girl who came to request it."

"One guess as to who," he muttered, his mood darkening. "Did your contractor say why it should be her and not her father?"

"Oh yes. My contractor came to an arrangement with the girl's father. A commodity for a fair price paid. She would poison Lady Kendall and my contractor would give her magic."

Verath blinked. Blinked again. Disgust pooled in the pit of his stomach. "Magic is not to be earned or paid for." His jaw tightened. "Tell me, how much did Caterina know? When you gave her the poison. Did she know of this trade? Of this exchange for magic? Did she know that the poison would kill her step mother?"

"No...no, my lord," Collier shook his head. "And yes. She was young and ignorant, after all. She knew about the poison but not about the trade. By putting an end to Lady Kendall, she and her father would secure a place of fortune. Undisputed. That was all she believed. She was eager for it—for a better life than the one she lived. To her knowledge, this was the final act that would improve her status. She understood that she had been selected to do it. She told me that being selected made her feel...special."

"Interesting." Verath rubbed the back of his neck. "So, she really had no idea about the magic? She believes that her ability is genuine? Something that came to her naturally?"

"Yes, my lord."

"What a farce," he scoffed.

"The deal of her magic was worked out between my contractor and her father without her knowing. Her father was eager to give her a place in the world. He demanded her safekeeping in exchange for becoming Kane's nask. The agreement was magically binding."

"Is that so?" He rubbed his chin. Safekeeping. The word stood out to him. What sort of magic did safekeeping encompass? Would it protect Caterina against King Talon?

"What you say is...enlightening. Very enlightening. It suggests that Stefan Rosen acted with his daughter's best interests at heart, as twisted as he was. A father's love..." He glanced at Imeir who shrugged.

A frown tugged at the corner of his lips. What would Caterina think when she realized what a fraud she was? As much as he wanted her to pay for what she'd done, he felt a small measure of pity towards her. For a person to believe they were special, that they possessed something as unique as magic, only to learn that their life had been a lie. That would be a blow indeed.

"What...what are you going to do with me? I've been truthful. I've given you what you want."

He grunted. "Nothing bodes well in your favor, Collier. There will be a trial. You will be expected to testify. There will be no lying from you. I assure you"—he nodded toward Imeir—"my witness has a great memory, as do I. Now...tell me about your contractor."

Collier's eyes widened. "My...my contractor?"

"Why, yes. You've already spoken so much about him."

"Oh..." Collier looked genuinely fearful now as he fidgeted. "His name...his name is Kane. But I'm sure you already know that. We... we crossed paths when my abilities with magic were newly discovered. He took me under his wing. Trained me. Sent me here, to peddle my wares and maintain my position until the time came when he would need me again."

"Excellent. Most excellent. You will be very useful to us. Perhaps we might just keep you alive for that reason."

"I...thank you, my lord. Thank you."

"Pray tell, what is your age?"

Collier cleared his throat. "One hundred and forty-eight, my lord."

Verath nodded. "Well, this has been most enlightening."

His gaze darted around, looking over the items in the room. He never enjoyed the screamers. Never wanted to be here longer than necessary.

He stood and took a final look at Collier trembling before him. "Truth has a way forcing us to face the deepest parts of who we are, does it not? When secrets meet light, there is nowhere to hide in the darkness, even for a squirrel like you. I think I've got all I need for today, though I'm sure you've got more acorns buried here and there. I'll get them eventually, or King Talon will once he returns." He ran a hand through his hair.

He and Imeir took their leave, making their way up from the dungeons.

"That was easier than I expected," Imeir admitted when they reached the upper levels of the keep.

"Agreed. I doubt it will be the case when we question Caterina."

"She's a young woman. It shouldn't be that hard to crack her shell."

"Perhaps not." He glanced about before making his way to the east wing. "I dare say Mage Targa will provide whatever shielding she requires. His presence alone will give her strength."

They reached Mage Targa's door and he knocked. Targa appeared moments later, frowning. "Ah. It's you. Good afternoon, my lord. Have you need of me?"

"Yes. Obviously. I wish to question Caterina, as is my right, as part of the ongoing investigation. Seeing as I'm not permitted to do so without you being present, I request your presence and hers tomorrow following the midday meal."

Targa's gaze narrowed. "I teach lessons during that time."

He tilted his head to the side. "Interesting..." He paused. "Are you suggesting your time is more valuable than mine?" Mage Targa's eyes widened at the accusation. "Good. I thought not.

Lessons can be postponed. This cannot wait. Tomorrow after the midday meal. I will meet you here. See that Caterina is present."

"Yes...yes, my lord." Mage Targa bowed his head.

He offered Targa a feral smile, holding the mage's gaze a moment longer before turning on his heel, Imeir at his side. He could already predict what would happen. Caterina would squirm and then she'd cave. And all the information he sought would come to light. Everything was falling into place perfectly.

CHAPTER 24
THE KING'S ARRIVAL

Brezen

Claire walked through camp, arm in arm with Tamara. Their night together had been a bonding experience, one she hadn't realized how much she needed until it had happened. Six guards trailed them, keeping a safe distance. The camp housed nearly three hundred people. White tents were browned with dirt, making sharp points against her line of sight, each big enough for two, making them ideal for mates.

Tamara introduced her to everyone. "It is important for them to see your face. It boosts their morale and shows that they matter. That what they *lost* matters."

"Don't you think it's ridiculous, though?" Claire couldn't help but ask.

"How so?" Tamara asked, shielding her gaze from the bright sunlight.

"I'm an outsider. They have no reason to trust me."

"You're the king's ward now. That makes you the next best thing, though, I suppose the king will be here soon enough."

Claire's stomach squirmed. Waiting for the king was fraying

her nerves. She wanted to get it over with, whatever *it* turned out to be. Scolding. Yelling, most likely. Anger. Another fight.

"Oh, here's Kivir and Amris. You should meet them too." Tamara took her arm, pulling her along.

At least it served as a good distraction.

When her feet began to ache, they crept away to an ancient oak tree on the outskirts of camp. Its trunk was massive, arms outstretched to offer shade and privacy. They sat against it. Tamara plucked a few leaves to keep her hands busy, twirling them around by the stems. The guards fanned out around them, keeping watch for potential threats.

"Do you always get stuck with such an entourage?" Tamara asked, eying them.

"I didn't used to, only recently. I hated it at first."

"I wouldn't like it much, either. I assume it was the king's doing?"

"Indeed." She told Tamara about her kidnapping and Talon's rescue. She might have embellished it in certain places, adding a few extra details about Talon's impressive display of swordsmanship. The truth was, most of her memories in captivity were a blur.

Conversation between them flowed easily.

They talked about her life before coming to Dragonwall and Tamara's life before running away to the fort. Her training with the mages and Tamara's aerial training with Byron. Life in Redport and Fort Squall versus life in the capital.

Tamara was six years younger, but she carried herself like someone a decade older. "Emmy trained you well," Claire found herself saying. "She would be proud if she could see you now."

Tamara brushed a tear from her cheek. "I wish she was here with us."

"Me too. I wish I could have met her." Her throat closed up. "So...what about you and Byron? Now that everything has happened, will you still be mated?"

Tamara exhaled. "Tomorrow would have been our bonding day. Now? I do not know."

"I'm so sorry," she whispered, unable to think of anything else. She put her arms around Tamara's shoulders, pulling her close. "I'm sure it will happen, when the time is right." Tears began falling down Tamara's cheeks. "I shouldn't have even asked. We can talk about something else if you want. Anything. More cars or airplanes. I can tell you about the movies. You'd love the movies. They're like moving pictures."

"No..." Tamara shook her head and pulled away slightly, wiping her eyes on the sleeves of her gown. She heaved a sigh. "Maybe it's good that you're here, good that I can get this off my chest. I haven't had anyone else to talk to."

"No one?" Claire frowned. "But...don't you have friends—"

"Oh, I do. It's just that they wouldn't understand. There's Sophie. She's my best friend now. She came to the fort when I did. You met her earlier, the one with the pretty auburn hair. She failed to find a mate. I can't...I don't want..."

"You feel bad that you got what you wanted and she didn't." It wasn't a question. Still, Tamara nodded. "I understand that. But she should be happy for you. She is, right?"

"I think so."

"And Lady Emmy? You couldn't talk to her about these things?"

"She was more of a mother. Though she did admit wanting to talk. It's just...she wasn't like you."

Claire barked a laugh. "Okay, I get it now," she said, poking Tamara in the ribs. "You just needed a modern girl like me. Well then, let's talk. Tell me everything about Byron. Everything that has happened between you. All the juicy details. We can dissect it."

Tamara's expression morphed into one of relief, and she wasted no time in launching into every detail, every touch, every embrace, every kiss she and Byron had shared. "Gods, you should have seen how mortified I was when I discovered that in order to solidify our bond, we would have to, *you know...*"

"Have sex?" Claire had to press her lips together to keep from giggling. Especially when Tamara's skin flushed a deep shade of pink. Honestly! Mothers in this world should have done better with their daughters. Especially about this kind of stuff. How were they supposed to prepare otherwise?

"Yes... I do not... That is to say," Tamara sputtered, "I know nothing about the actual sex part. I know where it goes and all that, but what am I supposed to do? Do I just lie still while it happens? And...well, have you ever...?"

"I have. And believe me when I say, a lot of it comes naturally."

Tamra's eyes widened. "But you are not wed, are you?"

"Gods, no!" She shook her head, huffing. "Everyone here is so old fashioned. I'm not a virgin. There was this guy...well, that's a story for another time. But yes, I've had sex a time or two."

Tamara squealed—actually squealed. "You must tell me all about it. Everything. I want to know. To be prepared."

"All right. But you asked for it."

She hoped the guards didn't hear as she stripped away Tamara's innocence with descriptions that would make anyone blush. Most of it appeared to mortify Tamara, who kept up a constant stream of interruptions. "What if he doesn't like it when I do it that way?"

"Oh, believe me, he will. He absolutely will." Claire nudged Tamara's shoulder and they both erupted into giggles.

A shadow fell over them and Koldis appeared. "Having fun without me?"

"Quite a lot, actually. Want to join? You might enjoy the conversation. Learn a few tips, even."

Koldis huffed, then shook his head. "I've been hunting for you both everywhere, you know. Our gracious hosts have extended an invitation for baths this afternoon. You had best get along to the manor."

"A bath?" Claire glanced at Tamara and they both giggled. Their minds were not yet scrubbed clean from all their dirty thoughts.

"Something funny?" Koldis crossed his arms.

"No. No, of course not. Who says I need a bath?" Claire added, her tone joking.

"You don't wish to clean up before King Talon arrives?" He shrugged and turned. "Suit yourselves."

They both cried out, jumping to their feet. "All right, all right. I was only giving you a hard time."

"You've been doing a lot of that since yesterday," he scoffed.

"Okay, okay. Sorry."

Their walk to Brezen's manor house took them through camp, to the outskirts of town. The manor had a great deal of land at its disposal. The sprawling town housed many of those who supported or worked in the manor. Koldis dismissed himself when they reached the entrance and were handed off to their hosts and servants. The guards remained, however, keeping a safe distance.

The manor was quite different from what she was used to in Kastali Dun. The biggest difference, she soon realized, was that there was no plumbing. Not like in the keep. She was mortified when she saw the line of servants going to great lengths, pouring hot water into two copper tubs. Probably the only tubs in the house. Sir Wentworth had gone to great lengths to offer such a luxury.

She and Tamara thanked their hosts profusely.

Female servants lingered about when the tubs were filled. They introduced themselves politely as Martha, Nelly, and Willa. Claire watched Tamara for cues on how to behave. It seemed she had no qualms about removing her clothing with the servants' help before climbing into the tub.

Claire did the same as Martha stepped forward. "Help, miss?"

"No, thank you. I'll manage." She certainly didn't need help getting out of her pants and tunic.

The moment she was naked, she realized her mistake. A gasp sounded behind her. Martha's mouth hung open, attracting every eye in the room, including Tamara's.

She glanced down at her sprite mark, then over her shoulder at the new one she'd earned. It was similar to the other. A swirl that spiraled outward, surrounded by flecks and dots. Both glowed a faint but noticeable luminescent aqua color. There was no hiding it now.

Ignoring their reactions, as if there was nothing wrong, she quickly stepped into the bath and sank low, hiding everything from view. The servants took this as their cue. They resumed their efforts.

She closed her eyes, groaning. The water was steaming, sending needle pricks through her cold feet. The heat began its work on her muscles. The water's surface was sprinkled with clippings of eucalyptus and lavender. It smelled heavenly.

At last, she relaxed.

The servants bustled forward with soap and she soon understood their reason for remaining. Tamara didn't find any of this odd, so she assumed it was commonplace, for nobles most likely. She didn't protest when two women came to her own tub and began washing her hair, but she did insist on washing her own body, if only to keep them from gawking at her marks. They'd gossip about it, regardless.

Mistress Kayla bustled in a short time later holding two gowns. "I had my handmaiden collect these," she said. "I couldn't allow either of you to don dirty clothing for the king. I'll have my servants attend to *that*." She pointed at the heaps of clothes in the corner.

Claire opened her mouth, then shut it just as quickly.

"Those will do fine." Tamara smiled. "You must give our thanks to the ladies who surely volunteered them. I'll see that they are compensated."

"Oh, I do not think that is necessary."

"Nonetheless, I have gowns of my own back at camp. And it would be my pleasure to ensure these are properly paid for."

Mistress Kayla nodded at last.

"The red brocade will fit Claire best and bring out her eyes. I'll take the silver one."

Claire cleared her throat and mumbled, "I had planned to just wear something I brought."

"You mean, something like what you were wearing earlier?" Tamara eyed her. "Don't you wish to look your best when King

Talon arrives? You are his ward, Lady Claire. It would please him to see you dressed the part."

"You sound like Desaree. But, you're probably right. That would be best, I suppose." She sank back down into the water to soak up the last bit of warmth. Maybe Talon would be less angry with her if she looked nice.

After they dressed, the servants insisted on doing their hair. Even Mistress Kayla's handmaiden helped, bringing little white flowers in from the manor's garden to weave into their braids. By the time they were finished, the sun was sinking towards the horizon. Talon wouldn't arrive for a few hours yet. They returned to camp in search of dinner.

"Well, well, well. Would you look at that!" Koldis said. He took Claire's shoulders, turning her this way and that. "I finally recognize you again." He winked and released her. Beneath his humor, she sensed his anxiety. She couldn't blame him. She felt the same. Even the air hummed in anticipation for the king's arrival.

They joined Byron, Jovari, and Koldis at the table, indulging in a modest supper of meat, potatoes, and boiled carrots. There was wine too—a much watered down version of what she was used to in the capital, more like grape juice, really—which she was still glad to have calming her nerves. The food, however, was difficult to choke down as her stomach fluttered.

"All right. Let's get this over with," Koldis said, standing from the table. He dismissed himself. Byron and Jovari followed after. They would ensure everyone was in place, assembled on the field to greet King Talon when he arrived.

Claire and Tamara waited in silence, waiting to be summoned. The longer they sat, the more her mind jumped to Talon. What would he say and do? What would she say and do?

Explanations raced through her thoughts. *I know I promised to stay out of trouble, but the villagers needed me*, she reasoned. *I was the only one who could stop the vodar. If not me, the villagers would have died. I was able to warn the fort. I made a difference in the battle.*

"You're fidgeting."

"What? Oh." She glanced down at her hands. Her fingers wouldn't stop tapping the table.

"Does he make you nervous?"

"No! I mean, not usually. I don't know. Normally I don't get affected like this. I have no problem standing up to him but I'm... anxious."

"Because he will be angry with you? Like that day in the throne room when you arrived?"

She blew out a breath. "Maybe. You know, I used to love making him angry. I think part of me did it on purpose."

Tamara reached over and squeezed her hand.

"I guess it's just because I made a promise to him, and now I've broken it. He has every right to be upset with me."

"But look at all the good you've done!"

She huffed. "Yeah, that's what I said when I showed up in Kastali Dun for the first time. A lot of good that argument did. Talon just..." She sighed. "Talon chooses to see what he wants. Usually he picks the one thing that gives him a reason to be angry and focuses on it. I promise you, the rumors of his temper are not made up."

The tent flaps opened. They jumped, as if Talon himself had waltzed in. Koldis eyed them a moment. "Time to go. Lady Tamara, Byron is waiting for you with the rest of the camp. Claire, you're with me."

"With...you?" She glanced at Tamara.

"Yes. With me. Come."

They followed him out. Tamara found Byron and went to his side.

"Where's Jovari?" she asked, glancing around. As if summoned, Jovari appeared beside her. Koldis moved away and transformed into his hulking green form. His scales glittered in the evening sun.

"Uhm. Am I missing something?"

"He's waiting for you to climb on his back," Jovari said, stating the obvious.

"But...we're meeting the king here, aren't we?"

"Just do as you're told." Tension echoed in his clipped words.

This wasn't the plan! She placed a steadying hand over her stomach. "And what about all these people? Won't they see me—"

"We are well beyond that now, Claire." Jovari pinched the bridge of his nose. "Just...go."

She nodded, too anxious to speak.

Koldis took flight as soon as she was settled. She placed a hand against his scales, hoping to steady her racing heart. As much as she wanted to know why they'd deviated from the initial plan, she did not ask Cyrus to remove the barrier on her mind. Her imagination had already drawn several conclusions of its own.

They flew little more than five minutes. The camp shrank away as the wilderness swallowed them up. Koldis descended into a densely packed grove of trees, one of many littering the landscape. She was off his back in seconds.

He transformed, crossing his arms. "You're to wait here until King Talon arrives. The rest of us will be back at camp to greet his entourage. See if you can butter him up a bit, eh? It was your idea to leave Kastali Dun in the first place, wasn't it?"

Her jaw dropped. "You're putting this on *me*?"

"That *was* the plan you agreed to."

"Well, yeah," she hissed, "but that was under the assumption we'd be back to Kastali Dun before he returned." Koldis shrugged. "So you just want me to what, wait? Here? By myself? In the middle of nowhere?"

"Don't be dramatic. Camp's an hour walk that way. It's not like you're unreachable. But yes, that's exactly what you are to do." He took several steps back, preparing to transform.

"Wait! Is he..." She swallowed against her dry throat. "He's angry with me, isn't he? That's why he wants to speak to me alone."

He eyed her, but said nothing, then transformed and took off into the sky. She watched him until the trees blotted him from view. Her stomach squirmed uneasily. She hated herself for caring. Since when did it matter what Talon thought?!

When things had changed between them, that's when.

"Ugh!" she scoffed, pacing back and forth.

The sun was almost at the horizon. Shadows passed overhead, winking in and out. Fort Kastali's Drengr. They flew low enough to send air rustling the treetops. She searched for Talon's monstrous black shape among them.

"Looking for someone?"

She gasped, whirling around. He stood little more than four feet away, watching her. Their gazes locked. For a moment, she could only stare. Was that *amusement* dancing behind his eyes?

She exhaled, and something inside her loosened at the nearness of him. He looked the same as always, dressed in travel clothes bunched tight over his muscled frame, with weapons strapped about his person like he was going into battle. He was alive and unharmed.

His head tilted to regard her. "You're wearing a dress, and you've done your hair too." Her lips parted in answer, but nothing came out. "Let me guess, guilty conscience?" She licked her lips, then swallowed. "What's the matter? Wraith got your tongue?"

"No," she said, but it sounded more like a squeak.

He stalked towards her, swallowing the distance between them.

Her breaths came faster. She took a quick step back. "I... I'm sorry, Talon. I shouldn't have—"

"I know."

She blinked. "You know? But, aren't you mad?"

He took another step closer, close enough that he could reach out and throttle her if he wanted to. "Oh, I'm *furious*." She flinched at the sudden change in his voice. He frowned. "You think I called you here to scold you? To yell at you? To gnash my jaws? I could do it, you know. I could transform and let my dragon handle you. Let it do what it so badly wants to do at this very moment."

"I deserve it," she whispered, surprised by her own admission. "Who am I if I cannot keep my word? I broke my promise to you."

"You did." His expression changed, softened. "What are we going to do about that? Hmm?"

"I don't know. I had a bunch of arguments lined up—good ones, too."

His lips pressed into a thin line. "Of that, I have no doubt."

"I suppose that a simple apology won't suffice?"

"Claire..." His voice was a low purr. Goosebumps erupted on her skin. She blinked up at him. "Trust is a fragile thing. I have found it difficult to trust you, just as you have found it difficult to trust me. It isn't something that simply exists. It must be built, stone by stone, brick by brick, moment by moment, through the choices we make."

"I..." She nodded. "I understand."

"But..." She held her breath. "There might be a way to fix this."

Her heart skipped. She unclenched her fists and wrapped her arms around her middle. "What do you have in mind?"

"Payment. In exchange for your broken promise. Perhaps a way to rebuild the trust we've worked so hard to establish."

"Payment? Like...never mind. Whatever it is, I'll do it."

"You will?" His eyebrows lifted. "Interesting."

"Why?"

"Your agreement was easier than I expected. Now I can name anything and you would have to accept."

"You wouldn't dare," she whispered.

"Wouldn't I?" His expression was unchanged. She glared at him. "Very well. Here is what I have in mind. One hundred nights, in exchange for your broken promise. You and I will take a walk together every night, an hour of your time given to me, and me alone." Her lips parted in surprise. "There was a time when you hated my company. If that were still true, this would be a fairer punishment. But, I like to think that after certain things between us, our letters, for example, that this might work."

A weight lifted and the tension eased from her shoulders. Without thinking, she threw her arms around him, pulling him against her. His body went rigid. She didn't care. She hugged him until he tentatively wrapped his arms around her waist. Heat spread everywhere they touched. Gods, he felt good against her.

"Talon, I'd be happy to walk with you in the evenings." She pulled away and scurried back several steps.

He smiled then, a genuine smile that put dimples in his scarred cheeks. "You mean that?"

She nodded. "I do. I think it will be good for us to get to know each other better. And if we enjoy it..."

He tilted his head. "If we enjoy it...?"

"Then maybe we can continue walking after the one hundred days are up."

He nodded, satisfied. "I'd like that."

They fell silent. She glanced around. It had become entirely dark.

"Wait." Realization hit her. "If you didn't bring me out here to yell at me, why *are* we here?"

"Ah!" He looked amused. "I wanted you to give me a full report. I'm about to walk into a nightmare. I would like to be prepared. Everyone will expect me to sweep in and become the savior. You can help with that, yes?"

She stared at him, then blinked. "Me? Didn't your shields tell you everything?"

He lifted a shoulder. "Snippets. I don't prefer to converse telepathically from a distance."

"Wouldn't Koldis be better for—"

"I want the truth from you, Claire. You, alone. From your perspective. I'll get their stories later."

"Oh." She swallowed, fidgeting with her fingers. "There's a lot to tell."

He stepped forward and held out his arm. "Good thing we've got a long walk ahead of us. Come."

She stared at him, not quite believing. A grin pulled at the corners of his mouth. This one screamed of mischief.

"We...we're walking back? But it will take an hour. Maybe longer."

"I am certain it will. Consider it our first walk together."

She huffed. She'd played neatly into his plan. Strangely enough, she didn't mind.

"Very well." She stepped up and slipped her hand through his elbow. "But it's not a pretty story, what I have to say. None of it."

He blew out a breath, his expression settling into stone. "I know. Perhaps coming from you it will be easier to bear."

Talon loved his kingdom. She knew that. There was little he wouldn't sacrifice to care for his people. What she had to say would be painful. And yet, he had chosen her above everyone else, to be there for that pain. She hardly knew what to make of it. But perhaps he still trusted her more than he let on, and wasn't that a relief.

CHAPTER 25
THE WALK BACK TO CAMP

Brezen

Claire leaned on Talon's arm as they walked back to camp, bone weary. She filled him in on everything, starting with their plan to destroy the vodar and ending with Kane's attack.

He listened quietly, flinching when she described the battle at Fort Squall. His scowl deepened as she continued. By the time she was done, he looked thunderous. For someone who didn't wear their emotions openly, he was doing a terrible job hiding how he felt.

When she finished, he was silent. "Well?" She pulled him to a stop, turning to face him.

He scrubbed a hand over his face. She studied him, peeling back layers to see the exhaustion lurking in his gaze. "I am ashamed of how deeply I misjudged you when we first met. Time and again, you put my kingdom before your own safety. I am unworthy of you."

She gaped at him. "Okay, who are you and what have you done with Talon?"

He huffed. "Oh, I'm still furious, but I appreciate your efforts nonetheless."

She swallowed. "I just wish...I wish I could have done more."

"What more could you have possibly done?"

"Hiondel and Lily."

"Claire." His expression softened. He lifted a hand, as if to brush her cheek, but dropped it before making contact. "There are always casualties in battle. I do not blame you for their deaths, and neither should you blame yourself."

"You really mean that?"

"I really do. It could have been worse, so much worse." She frowned. "I could have lost you," he said by way of explanation. "But you're safe. Alive. Whole. That's what matters."

She didn't contradict him—didn't tell him how broken she felt.

"Now come along." He pulled on her arm to get them walking. The camp glowed in the distance.

"What are you going to do?" she asked. "About...everything?"

"My ultimate priority is keeping you safe from Kane." He squeezed the hand she'd wrapped around his elbow, making her chest flutter. "Kane's proximity, just across the inlet, does not sit well with me."

"Me either," she whispered.

"As to all of this?" He motioned towards the looming camp. "Everyone will expect me to do something about it, as usual, and I'll never satisfy them. Some will want me to assemble our forces and form a counter-attack by morning, even if it means losing more of our own. Others will demand that we retreat to keep the city safe." He hesitated, glancing at her. "What would you do, if you were me? If you were king of all this?"

She opened and closed her mouth. He was asking her?! She took a moment to think, then said, "You will never make everyone happy. Your people should be your first priority, not the drengr from the fort. You must protect Squall's End. Kane will burn it to the ground if you attack. He probably expects it, too. He'll be ready."

"Good answer." They reached the camp's sentries. He turned,

dropping her hand from his arm. "That means I must remain here in Brezen for a short while, to ensure that everyone is safe. Fort Squall needs my support and I intend to give it."

"And...what of me?"

"Tomorrow, I will send Jovari and Koldis home. They will take their escorts from Fort Kastali with them."

"You're sending them away?"

"Yes."

"Because you're angry with them?"

He chuckled. "I see why you would think that, after they were willing accomplices in this scheme of yours. But no, I am not angry with them. I've been away from the capital too long. Verath is there managing everything alone. Jovari and Koldis will restore the balance in my absence."

"What about Bedelth?"

"He will remain here with you and I. While we are here, I expect you to present yourself as a face for our people."

"Me?"

"You."

She hid her surprise and said, "What about the fort?"

"Fort Squall will retreat south. There is plenty of room in Fort Kastali to house them, until they reclaim their home."

She opened her mouth—

"The road south will be long and difficult. They must leave much behind. Start anew."

"And we're going to escort them?"

"Us? No. We will fly home with my escorts from Fort Kastali."

"Okay." She blew out a breath. "And I'm going to fly with...with you?"

"Yes. Is that a problem?"

Something curled in the pit of her stomach. "I...no. No, of course not. I didn't mean it like that."

"Good." He took up her hand once more and placed it in the crook of his elbow.

He wasn't afraid to touch her. Not that she was complaining. It was just...

She scowled.

Something in him had changed.

They moved through the camp. The greeting party had long since disbanded, but there were still people milling about. Some gaped at them in passing, too surprised to bow. Even without his crown, Talon's presence was unmistakable. One glance at his scarred face said everything.

Voices drifted out of the central tent. An assembly had already been called, judging from the sound of it. "Well…" Talon said, dropping her arm as they came to stand before the guards. "Time to face this."

The guards stood at attention, greeting their king. He squared his shoulders, giving them a nod to open the flaps.

"Good luck," she whispered, unsure if he heard her as she fell into step behind him. But of course he had, because the drengr had excellent hearing.

All talking ceased. Those sitting jumped to their feet, then everyone swept into deep bows. She watched from the entrance, motionless.

She caught Tamara's eye across the tent, giving her a grin. Everything had gone well—better than well. Excellent, in fact. Koldis noticed her expression. His shoulders relaxed and he gave her a brief nod, relieved to see that Talon was not fuming.

Bedelth watched, smiling, as Jovari and Koldis strode forward to greet Talon. They clasped shoulders, then hugged and clapped each other on the back before leading him to the head of the table. Heat flared in her chest, pride, she realized, as she watched the interaction, the camaraderie.

They began by introducing Byron, Tamara, and the others. No one seemed to notice her. They were too focused on the king. Her toes twitched. She began to creep across the tent, towards her cot hidden behind one of the tent flaps. She'd nearly made it when—

"Claire?" She froze at the sound of her name. Talon motioned her towards him. "Join me?"

She hesitated, glancing towards the promise of peace and quiet. Then, her shoulders fell and she nodded, striding across the tent. Talon remained silent, even after she reached his side. Perhaps he didn't know what to say? Didn't know how to address everyone?

What would she say if she were in his position?

Her gaze swept the space, over each face turned towards their king with darting eyes. Eyes that never truly fell upon him. His expression was unyielding and unreadable. But the subtle set of his jaw meant he noticed. She didn't like that they couldn't bear the sight of him.

"Thank you for assembling," he said at last. "I came as quickly as I could. So much has been taken from you, from us. Loss of life, your home, your pride." He hesitated. She noticed the way his fists were clenched at his sides. "I have failed you. Failed to protect you. Any blame lies with me."

She looked up at him, surprised. How was this *his* fault? He hadn't been here.

"As king, every fort in Dragonwall is *my* responsibility," he continued. "This kingdom, its lands and people, you—my responsibility. Despite my best attempts to protect you..." He shook his head.

Something tightened deep in her chest. Hiondel and Lily had been her responsibility too. And she'd failed them. Failed to protect them.

She glanced around the table again. A tent full of people and they could hardly look upon him. Could hardly look upon their king who so selflessly carried the weight of a kingdom on his shoulders. Frustration boiled up inside of her. Didn't it bother him? Were his scars really that bad? Was the reminder of his past so uncomfortable they preferred to study the table?

Talon continued speaking. "I cannot imagine the kind of bravery it took you to abandon your home. But know this, your sacrifice will never be forgotten. Lord Byron," he said, turning. "Do we know the final death count of our kind?"

"Twenty-three pairs, my king, and six mates."

Talon closed his eyes, perhaps searching for a moment of tranquility amidst the grief in the tent. He opened his eyes and said, "I will pay my respects to those who lost their mates, if you will direct me to their tents once we are done here?"

"Apologies, King Talon, but they are not here. They have chosen solitude to grieve."

"As is their right. Very well."

Koldis stepped up. "Two patrols returned this afternoon, Your Majesty. We have made contact with six more. All have been advised to stay clear of Kane's dragons. They will rendezvous with us here."

"Their return will be most welcome," Talon murmured.

"And once they *do* return?" said a voice. "What then? Will we take back what is ours?"

"We should retaliate," someone else said, agreeing. A drengr of middling age with auburn hair and freckles. His mate sat beside him, anxiously avoiding Talon's face.

"What do the rest of you think?" Talon asked, seeking their opinions.

"If we move against them, the dragons will burn the city to the ground," Byron said, disagreement riddling his voice. "Kane promised it would be so."

"But we cannot sit back and let those beasts hold our people prisoner," another cried.

"Better that, then dead," Koldis muttered.

"They'll wish they were, with those beasts torturing them." A rider's voice this time. Claire glanced around, seeking the source. There were too many to tell.

"Kane promised no harm would come should we retreat," Byron answered. "We must hope he speaks the truth."

"How can we trust him at his word?" A burley drengr slammed his palm on the table. She remembered meeting him, meeting nearly all of them, but couldn't remember half of their names.

The table erupted in protests. Talon was right. Opinions were mixed; he would never please everyone. He watched passively, as if used to this. She opened her mouth to speak. He caught her eye and gave a subtle shake of his head.

The arguments continued until enough people had given up

and simply sat with arms crossed, scowling, waiting. She looked from one to another. These people were exhausted. Desperate. Heartbroken.

Talon lifted his hands and the room fell quiet. "I think, in light of your arguments, we can all agree on one thing. Kane must be stopped. We cannot allow him to control our lives." Nods rippled around the tent. "But we cannot expect to beat him in our current state."

People at the table shifted, perhaps trying to make sense of his words. She watched him out of the corner of her eye, trying to be discreet. She noticed subtle clues in his body language that spoke as loud as his words. The way he shifted his weight, the rise and fall of his chest, the twitch of his fists.

"When the time comes," he vowed, "we will make Kane pay for what he has done. We will make him pay for *everything.*"

"So...we aren't going to attack?" The speaker was clearly dismayed.

"Not yet. Our path forward will not be easy. If we do not attack, we look weak and our people in Squall's End are forced to cower beneath the rule of our enemy. If we do attack, the city burns. Thousands upon thousands of lives lost. No matter what we choose, the outcome is unfavorable. But—" He hesitated, looking around to meet their eyes. Many quickly glanced away. "In times like these, one governing factor must remain at the forefront of our minds. I am sure you can guess it? But if not—Claire?" She jumped at the sudden sound of her name. Talon turned to her, as did every pair of eyes. "You know the drengr's code, do you not? "

"I—yes. Why?"

"Recite it for us, please."

"Oh. Uhm..." She wanted to glare at him, but schooled her features. Instead, she recalled the words Mage Joren had taught her in one of their lessons. "Sure."

Her eyes swept the room in challenge. When she next spoke, her voice was steady.

A kingdom wants protection, in its time of need.
The drengr that were chosen, must pledge their vow to thee.
To uphold the code of honor, for which they take a stand.
To defend the weak and broken, sewing peace throughout the land.
Their words hold naught but truth.
Their might cannot be measured.
Their courage knows no bounds.
Their virtue ever treasured.
For so these words are spoken, must they not be lost.
Defend the kingdom and its people. No matter what the cost.

THE ROOM WAS SILENT. It was the reminder everyone needed.

"Thank you." Talon nodded, pleased. "As you are new to Dragonwall's ways, perhaps we might benefit from your insight. What do you make of the words?"

This time she *did* glare at him, discreetly, of course. "It's obvious, isn't it? Defend the kingdom and its people, no matter what the cost. Fort Squall is the cost of keeping those in Squall's End safe. Safe *and* alive."

"Yes." Talon offered a satisfied smile, the first he'd shown since entering the tent. His gaze swept over everyone. "Our answer is clear, you see. We must defend our people no matter what the cost. Even if it means sacrificing our homes to keep them from losing theirs."

No more protests came, and when the meeting finally ended, she was the first to scuttle off to her cot. She fell asleep dissecting every detail of Talon's return. Everything he'd said, every gesture, every grin, smile, and smirk. She needed to know what had changed. Most of all, she needed to know why.

CHAPTER 26

LATE NIGHT CONFESSIONS

Brezen

Claire opened her eyes, blinking at the darkness. Her ears pricked up the sound of hushed voices—probably what had awoken her. A faint glow came from beyond the canvas partition. Beside her, Tamara gave a gentle snore.

She tossed and turned, trying to find a comfortable position. What she would give for her feathered bed right now. It was no use —nothing was comfortable.

She sat up, discarding her blankets. Tamara gave another gentle snore. The ground was cold beneath her bare feet. She slipped out into the main tent.

Only a few candles were lit. Talon and Bedelth sat across from each other, speaking in hushed voices. They fell silent at her approach before Bedelth surged to his feet.

"I—" Her gaze landed on a pitcher. "Just getting some water. Please don't stand on my account." She grabbed an overturned cup from the stack and began pouring.

"No matter. I need fresh air anyway," Bedelth said, slipping away. She was about to protest but the tent's flaps fell back into place, leaving her very much alone with Talon. She replaced the pitcher and took a sip.

"Come, sit." Talon pulled out the chair beside him.

"I...I was just—"

"—going to drink that standing there awkwardly?"

"Right."

After a long pause, she sat down beside him, very aware that she was wearing nothing more than a spare nightgown. She made a show of drinking her water before setting the empty cup on the table.

"Couldn't sleep?"

"Something like that. You?"

He hesitated. "Something like that."

Silence stretched out between them, leaving her overly aware of his close proximity. She gazed at her cup as if it might turn into a teapot, trying to think of something to say. Each time she opened her mouth, the words didn't seem right.

When she turned to him, she caught him staring at her. Candlelight flickered over his face, throwing shadows and highlights across his scars. Her chest heaved at the sight. It wasn't necessarily pity she felt—he wouldn't want that. Perhaps it was sadness, especially after seeing how handsome he had once been, after knowing all that he had done for his kingdom, and how much he cared.

"You're frowning. If my presence bothers you, I can go."

"No!" She jolted forward. "I mean, it's not that."

"Then what?"

"I..." She shifted to better face him. "It just bothers me, I suppose. The others, from earlier. How they treated you. They couldn't bear to look at you. They avoided you even though they stood in the same tent as you. Even though you're their king. It's rude. Disrespectful, even. It made me—"

"Made you what?" He didn't so much as blink.

She exhaled. "It made me frustrated—and angry."

"Oh." Something in his expression changed, softening the stark lines. "I had not realized that would upset you. My scars are my own curse to bear, not yours."

"Talon... How can you...why would you see it like that? They're scars—nothing more. Certainly not a curse. It's not like you have horns growing out of your head, or a third eyeball. You're not a monster. Don't they see that? Don't they understand everything you've done for them? The sacrifices you've made?"

He tilted his head, perhaps trying to better understand her.

"Reyr told me about how you got them, about your parents and the Kalds and..."

He straightened. "I don't need your pity, Claire. I don't want it."

"No! I—that wasn't my intent. I'm angry for you, that's all."

"I see." He fell silent for longer than she liked. It made her squirm. She hadn't intended to have this conversation or make either of them this uncomfortable.

"Look, Talon, I won't apologize for wanting or even expecting others to respect you."

"Nor would I ask it of you." He leaned back in his chair. "The truth is, I am used to it, after hundreds of years of the same. One grows used to such things." He waved it away like a passing thought.

"So that's it, then? You've given up and accepted it?"

He deserved so much more. He deserved...everything. The thought made her frown. After all, why did she care?

"Claire, my people regard me how they choose to regard me because of the things I have done, the way I have acted and behaved throughout my lifetime. I might be selfless, but it often doesn't show." He gave her a knowing look. "Would you deny that I have a terrible temper?"

"Gods, no!" she cried. Her hand shot to cover her mouth, eyes wide. "I mean..."

"I know what you mean," he drawled. "You know all about my moods, perhaps better than most. Besides, those who *can* bear to look at me without flinching, they are the ones I care about. Like my shields. Like you. The others?" He shrugged. "That's their problem, isn't it?"

She huffed. "I suppose you're right. I didn't think of it that way."

He nodded. "The greatest prison a person can build is one of fear over what others might think. You could spend an entire lifetime fortifying the bars. I choose not to."

"I..." His words took a moment to sink in. He was right. She reached for his hand and stopped short, quickly pulling away. He glanced down at the action. Her skin flushed hot. "That's very wise of you," she managed. "But then again, you are a king. As long as you have the respect of those you care about, the rest doesn't matter."

"And what of you? Have I earned your respect?"

"You have. You should already know that."

He leaned towards her, propping his elbow on the arm of his chair. His face was mere inches from hers. Why was it so hot in the tent?

"You know," he said, his words low and deliberate. "Even before I had your respect, you never balked at my appearance."

"What...do you mean?" Her stomach fluttered. She could make out gold flecks in his silver eyes. Why hadn't she noticed them before?

"Don't you remember?" he was saying. "That day in my court? When you faced me? I wanted you to cower from me the way others do. I wanted you to fear me. You didn't. You stood and faced me. I will never forget the sight of you. Your pride. Your strength. It intimidated me. Still does, on occasion."

She managed to collect her thoughts. "I was intimidated by you too," she blurted. "Actually, I was terrified. I couldn't have done it without Cyrus. But, I was also angry. Gods! I was *so* angry." A laugh escaped her chest. "You were just so damn frustrating! You wouldn't listen to a word I said. Or didn't care. I wasn't sure which. I wanted to smack some sense into you right there in front of everyone, but of course, you don't go and smack a king in his own throne room."

"Smack some sense into me?" He tossed his head back and

roared with laughter, bellowing loud enough to wake everyone in camp.

Her eyes widened, tracing the lines of his exposed throat and chin, the way his hair fell back. The gesture was so carefree. As if nothing in the world were wrong. A smile tugged at the corners of her mouth.

"Yes," he said at last, straightening to look at her. "I suppose I would have deserved that. I suppose I have deserved everything you've thrown my way, and then some. Every scowl. Every glare." He huffed and his expression turned serious again. "I should have seen it. Even then, I should have seen it when it was right in front of me." He reached out and grabbed her hand, perhaps already forgetting that she'd been unable to do the same.

She hid her surprise, afraid to move. The gesture left her paralyzed.

"I've been *so* blind. So gods damned blind. There's something—"

The tent flap opened. "Gods, wake the whole damn camp, why don't—" Koldis froze at the entrance. His eyes widened, darting over them, over their proximity.

She ripped her hand from Talon's, but it was too late. Her cheeks burned with nervous embarrassment. The spell was broken. Koldis swore and turned on his heel, disappearing out of the tent without another word.

Whatever had just happened, or was about to happen, slipped through the cracks like water on a slatted floor. It was followed by a long, awkward silence. "I...should get some sleep," she mumbled.

"Of course." Talon jerked his chair back and stood, rushing to pull hers out as well. Things had gone from intimate to awkward in a matter of seconds. She wanted to run far, far away. She shouldn't have allowed him to take her hand. What was she thinking?! Why was this happening?

"Uh, you should try to get some sleep too," she added. What else was she supposed to say? "Good night, Talon." She gave him a sloppy curtsy and rushed away, throwing herself behind the tent's partition and beneath her blankets.

She stared up at the canvas ceiling. She missed the stars. At least the twinkle of them helped when she couldn't sleep.

Was Talon developing feelings for her? She burrowed deeper into her pillow, frowning. No. That was impossible. And yet...

The taste of blood filled her mouth. "Damn it," she muttered, releasing her lower lip from her teeth.

What had he been about to say? Part of her wanted to know, the other part was relieved that Koldis had interrupted. Would he have kissed her? Their faces had been so close.

No! She squeezed her eyes shut. No kissing. Absolutely not. He was the king, and a drengr. Nothing good would come of it. The worst thing she could do was get tangled up with him.

It wasn't as if they were mates.

Her breathing stopped.

Were they?

No. Definitely not. She would know—of course she would know. Besides, Talon had failed to find his mate. He *had* no mate. Right?

But, what if he did find his mate someday? Where would that leave her? Her pulse took off at a gallop.

Oh, gods!

Was she *jealous*? She groaned, flopping over onto her other side. She was! She was absolutely jealous! The idea of losing his attention made her skin prickle with anger. Which only made her angrier.

THE FOLLOWING MORNING, breakfast was sent over from the manor. Bacon, eggs, oatmeal, cinnamon apples, and bread. Aside from the constant stream of missives, delivered by errand boys, the event was rather mundane. Cutlery clattered and conversations were kept to a minimum. Every so often, the scratch of Talon's quill sounded as he answered each of the correspondences, issuing new orders.

She glanced up and found his gaze. It was the third time she'd caught him staring at her. His eyes darted back to the message in his hand and her cheeks warmed.

She stared at her plate. At least her appetite had returned. It felt like she could finally eat for the first time in weeks. Knots began unraveling—knots she hadn't realized she carried.

"Claire?" Tamara's voice drew her back to the present. "Did you hear me?"

"Sorry. I didn't."

"I asked if you wanted to join me for a walk?"

Talon lowered the parchment in his hand. "I think that's an excellent idea. Why don't the two of you get some fresh air?"

So they set out arm in arm, trailed by an entourage of guards. She took the opportunity to tell Tamara what had happened when she met Talon in the grove. "I expected him to erupt with anger over my broken promise," she explained. "Instead, he wants me to make it up to him with a nightly walk."

"Do you not think he has changed towards you?" Tamara wondered. "This doesn't sound like the male you described yesterday."

"I know."

They squeezed their conversation in between greetings as they traversed camp. Cook fires were lit as people gathered for breakfast. They were offered all manner of food, skewers of meat, boiled potatoes, bread, ale. Many begged for them to join in. After accepting the first few offerings, she politely declined all others. She'd already had a full breakfast, and her bodice was close to bursting.

She'd decided to wear another gown. Only because it was what was expected of her. As soon as she left for the capital, she'd be back in pants.

Eventually, she excused herself from Tamara's company in search of Jovari and Koldis. They were assembled with the other pairs who had accompanied them from Fort Kastali. A wave of longing passed over her. She missed Kastali Dun. But more than that, she missed Desaree and Saffra.

Faedrol and Hannah offered eager waves when they spotted her. "Are you flying back with us?" Hannah asked.

"I wish I could," she nearly groaned.

Hannah pulled her into a hug. "Too bad! We'll miss you."

"Thank you. Have a safe trip, both of you. And keep an eye on the king's shields for me. No carting bandits off in nets." They shared a laugh and bid her farewell.

Faedrol transformed into a glittering bronze dragon and Hannah vaulted onto his back. Many of the other drengr had already transformed as their riders fastened travel packs to their harnesses. She moved from pair to pair speaking with each of them, thanking them for accompanying her and bidding them safe travels.

Jovari and Koldis were last.

"Come to bid us a fond farewell?" Koldis smirked. "Admit it, you're going to miss us."

She stepped forward and threw her arms around him. He froze, then quickly returned the embrace. Jovari was next, but better prepared for her sudden show of affection.

"Just so you know, I am going to miss you." The backs of her eyes pricked with tears. "I can't believe you're leaving me here with Talon. What if he loses his temper? Neither of you will be here to take the heat."

"Someone's got to do it," Jovari teased. "Besides, we're needed in the capital. And anyway, our king is a new man. Whatever happened to him in the forest has left him changed. I say for the better."

She hesitated. "Then, I'm not the only one who noticed it?"

"Maybe you can find out why." Koldis winked. "You can tell us what you find after you return."

"Yes sir!" She gave him a salute. "Look, I wanted to apologize to you both before you left. I shouldn't have lost my temper with you after what happened. I know it's not your fault. You just wanted to know Reyr was okay. I did too."

Koldis cuffed her on the shoulder. "No hard feelings, hmm? We won't hold it against you. It takes a lot more than a few temperamental words from an unruly female to offend us."

She exhaled, relieved. "That's good."

Jovari stepped forward, squeezing her arm. "Goodbye, Lady Claire. May the wind be a steady current beneath your wings."

She smiled up at him. "And yours too, Jovari. We will trade stories when I return?"

"Aye, we shall." He stepped aside. Koldis gave her much the same goodbye, then they transformed into their glittering green and blue forms.

She stepped back, watching them assemble into formation, filled with longing, wishing she could go with them. Koldis gave a mighty roar and leapt from the ground. The others followed. She followed their progress as they rose into the sky, then disappeared against the horizon.

CHAPTER 27
CONFRONTING CATERINA

Kastali Dun

Verath listened to the subtle inhale and exhale of Desaree's breath, curled up beside him, her back against his front, nestled into the curves of his body. One arm was beneath her head, the other draped over her waist, holding her to him. He didn't sleep much, but he'd quickly grown fond of their nights together, the calm her presence brought him. Truth be told, he pretended he slept more than he did, if only as an excuse to be near her. His years of loneliness had caught up with him, driving him to form an attachment he knew was dangerous. It would only end in heartbreak. At his age, he knew better.

He had not worked up the nerve to claim her entirely. Not yet. Nor should he. His mind stumbled over that fact—fighting it. A time would come when he could no longer resist. How could he deny her? How could he hold her, but hold back? And when he did give in, what then? Would he treat her cheaply? He could not make her his wife. He could not be honorable in such a way. Not unless honor meant abstaining entirely. Even then...

Guilt clawed at him. His mind flashed back to Kendra and he

squeezed his eyes shut, trying to push her face away. *She's gone*, he argued. *You had your chance, and another will never come. She's gone.* The reminder was a difficult one. Kendra was similar to Desaree in looks and appearance. He only ever laid eyes on her once, but that single glimpse was burned into his mind forever. Ironically, he'd sought a woman similar, perhaps a reminder, if only to torture himself with a shadow of what could have been. The same brown eyes. The same velvety chocolate hair. He cursed under his breath, pushing these thoughts away—

An abrupt knock sounded. "Two hours before dawn," came the call. That damned guard! He'd flay the man next time he saw him, if these ridiculous wake-up calls didn't end. Desaree insisted on waking up early, even in Claire's absence. He could hear her voice even now. "There's an apartment to keep clean. I want everything spotless when she returns."

Desaree stirred against him, igniting a fire in his abdomen. "Is it time?" she murmured, her words sleepy. He liked her like this, unguarded, at ease in his arms.

He smiled, nuzzling against the back of her neck. "Not if you don't wish. Sleep a little longer. It's good for you."

"Mmm." She pushed herself deeper against him, into his arms.

He held back a growl of frustration, scooting his hips away so that she wouldn't feel his hardness against her back. "Besides," he added, "didn't you clean Claire's apartment yesterday? And the day before? How much cleaning does it need?"

"Mmm-hmm." Her eyelids were still closed.

"Good. Go back to sleep."

At this, she stretched, catlike as she scooted away from him. "I function better on a schedule. You know that." She moved onto her elbows to look up at him, holding his gaze. "Good morning," she whispered, offering him a shy smile. She leaned forward and gave him a chaste peck on the nose then got out of bed.

He turned on his side to watch her. "Any special plans today?"

"No. Not really. Madame Rosanne is going to drop off Claire's ball gown. I need to inspect it. Find some accessories for it. Otherwise, it should be a quiet day." She glanced at him. "What of you?

How did things go in the city yesterday? You said you had business there?"

"Yes, all went well. Nothing serious."

She stared at him. "Why do I get the feeling you're hiding something?"

He tutted, flopping over onto his back, placing his hands behind his head to look at the ceiling. The bed dipped. Desaree's face loomed over him. "I'm not," he answered. "Everything went according to plan."

"What plan? And I was referring to the 'nothing serious' part. This is about Caterina, isn't it? You are always open about everything else, except when it comes to her. It doesn't hurt me to talk about her, you know. I'm not a fragile little bird."

He wanted to argue. To him, every human was fragile. "I know." He sighed and took hold of her arm, pulling her down against his chest before she could protest. "Lay with me a minute."

"Only if you tell me what's going on." She craned her neck to better study him.

"Very well. But don't say I didn't warn you." He paused. "I caught Collier yesterday."

"What?! The poison maker? The one who—"

"Yes. That one."

"Oh. Well? What did he say? Did you question him? About my mother?" When he was silent, she grew frustrated. "Verath! Tell me!"

"I did—question him that is. He admitted to it. Your mother and your father too." He closed his eyes. This was not how he had pictured telling her.

"What?!" Her voice was a hiss. She freed herself from him and jumped from the bed. "And you...you're only telling me this *now*?"

"Desaree, please." He sat up, rubbing his temples. "I..." He had no good excuse. Though he had wanted information from both Collier and Caterina before presenting it to her. But mostly, he was afraid to see her hurt over the matter.

"You should have told me. I don't scold you often, if ever, but you know that I have a right to know everything pertaining to this trial."

He exhaled. "You're right. I'm sorry. Come. Sit. I'll tell you about it." She sat and he told her of everything that had transpired the day before, of how they'd caught Collier, and how he resorted to a truth serum to get answers.

"So, you'll question Caterina today?"

"Aye. After the midday meal."

"Can I...should I come?"

"I'm not sure that is a good idea." There was a pause. "Unless you truly wish to be there. But I would advise against it."

She remained quiet. "I suppose I would rather not see her. Not until...until the trial. Only when I must."

He pulled her close, covering her mouth with his. The kiss deepened into something that spoke of his reassurance. All would be fine, he would make sure of it.

There was a time when she protested his kisses, calling them improper and inappropriate. Now she gave in to him entirely, sighing into his arms. Opening wide for him. As his tongue roved over hers, a fire stoked in his chest. He pulled away before the flames grew too fierce. "Off with you then—to your duties. I have things of my own to manage."

Her cheeks were flushed. A result of his effect on her. He nearly growled in pleasure over the power he held.

She stumbled away to fix up her appearance, patting her hair back into place. He rose from the bed, strapped his sverak in place, donned his doublet over his tunic, and offered her a chaste kiss on her cheek before departing.

The guards across the hall stood watch at Claire's door. No one in the keep was any wiser to her disappearance. It was as he'd hoped. He nodded in passing.

A number of tedious tasks awaited him before visiting Mage Targa's apartments. There was the matter of taking King Talon's place in court, which he rued, and the correspondences he conducted in his absence, all of which required completion that morning. It would be yet another long day.

When the midday meal came around, he chose to take it in his chambers, desperate for a few moments alone. Then he met with Imeir and together they walked to Mage Targa's. When they were shown in to his apartment, he found Caterina sitting with her hands folded in her lap, an untouched cup of tea beside her, a blank expression upon her face. Good, she was anxious.

"Good afternoon, Lady Caterina," he said, keeping his voice neutral. "Thank you for meeting me." Peace was a delicate thing. Caterina was a favorite among the noble women of the court. He could not simply throw her out. He needed to be strategic about it. Talon would not thank him if he caused an uproar.

But if he could prove her guilt, which he technically already had, the public would disown her. If not, she would spread her lies and Desaree would be forced to live them. He needed to give her a reason to be afraid—something to catch her off guard.

"Good afternoon, Lord Verath." Caterina's manner of speech was stiff.

"I hope to make this short," he said, taking a seat across from her with Imeir. "I would like to hear your side of the story."

"Story?" She tilted her head, feigning ignorance.

"Yes. How you came to inherit the title of lady. Your father inherited Lady Kendall's title, property, and wealth. How did it come about?"

"Really, Lord Verath! How do you think? How are titles ever passed on? By death, *obviously.*"

"Yes. Yes, of course." He waved an impatient hand. "But I'm sure there's a story. Why don't you enlighten me?" On the sofa beside him, Imeir shifted. Targa chose not to sit. He lurked beside the sofa where Caterina sat, without offering them a drink or refreshment of any kind.

Caterina sighed, playing her part well. "Well..." She paused. "My father told me when I was younger that he had fallen in love with a woman. That he was to marry her and I was to have a sister. I was overjoyed. I always wanted a sister—a family." She glanced at Targa before continuing. "When my father married Lady Kendall, we moved into her home and became the family I always wanted. I had a sister at last." Her smile was unconvincing. "Then... then Lady Kendall, my...my *mother*...she got sick. A fever. It was so sudden. So fast. Everything had been perfect. Then it wasn't. It happened overnight. The fever shocked us. It took her in her sleep. We...we didn't know what to think, what to do. There was no time to call the healers—no time for anything." Her eyes glistened and a single tear rolled down her cheek.

What a great actress, tears and all. He held back a snort.

"Convincing, isn't she?" Imeir's sarcastic remark rang in his mind.

"Yes, convincing indeed," he scoffed, then said aloud, "That sounds rather tragic, my lady. I can imagine what a shock it was. The poison that was used to bring her fever about, *fire fever* I believe it is called? Or *kivilnari* in the old language of magic?"

Caterina's eyes widened before she recovered. "Fire...fire fever, my lord? You mean to tell me she was poisoned? But...why? Why would someone do such a thing? She was so...kind."

Mage Targa stepped forward. "Are you insinuating what I think you are, Lord Verath?" He pinned Verath with his dark gaze.

"Oh, I am. Caterina procured this poison from Collier and used it on Lady Kendall."

Caterina sucked in a deep breath. "Upon my word, Lord Verath. I...I never!" Her eyes were wide, no doubt in fear rather than feigned ignorance.

"Excuse me," Targa hissed, voice turning cold. "I was under the impression that this was a questioning session, *not* an accusation session."

Perhaps Targa needed questioning too.

"You're right," he conceded. "My apologies, Lady Caterina. Accusations will come during the trial." He exhaled. "Well, since I've had your story, how about I tell you Collier's? Squirrelly as that man is, he offered me all sorts of acorns, some he'd even tucked away for many seasons."

The color drained from Caterina's face. She was not expecting this—that he had caught Collier and questioned him. She probably hoped the poison maker would never be found.

Smiling, he launched into Collier's tale. He made sure to mention that the information was provided under the influence of a particular potent concoction of *sanidi*. Truth serum. This way, Caterina could not make excuses. He told them about the deal struck between Collier and Kane, and the deal struck between Kane and Stefan Rosen. "What I found most fascinating," he said, arriving at the story's end, "is that Kane gifted you with magic in exchange for your meddling." She sucked in a sharp breath, frozen under his intense gaze. "So it would seem, Lady Caterina, that your story isn't genuine, and neither is your ability for magic."

"What...what are you implying?" she whispered, the sound of her words hoarse. "That I have no magic?"

"Oh, you have magic, no doubt about that. What I'm *saying* is that your magic came from Kane. With the information we have, King Talon will be hard pressed to keep someone around who possesses magic from the very sorcerer trying to destroy our kingdom."

"But..." She abruptly stood. "No. That cannot be. My magic is mine. It came to me the way magic comes to all those who possess it." She looked down at Targa who had now taken a seat on the opposite end of the sofa. His face was unreadable. Was this as much of a shock to him as it was to Caterina?

"Your magic came to you, Lady Caterina, because Kane *gave* it to you. It did not flow in your blood as it ought."

"No." She shook her head. "I...I refuse to believe it." She backed away from the sofa, wringing her hands.

"Gods above, woman! Magic manifests at a young age. Look at your classmates. They're all younger than you by several years. Take Lady Saffra, for example. She was eight when her magic appeared. You can't possibly believe in the coincidence of yours showing right after you poisoned Lady Kendall."

"I'm just...a late bloomer. That's all. A late bloomer." This time, genuine tears pooled in her eyes. All sneering pretenses were forgotten.

A heavy shock indeed.

He and Imeir stood. "Well, believe what you wish. We have

enough proof from Collier to put you in the dungeons for life, perhaps even send you to an early grave. I think it best if you don't try anything before your trial. When the king returns, he will see fit to do with you as he pleases."

The trial was a few weeks away. Doubtful she would bother to do anything, except perhaps spread lies. Win other nobles to her cause. But the information he had against her was irrefutable.

"Please!" she hissed. "The king...he can't...he can't hurt me, can he?" She looked at Targa who had remained silent through all of this. "He can't, right?" she asked again. Targa swallowed but said nothing.

"Well, that's all I needed. I'll leave the two of you to bicker between yourselves." Satisfied, he took his leave, slamming the door shut behind him.

"Gods!" Imeir chuckled. "That was easier than I expected."

"I'll say. She took it as quite a shock."

"Indeed." Imeir paused. "But one thing intrigues me. If you had everything you needed from Collier, why question her to begin with?"

He fell quiet. "Because she ruined Desaree's life. I wanted to take something she held dear and rip it away from her the way she ripped Desaree's mother away. I would wager magic is the one thing—the *only* thing—she's felt sure about. Magic allowed her to feel special—entitled. Now she can truly see herself for what she is. A fraud."

They strolled through the east wing. A runner appeared, sprinting over. "Lord...Lord Verath!" He was out of breath. "This...is for you. Just came. High priority. Already paid for. From Brezen."

He frowned, eyeing the runner. "That wasn't cheap. Let's have it here." He grabbed the letter and the runner dashed away, adjusting his leather satchel as he went.

"From Brezen?" Imeir's eyebrows drew together. "What could it be?"

Verath thought of Jovari, Koldis, and Claire. But Brezen was too far north. There was no possible way.

He broke the seal and unfurled the parchment. His eyes darted over the contents. "Gods above!" he swore. His heart raced. "There has...there has been an attack. I...I don't believe it. Fort Squall?" He read over the contents twice in disbelief. And then waves of grief slammed into him.

"An attack?" Imeir's voice sounded far away. "You...you're sure? But how? When? *Who*?"

"I think I need to sit down." He walked into a nearby courtyard and sat down on the bench. It overlooked the bay below. He handed the letter to Imeir and put his head in his hands to think. How long was it since Claire's departure? Six days?

"It's from Koldis," Imeir said, "dated two days past. But how could a letter from Brezen get here so quickly?"

"A drengr flew it partway and dropped it at the closest runner station. Gods! How could this have happened?! And with King Talon away in the forest. What a disaster!"

Imeir fell quiet, reading the contents. "Wild dragons? But how did the fort miss them? They would have seen them coming."

"Keep reading." His head remained in his hands, elbows propped on his knees. He took deep breaths. It was all he could do to keep the agonizing sadness at bay. So many deaths. Fort Squall was too far away to have felt them, but now that the knowledge was there, the pain was too.

He'd sent Koldis and Jovari with Claire to eliminate the vodar. They were due to return as soon as tomorrow, assuming his calculations were correct. Yet, the letter had come from Koldis in Brezen. He could not say how Koldis had come to be there, nor what had happened in the meantime. All he knew was that Reyr was in Fort Squall. His death was not reported in the letter. "I would have known," he whispered, more to himself. "I would have known if he'd been killed. Just as Talon knew when Cyrus died." They were brothers, joined by blood oaths.

Imeir swore. "The fort was taken. Its people forced to retreat across the inlet. There is no mention of Reyr. You don't think..."

His head snapped up. He looked at Imeir. "No. Reyr is still alive. I don't know why he isn't mentioned. But you saw the words. Byron has taken over temporary leadership. You know what that means, right? It means Lord Davi is dead." A hiss escaped his chest. Reyr's twin brother. Instinct took over. He grabbed the letter from Imeir and stuffed it into his pocket, breathing hard. His crimson scales itched to break free of his skin.

Imeir had the same strained expression on his face. "We must give the signal, Verath." As if they had any other choice. "We must sound the call."

He nodded, swallowing hard. Sadness radiated outward from his mind, flowing through his veins in waves, like the aftershock of a quake. He couldn't hold back. His voice ripped from his lips as his scales broke free of his skin. His body swelled. He jumped from the ground, vaulting into the sky.

CHAPTER 28
A SPRITELY GIFT

Brezen

Claire finished her last bite of dinner. The moment she swallowed, the scrape of a chair brought silence to Sir Wentworth's dining room. They had been invited to dine in Brezen's manor house. Talon was at the head of the table. Sir Wentworth and his wife took places of honor on Talon's left. Bedelth sat on his right, while she and Tamara were several places down. The room was full. It took several seconds for everyone to rush to their feet after Talon stood.

Talon murmured something that left Sir Wentworth beaming. Then he walked around the table and stopped beside her chair. "Ready for our walk?"

"Now?" Her eyes darted around the room.

"You have finished, yes?" He motioned to her emptied plate. She nodded. "Good. Then let us walk."

"Okay." The word came out breathless. She took his arm and they left the room, walking through the manor and out into the evening air. It was already well past dark.

"How did your day go?" he asked.

"Fine, I think." She took a calming breath. "It was hard saying goodbye to Jovari and Koldis."

"They have grown on you."

She smiled. "They have, especially Koldis."

"Didn't you dislike him when you first met?"

"Dislike is putting it mildly," she said. He huffed. "What about your day?"

"Tedious."

She waited for him to say more. He didn't. "How did everything go on your trip to the forest? I never got the chance to ask."

"It was productive," he said, guiding them along the wagon tracks that led through an open field. He dropped her arm. "I got you something while I was in Esterpine. A few things, but this I'm especially proud of."

"From the sprites?" Her breath caught.

"From the sprites." He fished around in his pocket, producing a pouch made of shimmering silver fabric. "I wanted to give it to you tonight."

Her gaze didn't stray from his hands. He upended the contents into his palm. A tiny gasp fell from her lips. He cradled a tangle of delicate chain, like spun starlight. She tried to grab his hand for a closer look but he squeezed it into a fist.

"Ah ah ah." He clicked his tongue. "Patience."

He took the first item and held it up.

"A bracelet?"

"Yes." He fastened it about her wrist. "The sprites weave magic into their jewelry. This looks like it's made of silver, but it isn't."

She opened her mouth—

"Don't ask me what it is. I tried. They wouldn't tell me."

"Oh." She lifted her wrist to examine it. "I... Talon, it's lovely." It was a simple chain, elegant just like the sprites. "And the other?" She eyed his closed fist.

He slowly opened his fingers, palm up, this time allowing her to take his hand in hers. She examined the contents, brushing a finger over the piece of jewelry. A pendant on a silver chain.

"They call it a forest tear," he said. Indeed, the pendant was in the shape of a teardrop the size of a thumbnail, milky white on the outside, with a faint bluish glow from within. "It's a hollow moonstone that contains the forest's most precious entity." She looked up at him in question, still holding his open hand in both of hers. "Enchanted water from the river that flows from their king tree. Don't ask me how they got it in there. Another secret. Here—"

He unclasped the chain. She lifted her hair and leaned towards his chest as he encircled her with his arms, clasping it about her neck. They were almost hugging like this. Her nose brushed against him. She inhaled and smiled. Pine, flowers, and smoke. Like Cyrus had smelled the night she rescued him. The smells of Esterpine still lingered on his skin, mixing with his own draconic scent.

The pendent settled into place. It made her body hum like a plucked string. The sensation disappeared as quickly as it had come, but she was left with a heavy awareness of what she wore.

"I'm a sprite," she whispered, breathless.

"Yes and no." He stepped away to study her, his gaze hooded.

"No?" Her heart raced.

"I have discovered all that I can about you," he said. He took her hand and placed it around his forearm to guide her. They continued their walk. Her free hand darted to the pendent, fingers caressing its cold surface.

"Why yes and no? Talon! Tell me!"

He blew out a breath. "The information I received was rather contradictory."

She frowned. "How so?"

"Well, Queen Jade has her ideas, but so does Princess Taylynn."

"Princess Taylynn?" Her eyebrows knitted together. "I don't remember meeting any princesses while I was there. There was a Prince Feowen."

"Prince Feowen is her brother. She must have been away when you were there." He hesitated. "Queen Jade informed me of your meeting when you traveled through the forest, of your words alone together, of her knowledge that you carried the dragonstones from the beginning. She knew she could trust you because she sensed something spriten about you, though she didn't realize it at the time."

"Oh..." She tried to recall the details of their conversation together. It seemed so long ago now.

"Jade believes that spriten blood flows through your veins. She believes that you activated it when you were in your deepest time of need. That is the reason for your spriten mark. Every sprite must discover magic for themselves—that is why their children have no markings. You were correct in your theory on that. The sprites have a unique tradition in which they must make a pilgrimage into the forest alone, to discover who they are and what they are capable of. They return with fresh marks, badges, to show the magic they have mastered."

The necklace about her neck pulsed at the same rate of her heart. "So...it's all true then? I knew it!"

The track they followed took them to a copse of trees. Talon led her around the trees before returning to the track.

"There is more," he said. "It seems Queen Jade was not entirely open with me. She made me believe that whatever magic exists for you is something you must obtain on your own, through dire need, just as the sprites do when they venture out into the forest."

"Okay?"

"Princess Taylynn explained more. Sprites do not simply discover their magic, they can also master it through practice, through lessons with their elders that bring out certain parts of them. They can learn *new* magic this way, unlocking new abilities."

"So, they aren't just restricted to quests?"

"According to Princess Taylynn, no. Moreover, their blood magic is much like that of the drengr. The blood exists in one's body in various quantities, from various lines, sometimes diluted, and how you choose to strengthen it is up to you. Even the smallest trace of blood can be strengthened beyond belief. The more you learn and practice, the stronger you become." He hesitated. "There are also ways, according to Taylynn, ways to discover whose blood you carry."

Her jaw dropped and she stopped, forcing Talon to stop as well. "Are you serious?!"

"I hardly understand it myself. And Taylynn spoke in so many riddles I found myself struggling to grasp her meaning. But, I believe that if you were to allow them, they could trace your ancestry to whichever sprite you came from."

"Princess Irelia?!" she gasped.

Talon chuckled. "Let's not jump to conclusions. Princess Irelia wasn't entirely a sprite, remember? Her father was our first drengr king." He hesitated. "Besides, Taylynn mentioned nothing of Irelia. As far as we know, she died before she reached womanhood, regardless of what you believe. It seems more likely that another sprite, at some point in time, drifted to your world."

Her gut twisted. If ever there was a time to tell Talon about the cave under the keep, it was now. "There's something I need to tell you."

He stopped. "More secrets?"

"Yes." She sighed, as if this was just as much a plague for her as it was him. "There's something hidden under the keep. Something lost, forgotten in time."

"I'm listening."

"We found a cave."

"A cave?" His expression gave nothing away, but his voice echoed his surprise.

She told him how she'd discovered the door in her room and everything that had happened after that. Talon listened in silence. "Anyway, I haven't had a chance to see it myself. Yet."

"I see."

"You're not mad at me for keeping this?" she said at last.

"No. Thank you for telling me." He ran a hand through his mass of hair. "It's unexpected but...I believe you. Will you show me when we return?"

Her heart doubled its rhythm. "Yes, I would love to! Wait until you see everything. There's this shrine-thing, with a big tree made out of stained glass, and it moves by itself, and there is a passage to your tower, and passages that lead to the dining hall, and—"

He laughed. She froze, trying to memorize the sound of him. "I hope you know how absurd this seems."

She giggled, covering her mouth. "I know. But it's real. I promise."

"You have been busy in my absence. Have you discovered how to get inside the monument beside the broken gate?"

"Oh." Her face fell. "Not yet. I asked Des and Saffra to try in my absence. Maybe they managed it."

"And you think the broken gate explains why you could be carrying Irelia's blood?"

"It would make sense. What if Irelia went through and disappeared? I told you about Saffra's vision. I'm not certain they ever found her body."

"But how do we know the gate wasn't broken from the beginning?"

"Why would Queen Isabella build a shrine-thing beside it?"

"What makes you so certain that she did? It could be older than Isabella."

"I suppose anything is possible. I think she broke the gate herself, so that no one else would use it."

"Broke it out of grief for her missing daughter? Or, even anger?"

"I never thought about it that way. But as a mother, wouldn't she want to go after her daughter?"

"Hmm. Perhaps. People in Dragonwall have always feared your world. Some legends say that the gates were created for evil purposes by the asarlaí, long before Dragonwall was ever called Dragonwall. It is rumored that they were created to send all people of non-magical abilities through. A purge, if you will."

Goosebumps crawled over her skin. "Oh, gods! I saw them."

"Who?"

"The asarlaí." Her hand flew to her mouth. "That's it. How could I have missed that? When I came through the gate for the first time, I touched it and...and...I don't know. I think it gave me a flashback—like a vision of the past. I saw a line of prisoners in chains being led through it. And the asarlaí, one of them looked at me with his red eyes." She shuddered at the memory. "I swear he saw me."

"Gods above, Claire! How many secrets have you been keeping?!"

"I didn't mean to." She turned to him, brightening. "Thank goodness we have our walks together. Maybe I can finally get everything off my chest."

He huffed. "I should hope so."

"But back to Irelia, though. Do you think it's possible?"

He exhaled. "With you, I'm starting to believe anything is possible."

They fell quiet. Their walk was drawing to an end. They had already passed several quaint cottages lining the way back into Brezen. Talon led her off the path, in the direction of camp.

"Taylynn wants you to train with the sprites," he said out of nowhere.

"What?!" She faltered. Something squeezed her chest, a heavy longing, a desire to see the forest again. "You mean, I get to go back?"

"No." He scowled. "Absolutely not. Do you think I would let you out of my sight again?"

She opened and closed her mouth. "So, you'll disregard her advice? Why would you even bother telling me if that's the case? Or will she send sprites to the capital to train me?"

"No, she will not send anyone to you. She was adamant that you must go to them, that there are things to be learned in the forest. Teachers. Elders. The forest itself. Perhaps even the king tree."

She flushed. "And yet, you refuse? Talon, Hiondel died because of me. And Lily, too. I wasn't strong enough. Mastering my sprite magic means I won't make that mistake again."

"You are my ward, Claire. My responsibility. If I hand you off to those *tree-huggers*, I will never see you again. How, then, can I protect you?"

Something clicked into place.

"Talon, have you grown fond of me? Is that why?" His posture went rigid. The muscles in his arm tightened beneath her fingers. "Don't let your feelings interfere with what needs to be done."

"What makes you sure we should trust them, Claire? That we should trust Taylynn? Besides, you're not even full sprite."

"No, perhaps not. But drengr magic doesn't feel right to me. Sprite magic does. What good am I, if I cannot wield what I am meant to? It is my birthright, isn't it?"

"Birthright or not, I cannot allow it." He looked away, refusing to meet her gaze. "This...it is too sudden for me. And you know how stubborn I am."

She huffed. "You? *Stubborn?*" She gave him a hard prod in the shoulder to get his attention. "I'm stubborn too, you know."

"Oh, believe me, I do." He pulled her along again, leading her through camp to the command tent. "This is where I will leave you. Bedelth and I have business with Sir Wentworth."

"So that's it, then? End of discussion? Your answer is simply *no*?" She tried to keep her voice under control.

"Correct."

As angry as she wanted to be, she schooled her features. Two could play this game. He could not keep her from this.

"Well then, Your Majesty, I suppose there is always tomorrow. Perhaps I will convince you then. Or the day after. Or the day after that. Because you're stuck with me now, remember? Ninety-eight more nights to go. And I'm going to ask you over and over again until you're sick of it."

A smile pulled at the corners of his lips, transforming his hard expression. "Until tomorrow, then." He bowed low, holding her gaze, then turned on his heel and strode away.

"Talon!" she called after him, giving him pause. He glanced over his shoulder. "Thank you for the thoughtful gift. I love it." Her hand went to the pendant on her chest.

"I am glad," he said, then disappeared into camp.

～

THE FOLLOWING day passed in a blur. Everyone ate breakfast together before she and Tamara walked the camp, speaking with Fort Squall's people. That afternoon, she found a package on her cot wrapped in brown paper. Talon's other gifts. The first item was a pair of soft brown fabric boots with reinforced soles. She slipped them on, sighing. They came up to the top of her calves, gently hugging her skin. She paced around the tent, rolling her ankles and bunching her toes to get a feel for them. A perfect fit. More comfortable than any shoes she'd ever owned.

The next was a dagger with a blade half a foot long. She held it in her hands, staring in disbelief. She hadn't expected a weapon, but welcomed the thrill. Unlike Cyrus's sword, this truly belonged to her, was intended for her. She could feel it when she took the handle and pulled it from the sheath. The craftsmanship was beautiful. Luminescent markings spanned the length of the blade, glowing blue-green like her own. Magic woven into the metal. She tucked it away and examined the rest of the package's contents.

There were two spriten gowns like the silver one she had back in the capital. One was a light blue, the other a deep purple. Both fabrics shimmered with a silken sheen that caught the light with movement. They were nothing like traditional gowns worn by women in Dragonwall. More of a modernized toga, cut low in front, and nearly transparent. Desaree would not approve. Both showed too much skin. That wouldn't stop her from wearing them.

There was also a silver comb—Desaree *would* approve of that. She smiled and tucked the gifts away. Except for the boots. She kept those on her feet, and the dagger, which she fastened to the belt at her waist.

Talon was in a hurry to be away, to leave Brezen and begin their journey. She could tell as much during their walk later that night. He spoke of his longing to be back in Kastali Dun, his worries about the city. He loved his people more deeply than she had ever imagined.

A nervous energy settled over her at the thought of flying with him. It was hard to say why. While Dragonwall considered such acts as intimate as sex, she did not. Yet, he was Dragonwall's king. Not just that, he was a huge beast of a dragon. And she was going to fly upon his back like a queen. That made her smile with delight. Things had certainly changed so dramatically between them. Their past relationship seemed a distant dream.

When they reached the camp, she was almost sad their walk had passed so quickly. "Have you given our discussion any further thought?" she asked. The necklace at her throat hummed in response. "You know I must train with the sprites. I must master my magic."

"I have—too much thought." His words were measured. "But... ask me again tomorrow. Perhaps I will have a better answer for you." When he looked down at her, his face gave nothing away.

She nodded. "Very well then. Be sure that I will."

There were still a few bargaining chips left, after all, and he did not own her.

They reached the central tent. "Get a good night of sleep. I'll have Bedelth wake you at dawn. Our departure will be hurried. I hope to be back in the capital in four days, perhaps less if the wind is in our favor."

"You're not coming in?" She frowned, glancing between his hulking frame and the tent flaps. She had almost hoped...well, never mind.

"I have a few final matters of business with Sir Wentworth. I'll see you in the morning." He bowed and departed. She was left to watch his retreat until he disappeared among the tents.

CHAPTER 29

A BOND UNVEILED

Brezen

Claire jolted awake as something soft smacked her chest. Bedelth peered through the tent flap, smirking. She glanced down. "A pillow?! Really?"

"Time to get up," he barked, then disappeared.

She grumbled, stretching her muscles before getting to her feet. She was one day closer to sleeping in a real bed again—to waking up without aching muscles.

"Ughhh," Tamara grumbled beside her, rising from her own cot. "I could sleep for hours more."

"Same!" she agreed. "But preferably in a feathered bed."

"A feathered bed." A dreamy look stole over Tamara's features.

Tamara helped her get ready, packing up her remaining belongings. "You're sure you have everything?"

"Positive."

"Well, I suppose we won't be separated for *too* long," Tamara said. "I never imagined I would see the capital. Promise that when I arrive, you will show me around?"

"I promise."

They hugged then linked arms, walking to the field beside their camp. Her heart began to race. Talon and Bedelth were already assembled, along with Fort Kastali's other twenty pairs, those who'd escorted Talon to Esterpine. He walked between them, speaking casually with each pair. He looked tense. Their eyes connected and he froze, then nodded before moving away to transform.

Iridescent black scales sprouted from his skin like armor. His body expanded, swelling outward in a matter of seconds. A pleased roar escaped his jaws as his forelegs settled on the ground, talons ripping furrows in the soil.

"He's quite a bit bigger than the others, isn't he?" It wasn't necessarily a compliment. "How am I supposed to climb up something so large?"

"With poise and grace," Tamara whispered, nudging her. "Don't worry. You'll be fine. Good luck."

"Thanks," she whispered, giving Tamara's arm a final squeeze.

Adjusting her pack she strode across the field. Talon had settled himself a comfortable distance away from the others. She set her pack down beside his foreleg and looked up at him. Her head fell back, taking in the dark mountain she was supposed to climb. The harness straps were out of reach, but if she vaulted up his foreleg, she could grab ahold of them. There were also straps to fasten her pack.

"May I help you with that?" Bedelth appeared beside her. He eyed Cyrus's sword but said nothing.

"Sure, thanks."

He climbed onto Talon's forearm like a pro, fastening it in seconds, then strode off before she could thank him. Seconds later, he waited in his orange dragon form.

Talon's massive head swung around. His forked tongue flicked out like a snake's, tasting the air. She eyed him, frowning. He snorted, enveloping her in a small plume of smoke. "All right. All right. I'm going."

Taking several steps back for a running start, she sprinted

towards him and gracefully leapt into the air, placing her feet on his foreleg and vaulting upward to grab the straps of the harness. Her body collided with his. Her skin made contact with his scales. There was a brief instant where she felt the warmth of him before the jolting realization that she was still in motion. Falling. Falling. Falling....

Her heart stopped.

The world around her pitched and heaved, sending her right through the blackness of Talon's scales into something...more. She couldn't breathe. Why couldn't she breathe?!

"Claire...?" The richness of Talon's voice echoed in her mind.

"Talon?" She vaguely registered his presence. Where had everything gone? Where were the others? Where was *she*?

She panicked, taking in the world around her. Each breath was thick and heavy. She coughed.

"What's...happening?"

"It's all right." Talon's calm voice was meant to reassure her. It didn't.

"Where are you? I can't see you..."

She stood in a lava field, hues of red, orange, and black, stretched out in every direction, all the way to the horizon. She could feel the heat of it through the soles of her feet. *"Talon, I—"*

"Claire, stop panicking." The lava beside her gurgled and bubbled until it popped, burping up red-orange liquid.

She shrank away from it. Had he done this? Had he tricked her? Transported her to a Hawaiian volcano?

"Nothing of the sort. You are in my mind."

"Your mind?!" The landscape was harsh and inhospitable. She could barely breathe without choking on fumes?

"Claire, listen to me. You're in my mind. Please...stop panicking. Take a deep breath. Can you do that?" His words reminded her of the time she had been kidnapped, when he had coaxed her to calm down. Except this time, she was struggling.

"I..." She looked for him, for his glittering black form. It sounded as if he were right beside her.

"Deep breaths," he reminded her.

She nodded, inhaling deeply—in then out. She began to relax. None of this made any sense, but if she wasn't dead by now, she was probably okay. And Talon was there with her...somewhere. Somehow.

"*Wait...*" A sliver of realization dawned on her. "*You said this was your mind?*" Her voice echoed, as if she were in a vaulted chamber.

"*Yes. You are in my mind. You're safe.*"

"*But I don't...how?! Did I fall into your body? Where your dragon fire lives?*"

He chuckled. She felt it as a rumble that reverberated up through the soles of her feet. Several lava bubbles popped. She stepped away from them.

"*I can see why you would think that. But no, you are simply in my mind, not my body. Claire...I wanted to tell you. I tried...*"

She backed away without watching where she stepped. There was a squelching sound as her left foot sank into a puddle of lava. "*Ugh!*" It did not burn as she expected, but it was warm, comfortably warm. She caught a brief flash of a memory. Talon speaking to a woman with dark hair and silvery eyes like his. His mother.

She pulled free and the memory vanished. Her foot came away clean. She placed her hand against her chest to calm her racing heart. "*Was that...?*" She took another deep breath. "*How is this possible?*"

Her fear subsided, replaced by awe. She took a better look around, seeing her surroundings in a new light. Even though she couldn't see him, she could see everything that made Talon who he was. The entire lava field was alive.

"*It's magnificent. This place.*" Smiling, she turned in a circle. But why?! Why was she here?

"*Because you are my mate.*"

"*Your...your mate?*" She stepped forward, moving to a safer patch of dried, blackened lava. His words didn't quite sink in. "*But I can't be, Talon. That's...*"

"*Impossible? I know. I thought so, too.*"

Her stomach fluttered. Talon had failed to find his mate, failed after hundreds of years because his mate had never been born in Dragonwall. Her chest squeezed.

Buying time to think, she went down on one knee and dipped her hand into a pool of lava. She was enveloped in another memory. The forest surrounded her, familiar and inviting. She sighed with desire. With longing.

The face of a spriten woman swam into view. Princess Taylynn.

You're sure of it? Talon asked the princess.

Positive, Taylynn answered. *Claire is your mate as surely as I am a sprite. The king tree never lies.*

She ripped her hand from the lava, eyes growing wide. *"What is this?"* she whispered, not quite believing what she'd just seen.

"You weren't supposed to see that."

"She...she knew? Taylynn knew and she told you? And you didn't tell me?"

She stepped farther away from the lava holding the memory. The thought of it tasted like ash on her tongue, bitter and charred. She wanted to spit it out, to pretend she hadn't seen it. To pretend it hadn't tainted her.

"How could you keep something like this from me, Talon?"

"Claire, I—"

"No! You...you lied to me!" Her heart pounded.

He had kept this from her, this thing, this important piece that tied them together. If Princess Taylynn had been the one to tell him, then he had known for days. Known ever since arriving in Brezen, and even before then.

Pieces clicked into place. The way he'd treated her. The way he'd seemed so different.

Hurt spread through her chest, painful and piercing. It felt like betrayal. *"Am I worth so little that you couldn't tell me? Why...why would you do that?"*

"Claire, please! I never intended to hurt you. I tried—"

"No!" she hissed, shaking her head, backing away. Something pierced her mind—something foreign. She gasped. If she was in his mind, that meant he was in hers too! Or, he was trying to be. She

wouldn't let him. Her mind belonged to her and her alone! It was the last place she had to herself.

Cyrus, help! She cried.

In this, I can no more help you than you can help yourself, Cyrus said. *Remove your hand if it pains you so much.*

My...my hand? Realization swept over her. She wasn't *really* in a lava field. She was touching Talon's scales.

"*No, Claire. Please. Let me explain. I did not—*"

She jerked her hand away and the dark world vanished. She blinked against the dawn's light, against tears that blurred her eyes. She was still hanging, dangling from the harness strapped to Talon's back. How much time had passed? Seconds? Minutes? It felt like an eternity.

Shocked and confused, she released the harness, careful not to touch him again as her body slid down his. Her feet landed on his forearm. Without further contact, she jumped away from him, trying to understand what had happened.

He had lied to her! Lied by omission, yes, but it made little difference.

"Fly yourself back to Kastali Dun," she said, her voice cutting. "I'll walk the distance with Tamara and the rest of the camp."

She fled, sprinting away from everyone, away from the camp, away from the field, to be alone. An angry roar split the air behind her. Moments later she heard him, chasing after her. Hands from behind wrapped around her waist, stopping her.

Talon grabbed her and spun her around to face him. "Claire, please! *Please!*" His eyes were wide. The scars on his face were pale, white lines.

"No!" She struggled against him, trying to get free. He didn't budge, keeping a firm hold of her. "Let me go!" she cried, but he didn't. Her breaths turned shallow, coming faster, until she was on the brink of hyperventilating. "You hid this from me!" she gasped. "For days! You had so many opportunities but you...you—" A sob escaped her chest, cutting off the rest of her tirade.

He pulled her against his chest, pressing her against him. "Shh, please, don't…I didn't mean… It was never my intention… I tried—"

"You tried?" Her voice came out muffled against his tunic. "You had plenty of opportunities!"

"You're right." His arms tightened, as if afraid that if he didn't hold on to her now, he would lose her forever. "You're right. I may have failed the other night, but I should have told you. I should have made the time to say something. I…I made a mistake. I'm sorry, Claire. I messed up."

She stopped fighting him, going limp as his apology sank in. Apologies weren't something he did very well, but this time, he held nothing back. Not like the last time when it had taken months. This time it had taken mere minutes, and she wasn't prepared for that.

"You're sorry? You mean that?"

"Yes. I'm sorry. So, so sorry. I've done a lot of stupid things in my lifetime, but perhaps this might be the stupidest."

A strangled sound bubbled up from her chest, half sob, half laugh. She suppressed it. "It's too much," she said at last, over-whelmed by the elephant in the room. The fact that they were mates. "I had no warning. I…I wasn't ready."

"I know. Shh. It's okay." His hand stroked the back of her head.

"No, it's not! How can you say that? Is it *always* supposed to be like this? This *frightening*?"

He grumbled. "You're asking me? As if I have done this before? Two minds become one. It's different for every pair." He paused. "Claire…"

She pulled back to look at him. His arm was still around her waist, unyielding. She saw his face, his scars. His expression was strained.

"I really am sorry," he added. She nodded and wiped her eyes on her sleeve, aware of how ridiculous the two of them must appear to those watching. "I never wanted to hurt you. Gods! You're the last person in the world I want to hurt. It seems I have a good habit of it. Can you forgive me for this? I was scared."

"Scared of *what*?" She scowled.

"Of...of everything! Gods! Don't you see?! I have been alone for centuries. Convinced that living mateless was part of my curse, convinced that even if I had a mate, she would be forced to live with my...with my scars. With...me." His words came out bitter. "My life was exactly where I wanted it."

"Well gee, I'm sorry I came along then."

"No!" His arms tightened, keeping her flush against him. She arched to get a better look at him. "That is not what I meant. Look, as sudden as this is for you, can't you see it is just as overwhelming for me? I...I'm doing a poor job of explaining myself, aren't I?"

"I...no...I mean, yes. I think I understand your meaning."

Maybe she had overreacted. Perhaps a smidge. But he *had* kept a massive secret hidden from her. Then again, hadn't she done the same? More than once?

"I'm sorry I got so angry with you," she said at last. A strangled laugh escaped her chest. "I guess this is just a lot for both of us."

"Indeed." His chest deflated. "But thank you. That means a great deal. For what it's worth, I understand your reaction. I should have told you." He tucked her head beneath his chin, holding her against him. "I have known for five days and I'm still struggling to comprehend it. When my parents died, it took months to internalize the severity of it. I would wake up in the morning believing they were still alive. Then reality would sink in, and each day was as bleak as the last. And my scars—knowing that I would always be ugly. That took a long time, too. Big events sink in slowly for me. But *us*? Mates? I can't seem to fathom it."

"Me either," she whispered, her voice thick with emotion.

"I'm not used to having a bossy female in my life, you know. Not until you came along."

"I am not bossy!" She tried to push against his chest.

"You're not?"

"Okay, maybe a little. But only when I have to be. And maybe if you weren't so ridiculous all the time. Besides, you're bossier than me."

"Fine. Noted." He huffed against her hair. "You know, I thought perhaps our walks together might make it easier for me to tell you.

Admittedly, I did not want to believe Taylynn when she told me. I was certain that when you touched me, nothing would happen. That's partly why I didn't say anything."

"That…makes sense, I guess."

"Can you imagine me telling you, only to be wrong? I spent years hoping, searching, only to be let down, until I finally accepted who I am, what I am. I finally accepted my life. Being alone."

Her stomach sank like a stone. "Talon, you don't have to be alone anymore. Not with me. Don't you see? Everything has changed. *Everything*." She sniffled, brushing the last of the wetness from her eyes as she leaned away from him. She needed to see his face, now more than ever.

"Yes, it has." He sighed, looking down at her, studying her for several long moments. "I know this is a lot. It will take time, which we hardly have. All we can do is digest it in due course. And for the record, I'm not letting you walk back to Kastali Dun, even if I have to carry you in my claws the whole way. So you can either fly on my back, or choose a less dignified manner. Which do you prefer?"

Her lips parted. "You wouldn't dare!"

"Oh, I would."

She exhaled. "Fine. The dignified option, please. But does that mean I have to go back to the lava field?"

"Lava field?" His brow furrowed, making his scars more pronounced.

"Well, yeah. Your mind."

"A lava field? That's what you saw?"

"Um…I take it that's not normal?"

He kissed her forehead before releasing her. It was such a tender gesture, that she blinked in surprise. He didn't appear to notice the severity of it as he said, "No idea. But no, you don't have to go back to the lava field if you do not wish to. You were fighting me, fighting what was happening, which is why our minds didn't meld properly. I felt yours but I could not get inside of it."

"Why?"

"Perhaps because of your fear." He shrugged. "Normally,

people are prepared for this sort of thing. They long for it. They aren't fearful."

"Oh. Makes sense, I guess."

"I won't force you into anything, Claire. I will never force you into anything. Wear gloves if you cannot bear to touch me."

Her stomach hardened. "It's not like that, Talon. I...don't mind touching you." In fact, right now she wanted to quite badly.

Sparks filled his gaze. "Nor I, you. Shall we?"

She nodded and took his arm. They walked back to the others. Tamara and Byron lingered at the field's edge, watching. No one made any comment on their strange behavior. Thank the gods for that!

When Talon transformed, she noticed that her pack was still tied to his harness. She repeated the process of vaulting onto his back. This time she was quicker about it. As she came into contact with his scales, there was a brief flash of the lava field, this time accompanied by an overwhelming feeling of relief, which must have come from him, and then she was settled, strapping herself in. As long as she didn't touch him with her bare skin, they remained separate. When she fastened the final buckle, she considered everything.

Talon—her mate. *Hers.* Her thoughts scrambled and her heart fluttered with delight. She looked down at him, taking in his monstrous size, the way his inky scales shimmered from green to blue in the dawning sun.

"Mine..." she breathed, taking in the monumental reality of it.

She would never have to share him. What they had built together would always belong to them. All it had taken was a simple touch, and everything had changed.

She lifted her hand, tentative but determined, and let it hover just above his scales. A spike of exhilaration shot through her. And longing—a need to be complete—as if she had realized for the first time that part of her was missing. All she wanted, all she needed, was right here.

Her skin tingled. The forest tear upon her neck thrummed. She let her hand fall upon Talon's scales, this time, prepared.

The lava field rushed up around her, more beautiful than before. She did not fear it or fight it. She welcomed it. This was Talon at his deepest and most fundamental—a perfect reflection of the person that he was. Each rut running through the dried, blackened lava was a scar upon his soul. Each gnarled formation was a torment he had endured. Between these formations were the many memories that defined him. Some good. Some bad. It was like seeing him for the first time, his soul split open for the taking. Split open for her. In that moment, she knew that she wanted every broken piece, every misshapen fragment, every pool of memory. All of him.

The stifling heat cleared. Clouds rolled back to reveal a brilliant blue sky. Her acceptance gave way to awareness. The lava field evaporated around her until she was looking upon their world again as the sun rose higher. Her hand still rested on Talon's scales, but instead of seeing blacks and reds, she saw him. And he was there in her mind, too, and she was in his, sharing emotions and feelings. In her blood, she still felt the heat of his inferno, like a great pool of desire. And it was in this moment she understood what the drengr had meant about the intimacy of flying together—truly flying.

"But we are not flying yet," he said, reading her thoughts. *"Are you ready?"*

"Yes." Her heart skipped forward. Pure undulated joy clutched her. She was going to fly with Dragonwall's king. And she would fly with him not as an outsider, but as his mate.

Talon gave the signal, lifting his head to roar, and there was triumph in it. Not merely a signal to depart, but a signal of victory. The sound shook her body. He leapt into the sky, unfurling black, leathery wings. She exhaled, placing both hands on the harness, separating their minds to grip the leather. As the ground sped away, she spared a glance for Tamara and Byron. They were specks below her. She lifted her hand to wave before they disappeared from view.

Then, because she could, she placed her hand against Talon again.

"*Yes?*" His voice was rich, decadent, alluring.

"*Just wanted to make sure you were still there,*" she said. It was hard to keep the smile from her face.

"*I will always be here.*"

When she next looked down, the camp was a smudge. The entirety of Brezen disappeared until there was only barren landscape and open sky. For the first time in her life, she knew with absolute certainty exactly where she belonged. The calm that came with knowing was more profound than anything she could have hoped for.

CHAPTER 30

THE WAY OUT

Shadowkeep

Mikkin looked down at his plate of food, cringing. It was a pile of lumpy gray mush with a watery substance leaking from it. And of course, he was given no utensils.

"You call this food?!" he shouted after the guard, who had already disappeared down the corridor. His stomach rumbled in desperation, but he refused to give in. Not yet. He'd rather starve.

It was impossible to tell how many days had passed in a place like this. He'd taken to observing the frequency of food and water brought periodically. He'd received three servings thus far.

Each day felt like an eternity spent dwelling on his thoughts of what could have been. As he dozed in and out of delirious consciousness, he forgot Mardra was dead. He pictured what it would be like to come home to his sons after a day of hunting. What their cottage looked like. The garden out in front.

Then he remembered where he was and what he had lost.

He looked down at his food again. "Might as well call it poison instead of food," he grumbled.

A wheezing laugh sounded from across the corridor. "You'll be hard pressed to get much better round here," Berbik said, shuffling into sight. There was nothing but bitterness in the dwarg's voice. He had in been Shadowkeep's dungeons for years. One look at him was enough to see that.

Mikkin grunted. "Suppose you've just given up and eat whatever they give you, eh? Gray mush and all?"

"Might as well." Berbik shrugged. "It 'ent bad once you're hungry enough, you'll eat the dirt off your cell floor to stay alive." Mikkin grunted at that. "Fight it, but nothing will change. That's how things are down here. Be happy you haven't been entirely forgotten. All the other cells beside us have. You 'ent heard nothing from them, have you? Key master only brings two plates down."

"Maybe I *want* to be forgotten," he said. "Not like I have anyone to go home to. And anyway, when Kane returns, I'm in for torture and whatever else. Rather starve down here first." He shuddered. Torture would be bad, and the sorcerer would have tricks up his sleeve that took pain to another level. "What of you, Berbik? Anyone to return home to?"

There was a long pause. "Doubt it. I did, once..."

In the past few days, Berbik had painted a sad picture for himself. Mikkin knew little about dwargs, except that they were highly regarded for their mining and shaping of ice metal. The Northern Barrier Range was a vast place. It was said the dwargs had dwellings throughout the range, hidden underground. He'd heard more stories than most, being from the north, but they were still vague. Stories about the dwargs' metal-working skills. Stories about their ability to navigate underground mines and sniff out shafts. Stories about their strength. He never believed he would meet one.

He gazed at Berbik. "In all your time down here, don't suppose you've worked out a way to escape?" His eyes darted to the lock on his cell with a deep sense of longing. He knew what Berbik's answer would be, but decided it was worth asking, if only to make polite conversation.

"Escape?! You? Ha!" Berbik paused. "You got places to go? People to see? Thought you said there was no one left."

Mikkin snorted. "That may be, but I'd like to see the daylight again." Which told him there was still an inkling of hope hiding within him. He thought about Jamie out on his own, waiting for him. "Besides, I got work to do."

"The dragons? Yes, well, good luck there. Even if you managed to get your door open, you'd have a right time getting out of Shadowkeep."

"How do you mean?" He perked up.

"Well, to start, Shadowkeep was built by the dragons and their minions, carved with magic. It's a dragon fortress, a stronghold, with vaulted ceilings and single rooms as large as a king's hall. More importantly, it's high up on the mountain. You can only reach its entrance through flight."

A deep frown settled over Mikkin's face. "The dragons were already gone when I was brought up here. So then..." He fell silent. "How *did* they get me up? I saw servants. A man brings me my food. There are obviously others living here. They've got to get up and down *somehow*."

"Oh yes. They've built a lift, but it takes more 'an one man to operate it. One has to pull the rope for the other, and vice versa. You thinkin' you might convince some of them servants to let you down, huh? Or are you planning to throw yourself off the cliffs and hope the height doesn't kill you?"

A pit welled in his stomach. For a long time, he was quiet. Even if he managed to escape his cage, he would be stuck inside of Shadowkeep's fortress until Kane discovered him wandering the halls. Unless he could convince a servant to help. That would surely earn a more severe punishment. But he had to try something!

"Aren't dwargs supposed to be strong?" he asked after a while. His question earned a grunt. "Can't you bend your bars wide enough to squeeze through?"

"You're a daft one, you are."

"Suppose I am..." He shrugged.

"The sorcerer put magic on the bars. Otherwise, I'd have been out of here on my first day."

"I take it you already tried and failed?"

"Look here, if you can find a way to lift such a spell, well then yes, I could bend the bars. Don't suppose you got some hidden magical ability up your sleeve, huh?"

"What if you *did* bend the bars—hypothetically speaking. If two are required to operate the lift, one of us gets out and the other doesn't."

"Oh, goodie. You're not as daft as I thought."

"So, it's hopeless either way." Again, he fell quiet. He refused to believe that no solution existed. All his life he'd been trained to survive, living on the outskirts of Belnesse, looking to the forest for sustenance. He was trained to look at a situation from all sides until the proper outcome presented itself. That's all he could do here, until one became apparent.

He started to doze off, his back against the wall, when Berbik spoke again. "There could be another way." The dwarg's voice was so quiet he almost didn't hear. He jolted awake. "Suppose I do get the bars bent. Suppose we do get out. There could be another way out. Down...instead of up."

"Deeper into Shadowkeep? A secret exit?" His heart thudded against his chest.

"I wouldn't call it *that*. I don't even know if such a thing exists."

"What makes you think it does then?"

When Berbik didn't answer, he thought he had stumped the dwarg. But at last, Berbik said, "Stories. Stories from my people."

"Rumors?" Mikkin would hang his hat on a rumor, if it came to it.

"It's said that long ago, when the clans ruled this land, they had many dealings with the dwargs. The Ice Clan especially, coexisting peacefully with my people. We often traded. Many tunnels exist that link our great cities together beneath the mountains. We aren't suited for long periods above ground, especially not through snow. The sun isn't kind up there. And with snow, we'd freeze to death, most likely, before we ever made it anywhere.

"But in the tunnels, we found our best way to travel. If I managed, I might find those leading away from Shadowkeep. Those long forgotten. But even then, wandering around for days, maybe even weeks in the dark. Not even rats down that deep. We'd starve."

He ignored the starving part as his mind began turning over, slowly at first, and then faster. "So, you think that there has to be some way out—one of these tunnels? It would make sense. If your people traded with the dragons here, they had to get in and out of the fortress somehow. Like an old road. Hm..."

Berbik said nothing in return. He didn't answer for a long time. When he emitted a snore, it was obvious he had fallen asleep. At last, Mikkin did the same.

ANOTHER DAY PASSED. And then another. And another. Mikkin spent most of it curled in a ball drifting in and out of his waking dreams. Without food, his energy was too low to do much else. He turned lethargic. If he didn't get out soon, he wouldn't last much longer.

The familiar approach of the guard roused him. Perhaps this time he was hungry enough to eat. He pushed the old tray out of his cell in preparation. The appearance of the now spoiled mash turned his stomach. He would have vomited had there been anything in his belly. On second thought, perhaps never mind about eating. Tomorrow, possibly.

The guard's footsteps came closer, then stopped. A loud clatter echoed off the walls. He was slow to jump, slow to register the change.

"Gods above!" someone cried. "Mikkin?! Mikkin?! You down here?"

His eyes widened. He climbed to his feet, wrenching himself up using the bars. "Jamie? That you lad?" He kept his voice low. "How in the gods' hell did you get down here?" His heart raced. He wasn't sure if he should rejoice or despair. Had Jamie been captured too? He would never forgive himself if that was true.

He shoved his face through the bars, trying to look down the hall. Jamie came into view. "Found him!" Jamie called over his shoulder to someone unseen. Unka perhaps? If so, he owed that little goblin a huge thanks. Six people came into view behind the lad—three females and three males. His eyes widened. Behind the six newcomers trailed Unka.

"Jamie?! How in the gods' names...? I can't..." He was at a loss. "Gods, I owe you! Nice to see you again, Unka," he added.

Jamie offered a wide grin. His skin was chapped and cracked when he smiled. "I'll explain later. We've got to get you out of here. Lord Averaen believes Kane could be back any minute. We were lucky to find him gone."

"Lord Averaen?" He frowned.

"That'd be me," one of the males grunted, stepping forward. "Lucky is one way to put it. I will be no match for the sorcerer, if he returns."

Averaen was the oldest. His hair and beard were white, but his face showed minimal wrinkles. He was of a strong build, tall and muscled. Even in his old age, he was powerful. The female standing beside him was younger in appearance, but still older than all the others.

Mikkin frowned. "You...you're the leader of Fort Edge, aren't you? But...what the hell are you doing here?"

"As the lad said, we'll explain later." Lord Averaen closed the distance to Mikkin's bars. "Got to get you out of here first. Lucky we found Jamie, else you'd be stuck down here, since we had no intention of entering this place once we found it. Now, let me see about this." He placed his hand over the lock and began muttering words under his breath—magical incantations of some kind. He did this for a long while. The longer he took, the more strained his expression grew.

"Perhaps I can try?" A female stepped forward—a rider.

"Damn it to hell!" Lord Averaen exhaled. "No, Jenna, it's no use. It's not my strength—nothing to do with that. Damned sorcerer imbued it with some kind of anti-opening magic. Everything I try doesn't work." He slammed his palm against the lock.

A throat cleared behind them.

"Oh." Mikkin had forgotten all about the dwarg. "I should probably introduce you to Berbik. Berbik? Meet my...er...rescuers."

Lord Averaen turned. "Aha! A dwarg. No surprise. Suppose you want out too?"

Berbik let out a sound between a grunt and a laugh. "Unless I plan to die here, Master Drengr. Yes."

An idea came to Mikkin's mind. "Berbik can bend the bars! He said Kane placed some kind of magic that kept him from bending them. Perhaps—"

"—if we focus on removing the magic from the bars rather than breaking the lock mechanism, Berbik might bend them," Lord Averaen finished. "Is that possible, Berbik?"

"Just a hunch," Berbik admitted, shrugging beneath his cascades of hair. "I can bend the bars, most certainly, but removing the magic that makes them stronger—not sure about that."

Lord Averaen nodded. The female beside him remained watchful, a sense of deep intelligence lurking beneath her gaze as he doled out orders. "Ceget, Osorro, Jenna? You're some of our best with magic. Give it a try." Two drengr and the rider from before moved over to Berbik's cell and began muttering again. They placed their hands against the bars while they spoke. A faint blue glow spilled from their palms, washing over the bars.

"Well I'll be damned," Lord Averaen mused. "Looks like it's working." The three stepped away, their chests heaving. Whatever they had done had taken its toll.

Berbik stepped up and placed his hands on the bars. "I ain't got the same energy I once did. Poor diet and all. Let's see." He took a deep breath and then his arms tensed. His face grimaced. At first, nothing happened. Then a metallic groan filled the air. Ever so slightly, the bars began to bend.

"It's working!" Jamie cried. "Look at that!"

Berbik continued to strain. The more he pulled, the farther the bars moved, a small measure at a time. He had to stop twice to breathe, but at last, the bars were far enough apart for him to squeeze through.

Berbik set foot in the corridor. Almost instantly, a rumble shook the mountain like an earthquake. Everyone froze, eyes wide, motionless, listening, waiting. Silence followed.

"What the hell was that?!" Jamie whispered, looking back and forth.

"Don't look at me!" Mikkin held up his hands. "It's never happened before."

"It's him," Berbik hissed. "Kane. He's back."

"What?" Mikkin's voice was strangled. "How...how do you know?"

"Hurry, remove the spells on Mikkin's bars. Quick!" the fort leader barked.

"It's the mountain," Berbik continued. "Dragons never liked asarlaí sorcerers. Remember the old stories? They hunted them down. Butchered 'em. Shadowkeep knows it—remembers it. Every time he returns, the mountain trembles in greeting. In anger."

Mikkin's stomach dropped. "You're sure, Berbik? Sounds made up to me." If Kane was back, there was no way the drengr were getting them out without having to pass through Shadowkeep.

Berbik's nostrils flared. "I just know, all right? We dwargs guard our history and the history of Dragonwall fiercely." Berbik turned to Lord Averaen. "Kane's portal isn't far from here, much deeper beneath the mountain. If we're lucky, he will retreat to his chambers long before he realizes you are here. We leave as quickly as possible. But we cannot go up. Not now. He will catch us."

"You have another plan?" Lord Averaen's eyes narrowed.

"Depends on if you brought any food and water with you?"

By the look of it, yes. They had canteens attached to their belts. Pouches that most surely contained dried meat and other rations.

"Berbik said something yesterday about tunnels below Shadowkeep." Mikkin turned to the dwarg. "But how do you know where we might find them?"

"I'm a dwarg, Mikkin. I will use my nose."

Lord Averaen grunted. "Dwargs have supreme sense of navigation in dark places like this—places under the earth. Can I trust you, dwarg? You will not betray us?"

Berbik hesitated, then placed his fist over his heart. "You have freed me, Master Drengr. So too will I free you from this place. I will find us a road through the mountains. A road out. A debt for a debt."

Ceget, Osorro, and Jenna stepped away from Mikkin's bars, their work complete. Sweat dripped down their temples.

Berbik moved forward. He looked at Mikkin and said, "Who would have guessed our talks would amount to more than chat, eh?" Then he placed his hands upon the bars and began prying. His face turned a deep shade of purple. Beads of sweat poured from his brow, mingling with his overgrown beard. It took him twice as long as before, and once the bars were wide enough, he slid down onto the floor in a huff. "Just got to catch my breath, is all."

Mikkin squeezed through to embrace Jamie. "Good to see you, lad. Don't let me underestimate you again, eh?" He felt a rush of adrenaline coursing through him, feeding him energy he didn't think he had. In a few hours, no doubt he'd collapse. But for now, he was too jubilant to worry.

"Wouldn't dream of leaving you," Jamie said, grinning. The lad appeared to have matured a great deal in the past several days.

"Good to see you, Unka," Mikkin said, greeting the goblin who kept a wary distance. Unka nodded but said nothing.

"Enough with the greetings," the fort leader growled. "We can do that later. I don't want to die down here any more than the rest of you." He helped Berbik to his feet. "Any others worth freeing, Master Dwarg?"

"No one else alive on this level. As for the other levels? Who can say. I don't think I can pry any more bars today."

"Very well. Let's go." Lord Averaen motioned them forward.

They passed the guard lying on the floor. The trays were scattered on the ground. Mikkin's stomach growled. "Suppose you might have some food on you, eh, Jamie?"

"Not much. Lord Averaen and his party brought some with them. We left most of our belongings at camp. But we got enough for a few days, if we must ration it." Jamie reached into the pouch at his belt and offered Mikkin a slice of dried meat before passing along his water skin.

"Better than nothing," Mikkin said, taking a bite. The salted meat was delicious to his deprived tongue. It took three bites to finish the entire strip. He licked his fingers clean, not caring that they were dirty. Jamie passed him a second, and then a third. It barely sated his hunger, but he dared not eat too much.

"This way," Berbik said, leading them down a dark corridor. They traveled a ways, then took a right. Then a left. Then down again. Shadowkeep was a maze.

"How do you know which way is which?" Jamie asked.

"I can smell it," Berbik grunted, maintaining his pace. "Deeper places smell different. Dwargs have been trained to sniff them out. Even now, I can tell that *this* tunnel leads down farther than the one we were just in. But we shouldn't talk. Kane could be lurking anywhere."

They fell silent. The idea of Kane lurking in the shadows frightened all.

They went deeper with each turn, one hand on the shoulder in front of them since they couldn't see. There was no longer any light. The sconces and torchlight had diminished ages ago. They didn't want to draw attention by using magic for light.

By Berbik's reasoning, deeper was better. Once they went deep enough, they would find the road leading them away from the mountain. It was impossible for Mikkin to tell which way was which, so he kept his hand firmly planted.

"There," Berbik said after what felt like hours of navigating. "We are at the bottom...I think. *This* road leads west."

How the hell could he sense direction, too?

Mikkin did not bother voicing his surprise, and followed without complaint. It was clear that even the drengr—mighty as they were—were out of their element here. All they could do was take the dark tunnel before them and hope that someday, it might lead them to the light. Hopefully, before they starved to death. Until then, they could do little more than keep walking.

CHAPTER 31

TRAVELING WITH TALON

Eigaden

Claire slid from Talon's back, carefully avoiding skin to scale contact. Her feet stumbled on solid ground, body stiff from hours of disuse. "See you in a bit," she said, shouldering her pack.

He answered with a plume of smoke before taking flight with several others to hunt. She saw to her needs, with a group of females. Gods, she couldn't wait to have her privacy back, and a toilet. A real toilet, not some hole she had to dig in the dirt.

She shielded her gaze against the setting sun, looking out over the landscape. No tree cover for miles, flat land as far as the eye could see, with yellow grasses that grew nearly waist high. It was the kind of wide open place that reminded her of how small she was, of how insignificant. If she squinted, she could make out Talon's form in the distance, hunting. She watched him swoop out of sight.

She kept her sprite dagger attached to her belt, thankful that Talon had thought of such a gift. It felt safer having it in a place like this. Even though she was within shouting distance of plenty of pairs.

Their party selected a stretch of land somewhere on the Eigaden plains near a small stream. When she returned to the others, someone had already magicked the grass flat in the surrounding area and set up a large fire. Smaller cooking fires were spaced about it.

Living in the wide open wasn't easy, but it was made better by magic, thankfully.

"Nice sword," Bedelth said, eying her pack. "Had a chance to use it yet?"

She opened her mouth then frowned. "Not since the vodar attack in Talon's tower."

He nodded. "Some of us are going to practice. I need to get my muscles moving. Care to join me?"

"Me?" She glanced around.

"Yes. Why not?" He appraised her. "Let's see what you're made of."

"You don't have a practice sword? Koldis and Jovari always give me a practice sword, or even a wooden staff."

"Nothing like that around here," he huffed. "No trees. No sticks. If you're concerned, I can blunt my blade with magic." She opened her mouth, then frowned. "Or are you afraid I'll best you in front of the king?" He glanced at the horizon, as if searching for Talon's returning form.

"Like I care about that!" But she did, even though she'd never admit it.

The camp was a flurry of activity. Maybe she could brush off Bedelth's offer and help the others instead. "Well?" he said. "If you're not embarrassed, what are you afraid of then?"

"Nothing." She squared her shoulders. "I accept your challenge. Do your worst."

Bedelth grinned. "I thought so. Come with me."

Of all Talon's shields, Bedelth was the most unfamiliar. She knew next to nothing about him. Talon seemed to appreciate Bedelth's calm presence and often selected him for journeys like this. Yet, something told her a mischievous personality lurked beneath his brown skin and calculating eyes. Perhaps the next several days would afford her an opportunity to get to know him better.

There were others assembled with Sveraks drawn. A few of them were riders, which was less common. She blinked at them in surprise before dropping her things and retrieving Cyrus's sverak.

Bedelth took his blade and began muttering an incantation to blunt the edges.

This ought to be fun, Cyrus said, right on cue. She snorted. *Bedelth is a logical fighter. He determines a weakness and preys upon it. You will have to keep an eye on him, keep good form, watch where you step, do not leave yourself open.*

Is that all?

He ignored her sarcasm. *Bedelth uses feints and tricks. Just be wary.*

She watched the shield, assessing him based on Cyrus's advice. A worm of doubt gnawed its way into her stomach. *Don't suppose you could help me out this time? Since you're obviously so concerned.*

Cyrus was picky in revealing himself. Sometimes he did, sometimes he didn't. As it was, he was already doing her a huge favor by maintaining the mental block that kept her mind intact. It was a blessed relief to live in a quiet world, to hear her own thoughts and no one's words.

I'll step in if I need to, but you should try to do this on your own.

She took several practice swings, making slashes in the air. The blade was powerful and sleek. It was as if she were slicing the air in half.

"I'm ready." She got into position, both hands on the grip.

Bedelth stepped forward, still grinning. Like he knew something she didn't. Damn him. The blade of his sverak looked fuzzy along the edges, blurred, like it was in the process of disappearing into another dimension. She blinked, focusing on it before turning her attention to Bedelth's posture.

"Time to see what you're made of," he baited. They circled. His eyes didn't leave hers. He was looking for an opening, and he must have found one. He lunged forward, sword flicking left. She reacted, swinging to meet him. Too late—it was a trick. He swept around to the right and slammed his blade into her side.

She yelped and leapt backward. Pain radiated through her. She doubled over and waited for it to dissipate. "Gods! At least I know you won't go easy on me," she managed.

"And why would I do that?" he asked, voice flat.

She stood and lunged, bringing Cyrus's sverak down. Bedelth parried, blocking the blow. "Nice try." He shoved her away. "You would do better coming in from the side and taking a shorter swing."

She nodded and moved back, adjusting her grip. She took another swing, this time from the left. He blocked. She swung again. And again. He warded off every blow.

They danced back and forth. He let her take the offensive, letting her tire herself out, before switching roles. Defending each of his blows was trickier and trickier. He moved fast.

Just as Cyrus had warned, he tricked her over and over, drawing her attention away from his true target. She simply couldn't anticipate him. That was something that came from fighting him long enough to know him better. Which was likely what made him one of Dragonwall's most lethal blade wielders in human form.

They moved through cycles, each one ending in her defeat. It took little more than fifteen minutes to wear her down and make her sloppy. "Come on, Claire. Last round. Give it your all."

She nodded and took a deep breath, shaking out her muscles, urging them to hold up a little longer. And no thanks to Cyrus, who didn't bother stepping in. A little help would have been nice. But something told her Cyrus didn't plan on showing himself...not even this time.

Bedelth came at her, bringing his blade down over her head. She met it. The contact was jarring. He swept his blade edge along hers and brought it towards her face. She recalibrated and parried his next four blows in rapid succession. Sweat rolled down her forehead. Her breaths came in gasps.

He swung wide, appearing to trick her again. She responded

slower, waiting to see how his tactic would change. It didn't this time. Almost too slowly, she managed to pull her arm up, but the contact was too close to her body. The follow through sent her stumbling backwards. Tripping over her own feet. Her foot caught on a rock and she fell.

Bedelth continued forward, stepping over her to plant the point of his blade against her. "Dead. You lose." He grinned and stepped away. There wasn't a single bead of sweat upon his brow. The effort had taken nothing from him.

She glared up at him, shooting daggers from her eyes. She hardly noticed the clapping behind them. Their campmates had gathered to watch; she'd been too focused to notice.

Great. Just great. Now she'd made a spectacle of herself.

She found Talon among them, his silver eyes glittering in the setting sun.

"Damn it!" she muttered.

"Good match," Bedelth said, still standing above her. "Not bad, but no Cyrus this time." He offered a hand. She let him pull her to her feet.

"What makes you think that Cyrus wasn't here?"

He laughed. "Because you would have had me on my back in less than two minutes."

"Well, that was quite a show." Talon came up beside her. The small crowd dissipated, giving them privacy. "Perhaps tomorrow, you and I can match our blades?"

She snorted. "Crossing blades with Dragonwall's king? Sounds dangerous." She walked away to store her sverak.

He followed. "Afraid I might beat you?"

"Among other things," she said, shouldering her pack, turning to him. "I'm not sure Cyrus would do me much good against you. I've heard the rumors."

His eyes widened with mock surprise. "Rumors? Do they talk of my greatness?"

"Hah! Full of yourself much?" She gave him a teasing shove and stepped past him.

"Oh, come now. It would be fun, don't you think?" He fell into step with her.

"Fun? That's what you lot call it? I call it hard work. Look at this?" She pulled up her sleeve to show him the large bruise forming on her forearm. "Complements of Bedelth's sverak. Does that look fun to you?"

He growled, his eyes darkening. "Let me heal that for you."

She pulled her forearm out of his grip. "No. It will be healed by the morning."

"Gods, you're stubborn."

"So are you." She lifted her brows in challenge.

He exhaled. "Bruises or not, I want to spar with you."

"Isn't that what we're doing right now?"

"Gods above," he muttered.

"Fine. I'll think about it."

He chuckled. "I knew I'd win you over. Now come on, how about our walk? The food will take time to cook."

"Oh...right." She glanced around their camp. No one paid them any mind. She set her pack down. "All right, *Your Majesty*, lead the way."

He grunted and offered his arm.

They passed the sentries, striding through the tall grass. The silence grew before them. Now that they were alone, she didn't know what to say.

"Interesting day, don't you think?" Talon glanced at her. Just like that, the tension between them popped like a soap bubble.

"Is that the best you've got?" He lifted a shoulder. "I'm not sure discovering a mate bond with Dragonwall's king counts as *interesting*. Unbelievable might be better. Perhaps even impossible?"

"It is a bit much, I know."

She stole a glance at him. "How are you feeling about it? About everything?"

Despite spending their whole day in the sky, she'd barely touched him. It wasn't that she was afraid to share his mind. It was full of valuable knowledge, useful memories, and long sought after answers.

The problem was, if she could see every facet of his mind, he could see hers too. There were a few things she wasn't keen to reveal yet. The biggest was her unbreakable promise to Cyrus. Talon didn't know she was the one who had to kill Kane. As soon as he found out, he wouldn't be happy. She wasn't ready to upset him yet. Things were...surprisingly good right now.

Talon rubbed the back of his neck. "I'm feeling a lot and doing my best to internalize it." He stopped to look at her. "I'm old, Claire —by your standards, I mean. I spent the first hundred years of my life searching. I spent the next two hundred and eighty-three under the impression that you did not exist. That's a long time to believe something and then have that belief upended."

"Yeah, I suppose so." She swallowed. "Have you told Bedelth yet?"

He hesitated. "No. I don't plan to."

"Wait, you don't?" A hot ball of disappointment dropped into her stomach "What about the others, though? Shouldn't we tell them?"

He dropped her arm and rubbed his face with his hands. "We need to keep this between us, for now. No one can know. Not Desaree. Not Saffra. Not Reyr. No one."

She deflated. "Talon I thought...I thought you would be happy about this. That you would want to share it. I mean...you've waited your whole life. It's a big deal, isn't it?"

Was he embarrassed that his mate turned out to be some outsider from another world? Was he ashamed? She couldn't ask because she was too afraid to know the answer.

"Claire..." He took her hand in his, pulling her forward, almost flush with him. Her senses came alive, zeroing in on their contact, on his skin against hers. His fingers laced through hers and her breaths quickened. "Claire..." He said again, softer this time. "I am Dragonwall's king. If the world discovers what you mean to me, what you are to me..." He shook his head. "We are at war. Information is dangerous. Extremely dangerous. Until today, I possessed no obvious weakness. Now my biggest weakness is right here in front of me. You. I would hand over my entire kingdom if Kane found a way to use you against me. Don't you realize what this means? What Kane could do with such power?"

"I..." She had stopped breathing altogether. "But..." She swallowed, trying to form coherent thoughts. His damn thumb wouldn't stop moving against her skin, tracing circles, distracting her. "What if we limit who we tell? Make them swear to keep our secret?"

"It will probably come to that...eventually. For now, our secret may be our biggest weapon. Until we determine what to do with it."

"Talon..." Doubt snaked into her belly. "Everyone saw us this morning. Saw us embracing."

"Yes, they did." He hesitated. "And they will see more of it."

Her chest fluttered. "More?"

"Much more," he all but growled. "But, better that they believe I am fond of you than allow them to understand the full extent of what we are—of what you are to me."

"And what am I to you?" she whispered.

He looked down at her, fire burning in the depths of his silver eyes. The gold flecks in them smoldered. Slowly, he brought her hand to his mouth, kissing her palm, never taking his eyes off hers. "Everything, Claire. You are *everything* to me. And I will never let him take you from me."

They made a wide circuit around the camp, continuing on in comfortable silence as they walked. Talon did not relinquish her hand. Nor was she eager to pull away. It was a strange comfort, having a powerful figure beside her, knowing what she meant to him. It both fortified and terrified her.

Things between them were changing at an alarming rate, spurred on by the underlying strings that tied them together. She wasn't sure if her mind could keep up with her heart, or if her heart would race ahead of her and do something stupid. She wanted to kiss him, to take him in her arms, to run her fingers over every scar on his skin. To twist her fingers in his hair. To see if it was as silky and tangled as it often looked.

Those thoughts made liquid heat drop low in her belly.

When they returned to camp, dinner was ready. Stew and bread was served in excess. Talon stayed by her side, though he did not eat. Probably because he'd caught something while hunting. She almost thought to ask, but decided against it, since everyone would hear their conversation..

Everyone's words were hushed. Perhaps it was Talon's presence, or their exhaustion. They had pushed themselves to the brink, because it meant getting to Kastali Dun faster.

Once dinner was finished, everything was packed away. She would have to sleep on Talon's back, strapped into the harness. She feared sleeping against him would leave her mind vulnerable to him, to her secrets.

So once she was settled, she bundled up against the chill of the autumn sky. The night was frigid. She had a valid excuse for the gloves, cap, and cloak she removed from her pack. Desaree had also packed a scarf, which she wrapped around her face leaving only her eyes exposed. Only then did she lean against Talon's scaly neck to sleep, careful to keep her skin from him.

It was meager sleep at best.

~

THE FOLLOWING day stretched on for an eternity, made longer by exhaustion. She found herself dozing in and out of consciousness. Each time they stopped for a short rest, it felt like a dream. Talon remained in his form for each of these breaks. She did her best to stretch her muscles whenever they were on the ground.

By nightfall, she was glad to call it a day, even if they still planned on flying all night. They had a few meager hours to rest, but that seemed like a gift at this point. Talon did not venture out with the hunting party this time, perhaps too eager to spar with her. The thought of holding a sword overwhelmed her. She could hardly lift her own arms. But Talon was there, grinning and eager. She almost cursed his boyish enthusiasm.

"Ready?" He searched her features. She glared. "Oh, come now, surely you've got *some* energy. All that time spent sitting in a harness, doing nothing. I'm the one who did all the work today."

Her jaw dropped. "Oh, poor you! Flying *all* day. Fine. One match. But only on the condition that I get a few hours of sleep afterward."

He lifted a brow. "Sleep? Perhaps, if there is time after our walk."

"If I don't get some sleep, I'll fall out of my harness and you'll have to catch me."

"I will always catch you," he all but growled. "But very well. A few hours of sleep won't slow us down. I don't want you suffering."

She retrieved Cyrus's sverak from her pack. Everyone who wasn't occupied crept over, pretending they weren't interested in watching. She could feel their eyes, especially Bedelth's.

This was King Talon, ruler of Dragonwall, famed for his skill in battle, and here she was, a mere puny human blessed with a bit of magic, ready to square off against him. He was going to crush her like a bug.

Not this time. Not if I have anything to say about it...

She couldn't help it, but Cyrus made her smile. He didn't mind her losing to Bedelth, who now watched them with amusement, but losing to King Talon? Not an option.

Talon finished muttering, blunting his blade to protect her. "Ready?"

"As I'll ever be."

They took up their positions and began circling. Talon's face was a blank mask. She could no more anticipate his intent than she could the intentions of a rock.

If you don't mind....

Oh. Right.

She knew how to hand over control. She relaxed her mind as she'd done when the vodar had attacked. Cyrus's response was immediate. The sensation was jarring, as always, having one's muscles move on their own. Like being trapped without control. If she panicked, her brain would take over and Cyrus would be ejected. She couldn't let that happen.

Her body made the first move, plunging forward, sverak raised. Talon lifted to parry. She dodged him, spinning on her heel to trade positions. Her arms lifted, bringing her sword down to meet Talon's. Their blades met with jarring contact. He was strong. So was she—with Cyrus. She pulled her sword free and brought it down again.

Her first movements were reserved, tentative, as Cyrus grew accustomed to her. Talon had no reason to suspect her, not yet anyway. He came at her this time, sweeping his blade around, aiming for her side. She blocked and pushed him back, giving nothing away in her expression.

His eyes remained fixed on hers.

All right, time for some fun. Brace yourself...

She lunged, sweeping her blade to the left before switching directions. Quick and calculated. Talon blocked. She disengaged and came at him again and again. Their movements sped up. Soon she was moving faster than humanly possible. She let her body go, watching Cyrus display his skill for all to see. And what skill it was!

Talon's eyes widened when he realized it. "Not fair!" he hissed, bringing his blade up for another block. "That's cheating, *Cyrus!*"

"Oh, but is it?" It didn't feel like her own voice when she spoke, though it sounded like her. "Afraid I'll win, like I usually do?"

Talon snorted, but for all his feigned irritation, there was something more in his expression. Pure, undulated joy. He was sparring with a long-lost friend, one he missed very much.

Everything turned into a blur. Cyrus and Talon moved so quickly she could hardly follow with her mind. Gasps sounded from the gathered onlookers. She was vaguely aware of their surprise. All they saw was a young woman besting their king.

She lost track of time in a state like this, but she could feel her body tiring, even with Cyrus in control, calling upon his strength. It would take many months, perhaps longer, for her own magical growth to reach the level Cyrus required.

Beads of sweat rolled down her skin, and her breathing turned ragged, but she continued to match Talon blow for blow. His sword was blunted, but hers was not. Bringing it around in a sweeping motion, she dragged her blade's edge across his leg, slicing through his skin before jumping back. Blood oozed from the wound, soaking through his pants.

A war cry fell from her lips, mixed with Cyrus's pleasure and satisfaction. Talon's wound closed in seconds as he lunged, giving a shout of his own. This time he caught her blade against his and swept it around, flinging it from her grasp. She tried to keep hold of it, but her grip was weakened, exhaustion closing in.

In a single blink, Talon pivoted behind her and wrapped his arm around her shoulders, pulling her flush to his front. She was trapped. His blade came to rest against her neck. "*I win,*" he whispered for her ears only. "Well played, my old friend, well played indeed. But if you wouldn't mind, I'd like my mate back." His heavy breath sent tingles over her skin.

Their audience erupted into applause before slowly retreating.

Talon lowered his sword, but didn't release her. She felt Cyrus—overly satisfied with his tricks—fade into the depths of her mind. With his absence came a heavy exhaustion. She sagged against Talon. His arm moved to her waist, keeping her back flush to his front, holding her upright as her chest heaved.

"Let me know when you want a rematch," she teased. "Perhaps I won't be as easy to beat as you once thought."

He chuckled, burying his face in her hair, inhaling deeply. "I'll think twice next time, certainly. Cyrus was always a worthy opponent—one of the best I ever faced."

"Was it true what he said? That he usually beat you?"

"Sometimes yes, sometimes no. It depended on the day and our moods. I think he was trying to goad me, which he did quite well."

She smiled, allowing her head to fall back against his chest. Her eyes closed. She took several deep breaths, slower and steadier this time, reluctant to leave his hold, the strength of his arms.

At last, she stepped away. "I'm not sure I'll have much energy for a walk, but I'll do my best."

"Good. I would like that. Then perhaps you can have a nap."

They stored their sveraks, ignoring the onlookers who eyed her with newfound curiosity, and even respect. Talon reached for her hand and pulled her away, lacing their fingers together. Her heart fluttered. She allowed him to guide her into the growing twilight. When they were some distance away, he flattened the grass around them and sat down, bringing her down with him. "Perhaps less of a walk tonight," he decided. "Let's watch the stars for a bit."

"Okay," she managed, mumbling.

He laid down with one arm behind his head, and pulled her with him, positioning her comfortably in the crook of his shoulder. She curled against him, soaking up his warmth. The feeling of her body pressed to his ignited something deep in her core, but she had little time to consider the intimacy of it. Her eyes were too heavy. They fluttered and then closed. She was asleep before he could point out a single star.

CHAPTER 32

RETURNING HOME

Kastali Dun

Claire placed her ungloved hand against Talon as Kastali Dun materialized on the horizon. It was early morning, the sun's rays bathing the distant city in gold. Waves of relief and recognition washed over her. Talon's love of this city overwhelmed her senses. A smile pulled at her lips—his relief was her relief.

"Welcome home," she said. It was the only home he'd ever known, filled with hundreds of years of memories. This city was his lifeblood.

"My coronation tied me to this city, making it a part of me," he said by way of explanation.

Something told her he would love it regardless. She could see plainly enough into his mind to know that. *"Yes, perhaps you are right,"* he acknowledged.

She leaned forward, placing her forehead against his scales, grinning against him, grinning at the connection they shared. When their minds merged, most explanations didn't require an answer. Thoughts were simply unspoken but understood.

The ocean glittered on the horizon, wrapping around the

298

peninsula from the Bay of Bandu to the Dragonfire Sea. Beyond, she could squint and make out Irelia Island. *"I'll take you there sometime,"* Talon said, sensing her longing. She would like that very much.

She briefly removed her hand from his scales as she looked ahead. Kastali Dun. It felt like home for her, too. As much as home could feel like in a foreign world. The tall spires of the keep rose above it like pin pricks against the landscape. It was still a hazy smudge, but it would grow quickly as they approached. All too soon they would be landing, their journey at an end.

The past few days had flown by in a blur, quite literally. Very little time was spent on the ground. Scattered walks here and there. Brief spells of sleeping cuddled against Talon's body. Always away from camp, where others would not see them. Those affectionate moments meant everything to her. Even though they hadn't done more than cuddle, she felt fluttery every time she thought back on it.

Talon had a soft side to him, hidden beneath the chiseled stony face he showed to the world. Affectionate, even. Which was surprising, given that he had sworn off the opposite sex for so long. Perhaps the mate bond made things natural for him.

She had been careful to keep her mind separated from his. The thought of telling him about her promise weighed heavily on her. She needed to tell him. But when? And how would he react?

She pushed the thought away, buried it deep.

"I'm happy to be home," she admitted, replacing her hand against his scales. *"Very happy."* Her heart soared at the thought. Or was it his? *"I'll be happy to have my bed back, and a proper bath. And sleep! Gods, I'll probably sleep for days and days."* At this, a guttural chuckle rumbled beneath her. *"I will miss this, though,"* she added. *"Us...flying together in the sky."*

"I'll miss it too. But..." He hesitated. He wanted them to continue flying together. He wanted to show her what flying could truly be. He'd done nothing exciting—no swoops, dives, or rolls. Only tame formation flying. He would take her out when they could afford it, and show her why he loved his wings.

"Yes, I would like that. Very much." A thrill settled in the pit of her stomach.

At last, she removed her hand, mostly to think uninterrupted. Their return to Kastali Dun was going to change things. She liked the comfort of his company, flying with him, being around him. But he would go back to his kingly duties, and she would go back to her training.

Her insides squirmed. She frowned. Would returning to Kastali Dun build a wedge between them? No. She would keep that from happening. Whatever was necessary. Besides, they still had their walks together.

She snorted at the thought. What a strategic move on his part. She saw it then for what it was. Talon's way of fighting for them. He'd done it even before the confirmation that they were mates, because he had cared for her regardless. That left her feeling warm.

She thought back over their time together. Her memories stretched beyond the mate bond discovery. Talon wasn't the only blind one. There were signs—obvious signs. She'd missed them, too. Their little letters, the way they made her giddy. His heroic rescue when she was kidnapped. His defense of her honor in that cellar. Her bath afterward and how gentle he'd been.

Her mind flashed back to those moments in particular, when Talon knelt before her, washing her feet...her legs...her thighs... Heat erupted beneath her skin. Yes, in hindsight, his behavior towards her was obvious, even if he hadn't realized what he was doing. It merely came naturally.

And what of her behavior towards him? Mates were supposed to love fiercely, more fiercely than any other pairing. Did she love him more fiercely than anyone else in her life? More than her first and only steady boyfriend? Sure, he'd turned out to be a ballbag, but what about before he'd broken her heart? She had loved him, yes, but it wasn't the same as what she felt towards Talon. Whatever she felt for Dragonwall's king—perhaps not quite love, yet—was but a shadow of what it could become. In time. If they grew closer.

But that wasn't all.

What would their love become if they accepted the bond. If they mated? Her body shuddered. Warmth spread and pooled in her abdomen. *Would* they? Would it come to that? Would he want her in that way?

She wanted him, she realized. She wanted him entirely and completely. But, did she have the courage to claim him if he shied away?

A bitter thought filled her mind. It irked her that he wanted to keep things secret, even if she understood where he was coming from. But she already had enough secrets to keep. How long did he expect her to hide the truth? And why, if the truth was inevitable?

Unless…what if he never planned to solidify their bond? Her chest tightened. Surely that was not his intention.

Or, maybe it was.

Once they went back to their busy lives, Talon would be too busy to acknowledge the deep bond between them. His desire to keep it secret, while understandable, felt like a way for him to ignore what was between them. She pursed her lips. Maybe she was being silly. He cared for her, perhaps more deeply than she cared for him. Hadn't he already admitted what she was to him? He would *want* to spend time with her as much as possible.

She exhaled, louder than intended.

Something caught her eye, just outside the city walls. She gaped in surprise. There were tents. It was an encampment, crawling with people. The faint sound of music drifted to her ears, laughter, and merrymaking.

Before she could question it, they were flying over the city wall. Emotion welled up inside her at the sight of the keep. She was home.

Buildings slid by, places she recognized. The market near the docks, bustling as always. Ant-sized people making their way up and down the winding streets. Some stopped and pointed up at them.

The fort's drengr split away just before they reached the castle, Bedelth with them, leaving her alone with Talon. Talon did not circle around to the courtyard where people would see them.

Instead, he took her to the highest tower of the keep—his tower. It was flat on top, home to a private garden.

He landed, careful to avoid trampling the nearby flowerbeds. She placed her hand against his scales in question. *This is the queen's garden. No one will see you here. Best we avoid rumors.*

"Right," she muttered, removing her hand, remembering the need for propriety. She undid the straps of her harness and slid down from his back, grabbing her pack as she went.

They'd made it. She couldn't help her sigh of relief.

Moments later, Talon was beside her in human form, leading her to a trap door. She glanced around, curious, mesmerized by the private oasis towering over the city. "When you say *queen's* garden…"

"It was built by Queen Isabella when she founded Kastali Dun. I'll show you around some other time. Come, we have others waiting for us below." He threw open the door. "Here, let me take your pack." He was all business. Unsurprising, when other things occupied his mind.

She handed it over and followed. They descended and emerged in a small attic. It took a moment for her eyes to adjust. The room was empty, save the spears of light that fell across the floor from the windows. Talon led her down a wraparound staircase that took them directly into the main chamber of his tower.

"There they are!" Koldis said, striding over. Jovari and Verath followed on his heels. She grinned. "Good to see you!" he said. "Even if it has only been less than a week." He picked her up in a bear hug and twirled her around, making her laugh. When he set her down, she gave Jovari a big hug, too.

Verath's greeting was more formal. No hugging. But he did offer a small, polite bow. "Good to see you safely home, Lady Claire. I heard you were remarkable with the vodar." He winked before his eyes flicked toward the sitting area. She followed his gaze and squealed, sprinting over.

Desaree and Saffra stood, grinning. She threw her arms around each of them in turn. "I'm so happy to see you! You won't believe everything that happened. How…how have things been here?"

Desaree was about to answer when she froze, a deep blush tinging her cheeks. Talon had come up beside them. He held Claire's pack. "I suppose you're eager for that bath, hmm? And sleep? For days and days, if I recall?"

"I..."

"No no, take your leave," he said. "I have business with my shields." He glanced at Desaree and Saffra. "Good to see you, ladies. You'll take proper care of her, I hope?"

"Of course, King Talon," Saffra answered. "And...it is good to have you back."

"Aye. No alarming visions in my absence, I trust?"

"Oh. Well, yes. Of the attack on Fort Squall."

"Oh?" He tilted his head.

"It was too vague to do much...until it was too late."

"Yes, understandable. Fortunately we have Claire, who was able to warn Reyr and the others."

"You did?" Saffra's eyes widened. "That sounds like a story worth telling."

"Oh, it is," Talon answered for her. "I'll leave her in your expert care then." He caught Claire's eye and nodded.

"I...thank you, Talon." She shouldered her pack, glancing over at Koldis and Jovari.

Koldis lifted an eyebrow. "We'll catch up with you later?" he called. She knew exactly what he meant by 'catch up.'

"Absolutely," she said, grinning back.

Talon cleared his throat, eyes intent on hers. "Right. I'll see you later."

"Yep. Thanks." She turned to Desaree and Saffra, wishing more than anything she and Talon could give each other a proper good-bye, whatever that entailed. A hug perhaps, at the least, instead of whatever awkwardness was going on now.

As she left his tower, she glanced over her shoulder. He was already deep in discussion with the others. And so the wedge was already forming. Or, her fear of it.

"Tell us everything," Saffra demanded. They walked down the corridor to her chambers. "We heard about the attack on the fort.

But what happened with the vodar? And what's going on between you and King Talon? The way he looked at you..."

She snorted. "I think we're going to need all day for this."

The guards opened the door for them, greeting her respectfully. As she passed through, she set her stuff on the floor and paused in the entryway. "Gods, I've missed this." She glanced at Saffra and Desaree. "You don't mind if I take a bath first, before we jump into everything? I'll be quick, I promise."

"Of course." Desaree smiled. "I'll put your things away and we'll get you out of those clothes and into something more appropriate. Take all the time you need."

"We can wait," Saffra agreed, heading to the bookshelf to grab a book.

Claire smiled. "I really missed you guys. Like...a lot." Her chest squeezed at the familiar sight of them. It was hard to look away, like she'd been deprived of them long enough that she needed to keep staring to make sure they were real.

"We'll be right here," Desaree said, as if reading her mind.

"Okay, I'll be quick." She strode through her apartment, appreciating it more than ever before—

"Desaree?!" she screeched, coming to a halt.

"What is it?" Desaree rushed to her side, eyes wide, then she relaxed. "Oh. That. Gods, don't frighten me like that."

"Is this...is this my ball gown?"

"What else would it be?"

"It's just, I totally forgot about the fall tournament—and the ball." So much had happened; it was the last thing on her mind. She recalled the encampment of tents outside the city. The music, laughter, and people strolling about. "I'm not too late?"

Desaree laughed. "No. There are still a few days left."

She eyed the gown. It hung on a mannequin, a pool of black, shimmering fabric. The skirt had layers upon layers of tulle trimmed with iridescent beads along the edges. The bodice was strapless, resplendent silk fabric with a sweetheart neckline. Draped over the shoulder was a pair of matching elbow length gloves.

A million emotions fluttered through her chest, but mostly, immense relief. Talon was her escort for the ball. She had feared a wedge coming between them, but perhaps there was nothing to fear at all. The thought of spending an evening dancing in his arms.

"Des, I need you to teach me how to dance. Like, proper dance. Dragonwall's formal dances."

"Oh, don't you worry about that. Saffra and I will make sure you're ready. Everything will be perfect."

"And you?" She turned her full attention upon Desaree. "You and Saffra? You have escorts and gowns lined up?"

Desaree's face flushed. "Verath wishes to escort me. I had my gown finished last week. Saffra...I don't think she's going."

"I'm not," Saffra called from the sofa in an offhanded way, glancing up from her book. "If I can't go with Dax, what's the point?"

A chill settled in the air. Without Dax, Saffra wouldn't *want* to go. But that was no excuse to hide away in her room. This ball only happened once every five years.

She was about to protest when a look from Desaree silenced her. "Off to the bath. Hurry up."

She scurried into the bathing chamber, washing away the stink of travel. Desaree dressed her in a simple cream brocade, pausing to admire both the new spriten mark on her skin, and how much the old one had grown.

Saffra popped over, eying her with satisfaction. "Your sprite magic is growing."

Now that she had access to a mirror, she could finally see the new mark she'd earned for doing healing magic—magic she hardly understood. Like the other, this was made of swirls, though these were slightly different in how they interlocked.

Silky fabric settled over her skin. She sighed. It was a nice alternative to the scratchy travel clothes. She wouldn't dare admit that to Desaree, though. So what if dresses were growing on her? She could like both, couldn't she?

A platter of fruit and cheese arrived. Tess even wrote a little note of greeting. They sat down with wine in hand for an afternoon of storytelling and snacking. No detail was left out, except for the truth about her newly discovered mate bond. She told them exactly what had happened with the vodar attack, and how she had used her sprite magic. The hardest part was talking about Hiondel and Lily.

She explained how they had come to be in Brezen, and the outcome of the battle at Fort Squall. She even relayed in great detail Talon's appearance at camp. How he had struck a bargain with her. "One walk, every night, for one hundred nights. To make up for breaking my promise to him. *Punishment* apparently," she finished.

"Punishment?" Desaree teased. "Sounds quite *punishing*." Des and Saffra exchanged a knowing look, like they saw right through whatever was going on.

She desperately wanted to tell them about the mate bond. Withholding the truth felt wrong. They were her best friends. At last, she settled on a simpler truth. "We appear to have developed feelings for each other."

Saffra snorted. "You don't say! After so many walks together, flying together, and the way he's been looking at you for months, I don't find myself surprised in the slightest."

"I told Claire that she needed to open her heart to him," Desaree said. "You remember that, don't you, Claire? When he invited you to a midday meal after your kidnapping? Gods, it feels like ages ago."

"I remember." It really did feel like a long time ago.

Their discussion moved on to things she'd missed, which wasn't much, since they still hadn't found a way into the mysterious building in the cave. The biggest news was the capture of Collier. "The evidence Verath collected is concrete and absolute," Desaree explained. "We have enough to lock Caterina away for life, unless King Talon chooses to execute her—I'm not sure how I feel about that."

"It doesn't sit well with me either," Claire agreed.

"While I want her to pay for what she did, I just don't think I would feel comfortable with killing her. I suppose life in the dungeons might be a less favorable alternative, though. I want her to suffer, you know? But how much suffering is enough?"

Claire frowned. "What about banishment? Would that be a viable option? Send her away from Dragonwall forever. They do things like that, right?"

"They do," Saffra confirmed. "And frankly, that might be the best alternative. Though, Caterina is resourceful. She might see it as a way to sneak around and get revenge. We have no way to keep an eye on her once she leaves, unless King Talon assigns some poor soul to track her every movement."

"True..." Claire frowned.

In the end, none of them could decide on what was best.

CLAIRE'S NERVES flared when it was time for the evening meal. She would get to see Talon again. Yes, she was acting like a schoolgirl with a crush, but at least she could blame her feelings on the bond, so she didn't feel guilty, especially after hating him so much.

"Shall we walk down together?" Saffra asked Claire. "I assume you will have dinner in public tonight?"

"I...yes. Absolutely. Talon will expect it of me. Though, I'm sure my reappearance will spark rumors."

"Nobles love to gossip."

"Not as much as the servants do," Desaree said.

They meandered through the keep, making their way to the dining hall. Patrons were already filing in. As they entered, her gaze darted to the head table. Had Talon really become such a magnet? She caught him watching her, his face set. The tiny twitch at the corner of his lips was enough. She afforded him a small smile in return, before turning her attention back to Desaree and Saffra. They found a seat together in their usual spot near the hall's edge, beside one of the large fireplaces. Its warmth chased away the castle's drafts.

As soon as dinner was served, everyone began loading their plates. Talk was animated. Their table mates discussed the tournament and the stalls they had visited. Sir Codswald and his lady got her attention, asking her how her journey to Graymont had gone. A rumor Verath had recently spread.

She played along, giving them vague answers. Graymont was absolutely lovely! Especially during this time of the year. Its markets captured much of her time while she was there. She had even acquired a new gown. And the weather! It was truly fine. Desaree had to elbow her when she was obviously overdoing it.

"Will King Talon come by later to collect you?" Desaree whispered. Plates were scraped clean, the sound of cutlery dying down.

"I'm not sure." She wanted to pretend she hadn't considered it, but the truth was, she hadn't stopped thinking about what Talon might do. She glanced up at the head table and her cheeks flushed. He sat watching her—openly.

"Gods, could he be any more obvious?" she muttered, quickly averting her gaze. Desaree and Saffra both looked up then glanced away. She glared down at her plate. There were a few bites left. The rich food had been a bit much after days of bland travel food, so she had taken small portions and eaten slowly. Very slowly. Which was probably what he was waiting for.

She finished her last two bites at a snail's pace, if only to draw out the suspense. No sooner had she swallowed, did the king come to his feet. It created a ripple as everyone in the hall was forced to stand. She was tempted to remain sitting, if only out of rebellion, but Desaree hissed and nudged her.

"Fine, fine!"

Talon walked down the aisle, coming to a stop before their table. The hall was absolutely silent. "Lady Claire, our walk?"

She glanced at Desaree and Saffra. "See you back at my chambers later?" They nodded.

She took Talon's arm and he escorted her from the hall. A myriad of whispers followed in their wake.

"You did that on purpose." They strolled through the keep's corridors, towards the royal garden.

Talon's lips twitched. "I did. Does the attention make you uncomfortable?"

"Umm, well, yes, as a matter of fact it does."

"I see." He fell quiet. They entered the garden. He dropped her arm and took her hand instead, this time holding it without lacing their fingers together. Her heart still spiked out of excitement. It was dark, after all. Most patrons were still in the dining hall. No one would see them.

"Have you gotten settled in? Baths, sleeping, all that?"

"Oh. Yes, I suppose I have. Getting a bath was the highlight of my afternoon. That and catching up with Desaree and Saffra."

He faltered. "You did not...?"

"No, no. I didn't say anything about our bond, but I struggled. I'm not sure how long I can keep this secret. I don't like hiding the truth. Surely you feel the same way with your shields? Don't you want to tell them?"

"I do. But this is for the best. Ruling a kingdom isn't easy. You know that. Sacrifices must be made."

She swallowed, zipping the pendant of her forest tear along its chain. "I...I know. Sometimes I wish things were simpler. That you were just...well...just Talon. And that we could do whatever we wanted, whenever we wanted."

He huffed. "Welcome to my world. That very thought is one I spent years pining over when I was younger. When you become the ruler of a kingdom, you give your life over to something greater. Your life is no longer yours. You understand this, yes?"

"I..." She hesitated. "Yes. I suppose I do. That doesn't mean I have to like the rules."

He chuckled. "Always the rebel."

"Yep. That's me." She shrugged, offering him a knowing smile. "Rules are meant to be broken, isn't that the saying?"

To prove her point, she changed the way they held hands, lacing her fingers though his. He squeezed her palm in response.

"So...I saw my ball gown today. I'd forgotten all about it, with everything else, I mean."

"Oh?" He hesitated. "I usually dread the fall tourney ball. Every five years it comes, and every five years I'm reminded of being alone."

"I thought you had accepted your fate?" She arched an eyebrow.

"Despite having accepted it, it is still a reminder."

Her tone softened. "Well, you need not dread it any longer. You have me, now. Besides, it will be a good distraction. Though, it feels weird, you know, having fun like this after what happened to Fort Squall."

"Indeed. But diversions are necessary. Keeping thousands of people happy isn't easy."

"Right. What about the tournament? I've never been to a tournament—not like this. I get the feeling it will be nothing like ren fair. Probably a thousand times better." She recalled the sea of tents and stalls, longing to see everything from the ground.

"Ren...*fair?*"

"Yeah, you know, the renaissance festival? It's where people in my world get dressed up like people in your world." She struggled to keep the laughter from her voice. "They do jousting, and play fighting, and walk around with tankards of ale in one hand and turkey legs in the other."

"People in your world dress up like...like people in mine?" His eyebrows drew together. "Wait...you...you are being serious with me? Or are you making a joke? I cannot tell." His frown made that clear.

"I'm being serious!" She jabbed his arm.

"Ahh." He fake flinched, swatting her hand away.

"I used to go to the renaissance festival in college. I lived in New England for a while. Anyway, every October there was a local ren fair. My friends and I would get dressed up. Nothing as extravagant as this though." She looked down at her gown. "Gods, I would have been a sight to behold dressed like *this!*"

"And people do what at this fair thing?"

"Oh, you know, all the pretend stuff that you guys actually do for real. Pretend fighting, pretend jousting. Things like that."

"*Pretend?*" He snorted. "What is the point in that?"

"Oh, never mind." She grinned, glancing up at him. He still wore an expression of confusion. "Speaking of which, will we get to go? I would really like to see it. I guess I can go with Desaree and Saffra tomorrow—"

"No. I mean, yes, they can join us. But I will escort you. I had planned on tending to other matters, but I cannot let you see your first tournament without me."

"Certainly not! You'd miss all my surprise. Can't have that, can we?"

"No, we cannot." A smile broke free of his lips. The first real one that evening. Dimples and all. Rewarding her stomach with a flutter. "Morning court is canceled during the week of the tournament anyway, but I do have to meet with my lower council. Just a few hours. After that I can collect you and we can walk the stalls before heading to the arena."

"You're not going to compete?"

"Me?" He barked a laugh. "I stopped competing long, long ago. That is for the younger drengr and soldiers. Those with something to prove." He paused. "I do not remember the last tournament I attended. But with you here, it will be enjoyable. I am eager to show you a part of my world you have not yet seen."

She was, perhaps, more eager than he.

They talked of small matters after that, before he returned her to her chambers. As was usual, she asked him if he had thought any further about her training with the sprites. Yet again, he requested that she ask the following night. She promised that she would, because she wouldn't stop. Not until she got the training she needed to defeat Kane.

Then he bid her goodnight and left her grinning after him as he disappeared down the hallway.

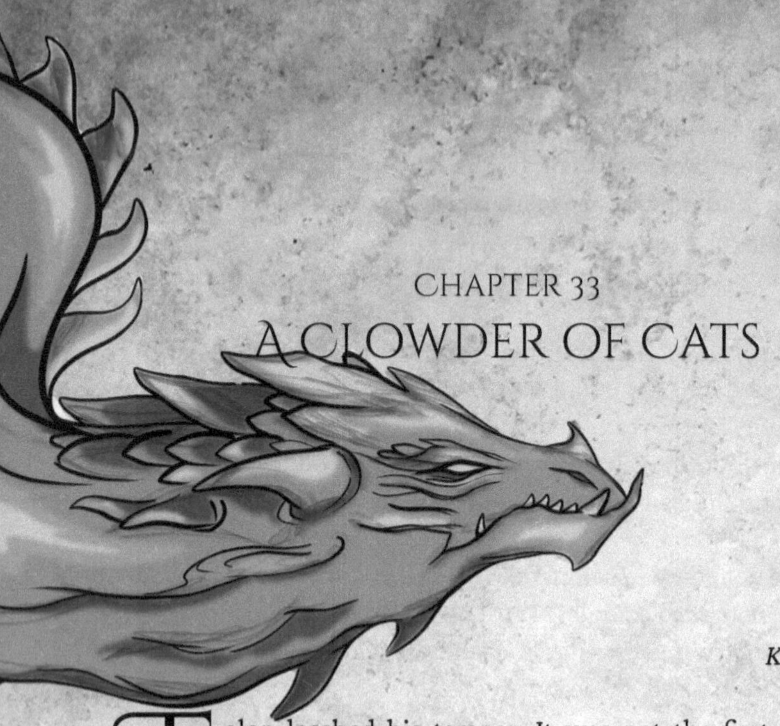

Kastali Dun

Talon leashed his temper. It was not the first time he'd forced himself to stop glaring at Lord Sion Aziz as the man droned on about affairs in Tayiqar. Gods, had council meetings always been this insufferable? Lord Aziz slammed his fist on the table. "Something must be done, or we will take matters into our own hands."

Tayiqar was mostly desert, though it had some rich land along the perimeters and a few valuable oases scattered throughout. During his absence, things had further deteriorated. Goblins continued to wreak havoc along the border and the lord governors of the south eastern territory were feeling the pressure.

"We've taken heavy losses and it is eating into our economy." Lord Abdus Morad was saying. "I see no way to get these villages back on their feet until this is over."

Morad represented Jipirat.

Talon inhaled, drawing himself up. "Tell me again, Lord Morad, why Dragonwall's armies are still having issues? I thought this was sorted when I made the trip to Lincastle. I worked with *your* lord governor on the matter."

"It was sorted, my king, but in your absence, three additional villages have succumbed, forced to evacuate. The loss of one hundred and fifty soldiers between them, loss of trade, of commerce. Karoch and Morak generally purchase large amounts of timber during the cooler months—or did, before all this happened."

"And why didn't General Kavish do a better job of defending those villages? How many damned goblins could there possibly be? We've killed thousands. They cannot keep coming." He smoothed his scowl. Goblins were like ants, so really, they could keep coming.

"General Kavish believed the attacks would occur in Dahrat, Manah, and Quar."

"Where did he get an idea like that?"

"He received intelligence on the matter." Lord Morad fidgeted.

"Of course he did." His mood darkened. Some generals were idiots. The human ones mostly. "I've been gone less than a month and already my work there is falling apart. What intelligence?"

"Spies, information from infiltrating their ranks."

An involuntary snort escaped his chest. "Is that really what he said? How did he infiltrate their ranks? Disguised a little person as a goblin? You don't believe that, do you? Sounds to me like he was acting off of feelings rather than facts. Feelings don't win wars, Lord Morad."

The room fell silent as some of his lords shifted uneasily. Saffra was, of course, not in attendance. His eyes slid over her empty chair every time he wished he could be elsewhere. He could have forced her to attend, but the others were less tolerant of her, and he felt that saving her from their snide comments was a small mercy he could offer.

"What would you have us do, Your Majesty?" Lord Aziz leaned forward.

"Remove him. Obviously," he drawled. Lord Aziz opened his mouth, eyes wide. Nothing came out. "Gods, man! Not that kind of removal. I'm brutal, but not needlessly so. I don't mean *kill* him. Demote him. Give him an honorable discharge. Whatever. I don't care how you get it done. Get someone else in place who will do a better job. Must I spell it out?" He took a deep breath. He'd been irritable all morning.

Claire's face swam into his thoughts, followed by needles of guilt. What would she think of his outburst? Thoughts of her steadied his temper. "Now, if that is the final matter, this meeting has run on long enough. I have another appointment for which I am already late."

He glanced at Matthis and stood before anyone could come up with another—

"One more thing, Your Majesty."

His fist clenched and unclenched, but he didn't groan, even if he wanted to. There was always one more thing. "I'm late, Matthis. It can wait."

The room came to its feet in unison, bowing as he took his leave.

Back in his main tower chamber, he spent a moment checking his appearance. His servants lingered nearby, waiting for an order. Everything looked fine, except—

His face. His eyes lingered over his reflection, his scars. Flames of self-loathing flickered in his chest, rising up. He pushed back against them, summoning frost to cool his veins. He would be out in public today. Gods, he hated the public. And Claire would be with him, radiating beauty while he scared everyone away. He held his own gaze for several heartbeats longer.

He would do this—for her. He would do this.

"Ready, my king?" Bedelth appeared and escorted him to Claire's chambers. He greeted the guards, Anderson and Derek. They knocked for him. Desaree's head popped into the hall before Claire and Saffra joined them in the hallway.

He only had eyes for his mate. Gods! It still took some getting used to. That word. *Mate.*

It didn't feel real.

"You look—" His gaze darted over the others before returning to her. Beautiful. Radiant. Alluring. Stunning. All of it. Everything. "—well."

She wore an emerald brocade, cut low enough that his eyes

lingered unnecessarily over her chest. Heat flared across his shoulders and the back of his neck and he lifted his eyes.

"Glad you didn't forget me," she said, arching an eyebrow. "We almost went on without you."

"Forgive my lateness. Council meetings will be the death of me."

"Gods, I certainly hope not!" she huffed. "What will the kingdom do without you? And your lower council. They'd be *so* lost."

"Always a wonderful sense of humor, my lady." But he heard the words she did not speak. The hint of what his death might do to her more than anything. His heart skipped. And just like that, his mood instantly improved. "Shall we?" He offered his arm and she accepted.

They made their way through the *Hall of Kings,* past each of the large paintings. He always disliked walking this stretch of the castle, seeing each drengr king happily paired with an equally fierce mate. An unnecessary reminder. But with Claire on his arm, that reminder was softened.

"Oh!" Claire said. "I forgot to tell you. Desaree invited Verath. He's agreed to meet us when we arrive."

"Ah. Excellent. A fine group we'll make." He glanced over his shoulder, catching sight of Desaree's flushed face. Bedelth had offered Saffra his arm.

Carriages rolled to a halt just inside the portcullis to take the five of them through the city. With the exception of the arena where the biggest fights were held, the tournament and its accompanying festivities always took up a great deal of space. Tents and booths, stages for playacts, sparring rings, and the like. There was no room within the walls for such a spectacle.

They made the drive out of the city in comfortable silence. He tried to think of things to say, but with Desaree sitting across from them, he was silent. He used the opportunity to steal glances at Claire, who had turned her attention to the window.

"Ready for a day of debauchery?" Verath was waiting as they climbed out. He strode forward to greet them.

"As always," he huffed in greeting. "Glad you could join us. Let's show these ladies a good time, shall we?"

Claire joined him and laced her arm through his. Verath chuckled, paying them a pointed look before stepping away to take Desaree's arm. Talon's eyes lingered over that look. He knew what Verath was thinking. And so what if Verath silently judged him? Soon enough, they would know the inevitable truth. Until then, Verath could go on guessing. Besides, his shield was hardly one to judge.

Bedelth and Saffra emerged from the second carriage a moment later.

A small crowd had assembled to gawk. All too soon, rumors of his presence would pass through the expanse of stalls. He clenched his jaw, staring at Claire, reminding himself that he was here for her—doing this for her. He was determined to act no different than any other patron, even with a crown upon his head and sverak at his hip.

Leading their party away from the carriages, they made their way down the first aisle. It was a maze of booths and shops. Shouts and laughter rang through the air. The scent of roasting meat mingled with the sweet tang of berry pies. It set his mouth watering. Jugglers and other street performers walked among the trampled lanes, stopping here and there to offer entertainment to any who might toss them a steely for a show.

"Oh! Look at that!" Claire pointed to a pair of entertainers in bright clothes who had stopped to climb atop one another. Acrobats, of sorts. The smaller of the pair had found his way to the shoulders of his comrade and stood erect, waving at the crowd, sometimes making obscene gestures when people walked by without tossing him a coin. "Let's give him something for his efforts!" she said, glancing up with a mischievous smile.

"A steely will do," he said, keeping his voice low.

Her smile widened as she opened her coin purse and tossed a steely up at the acrobat. He snatched it from the air and bowed, gracefully maintaining balance. "Why, thank you, fair maiden, king of kings, and lovely ladies and lords!" For their amusement, the performer popped on one leg, balancing with the other stretched out behind him.

No sooner had she clapped and laughed, was she distracted by another sight. If it wasn't a booth with a display of blown glass or jeweled hair nets, it was an orator reading poetry from a box.

"Oh, isn't that the cutest?!" She pulled him over to watch a clowder of cats trained to stand on their hind legs and roll cylinders across a table. She crowded together with Desaree and Saffra, giggling and placing bets on which cat would get its cylinder to the finish line.

"Gods above," he muttered. He stood back with Bedelth and Verath, exchanging amused glances. Cats rolling cylinders? What would they think of next?

She came away with three additional steelys for having bet on the winning cat, a sleek gray-haired fluff ball that had won by a hefty length. "You know," she said, looking up at him, "I wouldn't mind a cat of my own. Are we allowed pets in the castle?"

He took her arm. "Pets? Hmm. Not generally. The castle stewards work hard with our mages to keep rodents and critters out, so there's never been much need for cats and other animals. Besides, pets have generally been discouraged within the keep for cleanliness reasons under my rule. And excessive barking can be a downright nuisance in close quarters." Her expression fell, and he hated that. "Perhaps...an exception can be made?"

"I knew it!" She pinched his arm. "I knew I could convince you."

"Wait a minute," he said, "I haven't said yes, have I?"

She hardly heard him as she pulled him over to a ring booth where she proceeded to try on one of every size. Desaree and Saffra joined her, *oohing* and *aahing* over the various bands of silver and gold. Had it been any other woman in the world, his temper would have exploded.

They went from booth to tent and tent to booth. It was a never ending show of goods. He didn't get annoyed in the slightest. He enjoyed the distraction—enjoyed watching her frolic about in excitement—tracing the curves of her body, the way her shoulders rose and fell when she laughed, the slenderness of her neck, her hands as she held rings in the sunlight. Studying her mannerisms. Tucking everything about her away so that he could picture her whenever he was having a bad day. Picture these moments and remember them forever.

After exhausting the vendors' wares, they found a stage in the middle of the field. A group of comedians were set up to perform a rendition of *A Duck for a Hen*. The six of them grabbed seats near the front. He ignored the way people cleared out for them. He tried to pretend he was normal, no different than everyone else around. It was almost easy when he focused on Claire and nothing else.

Those in attendance got over the surprise at seeing him soon enough. Everyone settled down to watch the show. He was acutely aware of Claire beside him, the rise and fall of her chest, the delicate protrusion of her collar bones against her skin. They were close enough that her shoulder brushed his arm, sending heat across his skin. He kept his breathing steady to keep his mind from clouding with arousal.

He leaned in to whisper against her ear, noticing the gooseflesh that popped up on her skin. "A Duck for a Hen is a favorite tale at festivals like this. Have you heard of it?" She shook her head. Her breathing had quickened at his proximity, and he had the perfect view of her chest. His pants grew tight, but he kept his voice steady. "It's about an inexperienced young farmer who wants to build his own hen coop. He purchases a hen from a merchant after the merchant promises that the baby hen will lay golden eggs, but it's a trick. It's only a chick when the farmer buys it, you see. He treats it special, giving all sorts of attention, but the chick is really a duckling." A giggle fell from her lips, making sparks dance on his skin. She kept her gaze on the stage. "As the chick grows, the farmer quickly realizes it doesn't look anything like a hen, but he's never seen a duck either, so he has nothing to compare it to. He goes back to the merchant, who tells him that the chick simply looks different because it bears golden eggs once it matures. At last, the chick grows up and the farmer discovers that he's been duped. Arguments ensue. He eventually tries to run the merchant out of town. It's all rather funny, just watch. You'll see."

He was immensely pleased to earn a single grin for his efforts, and couldn't help but fix his gaze on her lips.

She watched the stage, unblinking, as the performers pranced around with raised voices, dramatically acting out all that he had explained. When they reached the part where the inept farmer confronted the merchant, the arguments between the two left her doubled over in laughter. He couldn't help but watch *her* instead of the performers. The way she laughed. Her smile.

He fought the urge to snatch her hand. Even simply imagining how she would react to his touch left him jittery. Would she lace their fingers together, like she often did? Would she pay him a gentle smile? But he couldn't—shouldn't. They were in public.

When the play act ended, they visited other booths on the far side of the field. Claire spent enough coin to leave him with an overloaded sack of wares, which he carried around without complaint, even when she tried to take it from him. The last item nearly split the seams. He glared at the heavy weight in his hand, lifting it pointedly.

"What?" she said, shrugging. "I'm giving back to Dragonwall's economy, aren't I?"

"I wasn't going to say a word."

Her eyes narrowed. He knew that look. Mock judgment.

"Really," he added, covering his heart. "I wasn't. Selling wares is what our merchants come here for. Most have very few opportunities like this. Your support will feed their families through the winter." His words appeared to satisfy her. "Now, shall we head over to the arena for some fighting? I could use some ale."

They made their way back to the carriages where they stowed their belongings and got comfortable for the ride back through the city's gates. The carriages stopped before the towering structure he knew intimately from his youth. It made him think of Reyr. His chest squeezed painfully.

"Wow, I've always wanted to see it up close." Claire's face was pressed close to the carriage window. "It's so much bigger in person."

"It seats thousands."

Her eyes widened. "Really?"

Desaree and Verath both nodded.

As they disembarked from the carriages, the clang of weapons echoed from within the arena. He led them through the front gates where Verath paid their entrance fee. Those around them quickly stepped aside to make way, bowing and whispering. Something about having Claire on his arm changed the way he felt about being on display. He usually entered through the back entrance that led directly to the royal box, but with her, he quickly noticed people's eyes were on her more than him. A far preferable alternative.

The royal box was shaded by an awning. They found their seats, settling in to watch. "The soldier fights take place in the morning," he explained, using the excuse to lean in close. "We already missed those. Right now it's mostly drengr. Well worth watching."

Mostly because he enjoyed seeing her reactions. She sat forward in her seat, her gaze intent on the dirt floor below. When a worthy blow was struck, or blood drawn, she emitted a tut of frustration or excitement, sometimes holding her breath. Her eyes flicked back and forth, perhaps memorizing each movement as an understudy might.

His thoughts drifted back to their sparring session. Cyrus had shown himself—much to his delight. But that was not what heated his blood. He remembered the way she leaned against him that evening, the warmth of her body against his, the smell of her hair, the way her curves lined up perfectly to his. Like she was made for him.

Merchants made their way through the stands, selling food and drink. Verath purchased refreshments and passed them around. They ate, and pointed, and speculated when one of the competitors made a blunder. He couldn't remember a time he'd had this much fun. For a few brief hours, he almost forgot what it was like to be king, to carry the burden of an entire kingdom on his shoulders.

The sun dropped towards the horizon and the fighting came to an end. The stands began to empty. The illusion shattered, and he found himself clenching his teeth, annoyed that it was over.

They waited for the crowd to dissipate before heading to their carriages. He allowed Verath to hand Desaree into their carriage before doing the same. The brief touch of her skin was hardly enough to satisfy him, nor the close proximity they now shared.

"Gods!" Claire was in raptures over everything. "That was so much fun."

They chatted away, talking through their favorite parts of the day. He let the sound of her voice lull him into silence, watching the buildings flash by as their carriage clattered through the city. He wanted to take her hand in his, but instead clenched his fist in his lap.

"I can't wait to wear my new hairnet. Maybe I can wear my red gown tomorrow and you can put it in for me?"

"Of course," Desaree was saying.

"I could do this every day," she sighed, at last turning to him, perhaps finally remembering he was there. "Couldn't you?"

"I could, if my responsibilities did not exist." Her face fell. He cursed himself for allowing his melancholy to take away from her enjoyment. "We still have the ball tomorrow night, don't forget."

"Of course! The ball..." Her expression brightened. She hugged her sack of wares to her chest. "It's going to be so much fun."

"Yes, quite," he said, letting the promise of it seep into his voice. His eyes lingered over her lips. Perhaps too long.

Their carriage clattered into the courtyard. Saffra and Bedelth emerged from the second carriage and bid them farewell, disappearing into the corridors. He gazed after Bedelth, noticing a tenseness in his shield's shoulders. What was that about?

"I'll just take these for you," Desaree stammered, grabbing Claire's overflowing bag of merchandise before disappearing into the keep with Verath.

He watched their retreating forms. "Well, they were quick to scamper away."

"Yes, I suppose so."

After an entire day pining after her, an entire day spent wanting to touch her, he had her to himself. It left his pulse racing. He wanted so badly to drag her off into some darkened corridor and pull her into his arms, to run his tongue over her lips, to taste her for the first time—

"Did you enjoy today?" She looked up at him with those eyes— those damn eyes.

His clothes were too tight, too warm. He forced his voice to sound calm. "I did. That was the most fun I've had at a tournament in as long as I can remember."

"Oh?"

"But only because you were with me." As soon as he said it, he watched her for signs of pleasure. There. She blushed and glanced at the ground, achieving the desired effect.

"Should we..." Her eyes darted towards the royal gardens behind them.

Their walk—but they had walked all day. And damned if he wouldn't have chosen to walk for an entire eternity, never ceasing, beside her. But then he thought of the pile of documents sitting on his desk, of the contracts he had promised to sign weeks ago. Gods. He wanted to gouge his eyes out at the mere reminder.

"If I could spend every moment in your company, I would be the happiest person that ever lived."

"But..."

He sighed. "But, duty awaits." She nodded, but did not seem upset. "May I escort you to your chambers? We can walk slowly."

She perked up and took his arm. They made their way through the keep. It was dark and the corridors were empty. He took her hand instead, lacing their fingers together, pulling her closer to him as they walked. His ears pricked at the faint sigh escaping her lips, almost imperceptible.

He walked as slow as possible without coming to a complete standstill. If only to keep hold of her just a moment longer. The guards at her door looked on, pretending obliviousness to their king's hand holding. Rumors would spark, if they hadn't already.

"You sure you don't want to come in for a few minutes?" she asked, glancing at the guards before looking back at him. "I can send Desaree away."

"I had better not, or else I might never leave." At this, she smiled. "Perhaps...perhaps another time?"

"Of course. Another time."

Perhaps tomorrow night, he wanted to say. After the ball. But he left the words unsaid. "I look forward to seeing you in your gown tomorrow." His words brought a flush to her skin. "I will come by and collect you at dusk, if that is favorable?"

"That—I mean, yes, it is." She glanced at the guards again.

"Don't mind them," he said, keeping his voice low, keeping a firm hold on her hand. "They are paid well enough to keep their mouths shut." He let the words hang in the air and saw the guards struggle to keep their expressions neutral. "Now then, goodnight, Lady Claire." He lifted her hand and kissed her palm, his lips lingering over her skin, eyes lingering over hers.

"Goodnight, Talon," she said in a breathy whisper.

He dropped her hand and stepped away, then retreated down the hall to his own door. Just before he reached his own guards, he glanced over his shoulder. She was still watching him, standing there with her arms at her side. How strange this was, to have someone so intently focused upon him. And not just *anyone*, either. Gods, it made his insides squirm with a feeling he hadn't felt in a long, long time. Giving her a final smile and an awkward wave that made him feel absolutely and completely stupid, he disappeared into his tower.

CHAPTER 34

THE BATHING POOL

Esterpine

Jeanine placed her hands on her knees, doubling over to breathe. Stars popped in and out of her vision. A bead of sweat rolled down her back, despite the coolness of the forest.

"By all means, take as long as you need. I've got nothing but time." Feowen sheathed his blade and crossed his arms, but the corner of his lips curved. She wanted to wipe the smug grin right off his pretty face.

They'd been sparring for nearly two hours. Training to the rigors of Feowen's standards, which were less strict than Lykan, but also more helpful. She still trained with Lykan a few times a week, to keep up appearances. But Feowen offered better tips and feedback. She was learning in a constructive way, rather than merely practicing.

A subtle movement caught her attention. She glanced toward the edge of the clearing. A pair of eyes met hers. "Your sister is watching us."

"I know. She's been there for nearly ten minutes."

324

She brushed away the locks of hair sticking to her forehead. "Oh. Well, sorry if I was too busy trying to stay alive to notice."

"Relax." Feowen turned away. "Hello, sweet sister. No need to keep gawking. Might as well join us and say what you've come to say. Not that we'll make much sense of it anyway."

He shared a secret smile with her.

Taylynn swept from the undergrowth. Her keen gaze pinned on them. "I'm pleased to see you practicing so diligently." She glanced at Jeanine before looking back at Feowen. "Her training is progressing well, yes? Good. In time, she will come to need it."

Jeanine's brow furrowed.

"In time?" Feowen's head tilted, predatory in nature. "Always the cryptic one, sis. I'm surprised you even care, given your stance on violence."

"I need not like violence to know when it is necessary. Swords win arguments as well as words." She was met with silence. "Oh, all right. I came to say goodbye."

"You're leaving again?" The tone in Feowen's voice changed from annoyance to concern.

"I must. You know I must."

"And what is your excuse this time?"

"The stones. I must return them."

Feowen's expression clouded. "Mother gave them back?"

A faint tut escaped Taylynn's lips. "Only after another argument."

"About?"

The princess glanced at Jeanine before saying, "It was as we expected. She refused to hand them over. Even after I reiterated my role." Taylynn screwed up her face, mimicking Queen Jade as she said, "'You cannot expect me to give them to you. How can I trust you won't give them away again?'" A perfect impersonation. Absolutely perfect. Jeanine hid her wicked smile.

Feowen shrugged. "You can hardly blame her."

"Can't I, though?"

"She is bitter over Cyrus. You know how she holds grudges."

"I did what I had to do, Feowen. She knows that. You know that. I know that. We *all* know that."

"True. But I'm not sure she will ever forgive you for it."

"Probably not. But his claim was valid. What choice did I have?"

"What choice? Even though you knew what would happen if you handed them over?" Feowen arched a knowing eyebrow. "You knew what would happen to Cyrus. To Dragonwall. To all of us." His words were damning.

"What happened was necessary," she snapped. "And we both know why." Her gaze flicked to Jeanine again. "Anyway, I shan't be away *too* long...not this time."

He studied her. "You mean, I'm not going to have to drag you out of the forest like I usually do?"

"*Drag me*? I would hardly call it that."

His expression darkened. "And what would you call it? Every time I fetch you, I worry it has finally happened. You go in there,"— his eyes flicked towards the undergrowth—"and you come out more forest than sprite. Every. Damn. Time. Tay. It's going to claim you if you aren't careful. Once that happens, I won't be able to save you."

"You worry too much, little brother. I can take care of myself."

"Take care of *yourself*?! Don't make me laugh."

Jeanine's frown deepened, trying to make sense of their words.

"I will return. I promise. And while I am gone, keep our mother in check."

He scowled. "And why would I need to do that?"

"Upon the wind rides the current of change. I sense it in my bones. So does our tree. Before long, we shall have a visitor."

Feowen scowled. "And who might that be? Not King Talon again?"

Taylynn laughed, like a chime caught in a breeze. "Oh, no. I do not think he will ever return. Just make sure mother behaves. You know how she is around those who threaten her."

"That's all you'll give me?"

Taylynn glanced at the undergrowth and inhaled, fully

ignoring the question. "I cannot say how long I will be gone, Feowen. Just do as I say." With that, she turned to Jeanine. "You will play a role, too. Watch over our guest when she arrives. She will need a friend. Farewell." She strode to the foliage and disappeared from view.

Jeanine's lips parted with surprise. "Take...take care of who? Why would she ask...?"

"Because she's mental, that's why." Despite what he said, there was fondness in his words. He sighed. "I didn't think it would happen."

"What? What would happen?" None of it made any sense. Why was it always like this? Like trying to solve a riddle every time Taylynn spoke. Like the princess wanted to say more, but never said enough.

Feowen's eyes shuttered. "I think we'll know soon enough."

"Great. That's it? You too, huh?"

His gaze lingered over her and then he laughed, long and loud. "You look like hell, Jeanine. Absolute hell."

She cursed under her breath, words she'd picked up over the years from Jahl. She framed a cutting reply—

"Come on. I know exactly what we need." He led her away without waiting for an answer.

"Well, fine then!" she muttered, sheathing her sword. She followed him through the dense foliage until they reached a path. The forest was full of these twisting dirt paths, each leading to a different destination, many leading nowhere at all. She often wondered if their purpose was to trick brave travelers who managed to get near Esterpine.

"Where are we going, exactly?" she called after Feowen. Her exasperation dissolved the farther they walked. He was far enough ahead that she lost sight of him. She refused to increase her pace. Her skin was sticky enough.

They certainly weren't heading back towards the city. Then again, much of the forest looked the same. She could have been somewhere she'd been hundreds of times before without knowing. The tall trees were covered in vines and dense foliage. Flowers scattered across the green tapestry before her like stars smeared across the night sky. Birds welcomed them in passing. Insects chirruped. A light breeze caressed all it touched, including her heated skin.

"Just up ahead," Feowen called, even though they continued to walk for another ten minutes.

She caught the sound of trickling water. Feowen stopped. "We are here. Close your eyes. I want it to be a surprise." There was excited impatience in his voice, which intrigued her. "Come on, Jeanine. You'll have to trust me."

"Fine, but this better be good." She squeezed her eyes shut.

She almost gasped when his hand slid into hers. Her body stiffened. If he noticed, he ignored it. Instead, he pulled her forward. "Careful—" He put his other hand on her waist, guiding her. "There's a log there—watch it." The sound of water loomed closer.

She let her other senses take over, giving in to his gentle touch. The path beneath her feet softened. She smiled at the feel of moss between her toes.

This close, Feowen smelled like the forest, a mix of flowers, soil, and pine.

Weeks ago, she pondered his attention. The increasing amount of time he spent around her. He continued to ask her strange, off-handed questions. To study her as if she were some zoo exhibit. She saw a zoo once, in Lincastle, as a child. All manner of animals and beasts she never thought real. Was that it? She was the human he wasn't used to interacting with? The human he'd seen so little of during his sheltered life in Esterpine? She knew that few of the sprites left the forest, if ever.

Only those who manned the outpost got to interact with humans.

But there was something else to his attention. He laughed at the awkward things she said, but never in a mean way. He watched her when she pretended not to notice. He teased her, but there was never any bite to the words.

She'd grown used to his oddities. Where his sister was cryptic, he was openly curious. Where his sister was soft and flowery, he was rigid and unadorned. Where his sister preferred to hide away, he flaunted himself out in the open. His sister didn't mingle with the people of Esterpine. He did. More and more he seemed the opposite to Taylynn in every way. The two of them struck a stark balance. A curious linking of blood. Yet, the love between them was painfully obvious. Their earlier conversation had only reinforced that.

She wondered what Feowen had meant when he mentioned rescuing Taylynn from the forest. Had there been something within its depths that harmed her? Perhaps she would never know.

"All right. It's here." Feowen released her, though his hand lingered over her a second longer than necessary. "Open your eyes."

She did. A gasp fell from her lips. "Oh! It's...wow."

That something *so* exquisite could exist this close to the city shouldn't have come as a surprise. But it was, entirely. Hours, days, spent wandering the outskirts— "Why have I never found this before?"

They stood before a deep pool of clear water fed by a small creek. It emptied into the pool by way of a small waterfall. It exited at the other side through a narrow gap in the rocks, trickling away into the undergrowth. The lyrical sound whispered as it pulled her gaze from one side of the forest to the other. All around was soft moss and flowers, like a carpet for bare feet to tread over.

"Only those who know of its existence may seek it out," Feowen answered. "We have many pools like this, filled with living water."

"Living...water?" She glanced at him.

"Yes. It isn't like the water you are used to. Come, let's enjoy it." Without waiting for an answer, he stripped away his knee-high pants, the only bit of clothing he'd been wearing, and jumped naked into the pool. His midnight blue hair fanned out around him.

She watched, speechless. He laughed and sent a torrent of water splashing in her direction. "Come on!" he called. "You could use a swim."

Her eyes darted. She could say no, that she had no interest in swimming. She didn't know how to swim. There were no pools of water where she was from and this one was fairly deep at its center. But it was the nakedness that left her nervous.

"Uhm." She cleared her throat. "While *you* might be comfortable in *your* skin, where I come from, females don't shed their clothes for males but on their wedding night."

"Oh?" His expression turned to one of mock surprise. "Since when have you *ever* played by the rules?" His eyes darted to the sword at her waist.

"I..." She swallowed, knowing full well he'd snared her.

Feowen was old, very old. That alone was unnerving. A female's body wasn't foreign to him. He'd probably seen numerous beauties among his people, given how open they were, given how little they wore.

But she wasn't a sprite.

She glanced into the pool again. The water was tempting—so terribly tempting. Another bead of sweat rolled down her back, as if taunting her.

A small smile crept over Feowen's face, as if he could sense the sweat beading her skin. "A swim will do you good. Quit being shy, *human*." The last word hung in the air like a taunt. He said no more, swimming away to the other side of the pool where he disappeared under the waterfall.

She opened her mouth, but nothing came out. Her resolve hardened. She was no prude. What did she care? Her body was nothing more than flesh, blood, and bone. And lately a great deal of muscle, honed by hours practicing with Feowen.

"Here goes nothing," she muttered.

Feowen was still unseen, somewhere beneath the waterfall, as she shed her clothing. She moved quickly, removing her sword and tossing it away, then her tunic and pants. She rushed to get in.

She had just stepped into the pool when a torrent of water splashed over her. She screeched and lost her balance, slipping. Cool water rushed up around her. It was a balm to her aching muscles and sticky skin, washing away her discomfort in an instant.

Her feet found the sandy bottom and she stood, scrunching her toes. The water reached her shoulders. Feowen's wicked face popped up above the water's surface. "You did that on purpose!" she hissed, sending a splash his way.

"Maybe. You humans are so stiff!" He swam away before she could argue. "Come, enjoy the waterfall," he called.

She glanced across the pool. She wasn't eager to attempt swimming, so instead, she edged her way around, keeping to the shallow side, keeping her body submerged. Feowen was right, though. The water felt incredible. Refreshing. Unlike any bath she'd ever taken.

When she reached the waterfall, bliss settled over her. The water cascaded around her, dousing her hair, rushing down her face. She wiped it from her eyes, but let it continue to wash over her.

"The water in the forest is connected," Feowen explained. Behind the waterfall, there was a small indent in the rock wall that made his voice echoey. "Everything flows away from a single source, out into the world like arteries from a heart."

Her brow furrowed. "A single source? Where does it come from?"

"The king tree, of course."

"Oh..." She frowned. Her upbringing had been sheltered, but she knew enough about geography to know that most bodies of water needed a true source, like a glacier, or mountains covered in snow. Rain. The forest lay at the center of the continent. Water didn't come from nowhere...did it? "You cannot expect me to believe a tree produces its own water."

"At the base of its roots there is an eternal spring that bubbles up from the depths of the earth, and from this spring flows all water, all life, feeding the world." He dipped lower and took in a mouthful, swallowing. "Here in the forest, its properties are limitless. But once these tributaries leave, they lose their potency."

"Turning into the water that we humans are used to? Normal water?"

"Exactly." He took another mouthful, but this time sent a

stream at her face like a child might. She laughed and fell back-wards out of range, splashing a torrent of water in his face before dipping back out into the main pool. He followed.

"So, what happens if I drink this water?" she asked. "Will I become a sprite?"

"I doubt it. Though, I've never heard of a human drinking our water. We don't bring humans into the forest, let alone lead them to our hidden secrets. Perhaps you might be the first." He hesitated. "Go ahead. Give it a try."

She paused, studying him. Was he making a joke? There was no hint of mischief in his face.

She filled her mouth, letting the cold liquid flow in. It tasted like water—clean and refreshing. But it also tasted like more. She swallowed. The cold traveled down her throat and into her stom-ach. She could almost track its progress through her body. She waited. Nothing happened.

"How do you feel? Funny in the head? Dizzy? Alive? What?"

"Normal...I suppose?"

He arched an eyebrow. "Your mind doesn't feel addled? Perhaps you should start singing and see what happens."

"Hah! No, thank you. I'll pass."

"Well..." He shrugged. "It was worth a try."

She watched him swim out into the middle, almost envious. He moved his arms and feet in a paddling motion, staying afloat. If she tried, not only would she look foolish, but she'd sink to the bottom like a rock. The boulders beneath his feet looked quite a ways down. She wasn't keen to take her chances.

"Come on. Give it a try," he called, as if reading her mind.

"No thanks," she said, finding a spot shallow enough to sit, while remaining fairly submerged. A dart of sunlight made its way through a gap in the trees, lighting up the glow that permeated the forest. Turning the air golden. It fell upon her skin, warming her. She smiled, leaning into it, letting her head fall back, aware that her shoulders had lifted out of the water, that her breasts were probably visible. But it was so warm, so welcome.

She became extremely aware of Feowen's attention on her. She peeled open an eye, catching him staring, his eyes dark with something unreadable. She shrank back down to her shoulders. He looked away and began swimming back and forth across the deeper reaches of the pool, leisurely occupying himself. She studied his body, the markings on his skin, the way they swirled and glowed. His blue hair followed him, fanning out each time he stopped. The infuriating desire to run her fingers through it made her hands twitch. She pushed the desire down deep.

Her face turned red when she caught a glimpse of his nudity as he plunged face first beneath the surface. She turned her gaze to the forest, looking for other things to study. But his movements continued to draw her attention, as if he was doing it on purpose.

"Show off," she muttered, certain he'd heard when he snickered.

They remained in the pool for quite a while. He asked random questions. Like, why didn't humans know how to swim? Or, why were they all such prudes? And, how come a woman only showed her body to her partner? "Our women enjoy displaying their markings openly," he explained.

"Believe me, I'm well aware."

"A sprite's markings are a display of power," he went on. "It is a part of our identity, who we are, what we are capable of. Our strength. How do your people display such things?"

She considered, letting her head fall back again to catch the sunshine. "Through wealth, I suppose. Layers of fabric. Jewelry. Men like carrying well-crafted weapons. Women like flaunting well-made gowns." She turned to look at him.

"Yes, but none of that speaks to a person's abilities."

"True, but what abilities have we to show that might measure up to your judgmental standards? We cannot sing magic into the air. We cannot perform spells." She hesitated. "We can work with our hands, I suppose. Crafters can boast their wares at the marketplace. A musician can perform. But for the most part, it is all hidden. We cannot look upon another and say, 'Oh, she is good at singing flowers into existence. He is good at healing a broken tree root.'"

Feowen snorted. "That was only once. And only because it was one of my favorite trees." She arched an eyebrow. "Besides," he added, "I do not have a marking for it, so how would anyone but you know what I accomplished?"

"Well, you get my point."

"I suppose I do." He swam over, taking a place beside her.

She was highly aware of her nakedness—their nakedness. Heat erupted across her skin, leaving her flushed. She kept her face forward, hoping that he wasn't studying her. The water was perfectly clear. He need only look below the surface to see her hardened breasts.

"It makes you uncomfortable, doesn't it?"

She nearly jumped, glancing sidelong at him. "Yes," she said at last.

He snorted. "Humans..."

She opened her mouth—

"You have a beautiful body, Jeanine. So if that's what you're concerned about, you needn't be."

Her mouth snapped shut. That was *not* what she was concerned about. Hardly at all. Not even a little bit.

"If I bring you a gown, will you wear it to the autumn moon feast tomorrow night?"

"So I can show off my naked body to everyone else, too?" Her voice was louder than intended. "Bad enough that you have seen it. No, thank you."

He turned to stare out over the pool. "I...perhaps you are right. I simply thought you would look lovely in it, that is all. Never mind. I knew you would refuse."

"Wait..." Her chest pinched uncomfortably. Had he gotten a special gown made for her? He meant well, it was just that his views of propriety were simply too different from hers. Their culture, so dissimilar. But this was her home, for now. Perhaps she could learn to be understanding.

"You really have a gown for me?" she asked, her voice tentative. "Even if you knew I would say no?" He shrugged and turned away, as if it was unimportant. "Will it...will it show my female parts?"

He snorted. "Your breasts, you mean?" His eyes glanced down in obvious appraisal, sending a wave of heat straight to her core. But it was only a quick glance. "No, it's a bit more conservative than most. Because I knew how you would feel about that."

"Oh…"

"But it's fine. Just thought I'd try anyway. You humans—"

"That's enough, Feowen." Her voice turned deadly quiet. He glanced at her, wide-eyed. "I'm tired of the *you humans* this and *you humans* that. I know you think you've got me all figured out. And perhaps to some measure, you do. But enough is enough."

"I—you are right. My apologies."

Her lips parted in surprise at his apology. She exhaled. "Since you think you've got me all figured out, Prince Feowen, then I will surprise you by accepting your gown, if only to simply prove you wrong about me."

Then, to further prove a point, she stood from the pool, naked and dripping, her body displayed for the world to see, and left him to find her clothing. He watched, open mouthed, eyes trailing up and down her flesh as she began dressing in front of him. "Oh, and by the way," she snapped, "you left your jaw in the water."

His mouth snapped shut. The grin that followed was enough to steal the breath from her chest. He withdrew from the pool. It took every measure of self control to keep her gaze on his face and not on the rest of him. Especially the well endowed parts.

"Interesting," he said, passing her to collect his single item of clothing.

She tightened her fists. "What?"

"It would seem we were completely and utterly wrong."

"About what?" Gods, his back was covered in muscles that contracted as he slipped into pants. She strapped her sword to her waist, using it as an excuse to focus on something other than him.

"The water *has* addled your mind. We'll make a sprite of you yet."

A smile rushed to her face; she fought to hide it. The tension between them dissolved. "Yes, I suppose so," she found herself saying. Why was it so *difficult* to be annoyed with him?

"After you," he added. He held out his arm. She stepped forward onto the path, glancing over her shoulder to find the foliage had already fallen back into place, shielding the pool from view. Something told her that should she want it, she would find it again.

CHAPTER 35
AN IMPOSSIBLE CHOICE

Kastali Dun

Claire collapsed onto the sofa, breathless with laughter. Her friends did the same, their faces lit with excitement. The furniture had been pushed aside, leaving enough space for dancing. They'd spent the last three hours going over choreography for quicksteps, reels, spirals, tromps, waltzes, and more.

"I can't breathe," she gasped, clutching her side. It pinched with each inhale. "How will I manage in a ballgown?"

"You'll manage," Saffra said. "As King Talon's ward, everyone will expect it."

"No they won't," Desaree scoffed. "She's an outsider."

"All the more reason for her to surprise them," Jocelyn said, sharing a conspiratorial look.

"I'll be ready," she said. "The last thing I want is to give them another reason to gossip about me."

"Good." Jocelyn stood. "I'm famished. Let's have something to eat." Breakfast had been delivered at dawn, but they hadn't touched it.

With the tournament's ball taking place that evening, they'd all but run out of time. She was decent on her feet; her lessons with Jovari and Koldis had gone a long way in that regard. Plus, she'd had some dance lessons growing up, when her mother wasn't sure what her calling might be. A few years of jazz, ballet, and tap. Of course, that was before her teen years. But she'd gained a good sense of self and coordination.

The thought of being on display for the first dance of the evening set her nerves on edge.

"If you're still feeling uncomfortable, we can run through everything again, after we eat," Saffra said. "Another hour and you should be as good as the rest of us."

Claire snorted. "I very much doubt that. You've got a lifetime of experience on me. But...we'll see."

They gathered around the table, laughing and speculating. She'd just filled her plate, when a knock came at the door. "I'll get it," Des said, jumping to her feet. Bedelth swept into the room.

Claire dropped her fork. "Bedelth? Is everything all right? Is it Talon?"

"Our king is fine. Please, sit. Forgive me for the unexpected interruption." He hesitated, taking in the scattered furniture and table full of food. His gaze settled on Saffra. "Might I have a word?"

Saffra frowned. "Surely it is nothing that cannot be said before the others."

Bedelth glanced between them, his posture rigid. "Right. Very well. I understand that this is rather last minute, but I have found myself without a partner for tonight's ball. I was hoping that...well, I understand that you do not plan to attend. I thought perhaps you might...?"

"Oh..." Saffra's blink was her only show of surprise. "I had not planned on going. But Jocelyn doesn't have a partner yet. She would be more than happy to accompany you."

"Actually, I..." Jocelyn hesitated before sinking lower in her chair. "Forgive me, but I do already have an escort for tonight. I just didn't tell you as I thought the reminder of your—I thought it might be painful."

"I see." Saffra fell quiet.

Bedelth adjusted the collar of his tunic, as if it was too tight. "I apologize for making this awkward. Forgive me, I should not have come." He turned to leave.

"Bedelth, wait." Saffra stopped him. "It is... That is to say, I appreciate you thinking of me. You have always been thoughtful." She looked uncertain. "I don't have a dress commissioned for the occasion. But, never mind about that, I'm sure one of my other gowns will do."

Bedelth's face changed, brightening. "You're sure? It is not too much trouble?"

"It is no trouble at all. I would be honored to attend with you." Saffra paid him a kind smile. Something unspoken passed between them.

Claire watched, curious. "I think I have an idea," she decided, catching Saffra's eye. "I know where we might find you something better suited for the occasion."

Saffra studied her before turning back to Bedelth. "Very well then. As you can see, it shouldn't be a problem. Thank you—for asking."

His relieved smile lit up his face. "That's excellent. I look forward to it very much. Oh—" He hesitated again. "I almost forgot." He handed Claire a folded note. "From Verath. He asked that I deliver it since I was already on my way here." She took it, frowning. "Well, that's it, then. I'll collect you at dusk, Lady Saffra. Until then..." He nodded at the rest of them before making a quick exit.

"Uhm..." Claire glanced at the empty place he'd left behind, then at the note. "Did that just happen?"

"It did." Saffra's voice sounded far away, as if she too couldn't believe it.

Claire handed the note to Desaree. "He probably meant to give this to you, not me. Verath doesn't send me letters."

Desaree took the note and scowled. "No, it has your name on it." She handed it back. "Why would he be writing to you, I wonder?"

"Hmm." Claire read over its contents, frowning deeper.

"Strange. He requests I dine with him for lunch. As if we don't have enough going on already. But, why me? Why today? I don't understand."

"Let me see." Desaree took the note, chewing absentmindedly on the skin of her bottom lip. "Now that I think of it, I do recall him mentioning something off hand—needing to talk to you about another drengr, I think?"

"Very well, then." A wicked smile came to Claire's face. "I'll join him for lunch. But only because I bet he wants to talk to me about *you*, Des." She poked Desaree in the shoulder. "Maybe he wants ideas for tonight. Or...I don't know...something."

"About me?" Desaree shook her head. "I doubt it. But you had better answer his reply. I'll be busy this afternoon, anyway, getting everything ready for us. Now that Saffra's going, we must get her ready, too."

"Jocelyn can attend to me," Saffra murmured. A set of lines had formed between her eyebrows. "You two worry about yourselves."

"Oh, right! That reminds me," Claire said. "A gown. Did you know that the king's tower has a whole wardrobe set aside for the queen?" Everyone in the room fell silent. "I'm serious. An entire room!"

Saffra's brows drew together. "The queen? You're sure? But there *is* no queen."

"Well, yeah." Claire's smile was wicked. "But that's not what I meant. Remember when I found the passageway to the queen's private parlor, the one we used that night the vodar attacked? Well, I had a peek around the first time. Let's just say, the king probably isn't the only one who has an extensive wardrobe. Wait until you see it. I'm positive we can find something there. And, you'll look like a queen!"

"Oh." Saffra hesitated. "I'm not sure I should...but...well, it would be fun to have a look, wouldn't it?"

"We'd be caught, wouldn't we?!" Jocelyn glanced between them, obviously worried. "Everyone would know your gown belonged to the queen."

"Jocelyn, there hasn't been a queen in hundreds of years,"

Desaree said, surprisingly open to the idea. "Most of the nobles attending the ball were not alive during the last queen's reign. Those who were probably didn't pay close enough attention."

"Yes, but..." Jocelyn frowned. "Well, all right."

THE QUEEN'S parlor was deserted, as expected, its furniture draped with sheets to protect against dust. Windows cast square patterns of light across the floor. "What level of the tower is this?" Jocelyn asked.

"One of the lower levels," Claire answered, glancing around. "We had to climb several flights of stairs to reach the main floor last time we were here." It was dark then. She spotted the door she wanted. "Here, this way." It led to a staging room with mirrors and padded stools. Likewise, everything was covered to protect against dust. "This must be where the queen's ladies got her ready. The wardrobe is through here."

The wardrobe's interior was pitch black. A dusty smell left their noses crinkling. Saffra sneezed before sending out glowing orbs to light their way.

Claire's eyes widened. "I almost forgot how large it was. The biggest walk-in-closet I've ever seen." She stepped inside. "Fit for a queen."

"The queen's wardrobe," Desaree murmured, awed. Her voice took on a dreamy tone. "Can you imagine, Claire? If *you* were the queen and this was *yours*? I'd have something new to dress you in every day!" Des let out a little squeal of delight.

Claire's face burned. She hated that none of them knew about her bond with Talon. "Yes, I can only imagine."

If she and Talon acted on their bond, if she became Dragonwall's queen, this could all be hers. Or, perhaps it already belonged to her simply by being his mate. Either way, her heart began to pound with yearning.

"Well, what are we waiting for?" Desaree pushed past them.

Besides gowns, there were wooden jewelry boxes—one of

which had probably held the blue sapphire necklace Talon gifted her—shoe cubbies, racks for shawls, and everything else a queen's attire might need. Everything was meticulously shielded from dust. "There must be magical enchantments placed on this room, to protect from the ravages of time." Claire ran her fingers over everything, needing to touch it, to feel it. To connect with it. Hers... what if all this became hers?!

They rustled through the contents of the wardrobe for what felt like hours, gushing over the beauty of the fabrics, the elegance of the gowns, and the sheer collection that had amassed over multiple reigns. "These gowns were definitely worn by multiple queens," Jocelyn pointed out. "Look at this one." She had uncovered a dress of black lace. "This style is positively *archaic*." Her nose wrinkled. "I would *never* dress Saffra in something like this. Perhaps it was relevant thousands of years ago, but certainly not now. Who wears high collars that cover the neck in such a way? Not a single measure of chest showing."

"Hmm, you're right." Saffra eyed it. "Dragonwall's queens must add to the collection over the course of their reign. I bet some of the gowns date all the way back to Queen Isabella."

Claire's heart raced—something to connect her to the ancient queen. A woman who might possibly be her ancestor.

"Well, let's find something and get out of here," Claire said. "I don't want Talon catching us. We're stealing from the queen's wardrobe, after all."

"Not stealing," Desaree amended. "Only borrowing."

Claire hardly heard her. Something had caught her eye. "Look at this!" Triumphant, she removed a pink and orange brocade, its hem tinged with red. Like the colors of the setting sun. It looked almost identical to Bedelth's scales. "This is the one. It's perfect—an excellent match."

"There are ties." Jocelyn examined the gown, holding it up against Saffra's slight frame. "I should be able to adjust it this afternoon. Yes, this should do nicely."

Claire couldn't help but wonder if it was a sign that they were meant to find this exact gown.

CLAIRE STOOD outside Verath's chamber and knocked. Verath answered, a pleased smile on his face. He wore a sleeveless doublet of blue brocade, with a billowy tunic beneath, and casual tan pants. Her eyes lingered over his bare feet. This was his apartment after all, and one did go barefoot in one's own living quarters. She liked his dressed down, informal appearance.

"Leave us," he said to her trailing guards. "I will escort her back when we are through." They nodded and departed.

He turned to her. "Good afternoon. I appreciate you joining me under such short notice."

She smiled but otherwise remained silent as she slipped into his living quarters, taking in the space. It was smaller than her own chambers, but no less comfortable. There were separate living and sleeping areas, and a door off to the side for his bathing chamber. She immediately approved of his love of books. Everything was neat and tidy. Clearly someone who appreciated organization. His room also had doors out to a balcony. All the rooms along the outer wall of the corridor had such a luxury.

A small table in the center of the room had been set with their meal. Verath rushed to pull out a chair, motioning for her to sit. She did, but remained silent, continuing to eye him. He did not appear to mind her silence.

His hulking frame was nearly too large for his chair.

"I admit, you have me at a loss. To what do I owe the pleasure of your invitation?" Her words came out more formal than intended.

"Direct and to the point," Verath said, nodding. "Shall we not dine and indulge in a few snippets of small talk before we get to business, my lady?"

She snorted. "Cut the bullshit, Verath. We both know I'm not a lady by Dragonwall's standards. I did not hesitate to call you Verath, as I'm sure you noticed."

"Claire, then." His lips twitched. "I admit, I have never met another woman with so little fear of speaking her mind. Not an ounce of timidity in your bones."

"Modern words for a modern gal." She offered him a grin. "Besides, how else does one learn to handle a great king like Talon?" She glanced down at the table. Their plates were covered with silver covers. Out of curiosity she lifted hers to find sliced ham, potatoes, and honey wheat bread.

"I do appreciate modern words," he mused. "Our formalities can be exhausting. That's why I like you, Claire, a great deal."

"But it did take some winning over on my part, no?"

He fought back a smile. "Not much. But I tend to mistrust strangers, especially outsiders."

"You've met a fair few of them, I take it? Outsiders?"

"Very funny. But you understand my point?"

"I do. But you still haven't answered my question." She eyed him.

"Indeed." He lifted his glass and took a sip of water. "I wanted to speak with you regarding a certain matter that has come to my attention."

"Oh? Little old me?" She placed a hand over her breast and feigned surprise.

"Yes. I need your help. Or at least, I believe you to be a suitable person for the job."

"This isn't in regards to Caterina, is it? Because I want nothing to do with that woman."

"Caterina?" His head tilted. "Oh. No. Not at all. No." He hesitated. "As you know, the king's collection of shields is short in number. Cyrus was a crucial part of our circle."

"Oh..." This definitely wasn't going where she'd expected. She exhaled, forcing her shoulders to relax.

"He will be difficult to replace, but there should always be six."

"Right. I thought... Well, never mind."

"Thought what?"

"I honestly thought you called me here to talk about Desaree."

"Desaree?" His expression brightened. "While that is a topic I never tire of, no. We have a potential contender for a king's shield."

"That's...great. But what does it have to do with me?"

"I need you to talk him out of it."

She nearly choked. "Me? But, why? What makes you think I'll have any sway?"

"Come. Let's eat and I'll explain." He cut into the ham on his plate. After a beat, she exhaled and did the same. "It is a young drengr by the name of Dallin. Just after you departed north, he appeared in the capital from Fort Edge, requesting to be considered."

Through a mouthful that was utterly unladylike, she said, "Okay. And what's so wrong with that?"

"What's so wrong? Claire, he's young, extremely young. He fledged four, maybe five years ago? That's too young."

"So what?" She shrugged. "His age may be indicative of inexperience, but he still deserves fair consideration. Is he competing against any others?"

"No. No others. Twenty-four is simply too young."

"I see." She set down her utensils and crossed her arms. Twenty-four was merely two years older than her own age. Did Verath consider *her* incapable too? "Tell me, is there a rule in the charter that sets an age requirement?"

"No. But surely you—"

"Look, Verath, I get that you're nervous about giving such a responsibility to someone so young. I am, too. Talon's life means a great deal to everyone, myself included. We want him adequately protected. That doesn't mean Dallin can't learn, that he can't grow in time. You can train him up a bit." She hesitated, eying him. "You'd make a great teacher, you know."

"I..." His chest puffed up. "That's beside the point."

She sighed, picking up her fork again. "I just don't think you should turn away a candidate that might be a worthy contender simply because of age."

His jaw tightened. "I don't think Dallin has fully considered what he would be giving up. A shield's position is for life. We take no mates."

"Oh. The mate thing. That's what this is about?" She considered his words. "All right, besides all of that, why do you think I'm a good fit for this? I'm guessing it has something to do with my age? He'll relate to someone younger?"

"Precisely." Verath leaned back in his chair.

"I don't really feel comfortable with this." She picked at her potatoes. "Mostly because I don't agree with you."

"What do you mean?"

"I don't agree that his decision is rash. I just don't. Everyone understands the severity of the oath. He will have already considered what it means. Why else would he journey so far to toss his name in the hat?"

"Just because he knows the rules doesn't mean he understands the full extent of them." Something crossed his expression. Pain? Regret? It was gone before she could decipher it.

"Fine. What makes you an expert on the matter, then? Have you even asked him?"

"I don't need to ask. Young people are stubborn. I'm sure he *believes* he understands the cost. I can assure you that he does not. He can't. Not until..."

"Not until what?" Her eyes narrowed.

"Not until he becomes a shield and then discovers that his mate is out there, waiting for him."

She frowned. The severity of his words came crashing down around her. Everything clicked into place. "Desaree's not your mate, is she?"

Even as she waited for him to answer, an ache penetrated her heart.

"No. She is not." His voice was low.

"What...what happened?"

"I'd rather not talk about it." He fell silent for the span of several breaths. "Claire, just because Dallin thinks he has life figured out, does not mean he does."

"Tell me what happened," she demanded. He did not answer. "Verath, you're courting my best friend, and now I find out that she's not your mate? I knew it was a possibility, but still. You're asking me to speak with Dallin over a very serious matter. Convince me that it's serious. You owe me that much."

He opened his mouth, then closed it. After a long hesitation, he said, "If I tell you, you must promise that you will not speak of it to Desaree. I cannot bear...it's something she should hear from me, not you."

"And will you tell her?"

His eyes fell to the table. "I cannot make that promise. Some demons are better left buried."

"Fine. That's between you and her. I promise I won't say anything. But just so you know, I hate keeping secrets." He arched a brow, like he was about to argue. "Okay. The *new* me hates secrets."

"All right, I'll tell you. Please be gentle with your judgment."

"I will. I promise."

"I was in my eighties when I decided to seek glory." As he spoke, his eyes were pointedly fixed upon the wall behind her. "King Tallek had an opening in his ranks. Becoming a shield was the ultimate achievement in my eyes. I see so much of myself in Dallin. I hadn't found a mate, and frankly, I didn't care about it. I could bed whomever I wanted. Being free had a nice feel to it. But my life lacked purpose and becoming a shield would mitigate that. So I applied and was accepted into King Tallek's ranks. It was an honor. I swore my oath. I was happy. I had everything figured out.

"A mate was the farthest thing from my mind for many years. I felt a sense of purpose, of fulfillment. The years ticked by. Eventually, King Tallek died, and I swore myself to his son. Then something changed. I felt it in my heart first, and then the rest of my body. It was like a subtle pull, like something was missing. It made no sense for a long time. An itch that no scratch could suppress. Ten years passed. And then fifteen. And then the realization hit me."

Disbelief broke over her like someone had cracked an egg over her head. "Your mate had come into existence."

"Aye. Kendra." His face twisted and he clenched and unclenched his hands as they rested on the table.

"You...you know her name?" A million questions bubbled up

inside her. She dared not voice any others and risk disturbing his explanation.

"I knew more than her name." He rubbed the back of his neck. "When I figured out what was happening, a sense of fear settled over me. I didn't know what to do—how to react. I thought if I ignored it, it would simply go away, but as the years passed, the inclination became stronger. She was nearing twenty when I sought her out. I made up some excuse to leave the capital, to check on troops in the countryside. I followed the pull to a town in the heart of Dragonwall. Orhaven." His eyes took on a faraway look. "Gods she was beautiful, with hair the color of chocolate, and a smile that could disarm the coldest male. The first time I saw her, I watched her playing with the village children, so motherly in her affections. She doted upon them and they adored her. I could tell that she was unmarried. The thought left my heart soaring."

Her insides turned to ice. "What did you do?"

"I watched her. I memorized her face. I imagined all the things we might do together. The life we might have together. Then I left."

"What?" she choked out.

"The years passed and with each day, I felt more and more like the wretch that I was. The day she died, I felt it in my heart like a knife. I knew then the full severity of my actions, of what I had done."

"You didn't...you didn't go to her?" she whispered. "You didn't talk to her?"

A harsh laugh escaped his lips. "Oh, believe me, the thought crossed my mind. I stood in the shadows and a million possibilities fluttered through my mind. But they each boiled down to two options. I could take her for my mate, abandon my honor, and banish myself from Dragonwall never to return, or I could accept the oath I had given, maintain my honor, and return to my duties."

Absolute horror settled in the pit of her stomach. "So you...you just *left* her there?"

"How could I be so cruel as to speak to her? To seek her out when I could not claim her? She was better off not knowing of the life she might have had. Not knowing what I robbed her of. It's...it is not so easy, Claire. My honor was at stake."

"Honor be damned!" She slammed her palm on the table, making the plates jump. "You should have gone to her! You...you deprived her of her destiny. You forced her to live a life she was not meant to live!" She was yelling now. "You...you stole from her, Verath! That alone is dishonorable!"

"You don't think I know that?!" he roared, leaping from his chair to pace. "You don't think I live with the decision every single day of my life? That I don't suffer from it? That I don't hate myself for it? That I don't fall asleep each night wondering how things might have been different had we fled to Kalderland, or Pavv, or Oshea across the sea? Fled to live our lives together?" His words slowed to a calm. "You think I go untortured?"

"I..." She took a deep, steadying breath. Shame washed over her. "I'm sorry. I should not have reacted like that. You asked me to be gentle in my judgment and I overreacted."

He exhaled, then reclaimed his seat.

She thought about what she would have done in his shoes. At first the answer seemed simple. But it wasn't. She knew what it meant to make a promise, and what it meant to break a promise. And Shields made oaths—life binding oaths. The shame would have ripped him apart the same way had he chosen her.

Verath had suffered and still suffered. His face was a tableau of overwhelming emotion. He dropped his head into his hands and gave a shuddering sigh.

"Verath, I...I'm sorry," she said. "For what you lost. You were presented with an impossible decision between honor and love."

"Yet, those were my choices," he said. "All because I made a rash decision in my youth to chase glory." When he lifted his head, his eyes glittered. "Now do you see? Now do you understand?"

She swallowed. "I understand, but I don't think Dallin will. It is not something you can tell a person, something that will sink in. They must live it. That is the cruelty of it all, don't you think?"

"Cruel. Yes. Life is cruel."

"But you have Desaree. She makes you happy, right?" Her voice shook.

"I have my Desaree. She makes me happy."

Not Desaree, but *my* Desaree. But she did not make him as happy as his mate would have. He didn't need to say it for her to hear it in his voice.

"And...you're certain Desaree is not your mate? That Kendra was indeed your mate? You never went to her. She never touched your scales."

"I know it in my heart," he whispered.

She reached across the table and put her hand over his. "Verath, I'm so sorry. I almost regret asking, regret causing you this discomfort. Does...does Talon know?"

Verath shook his head. "No one knows. I couldn't bring myself to tell anyone, to face the judgment that the truth would bring."

"You cannot blame yourself," she said at last. "Sometimes no choice is a good choice. Some of our choices fill us with regret. Some will haunt us unto death. We must get by as best we can. Life is unfair in many cruel ways. You must now choose to let it go. Don't let it chase after you."

He held her gaze. "Thank you. I...you're right. But such a thing is easier said than done. I will think about it."

She leaned back to regard him. "So, what do we do about Dallin? I understand the gravity of the situation, of what could befall him should he be accepted into Talon's ranks. Yet, I still believe that it is not our decision to make. Will you...might I share your story with him in confidence? So that he understands what is at stake? After that, all we can do is trust him to make his decision without our added interference."

"I'm not sure I want him to know."

"He looks up to you, doesn't he? Else he would not have approached you. I do not think you should fear his judgment. This is something he ought to know, and he will never fully understand until then."

Verath grappled with the idea then said, "You may tell him, then. I do not have the heart to."

"I think it is for the best."

They fell silent. Her appetite fled, so she came to her feet. "I ought to leave you. Give you some time to recover before tonight. That reminds me, have you seen Desaree's dress?" It was her best attempt to lighten the mood.

"Oh." His expression changed. His eyes brightened. "No. She refused to show me."

"Well..." A wicked grin came to her face. "Wait until you see it."

A smile tugged at his lips. "No hints?"

"My lips are sealed." She made the motion of zipping her lips and throwing away the key. When she walked to his door, he followed, escorting her down the hall where her guards waited outside her chambers.

"Thank you—for listening. I...it is a relief to get that off my chest. I hadn't realized until now."

She reached out and squeezed his arm. "Unburdening your heart is the first step towards healing. I'm happy to listen anytime you need to talk." She curtsied sloppily, reminding him of the outsider she was. "See you tonight, Verath."

He bowed formally. "See you tonight, Claire." She watched him go with heaviness in her heart, hoping she would never need to make a decision like his.

CHAPTER 36

DANCING WITH TALON

Kastali Dun

Claire gazed at her reflection, mesmerized. Layers of tulle and iridescent beads shifted color each time she moved, from dark green, to purple, to deep blue. Her gown was exquisite.

Dusk was approaching and with it, the start of the ball.

She inhaled. The air was electric with excitement. She could almost taste it.

Desaree wandered around lighting candles and wall sconces, her gown a blood red number with fitted sleeves and a bodice that came to a deep point over her abdomen. A red waterfall trailed in her wake.

Desaree's transformation was masterful. Seeing her like this—it made Verath's affection easy to understand. No wonder he had struggled for so long to resist the temptation of her. That didn't make his truth any easier to bear.

She turned away, back to her own reflection. Her golden hair was piled high atop her head. A jeweled comb was wedged against her coiffure in a crescent shape. It sparked with iridescence to match her gown. The contrast against her hair was astonishing. Desaree had even added kohl to her eyes and rouge to her cheeks.

A small smile pulled at the corners of her lips. She would have killed for some real makeup. Never mind the other modern comforts she missed.

She put a gloved hand against her skin, flushed with excitement. The glow of her spriten necklace pulsed, as if sensing her nerves. Her sweetheart neckline was cut low, highlighting the curves of her breasts and chest, showcasing her delicate collarbones.

Tonight was the first time she would show everyone what she was. The mark on her back was on display for all. The world would discover her secrets sooner or later.

Desaree appeared beside her. "King Talon won't be able to keep his eyes off you. Not that he ever can."

Claire's stomach fluttered. "You're incredible, Des. I have never felt this beautiful."

Desaree wrapped her arms around Claire's waist, bringing her chin to rest on her shoulder. They both gazed into the mirror. Desaree's face shone with nothing but love and admiration.

"Wait until the ladies of Dragonwall see you. The kingdom's dressmakers will have their hands full."

"You're saying I'm a trendsetter?"

"Something of the sort," Desaree murmured, eying the gown. "Madame Rosanne did a splendid job. I hadn't expected such a close match to Talon's scales. Even my own isn't as close to Verath as it could be—and for good reason. With a gown like yours, you might as well be attending your bonding ceremony in the throne room."

"Des!" Claire squealed, pushing herself out of Desaree's embrace. Desaree's words hit too close to home. Her heart pounded. It was a coincidence—merely a coincidence. Desaree couldn't possibly know about her secret.

Desaree shrugged, backing away. "You can't blame me for voicing my opinions. The two of you would make perfect mates. You balance him—warmth to his cold. It's a shame he never found...well, never mind. Anyway, I must be away. I'm supposed to meet Verath, you know, to give King Talon the opportunity to collect you alone." Her voice dripped with mischief. "You'll be fine until then?"

"I...yes."

"Good." Desaree bid her goodbye.

She wandered around her chambers, stomach aflutter. At her wine cabinet, she uncorked a red that smelled of cranberry and oak. It trickled into the goblet, the only sound besides the crackling fireplace. She swirled the liquid and inhaled before taking a sip. The tarte taste exploded on her tongue. She closed her eyes and took another sip. Warmth spread through her stomach.

A brief knock made her breath catch. "Come in," she called, clearing her throat. She set the goblet down and turned. Talon stepped into her chambers, closing the door.

One look at him and she couldn't move. Couldn't breathe. Couldn't think. He looked every bit Dragonwall's king and more. Like midnight, personified. Like a god in a human's clothing.

His unruly hair was combed, though signs of misbehavior were still obvious beneath his crown of gold. This one had onyx accents set into its band. His doublet was the same black brocade as her bodice. It fanned out at his hips, entirely flattering his muscular frame. Its long sleeves were attached with ties. The black silken tunic beneath peaked through the gaps. The hem along the sleeves and neckline were trimmed with the same beads as those decorating her gown. His black pants were fitted and tucked into a pair of black boots. He wore a cloak pinned at one shoulder, like a dashing knight from the stories she'd grown up reading.

She hardly noticed the scars on his face, too distracted by his silver eyes pinning her in place.

"Claire, you look..." His eyes carved a path over her body. She burned beneath his scrutiny. He stalked over to her, swallowing the distance between them. Her breath caught as he took her hand, kissing the center of her palm. "I could take you to the throne room this very minute. Declare you my mate. Have Verath perform the ceremony. Make you mine."

Tongues of golden flame sparked in his silver eyes.

"Do it, then?" she baited. "Right now. How soon can the others meet us there?"

"Gods..." He took her face in his hands, rubbing the lines of her jaw with his thumbs. "How I wish for it, more than you can even imagine..."

His lips were close—so close. Was he going to kiss her? Her heartbeat ratcheted up.

"You exquisite creature. I have never felt more unworthy in all my life. A beast like me should not be allowed to touch you, to have you." Something flashed in his eyes, too fleeting to decipher. "But here we are."

Her gaze traced the shape of his face, the lines of his scars, the point of his chin.

"If only things were simpler," he added.

"They can be." Her throat bobbed. "*You're* the one making everything difficult, Talon."

He gave a sharp exhale. "These matters are not as easy as you think. Being mated to me has consequences, the likes of which I am not sure you understand. You don't know what—" He stopped abruptly and cleared his throat. "Never mind that just now. Let's talk about it later. Tonight, you are far too stunning to quarrel with."

"Why? Because I'll win every argument we start?"

"Precisely. I cannot think straight around you, especially now." He hesitated and dropped his hands. "I have something for you. Then we must go. The others are waiting in the hall." He reached into his pocket to retrieve a piece of jewelry. It dangled heavily from his fingers.

She eyed the necklace. A thick gold chain, a collar, set with onyx stones. An exact match to his crown. A statement. And a much better fit with her gown than the small, barely visible pendant she wore now. Even though she hated to part with the spriten necklace for the night, she longed to don the one he held in his hands. Perhaps she couldn't be his queen just yet, but she could be something close.

"May I?" He motioned her over to the mirror.

"Of course," she whispered, following him and placing herself before it. She watched his languid movements as he removed the delicate pendant, grazing her neck with his fingers, and handed it to her. She closed her palm around it, almost reluctant to let it go. Just one night. She could put it back on in the morning.

He unclasped the catch on the collar and reached around her, draping the heavy gold and onyx over her collarbone. His fingers brushed against her. Shivers raced down her spine.

"There." He traced his fingers along her skin, over the mark at her back, humming at the sight of it, before bringing his hands to rest on her shoulders. "A perfect match."

He was right. Even without a crown, she looked like she belonged beside him.

He leaned forward and brushed his lips against the back of her neck, trailing kisses along the curve of her shoulder. Warmth spread through her. She watched him in the mirror's reflection, barely breathing. He came to a stop, mid kiss, and captured her eyes with his. "Kissing you feels like a sin," he murmured before stepping away. "I am so unworthy."

She opened her mouth to speak, but words failed. Why should *anything* between them be a sin? They were intended for each other. Mates. Unless...unless he didn't plan to act on their bond? The thought terrified her. There were so many things she wanted to say. Everything and nothing at once. But she feared ruining these moments between them. She wanted tonight to be perfect, no matter what happened.

"Come. Let's not keep the others waiting." He held out his hand. She took it, allowing him to lead her from her chambers.

The others stood patiently. She was unprepared for the sight of Koldis and Jovari without escorts, making Bedelth's request to Saffra all the more intriguing. There was no time to speculate over it. Desaree and Saffra gave her wide, encouraging smiles.

Saffra's arm was draped through Bedelth's. He looked especially pleased with her beside him. She looked like royalty in the gown they'd found for her. The orange left her caramel skin glowing. Her hair had been done up expertly by Jocelyn, who was probably somewhere downstairs with her partner, waiting for them to make an entrance.

Talon took up his place at the front of the group. She hooked her hand through his arm, anchoring herself to him in more ways than one. He proceeded down the hallway, the others following in a procession behind them.

"Saffra looks especially stunning tonight," Talon murmured as they descended a staircase. "Don't you think?"

"Especially stunning," she agreed, trying to keep a mischievous smile from her lips.

"I wonder how she managed a gown like that on such short notice?" Nothing slipped past him.

"Easily enough. I had the presence of mind to lend her one." Talon faltered, quickly recovering. A flush crept up the sides of his neck—rare, so very rare to catch him by surprise. "No need to fret," she added, patting his arm. "We can discuss it later."

She knew exactly why her words had unsettled him. It was not Saffra's wearing of a queen's gown that flustered him. It was because they were not yet mated. Technically, gowns in the queen's wardrobe did not yet belong to her. By acting as if they did, she was acting as if their bonding was inevitable. For her, it seemed so. But clearly, that wasn't the case for him.

"And how did you manage to slip past my guards?" he asked, throwing her a sidelong glance.

"The secret passageways, remember? There are a few leading into the tower. The queen's parlor, in particular."

"Ah. Yes." His expression changed to one of interest. He glanced at the wall beside him as if he might spot a hidden door that very minute. "You said you would show me. With everything...it slipped my mind."

She smiled. "Not to worry. As soon as you're ready, I'd be happy to show you. I have yet to see the cave beneath the keep, so you're not the only one eager to explore." The truth was, she'd wanted to explore the cave since its discovery. But something always came up —or perhaps she was avoiding it more than she cared to admit.

Afraid of the answers she might find. Afraid they might contradict her suspicions.

They reached the landing overlooking the entry hall and came to a stop. Her breath fled her chest. A sea of people stood below, elegantly dressed in every shade of fabric imaginable. Except royal blue. Though, it was obvious they preferred bright colors. She and Talon were the only ones in black. That left her immensely pleased.

The tournament ball was open to nobles and distinguished drengr. The guest list was limited because of space, but some five hundred patrons had received an invitation. The sound of their excited chatter filled the air. Servers in castle livery of white and gold walked through the crowd, carrying carafes of wine and finger foods.

At their appearance, a hush spread over the room. Talon lifted his free hand to signal for silence. "Good evening, one and all! Welcome to the Fifth Year Tournament's Ball." A smattering of polite applause sounded. "Tonight is meant to be a happy celebration as we ring in the approach of winter. But we already know that. I'll save my words and get this beautiful woman down to the dance floor." He glanced at her, eyes aglow, before turning back to the crowd. "I never liked speeches anyway. Enjoy yourselves tonight, and let the madness of the world go unthought of for now." He nodded—a show of finality to his words—and the crowd applauded.

"Ready?" Talon murmured.

"As I'll ever be," she said, gazing at the vast number of people below. She could feel his eyes intent upon her.

He led them down the stairs. She was vaguely aware of the others trailing behind them as they descended. The crowd parted. She plastered a smile on her face and nodded greetings, trying to appear friendly. Everyone gazed at her with open shock, taking in her show of bare shoulders and the exposed mark, whispering as she passed. She caught a brief glimpse of Caterina standing beside Mage Targa. Caterina's lips curled and her eyes flashed with hate. Had her face not held such an ugly expression, she would have looked beautiful in her silver gown. The color of Talon's eyes, she realized. Tonight was probably one of the last nights Caterina would spend as a free woman before her upcoming trial.

She and Talon proceeded into the throne room as the doors swept open for them. She gasped and faltered. Talon's arm tightened, spurring her on.

The room had been unexpectedly transformed. It reminded her of the way Talon had decorated the servants' dining room for Verekblot. The cathedral style ceiling was weighed down by the presence of massive garlands. Glowing lights twinkled within them. The pillars were wrapped with orange, red, and yellow tulle splattered with more glows. The colors of autumn. She inhaled, sighing. It smelled of floral fragrances and wood from the Gable Forest.

At the far end of the throne room near Talon's dais, a small group of musicians dressed in castle livery assembled with their instruments, waiting. Talon took her to the middle of the open floor as guests piled in, filling the spaces along the perimeter between the pillars. Talon's shields set themselves at the front of the crowd, watching. Desaree and Saffra offered her nods of encouragement.

"You can perform a *Tromp*, yes?" Talon asked. As if the *Tromp* was a dance common in her world as it was in his.

"You're only asking now?" she whispered. "What if I can't?" She didn't bother telling him she'd learned the steps that morning. He opened his mouth, then closed it when she grinned up at him. "I'm only teasing. Yes, I can." Nervous jitters settled over her. She took a deep breath, willing herself to relax.

"Perfect." His face was motionless, a mask. He didn't like other people knowing his thoughts, especially not a room of this size. But his eyes crinkled slightly at the edges as he said, "Let's show the world how it's done then?"

The torchlight danced across his skin. Only the deepest scars stood out. The one running diagonally across his face. It was impossible to imagine the pain he must have felt that day. She couldn't stop herself from tracing the lines, memorizing them.

They positioned themselves several arm lengths apart for their first set of steps. A hush fell over the room. She could hear her hushed breaths. Talon offered the musicians a subtle nod and the music began.

A stringed instrument sent a trickling of low notes into the air. That was her cue. The only music that morning had been Desaree's humming. This was different—more potent. She took two steps forward, right foot, left foot, then two steps backward, right foot, left foot, then two forward again and curtsied, holding her curtsy with her gown slightly lifted off the ground. Her skirts were heavy, but she remained motionless. The picture of grace and poise.

Talon repeated the same steps, coming towards her. *Step, step.* Then backing away. *Step, step.* Then towards her again. He swept into a deep bow, keeping his eyes locked on hers.

This time they both stood and faced each other again. Now they were close enough to touch. She lifted her right hand to his, their palms and fingertips nearly touching. She felt the heat of his skin through her gloves. She lifted the left side of her skirt and they circled one full rotation before switching hands and circling again. Clockwise then counterclockwise. And again. Their courtship was progressing. They stepped apart. She curtsied and he bowed again. A second greeting. This time he wrapped his arm about her waist and she placed her hand on his shoulder. He swept her around into what was closer to a waltz. The steps continued to mimic the forward and backward movement of the first two phases, as the music carried them. They were like birds in a mating dance, tentatively approaching and then retreating, begging to get closer.

As the tempo increased, they found themselves all but skipping across the floor. A giggle slipped from her lips as he supported her. She clung to him with no regard for their close proximity. Her eyes remained on his face, drinking him in. All stiffness abandoned, his lips split into a deep grin, one she wanted to freeze in her memory forever.

The floor remained empty, fully open for them. At the pace they moved, with no attention for what was around them, it was a blessing. The world disappeared. Time ceased to exist. She almost didn't notice when the music slowed. They came to a stop, but even then, she was oblivious. It wasn't until the roar of applause echoed through the throne room that she blinked. The spell was broken.

"Beautiful," he murmured, looking only at her.

She dropped her hands and clapped with the audience, laughing as she looked between everyone else and Talon. His chest rose and fell with heavy breaths.

"Come! Join us!" He spread his arms wide, inviting other couples out onto the dance floor. Desaree and Saffra appeared with Verath and Bedelth to dance beside them. There was only a matter of moments before the musicians launched into the next song. As it started, those who recognized the melody knew it was another waltz. Nerves washed over her, but she had Talon to guide her, and that counted for a lot.

Talon pulled her against him. A gentle squeal slipped from her lips at the sudden possessiveness of his movements, of his hands gripping her. She was already drunk from the excitement of the moment. He rushed her into the next set of steps.

Two more songs continued this way, with little more than a few moments to breathe. Soon she found herself clutching her side, laughing, nearly bent over to catch her breath. It felt like a fever dream, so unreal.

"The musicians only play four songs at a time," Talon explained, taking her hand and pulling her from the crowd. His voice rang with elation. "Come, let's take a moment to breathe. If I don't get some food in you, you'll faint before the night's end."

He led her to the dining hall. She gasped at the sight. Tables were piled with food for self-service.

"Your gown is incredible," he said, noticing the way others looked at them—at her. "You certainly managed to capture every-one's attention tonight. I can't decide if it's your beauty or your boldness that entraps them."

"Or both," she said, teasing.

They drew plates and dished up food before he led her to the head table. She took a seat at his left. "So *this* is what it feels like to sit up here."

"Indeed. High and mighty. The best place to rule over my subjects." His eyes danced .

"Right. It all makes sense now. Best view in the house."

Her plate was filled with slices of succulent beef and roast goose, garlic potatoes, diced vegetables in a mustard crème sauce, and honey bread. A cupbearer came by to fill their goblets.

By now, other guests were filing into the hall to eat. The noise escalated, turning to a frenzy of excitement. In the background, the instruments of the musicians struck up another tune. "Having fun?" he asked, leaning in close. His breath tickled the shell of her ear. But that wasn't what distracted her. His left hand found her thigh beneath the table. His thumb caressed her over the fabric of her gown. A thrill shot straight to her core, making her toes scrunch up in her slippers.

"More fun than I've had in days," she managed, breathless. "You?"

"Absolutely. The best time I've ever had at a ball." His face glowed in a way she'd never seen before. He pulled his hand away to take up his cutlery.

She watched his movements, eyes lingering over that hand, reluctant to see it newly occupied. "Hmm...more than any other ball? That's saying a lot, you know, considering you've attended *how* many?"

"Hmm. Over a hundred, give or take."

She snickered, then picked at her food, eating a little here and there. Being in his presence, with so much of his attention, left her fidgety.

"You dance well," he said after a few mouthfuls. "I am impressed."

"Oh? I have good teachers."

"I should have known you'd come prepared for war." A deep, draconic laugh rumbled in his chest. "Desaree and Saffra?"

"And Jocelyn."

They fell silent, eating.

A few minutes later, her eyes landed on Caterina waltzing in with a group of courtiers, chattering as if nothing in the world were the matter. She was the center of their attention. Of their universe.

Hot anger heated her cheeks, seeing Caterina so happy and carefree. She didn't deserve it. "What are you planning to do about her?" she asked, eyes flicking in her direction. "Verath told you about what he discovered?"

Talon followed her gaze. "Yes. He told me. Rather unfortunate, but not surprising. She always was a snake—albeit an unthreatening one." They watched her as she made her way to one of the tables and began loading a plate of food. "The trial will continue as planned. She will be found guilty and sentenced to death." His words left no room for discussion.

She hesitated. "Caterina was very young when she committed the crime. Will that be taken into account?"

"A crime is a crime, Claire. She knew what she was doing. Come now, let's not talk about heavy matters this evening. I'd rather enjoy your company and keep the mood light, wouldn't you?"

She blew out a breath. "Yes, you're right. Problems for another time."

Koldis and Jovari swept up to the table, faces aglow. "Shouldn't you two be out *dancing*?" Koldis said, arching a brow.

"Yes, yes," Talon muttered. "I wanted to make sure she ate first."

"I see." Koldis eyed her plate. "And you're finished, then?" he asked her. She shrugged. "Well, in that case, may I have the next dance?"

Jovari tsked. "I thought we agreed that *I* would dance with her first?"

"Well, too late. I already asked. You can dance with her second."

"And where does that leave me?" Talon asked, amusement coloring his voice.

Koldis chuckled. "Well, *my king*, you may have her for the rest of the night. But only after we've had our turn," he taunted, holding out his hand. "My lady?"

She glanced at Talon. His eyes darkened possessively before he relented. "You had better go ahead, before I change my mind."

Back in the throne room, they took up a position with the other couples. "This next is a *Gallop* I think," Koldis said.

He put his hand on her back, holding her at a comfortable distance. They waited for the others to get in position. The first notes of music started. "As suspected," he said. "Brace yourself." A moment later, they surged forward, skipping across the floor with the other couples. It was exhilarating. She couldn't control her laughter as they weaved their way through the dancing bodies.

It wasn't a dance for talking, but somehow Koldis managed. "You and Talon look awfully comfortable together as of late."

"Noticed, have you?" She all but yelled to be heard over the merriment.

"Yes, we certainly have. Don't think we aren't whispering about it. Bedelth said the two of you were sneaking off together the whole way home from Brezen."

"No?! Did he really?" She feigned surprise. "Well, maybe you shouldn't believe every rumor you hear."

"Rumors? From Bedelth?" He scoffed. "It's not a rumor if it's from Bedelth. And for the record, don't take this as my disapproval. Our king is a changed male. Whatever you're doing, keep doing it. None of us are complaining, believe me."

Happiness made her chest swell. She kept her voice serious as she said, "Glad I have your approval."

"Come now, I've been an admirer of your ways for some time now."

"My *ways*?!" She laughed, breathless. "You act as though I've been here working magical manipulations over him."

"Haven't you, though?" His mouth twitched. He steered them around another set of couples.

"Maybe I have," she admitted. "That's why he's been so different, you know?"

"Oh? Are you saying that our king is infatuated with you?"

Koldis sent her into a spin. "You could say that."

"Seems strange, don't you think?" His voice filled with suspicion and her smile fell.

"What do you mean?"

"King Talon doesn't get infatuated." He held her gaze, searching for answers she could not give. "I've known him for nearly two hundred years, Claire. Our king does not follow the whims of his feelings, no matter how beautiful you might be. He hasn't had a woman in...forever."

Her heart pounded in her chest. "Well, maybe he's just never met a woman quite like *me*?"

Koldis roared, throwing his head back. "Point taken. I cannot say that he has."

She breathed a sigh of relief, glad he was willing to play her game. For now.

She was handed off to Jovari. He was less suspicious and instead opted for small, polite talk. How was she enjoying the ball? Were there balls in her own world? How did they compare?

"Our dances are a bit less formal," she explained. She considered what his reaction might be if he saw her in a packed club with strobe lights. Instead, she changed the subject. "Why no partner tonight?" she asked.

His smile was sly. "So that I can dance with whomever I desire. No sense in being tied down."

She was handed off to Bedelth instead of Talon, who was now dancing with Saffra in exchange. She took full advantage of this opportunity to ask, "What's your relationship with Saffra?"

He tried to appear surprised. "I've known her since she was a child. I care for her, that is all. What happened with Commander Daxton is a tragedy. I wish her nothing but happiness."

Even though his words were sincere, she couldn't help but sense something deeper in them. There were feelings lurking beneath the surface, even if he didn't care to admit it.

After a short break, she was handed off to Verath. "Am I to dance with every shield in attendance before I get Talon back?" she complained when he swept her into a new dance. It was hard to keep the laughter from her voice.

"It would seem so, my lady." Verath's eyes sparkled. His earlier melancholy was gone, as if it had never happened.

Des looks happier than I've seen in a long time," she said.

"You think?" He glanced over to where Desaree danced with Koldis, also noticing that Jocelyn was now in Jovari's arms.

"I haven't seen her smile this much...ever," she said. Verath merely hummed. "You make her really happy, you know." He nodded but said nothing more. His eyes frequently darted over to Desaree for the remainder of their dance.

At long last, she found herself in Talon's arms. "I almost thought I wouldn't get you back."

"You think I would allow that?" He tucked a strand of hair behind her ear, studying her. When he next spoke, his voice was low, "I've done my duty for the night, sharing you with the others. The rest of your night belongs to me." His words sent fire licking straight to her belly.

They spent the rest of the night together. It was impossible to count the number of dances they shared, the number of smiles, the number of times his hands traveled to places they shouldn't, but only when no one was looking. It left her breathless and lightheaded.

She was nearly faint with exhaustion when he pulled her from the floor at last. "I think it's time to retire for the night. What do you think?"

She tried to protest, but words failed. The thought of getting him alone was more enticing. So instead, she nodded and allowed him to lead her away, back up the stairs and into the south wing of the keep, straight to her door. The guards looked on in silence.

"I'm not quite sure I'm ready to sleep yet," she admitted. "I... would you like to come in and share a glass of wine with me? Or perhaps two?"

He glanced at her door. Indecision played across his features. She thought he might decline. He surprised her by saying, "Thank you. I would like that."

She blinked several times, then grinned.

He motioned her forward. The guards took this as their cue and opened the door for them, stepping aside. Talon followed her in, just as the door gently shut behind them.

ANYTHING BUT SIMPLE

Kastali Dun

Talon followed Claire into her chambers, chasing after her calming scent. He should have declined her offer. It had been on the tip of his tongue to do so, but his words had betrayed him. *Just a few minutes*, he told himself, then he would bid her goodnight and depart.

"I opened this earlier," she called from across the room. "I think you'll like it." She lifted a bottle of wine to her nose, breathing it in. Her eyes fell shut, a soft smile playing on her lips. He stood motionless, watching her like prey. He blinked and cleared his mind. She wasn't that. Yet, the dragon inside him stirred as she stoked his instincts, capturing his attention and ensnaring it.

"Is red all right?"

"Red is fine," he said, stalking across the room. He kept her in his sights as she turned to gather another goblet. Her slender shoulders were bare. He traced the lines and planes of her body, his gaze lingering over her spriten mark. It was beautiful against her skin, much as he hated to admit it. His attention fixed upon her neck and the wisps of hair that had come free of her coiffure.

He stepped up behind her, as close as was possible without

stepping on her flowing gown, and pretended to watch her movements from over her shoulder. His hand brushed the loose strands of her hair from her neck. An excuse to touch her. She stilled beneath his fingers, responding to his touch. He pulled his hand away.

"Here," she said, turning. She lifted her goblet and clinked it against his. "To finding what was once thought lost."

"And carving new beginnings," he added and then took a sip, keeping her hypnotic green eyes locked on his. "Mmm." He rolled the liquid around on his tongue before swallowing. "From up north, if I had to guess?"

He reached around her for the bottle, allowing his body to brush against hers. He didn't care *where* the wine had come from, even though he made a point of reading the label. Her breath grew louder and more staggered. Was this the effect he had on her? Pleasure over the idea dumped into him.

"Hmm...Yes," he said, setting the bottle down. "I've had this one before." He wasn't sure if he had. He didn't care. His words were mindless—an excuse to speak. He was too distracted to make sense.

She sipped from her own goblet, regarding him over the rim. Heat flushed his skin. Had someone added another log to the fire?

"I could use some fresh air," he blurted, pulling at the collar on his tunic. "Care to join me?"

"Oh. Yes. Sure." She blinked. He was already stepping away, striding in the direction of the double doors leading out onto the terraced balcony. He exhaled to ease the tension in his shoulders. Along the way, he unclipped his cloak and tossed it over the back of a chair. Why was it so frustrating to want two completely different things at once?

The cool evening air kissed his skin. He inhaled the salty sea breeze, letting it calm his nerves.

Claire came up to stand beside him. "Only two minutes alone with me and you're already avoiding me," she teased, her voice overly bright. She stood close—too close.

"Avoiding you?" His eyes darted towards her, then away. "We've spent nearly the entire evening together."

"That's not what I meant. Every time you catch yourself getting too close to me, you pull away."

Was he? He opened his mouth to argue, but she was right.

"Why?" she asked. "Is it because you're afraid of me?"

An embarrassingly high-pitched laugh escaped his lips. He clamped his mouth shut. "I'm not afraid of you, Claire, but I am afraid of the way you make me feel."

She tilted her head, regarding him curiously. "I get that, but why do you fight it? Why do you fight *me*?"

He scoffed. "Because I don't understand why you have so mindlessly accepted me. You hated me, remember? And for good reason. The moment you discovered our bond, you stopped fighting me, stopped challenging me. We don't even argue anymore—not that it's a bad thing. You know I dislike arguing with you. Sometimes, I even catch you looking at me like...like..."

"Like what?" Her expression turned defensive, guarded.

"Like I'm the most wonderful thing you've ever seen in your short span of twenty-two years, when I know quite well that I'm not." His jaw flexed in irritation. "Sometimes I fall for it, you know, those looks you reward me with. Then I look at my reflection and remember what I am. Who I am."

This wasn't the conversation he wanted to have—not tonight. Tonight had been perfect. He'd hoped it would end that way. He should have declined her invitation to stay. He ran a hand through his hair, only to remember he was still wearing his crown. He nearly knocked it over the balcony wall. Catching it, he set it beside his goblet on the parapet. It clanged down with more force than intended.

"What exactly are you implying, Talon?" She held her goblet clenched in her hand.

"I'm saying you are befuddled by our mate bond. You wouldn't look at me twice if it wasn't for that."

"Are you kidding me?" Her lips parted. "Is that what you think?!"

"It's what I know."

She huffed and walked away from him, nearly sloshing her wine, then rounded to face him, frustration rippling in the air around her. "You think my discovering our bond simply *transformed* my feelings? Just like that?" She snapped her fingers.

He opened his mouth to agree—

"You're wrong."

"You cannot expect me to believe that a few heartfelt letters, passed between the two of us, was enough to win your heart," he all but growled. "So forgive me if I fail to believe it."

"It wasn't just the letters."

He stopped short. "Oh?"

"It was more than that."

"Oblige me, then," he demanded. "What grand act have I done to wash away all the horrible things that made you hate me?"

He couldn't move, rooted to the spot, desperate to understand how she could feel anything for him beyond the bond between them.

"Talon." Her voice came out gentler than he expected. She worried at her lower lip, something she did when nervous. "It started with the way you cared for me after I was kidnapped. But I didn't—the feelings weren't there yet. That was only our turning point, when you opened my heart to you. Brezen was simply the moment that you fixed yourself there permanently."

"Brezen?" He scowled, trying to recall some monumental moment he must have missed between them.

"When you arrived, you weren't angry, even though I expected you to be. You...you were different." She shrugged and turned out towards the water. "The way you handled everything at Fort Squall. The time you spent walking with me in the evenings. Your thoughtfulness. Your gifts. Your tender moments. Each of those things imprinted themselves upon my soul. But it was the night in the tent, ultimately, that made up my mind."

"In...in the tent?" His throat bobbed as he swallowed.

"When we talked about your scars. It allowed me to finally see you differently. After that, my mind went back through everything that had happened between us. From the time of my arrival in your kingdom to...afterward. Everything clicked into place. I thought about the way you..." She hesitated.

"The way I what?" He couldn't breathe, couldn't think.

"The way you washed me after rescuing me from my kidnappers." Her skin flushed a deep shade of red; he wanted to memorize the sight of it. "You gave me a bath and put me to sleep in your own bed. No one has ever done anything like that for me before. But you're not just anyone, are you, Talon? You're a king—Dragonwall's king."

He blinked, trying to think of something to say.

"Sometimes, when I close my eyes, I see you standing there," she whispered, "hunched over me, washing my feet. It took that night in the tent to put everything into perspective. I think...I think I felt something for you then. Something more than adoration, even if I wasn't ready to admit it to myself. I felt..." She clamped her mouth shut. The fingers clenching her goblet had turned bloodless. "What are you doing to me, Talon?" Her words were barely a whisper.

He licked his lips. "So...it wasn't simply the mate bond?"

She turned, sloshing wine this time. "Didn't you just listen to a word I said? Look, Talon, if the mate bond didn't exist and we were standing here as we are now, I would *still* want to kiss you."

"You..." Warmth blossomed in his chest, traveling down. His pants were suddenly too tight. Hunger clawed at his insides. "You want me?"

She groaned. "You *frustrating* man!" It almost made him smile, the scolding tone in her voice. She lifted her goblet and drained it, then slammed it on the parapet and turned to him, holding him captive with her gaze. Suddenly, she'd become the predator and he the prey.

Only a few seconds passed, but it felt like a lifetime of silence. Her eyes darted over his face, tracing each imperfection in his skin. He'd never felt more exposed in all his life. He fought the urge to cover his face, to turn and hide it from her.

"Come here, Talon."

The command left his insides curling. His feet moved before he could stop them, closing the distance between them until he was before her. She lifted a hand and he flinched. She froze, fingers hovering over his skin. "You have no reason to fight me anymore. No reason to fear me. Please...don't be afraid."

He exhaled. "I'm...I'm not afraid."

She'd won.

His heart stopped beating when she laid her hand against his scarred cheek. The warmth of her skin mixed with his. He closed his eyes and leaned into her touch.

"You might hate your scars, but I do not. They tell a story. Perhaps not the story you wish, but every tale has two sides. You hear one of loss and heartbreak. I hear one of bravery and heroic deeds." She traced her fingers along his skin, sending sparks shooting through him.

His eyes fluttered open. "But they are ugly. My face is ruined. How can you...how can you bear to look at me? Your beauty. Your pure heart..." He shook his head. "You could have anyone you wanted. Why me?"

She reached up with both hands this time, using her thumbs to smooth away the scowl that had formed between his eyebrows. "Talon, yours is the *only* heart I wish to conquer."

He nearly fell to his knees.

"You already have," he managed. His throat constricted, making it hard to speak. "My heart was yours the moment you walked into my throne room. I just didn't know it yet."

She took a step forward, keeping his face in her hands, until her body was flush with his. His world froze—*he* froze—caught in the snare of her smoldering regard. She pulled him to her, stepping barefooted onto the toes of his boots to reach him. She brought her lips to his, gently at first, destroying the world around him with one single action.

His body exploded into sensation.

He pulled her against him, growling. His fingers tangled in her hair. Their bodies pressed together, his hard and unyielding, hers soft and pliant, like clouds flowing through a mountain pass.

It left his insides humming.

Their kiss didn't stop. It deepened into something needy. She pressed her fingers into the nape of his neck. A low groan rumbled in his chest. There was a flash of red behind his closed lids. The dragon inside clawed to break free, begging him to let go. His arousal heightened, pressing against the ties of his pants as he hardened. The itch of scales rose like the hairs of his skin, standing on end.

Claire let out a gasp and pulled away, breaking their kiss.

He did not release her—would not, could not. "Claire..." he warned.

"I...I'm sorry," she gasped, eying the scales that had erupted along his skin. "I didn't realize. I didn't mean to agitate you."

"I am far from agitated."

"Oh." Her gaze dropped to his neck where he was certain a patch of scales had not yet receded. She kissed him there, kissing them away. A tremor raced through him. "How curious," she whispered against him, lips lingering over his skin. "So very curious." This time he erupted in gooseflesh where she kissed him.

"Curious indeed," he muttered, his mood darkening. His arms had turned to iron, fixed around her, unwilling to let go. She still stood on his boots, her forehead high enough so that he could kiss it, which he did.

"Does your skin always do that when you kiss someone?" she teased.

"I do not remember the last person I kissed. But, no. Only you. And don't mind the dragon," he added, annoyed with the beast inside. "It doesn't like it when I exercise control."

"You mean *you* don't like when you exercise control." She poked his chest.

"Yes. Something like that."

"Why do it, then? We both know what we want." She pushed herself away from him and took his hand in hers, pulling him towards the balcony doors.

He took a few steps, drunk on her attention, then stopped short. "No. No, Claire, I cannot. We...we cannot."

Hurt crashed over her features. She dropped his hand. "I told you to stop fighting me, Talon."

"I'm not *fighting* you. I must control myself. You should as well. Otherwise, we will be mated before dawn. It's not...this isn't..."

He'd never hated himself more than at this very moment. The most intoxicating woman in the world stood before him, ready and willing to submit. Yet, he was refusing her?! His black dragon clawed at the confines of his chest.

"There's a process," he gritted out.

"Oh." Her shoulders fell. "Right. The ceremony. But, why do we have to go about it in that order?"

"Because I am the king and it is expected." He took a step towards her. "Besides, it is more than that. We cannot seal our bond tonight, Claire. Not before you understand all that comes with it."

She crossed her arms. "Then tell me."

He turned and walked back to the parapet, picking up his goblet. After a sip, he turned to lean against the wall, regarding her. "If I were any other, the matter would be simple. But I'm not simply anyone, and the matter is not simple."

"I know that. You're the king. This is the part where you tell me I've got to become Dragonwall's queen, right?" She challenged him with her stare.

"Well, yes, there's that. But it gets worse. Becoming Dragonwall's queen sounds easy until you understand the responsibility attached to it. You've said so yourself, you don't know how I manage to handle it, day after day, year after year. The responsibility of being a servant to my people. The freedom I sacrifice for it. It would be no different for you."

"I'm okay with that, Talon." She seemed to grow taller. "If it means being with you, I'll take whatever responsibility life throws at me. Look at what I've already been through. I left my home. My family. My world. I've faced you. I've faced the screamers. I've faced Kane's attempt at kidnapping me. I defeated the vodar. I think I can handle responsibility if I put my mind to it."

He chuckled darkly. "Yes, you've proven as much."

"Exactly. So if you think I'm going to abandon our mate bond simply in fear of responsibility, you're mistaken."

His heart burst free, soaring high over the clouds as if he were flying, but the feeling was short lived. "What if it means that you can never go home? That you will never see your family again?"

Surprise flashed in her features. "What are you saying?"

He clenched his jaw, hesitating. "I know how much you miss your home, your family. You once begged me to return and I refused. I've kept you here for your safety, but also because I'm selfish. None of this is fair. Yet, neither can I allow you to leave. Not yet. Not until Kane is dealt with. Not until I know he won't follow you through the gate and use you against me. But when this is all over and Kane is defeated, I have every intention of allowing you to return home, even though it will hurt me irrevocably."

"What are you saying?" she hissed as the color drained from her face. "You...you want me to leave?"

"Gods, no! But I also cannot keep you here against your will."

"But...but I don't want to go home." She shook her head. "Not yet, anyway."

"You don't?" He lifted his eyebrows. "You don't want to see your family again? Your friends? Have pancakes and coffee? Watch the sun set over the cornfields of Indiana?"

"I..." A frown exploded across her features. Her shoulders sagged. She came over to lean against the parapet beside him. "I mean, I thought maybe I could go back to say goodbye. But I couldn't actually *live* there again. I'm part sprite, Talon. And with Cyrus, with everything—" She shook her head. "My place is here now."

"I see." He didn't allow his elated emotions to color his response over her admission.

"But, why couldn't I just pop through the gate for a few days to say goodbye? Why must accepting our bond mean I am alienated from my family?"

He exhaled. "If you become queen, the people of Dragonwall will become your chief priority. It wouldn't be safe for you to abandon them, even if for a few days. Here, it's easy to make promises. You possess a great deal of power and authority."

"So...?"

"That authority will not follow you through the gate. If you go through, you might never come back. That is not a risk I'm willing to take."

"I..." Her throat bobbed. He could see her thoughts turning over. "You're right," she said at last.

He nodded. "Once you are my queen, your life no longer belongs to you."

"I will belong to Dragonwall," she whispered.

"Exactly." It crushed him to see the realization sink in. To see her realize what she would be giving up. It was the reason he'd avoided this conversation. Especially earlier, before the ball. "And now you understand that this is no simple matter. You face a difficult choice, Claire. One I wish you didn't have to make."

She opened her mouth—

"No, before you speak, let me finish. You might think you know the answer right now, in this moment, but I cannot trust it. I cannot, in good faith, accept whatever you are just about to say. A decision like this takes time and consideration. I want you to think about your future, about what you want. I want you to think about what I'm asking of you. It isn't fair, but ruling is selfless. Anyone who believes otherwise wouldn't make a good ruler." He reached over and tucked a strand of hair behind her ear. Even now, she leaned in to his touch. "I feel like a monster for placing this difficulty upon you." He hesitated. "Am I?"

"No," she whispered. "Of course not."

He exhaled. "If I could bear this weight for you, I would. I would bear everything so that you might be freer, happier, lighter."

"No, Talon." She shook her head. "You've been through enough. This...this is mine to bear, and I can." She grabbed his hand and laid it across her cheek, leaning into it. Her eyes squeezed shut. A single tear freed itself and slid down her other cheek. His chest fractured at the sight of it. He wiped it away with his thumb, then pulled her against him, resting his chin on the top of her head. "I'm sorry," he whispered. It felt like the only thing he could say at a moment like this.

"I know."

He lifted her off her feet, pressing his lips against hers. She hesitated, but at last she responded, kissing him back, relaxing against him. It helped to quell some of the lingering anxiety. She still wanted to kiss him. Thank the gods for that.

His biggest fear hovered over him like an oppressing cloud. What if she chose her family over him? What if, after coming so close to finding his mate, everything fell apart?

She must have sensed his unease, because she wrapped her arms around him and pushed more deeply into his kiss. She tugged on his bottom lip as she pulled away, sending fire through him.

"I'm not going anywhere, Talon," she murmured, rubbing her nose against his. "I told you before and I'll tell you again. You don't have to be alone anymore. I would give up everything. All of it. You know that."

Emotion slammed into him, nearly knocking him backwards. His mate. This wonderful, brilliant, amazing woman. His mate. She knew exactly what he needed to hear.

"Even still," he murmured against her lips, "promise me you will think about it. When you give me your final answer, I will know it is genuine. I cannot bear for you to have any regrets. I may be selfish, but..." He sighed.

She placed her hands on either side of his jaw, stroking his cheeks with her thumbs. "I already know what I want, but I...I'll think about it. I promise."

"Thank you." He kissed her forehead.

She stepped down off his boots and he smiled as he watched her retrieve her goblet and walk back into her quarters. The interior danced with the orange glow of candlelight. Retrieving his goblet and crown from the parapet wall, he followed after her.

"Another cup before the night ends?" She held up the wine bottle, a smile on her face, as if the conversation hadn't happened. "It's not empty yet."

"I should probably go." He wanted to stay, but he also felt the heavy toll of their conversation. It weighed on him. He'd made things harder for them, and that was his fault, because of who he was.

She blew out a breath, as if his reluctance was exactly what she expected. "Please don't go, Talon. I'm not going to be able to sleep yet. Stay for one more, and sit with me by the fire." She held out her hand to him.

He eyed it. "All right. You win. You always win."

He went to her, handing over his goblet. She refilled it. Then, with movements that surprised him, she took the crown from his hand, looking it over before setting it beside the empty bottle on the wine cabinet. The familiarity and ease of her movements loosened something in him. Like he could see a life with her, a normal future, where the two of them did this regularly, enjoyed each other's company every night. A glimpse of what life might be like if she accepted him. He wanted it more than anything in the world. He understood the power she had over him. What he would do for her.

She took her goblet and led him to the sofa. Her gown fluffed out around her when she sat down. She looked down at herself and giggled. "I feel like a cupcake in this thing."

"A cupcake?" He couldn't help but smile. "As in, a cake that's in a cup?"

She laughed. "You don't know what cupcakes are?! Tell me you're joking!"

"Not joking."

"We must remedy that immediately." Cupcakes, as it turned out, were just as the name suggested. Cakes baked in small cups, iced with a heap of frosting. They sounded delicious. "I have a weakness for cupcakes, actually," she admitted. Her voice turned dreamy. "I don't even care what kind. Carrot, German chocolate, vanilla."

He put his arm around her, pulling her into the crook of his shoulder. "Is that so?" he murmured into her hair. "Tell me more about these cakes in cups, then."

She giggled. "Fine, but you asked."

He kissed the top of her head as she launched into a detailed explanation about confections. They stayed like that for a long while, their conversation morphing into other things. She told him about all the different foods in her world. Foods that she missed or disliked. He was happy to sit and let her talk and talk and talk, resting his chin against her hair, smiling at some of the silly things she said, inhaling the scent of lavender every so often.

And then she fell quiet. It wasn't until a gentle snore broke the silence that he realized she had fallen asleep, long emptied wine goblet still in hand. He chuckled, drained the rest of his, then set both on the table beside the sofa. The movement roused her, but she only offered a pleased sigh. A worry line had formed between her eyebrows. He smoothed it with his thumb. Her lips pulled into a tiny smile as she sank deeper against his shoulder without waking.

He sat for hours, just so that he could watch her sleep.

At the first inklings of dawn light, he gently adjusted her so that she was comfortably spread across the sofa. It was difficult with her gown spilling over onto the floor, but he managed, propping a pillow under her head and tossing a blanket over her bare shoulders. She mumbled something but continued sleeping. It made him smile. Leaning over her, he softly kissed her lips. Another quiet sigh broke free of her.

He retrieved his cloak and almost grabbed his crown before thinking better of it. Leaving it behind would give her an excuse to come and find him. Smiling, he quietly slipped through the door and left her to her dreams, hoping they were entirely of him.

CHAPTER 38
PASSAGE NORTH

Kastali Dun

Bennett drained his tankard and slammed it on the table harder than intended. A belch erupted from his chest. He let it loose, pounding his sternum with a fist. Nearby drinkers lifted their tankards and cheered.

The night was nearly over, and it had been a rowdy one. While all the pretentious nobles were up in the castle having their *fancy dance*, all the common folk were drinking away their worries on cheap ale. He wasn't necessarily poor as far as poor went. He made a decent living as a merchant captain—quite decent after the king had paid him for the transport of precious cargo from up north. But a good deal of what he made was often spent on the meager entertainment he could scrounge up landside.

"Beggin' your pardon, captain, but there's a woman here to see ya." The bar wench leaned over the table to collect his tankard. "You'll take another, I presume?" He nodded. "Good. So...the woman. Shall I send her over?"

"I'm not looking fer a bed tonight," he growled. What was it about ship captains? Perhaps word got around. He always paid his women well.

"Oh!" Morita laughed. "I don' think she's peddlin' herself that way."

"Then who is she and what the damn hell does she want, eh? I'm not in the mood for antics tonight." He followed Morita's gaze across the room. His eyes landed on a cloaked woman. She sat alone at a table, her head down. Entirely out of place.

"Humph. Don't look like anyone I know. I'm not lookin' fer business tonight," he slurred.

"Give her a chance, hmm? She paid me well to come and talk to you. Seems pretty desperate. I'll send her over."

"Ugh, woman! You're bold tonight. Fine. Send her over so I can send her away." He gritted his teeth as the tavern walls around him tilted and lurched back into place. Morita disappeared, heading for the bar to refill his drink. She stopped beside the cloaked woman and whispered something. The woman glanced at him before nodding. A moment passed, then she stood and came over. At least she had succeeded in piquing his curiosity. He pulled out the chair beside him. She took it.

"Captain Bennett?" Her voice was low.

He tried to make out her face under the shadowed hood. She was young.

"Aye. Yer lookin' at him. Who's asking?"

"I am."

"Obviously, *girl*. That's not what I meant. What do you want?"

"I heard that you are the best merchant captain in Dragonwall. I'm looking to transport valuable merchandise north."

"Valuable merchandise?" His eyes narrowed. "How far north?"

"Ice Port."

"Gods, girl! What the hell do you need to take up there? There are plenty of adequate vessels captained by reliable folk. I can refer you to a few if you like...for a price." He eyed her. Her cloak alone would fetch a pretty steely.

She tutted. "I came to you for a reason, Captain Bennett, not a referral. I seek discretion."

"Right. For your *valuable cargo*." He snorted. "Of course. Tell me what it is, and I might consider it."

"I can see there's no lying to you." She crossed her arms. "The cargo is me."

He threw his head back and roared. "Valuable cargo indeed!" Tears leaked out of his eyes.

Morita chose that moment to bring his refill. He took a drink before returning his attention to the matter at hand. "I don't operate a passenger ship. You'll have to try elsewhere."

"I can pay well." She removed a sack of coin from beneath her cloak and dropped it on the table.

"Are you daft?!" he hissed, swiping the bag out of sight. She sucked in a breath. "Don't you know where we are? A bag of coin like this will get you kidnapped, robbed, or worse..." He tossed it back to her under the table and glanced around. No one was looking in their direction.

A flutter of wings sounded overhead. Beaky flopped down on the table, squawking. The woman shrieked and toppled backward in her chair. The clattering brought the tavern to silence. Everyone around them burst into laughter, watching Beaky as she hopped from foot to foot on the table, cawing at the woman on the floor. He joined in, bellowing. "Now, now, Beaky. Don't frighten the poor girl." His scolding was only half hearted. He didn't bother helping her off the ground, nor righting her chair. He was no gentleman, after all. And a noble woman like her—for he was certain she held a title—was probably used to all manner of simpering and fussing. She would get nothing from him.

She sputtered and rose to her feet. "Is that...does that *thing* bite?" she asked, righting and returning to her chair.

"That *thing* has a name. And you'd best not insult her or she just might." He reached out and stroked Beaky, but Beaky scooted out from under his hand and stepped away.

"Pretty girl. Pretty girl," Beaky chirped. "Scared. Scared, pretty girl."

"Shoo! Shoo." He swatted at her. "Away with you, you gods-damned bird." Beaky gave a final squawk and leapt from the table, returning to the tavern's rafters. "Now..." He turned to the woman.

"Right." She brushed the wrinkles from her cloak. "As I was

saying. I can pay well. One hundred gold dragons now. One hundred when we reach our destination. That's a handsome sum considering you're headed north anyway."

"Why in the gods' hell do you want to go up there? You got some kind of death wish or somethin'? Curious about the dwargs?" He hesitated, eyes narrowing. "Tell me you at least know there's dwargs up there, among other things. The north is a harsh place, girl. Plus, rumors that Fort Squall's been taken. We'd have to pass by that way along the coast. They say there's dragons there—wild dragons."

She tutted. "I know what a dwarg is, Captain Bennett. I might be rich but I'm not ignorant." She hesitated. "We can steer clear of Fort Squall. I wish to go to Ice Port."

"Yes, yes. You've made that clear, but you haven't said why."

"My business is my own." Beneath the hood of her cloak, her mouth pulled into a frown.

He sighed, thinking it over. One hundred gold dragons now and a hundred later was a fine price, especially since he already had a heavy cargo to take along the coast, though not as far north as Ice Port, but what were a few additional leagues in the grand scheme of things?

"Hmm..." He drummed his fingers on the tabletop. It was sticky with old drink. "Shouldn't you be up at the keep? Enjoying the ball with the rest of them nobles?"

"I left there to come here. And don't change the subject. Ice Port."

"Aha! So you *are* a noble then." He leaned back in his chair, balancing on the back legs, proud of himself. "What's your name, girl?"

"You really think I'd tell you?" she huffed. "Will you take me? Or shall I go find another captain?"

"I thought you said I was the best?" He fought the smug smile pulling at his lips. Gods, this girl was easy to taunt.

"How dare—" She stopped herself, glancing around to see if anyone noticed her hiss.

"Careful, *girl*." This one had claws. "You may be a noble up at the top of that hill." He waved his arm. "Down here with that cloak on, you're nobody, especially once you hand over that sack of gold and get on my ship. Now...what should I call you?"

"Does that mean you'll take me?"

"Hmm... Bad business, bringing a woman on board." He lifted his tankard to his lips and finished what remained. "I can't answer for my men's behavior. They don't usually get pretty lasses like you to eye while they work. Last thing I want is to be pulling 'em off you at every damned moment of the night."

She squared her shoulders. "I don't think you need to worry about that. I can take care of myself."

He snorted. "Riiight."

"Fine." She scooted her chair out to leave.

"Oh, sit down!" He slammed his fist on the table. "Give me your name. I'll take you."

Her posture relaxed as she sank back into the chair. "You can call me Cat."

"Cat. Hmm. Very well, *Cat*. Tell me, what are you runnin' from, eh?"

"What did you say?"

"You're obviously runnin' from something, or someone, else you wouldn't be so eager to broker passage with me. A man, perhaps? Your husband?"

"I'm not married." She said this almost too quickly.

"Ah, well, guess that's your own business even if you were. Very well then. I'm planning to leave at dawn. You're lucky you caught me." He rose to leave. "The gold?"

She hesitated, placing the sack into his open palm. "Where... where can I find you, Captain Bennett?"

"*Lady Faith* is docked in the bay. You'll meet my first mate, Jonah, at the docks at sunrise, Pier Twelve. Shorter fellow, good lookin', better lookin' than me, that is." He turned from her, looking up at the rafters. "Beaky! We're leaving, you damned bird. I need some sleep."

Beaky fluttered to his shoulder. "Pretty girl. Pretty girl."

"Shut it." He placed a few silvers in Beaky's beak. "Take that to

Morita. There's a good bird." Beaky took flight and dropped the coins at the bar before returning to his shoulder.

He looked at Cat, still sitting at the table. "See you in the morning," he said, a wide grin splitting his lips. This woman had no idea what she was getting herself into.

~

"Argh!" He woke at dawn with a splitting headache. Beaky was on his chest, pecking him awake. "Argh! All right! All right! Blasted bird. I'm up!"

"Wakey wakey," she cooed. "Wakey wakey. Wakey wakey. Wakey—" *Swak!*

"I get it!" he snapped, swatting her away to sit up, taking it slow. His hands flew to his temples. "Argh!" He groaned again. Every attempt to massage the pain away failed. There was a heavy lump in his trousers. He looked down at the bulge in his pocket. Gold. Lots of gold.

Memories from the night before swam into his mind's eye. The woman. *Cat.*

"Think she'll show?" he asked, looking at Beaky. She was at the window, fluttering around with impatience. The bird was well trained and knew to do her business out of doors. She even did most of her foraging alone, though she still relied on him for certain...luxuries.

"Right...all right. Just a moment." He reached into the canister at his bedside table and produced a handful of nuts and dried berries for her. She pecked each one delicately from his palm like a little lady before fluttering back to the window. He gave her an affectionate stroke along her back, chuckling. She was out the moment he cracked the window open. "Find me later," he called to her. "And don't be late. We leave with or without you.

All he received in return was a squawk.

A knock sounded at the door. "Enter," he called, fastening his belt and other belongings, pulling on his boots.

Laura, the servant girl, peeked in before opening the door wider. He'd seen her most mornings. "Water for you, sir."

"Well, bring it in, then." He stood to gather the remainder of his things. "That's a good lass. Thank you. I'll be checking out this morn' if you wouldn't mind letting Marcy know."

"Aye, sir. I'll tell 'er." She set the pitcher beside his water basin and hesitated. "I...I warmed it this time, sir. Since I know you like it scalding at the early hours."

"That's a thoughtful girl." He tossed her a steely from the pouch at his belt. "On second thought, just a mo'." Reaching into Cat's pouch of gold in his pocket, he pulled out a dragon. "Because you're a good lass, and because I know the medicine for your ma is expensive."

Laura's eyes went round. She couldn't have been older than fourteen, and had probably never seen a gold piece in her life. "You..." Her face turned red. "Wow..."

"Don't worry, girl. I ain't be needing anything in return—nothing like that. I'm off to the sea today, as it is. Now, run along."

Laura took the coin, stammering her thanks as she departed. He turned to his basin and poured the water from the pitcher, watching the steam rise up as it filled. With winter close, warm water was a luxury for a place like this. Most were lucky to get any fresh water at all, considering the walk to the street's well. But he paid Marcy well, and her servant girls, like Laura, were obedient. He washed his face, neck, hands, and hair, using the last bit of soap he had saved for the occasion. There wasn't much bathing to be done at sea. Were it warmer, he'd just take a swim, but the air was too frigid for that. Especially up north. And fresh water was generally rationed. So baths were saltwater or nothing.

He was out of the Brickyard Inn within the next ten minutes, striding to the dockyard. A few acquaintances greeted him from opposite sides of the thoroughfare, wishing him well on his next voyage. His crew was probably well underway with preparations. They had reunited just two weeks past when those injured in the battle near Stormy Bay were returned to him. He was glad to have them all back safe and healthy. Especially complements of Lord Davi's coin.

A pang of sadness clutched his chest. He'd heard the rumors of Fort Squall's demise. Including the rumor about the fort leaders, lost in the battle. It was all hearsay, but something told him it was true.

Jonah waited at the docks, hands on his hips. "Really, Bennett, sir? A woman? You cannot be serious!"

He chuckled. "*So*, she showed her face after all, eh? I almost wondered if she'd get cold feet."

"Oh, she showed up all right, and proceeded to make all manner of demands as she was *handed down* into the rowboat and taken out to the ship. Gods, man!"

"What? She paid well." He shrugged. "I took pity on her. But she's hiding something."

"All the more reason to leave her behind. What'd she pay?"

"I'll tell you in a moment. Let's go." He peered out over the bay. The *Lady Faith* sat low in the water. All her cargo was stowed the day before. With the exception of the woman named *Cat*. He followed after Jonah into the rowboat and told him about the night before. They made their way to the ship.

"She offered *that* much?"

"Aye." A frown pulled at his lips. He scanned the sky, taking in the formations of the clouds and the direction of the wind. His gaze darted from bird to bird. Beaky wasn't anywhere in sight. No doubt she was taking advantage of her last moments on land.

Jonah was still talking as his muscled arms kept busy with the oars. "She could have paid a passenger fare for a fraction of that price," he was saying. "She's definitely hiding something."

"That's what concerns me," he mused, continuing to scan the sky. The sun was due any moment. A wonder he'd managed to get up so early. But the sea waited for no one. "There're only a few reasons someone would pay that much to get out of Kastali Dun."

"Think she's wanted for a crime?" Jonah asked.

"Gods! Hope not. Although, that was my first thought. Second thought is that she's just running from someone. Abusive husband, most like. Though she claimed to be unmarried."

"Well, did you ask her?" Jonah studied his face.

"Believe me, I did." He grunted. "She wasn't forthcoming. I didn't push. 'Sides, if she is a wanted criminal and she tells me and I take her knowin' that she's wanted, then I'd be aiding and abetting. Don't want that to my name."

"Right. Two hundred dragons is a tempting bargain. And she's going to Ice Port, so it isn't like the king'll send his men that far north if she *is* wanted. Not unless she done something real terrible. I ain't heard nothing of it from the gossips, so it must not be too concerning." Jonah hesitated. "Why not flee somewhere else though? Oshea? Harrah? Them countries would be more favorable than the icy north."

Bennett agreed. "Maybe we'll find out more on the way. For now, let's just focus on getting out of here."

He was no sooner on board than the woman *Cat* was atop him —figuratively speaking, since he would have much preferred the literal case. "What can I do you for, *Cat*?" He tried to appear pleasant, but he had a ship to run and no time for her antics.

"My cabin has no window. I would like a windowed cabin for the price I paid."

"Oh. That so? Well then, come with me." He led her to his cabin and fought back a frown. Perhaps he should have tidied it better before disembarking a few days ago. The bed was made, but his things were strewn about, and the desk was cluttered. "How about this? Will it do?"

Her face brightened, though she didn't smile. Free of her hooded guise, he could tell now that she was uncommonly pretty. Beautiful, in fact. And she knew it.

Her dark hair had been pulled back with a ribbon and hung in thick curls down her back. Pretty brown hair with streaks of gold. Her gown was far too fancy for a ship, but he wasn't going to say anything. So he bit his tongue and waited.

"This will do nicely," she said, lifting her chin as her eyes danced around the room.

He smiled a dark, wicked smile. "Good, then you can share it with me. Try not to hog all the covers while we sleep, eh? I don't share well." A look of disgust morphed across her features. She sputtered, shocked by his audacity. He doubted there were many people who crossed her or would dare say such a thing. He arched an eyebrow. "You wanted a window. This is the only private cabin with windows, and it's mine. So unless you want to be *sharin'* it with me, and you'll find no complaints on that matter,"—he winked at her—"then you best be happy with the one you got."

Her face turned red with anger. She harrumphed and stormed away, back down the narrow corridor, jamming her hands out along the walls to keep her balance. The ship rocked and she yelped, falling against one wall before regaining her legs. He chuckled, watching her teeter to the cabin she'd been given— Jonah's as it turned out. Poor man had sacrificed it and would shackle up with the crew. She threw him an annoyed glance over her shoulder before disappearing from sight. And good riddance, too! Maybe she'd stay tucked away for the entire journey and rid him of her annoyance.

Satisfied, he returned to the deck. He had a ship to manage, and it was high time to be getting underway. His crew greeted him, with questions on their lips about the lady they'd seen. He gave them a stern talking to and told them to keep their dirty paws off her. Should they get her safely to Ice Port, there'd be ten gold dragons in it for each of them. A share they'd never seen before. That shut them up immediately. He could see the thoughts of how much drink and pleasure money like that could buy, flashing across their hungry gazes.

They had just stowed the anchor and unfurled the sails when he heard a bird's caw. He turned his eyes skyward to find Beaky making lazy circles around the ship, coming in for a landing. She settled down near the eagle's nest to keep watch. "Bout time, you daft bird," he muttered up at her, unable to keep the smile from his lips. She only chirruped down at him. He grunted and returned to his work. The sea waited, and it was time to set sail.

CHAPTER 39
THE AUTUMN MOON FEAST

Jeanine jumped at the sound of knocking. She set down her book, careful to set the ribbon so as not to lose her place. Growing up in Lincastle, she was fortunate enough to have tutors as a child. The children of Kaljah didn't know how to read. They'd never had any reason to learn. Perhaps because the number of books in the village, excluding her own, could be counted on two hands.

Even after moving to the middle of nowhere, her mother had insisted they continue her education. Reading, writing, numbers, and history. Up until her mother's death.

She hadn't very many books to her name. None of them had survived the attack on Kaljah, but Esterpine had a massive library. Feowen had given her leave to visit when she liked. Most of the books and scripts were written in other languages, spriten dialects that dated farther back than the Third Age. But there were enough in the common tongue.

The knock sounded again.

"Coming. Just a moment." She rushed to the door, taking in the appearance of an unfamiliar sprite through the glass. A messenger with a bundle.

"I was sent to bring you this," he said, offering a parcel wrapped with brown cloth.

"Oh. Thank you." It wasn't as if she could have forgotten Feowen's *gift*.

She watched the messenger depart before shutting the door. It was late afternoon, and the surrounding city was abuzz with activity, all in preparation for the Autumn Moon Feast. Her lessons with Feowen had been canceled. *His Highness* had been required for matters of politics. Probably an excuse to avoid her after their time together the day before.

She set the package on her small dining table, pulling away the strings and wrapping. Gauzy fabric tumbled into her fingers, smooth like water, in a shimmery, midnight blue. The same color as Feowen's hair—a direct match, in fact. She clenched her jaw, studying it.

It was stunning, even if it wasn't something she would normally wear. The silver ties at the waist, the beading along its hem, the swirls of silver foil across the fabric like spriten markings. It took her breath away. It was a gown that would transform her. She knew it without needing to try it on.

She held it up, examining the fabric, pleased that it wasn't entirely transparent as she'd expected. What did Feowen mean by giving this to her? Was it a ploy to see her in a dress? To determine a new side of her? Or perhaps to see how much sway he held over her?

She frowned.

The last fancy party she'd attended was as a child in Lincastle. Gatherings in Kaljah were a casual affair. And even the nicest clothes worn by the villagers paled in comparison to what she held in her hands.

She blew out a breath, well aware that she could not put this off.

She went about bathing before attacking her tangled mass of brown hair, combing it until it shone, then braiding and twisting it in a chignon. The vanity had a supply of pins, which she used to tuck it into place. There was even kohl and rouge available for her use.

Most of her dwelling was exposed, made of glass beneath massive tree roots, just like the rest of Esterpine's dwellings. Privacy was scarce, so she utilized the folding, opaque walls, amply supplied, to block off the private areas where she slept and bathed. She stayed sheltered in seclusion as she donned the gown and gazed at herself.

"I don't even look like me," she muttered, lifting a hand to her face, just to be sure that her reflection was real. The markings that flowed over the gown's fabric shimmered as they caught the light of the orbs hanging from the root ceiling.

Tears pricked her eyes. She wished her mother could see her, all grown up, dressed like this. Elsabeth would have been proud. Her father, too. To see that she could look the part of a lady even if she preferred weapons to dresses and dolls. Maybe they *would* still see her, wherever they were resting, with the gods in their afterlife.

A knock stilled her. Feowen always used the same double tapping pattern. She hadn't expected to see him until the feast, but maybe he wanted to gawk, to give her a hard time after she'd agreed to wear the gown. She stepped around the paper wall, exposing herself.

Even from across the dwelling, she saw the smile curving his lips, making little dimples in his cheeks. She faltered, looking him over through the glass. He'd chosen a more traditional spriten garb, leaving his chest and legs exposed. She couldn't help but stare, yet again, at the markings flowing over the skin of his lean body. She'd seen him yesterday, but tonight, with his blue hair pulled back, wearing the same fabric as her, it was a different story.

"May I come in?" he called. "Or are you going to gawk all night?"

She opened the door, glaring at him. "Looks like you failed to mention a few things about my dress. How is *this* a good idea?" She gesticulated between them, their matching fabrics. "Your mother is the queen. A fact I'm sure you haven't forgotten. I'm just an outsider. You cannot dress me up like this and match what I'm wearing."

"Afraid we might give the wrong impression?" He gave a challenging arch of his eyebrow, eyes dancing as he waltzed in. He glanced around before settling his gaze on her, lingering over her curves, making her cheeks burn. "I almost didn't think you'd wear it."

"Very *funny*. Ha ha. I'm laughing so hard." She adjusted the tie on her gown, suddenly self-conscious. "And so you know, if it showed any more skin than it already does, I probably wouldn't have."

Feowen chuckled. Then his eyes snapped away, fixing over her shoulder. She turned, following his gaze. Jahl stood just outside of the doorway, open mouthed. Her insides went cold, watching his eyes take in her gown and Feowen's matching...attire.

Before she could say anything, he turned on his heel and stalked away. She glanced between Feowen and Jahl's retreating figure. "Better go after him," Feowen said, shrugging. "I'll wait." He took a seat on a nearby chair.

She sprinted out the door and caught up to Jahl. He stomped onward without stopping. "Jahl, please." She took hold of his arm, forcing him to face her. Several sprites passed, paying them strange looks. "Why are you being like this? You've been weird all week."

He huffed. "Nice *dress*."

"What's that supposed to mean? Why are you so upset?"

He sighed. "I came to see if you wanted to accompany me to... never mind. You're clearly going with *him*. Looks like you've assimilated to sprite life well enough."

"Jahl..."

"No. It's...it's fine. I'm leaving anyway, so what does it matter?"

"Leaving? What are you talk—?"

"I don't belong here, Jeanine. I did not think you belonged either but..." He looked her up and down, as if proving a point. "I was going to ask you to accompany me to Kastali Dun, but maybe you are better off here, with him."

"You...but our people. What of Kaljah? You cannot just...and what would you even do once you're there? You haven't any money. You—"

"King Talon offered me a position with Kastali Dun's city guard and a handsome salary. Who knew our king could be so generous?" Her mouth fell open, speechless. His face softened. "I was going to tell you. Actually, I was going to speak with you about it tonight, and invite you to come with me to the feast. But..."

"I..." She exhaled. "Queen Jade appointed us to represent our village, Jahl. And you're...you're just going to *leave*?"

"Just because you and I speak for our village, doesn't make Kaljah our responsibility. We have lives to live, Jeanine. I was going to leave before all this—" He waved an arm through the air. "I was going to go out and forge my own path, anyway. Now, I've been offered a comfortable living, a prestigious position with the capital's city guard, with the highest recommendation. You don't turn down a king's recommendation."

"It's what you always wanted," she whispered, letting the news sink in. "I..."

He shook his head. "I wanted you to come with me. An adventure for both of us, like we often talked about. But, also so that you didn't feel like I was leaving all the responsibility with you. We dreamed about this! Remember? How many times did you wish you might accompany me when I talked about leaving Kaljah? How many times?" She opened and closed her mouth. "Don't worry about Kaljah. We can select others to care for the villagers, to speak for them until they can return home. Come with me, Jeanine." Hope lined his features. "This is our chance."

Her stomach dropped. Jahl was right. They'd spent so many hunting trips dreaming of a life away from Kaljah, dreaming of running away together, even if she always knew deep down that she could never leave her father behind. But, her father was dead. She had nothing tying her to Kaljah anymore. And yet...there was something.

She shook her head. "Jahl...I...I can't. I don't think I can leave Esterpine. Not yet, anyway."

Even as she said the words, she frowned. Something nagged at her. A feeling. Like an itch. Princess Taylynn's words came back to her. She was to play a role in something, but what role? An inkling told her that leaving with Jahl wasn't her path.

Jahl's shoulders dropped. "It's because of *him,* isn't it? Don't be so naive, Jeanine. You know you're just human. He's immortal. A fairy prince or whatever."

"Sprite, prince, Jahl. He's a spriten prince. And I'm well aware." Her jaw hardened. "I can't believe you're even suggesting it. You think I would stay simply...?"

"For a prince? Why not?"

"That wasn't what I meant. And that's not why I'm staying."

"Fine. Your reasons are your own." He made a sound of frustration. "I won't force you to come. But this—it's not my life. And if you don't plan to join me, then so be it. I leave in the morning, with or without you. The queen has promised an envoy to take me to Ellia outpost. From there, I will travel on foot to the capital. I'll see you at the feast."

He retreated, disappearing into the foliage before she could say another word. Before she could ask him how he planned to travel all by himself to the capital. The notion was silly. Outrageous, even!

She snorted and walked away.

She found Feowen lounging, flipping through the book she'd set down. Her cheeks turned hot. It was one of the few romantic books she'd found, and she hated the idea of him knowing.

He snapped it shut and stood. "Well?"

She shrugged.

"You've lost all your color. What did he say? Want me to knock some sense into him?"

"I think that would be the *worst* idea," she muttered, moving about the dwelling to tidy things, simply to give her hands something to do. They were trembling, she realized. With anger. Or perhaps fear. Or some other emotion she couldn't pinpoint. Jahl had always been her rock. And now he was leaving.

"Fine." Feowen sounded bored. "Whatever you wish. Shall

we?" He waited for her. She nodded and took his arm, following him out of the dwelling and through the woods, well aware of his frequent glances. "You look...nice—for a human." She jabbed his arm, earning an *ouch* sound. "Only teasing," he added. "But you really do look lovely."

"Thanks, I suppose?"

"The color suits you."

"Right." She almost snorted.

He paid her a sidelong glance. "It is also my favorite color."

"I couldn't tell."

He grinned, and they continued their walk in comfortable silence. Each step left her highly aware of his presence beside her. Of her skin against his, her hand draped through his *bare* arm. She kept her eyes forward, even when she saw the frequent glances he shot in her direction.

She really had no idea what to make of him.

They made their way to the large clearing where the feast was held. The trees opened enough to show a small swath of clouds and sky. The full moon would rise, framed by the clearing at midnight. Or so she'd been told.

Groups of sprites stood about, mingling and chatting, most dressed in more revealing garb than her own, with material that was virtually nothing more than a soft shimmer over their skin. Light music drifted to her ears. She sought it out and her gaze landed on a group of musicians who held flutes and stringed instruments. A few revelers danced holding hands, forming a ring, laughing with gentle voices.

Those she passed looked at her, eyes widening when they took in the prince beside her. It left her uncomfortable. She never liked this kind of attention. Then again, they looked at her when she walked around in pants, too.

"Everyone's staring," she muttered, paying Feowen a glare. His fault, after all. He gave a low chuckle and said nothing.

"Well! Aren't you lovely!" Queen Jade appeared before her, arms spread wide, smile on her face. A smile that didn't touch her eyes.

"Your Majesty! Thank you. Not nearly as lovely as you." She dropped Feowen's arm and offered the queen a curtsy, careful not to let her eyes drift over the queen's body, over the lack of modesty.

"Mother," Feowen said by way of greeting.

"And where is your sister?" the queen asked, looking him over but saying nothing about his attire. "Out on another of her ridiculous forays, I suppose?"

"Something like that."

The queen's face hardened. "*Tiresome* girl!"

"She's hardly a girl anymore, Mother, not for some several thousand years at least."

The queen sighed, glancing around. "Yes, I suppose. Oh look, there's Lord Marquin. Do excuse me." She nodded at both of them and swept away.

"Yes, yes, go and mingle. Do what you do best," Feowen muttered, watching her go with a frown.

"You and your mother don't get along very well, do you?"

Feowen glanced down at her. "What? Oh. Well enough, I suppose. Far better than she and Taylynn do." He hesitated. "It wasn't always this way, but..."

"But what?"

"But you ask a lot of questions, don't you?"

"Well, you're always so secretive. What do you expect? Wouldn't it just be easier to speak freely? Or do you still not trust me?"

"It isn't that." He guided her to a table where they sat. No one had joined them yet, so they were still largely alone. "I suppose it's hard for a human to understand—"

There it was again! *Human* this and *human* that. "Try me," she said through gritted teeth.

"Fine. Fine." He waved a hand in dismissal. "A queen should know when her time has come. When it is time to pass the mantle to her daughter. We are immortal beings, yes. But nothing should walk this earth forever. Our mother cannot seem to let go. It has created a rift between her and Taylynn. Among other things..."

Jeanine opened and closed her mouth. "I...didn't know. How long does a sprite queen usually rule?"

Feowen shrugged. "It depends. Queen Jade has ruled for nearly thirty-five thousand years. Far, *far* too long. My grandmother ruled for fifteen thousand. Queen Isabella before her, my great aunt, close to ten. Isabella's mother, only six. You see the problem here? Generally, our king tree makes the decision, when the time is right. And in Jade's case, I'm certain the decision was made a good fifteen thousand years ago. At least."

"Fifteen...but." It was hard—almost impossible—to fathom time on this scale.

"Yes, yes. That would make me very old, I suppose."

"*Ancient.*"

He shrugged. "Not to me—to us. Time doesn't move here, and yet, it races by. Ten years in a single blink. One hundred in the span of an exhale. Five hundred in the time it takes for the sun to rise. A thousand in the span of a day. Two thousand...you get the point."

"And all of this is decided by some...some *tree*? Isn't it just a legend?"

Feowen tutted. "Not just legend. The tree is real, I can assure you."

"Oh, so you've seen it, then?" She lifted an eyebrow.

"I? No. But Taylynn has. Those who have seen it, generally only see it once. It is where we go to die. Close your mouth, you're letting bugs in."

"I...to die?"

"To die. When it is my time, I will seek it out. The tree bears a special fruit, the fruit of passage, some call it. When we are ready to pass from this life, to be reborn as part of the forest, we partake of the fruit. We fall into a peaceful sleep among the roots, where we are taken into the tree's bosom and reborn as nature. As part of the forest."

"You mean, I'm surrounded by a bunch of dead sprite tree foliage?" She glanced around, glaring at the tree beside her.

"Shh." Feowen jabbed her arm, incredulous. "Don't let others hear you speak of it like that. But...yes." A small smile pulled at his lips. "I suppose so."

"How come Taylynn has seen the tree then, if she wasn't ready to die? And what about everyone else? No one changed their minds after seeing it? No one decided they weren't ready to die after all?"

"The tree shows itself when it is time. For those who wish to pass this life, they journey out into the forest and the tree finds them. They must be truly ready for such to happen. I don't think the tree would show itself if it knew they planned to change their minds."

"*It*, or *he*? You called it a king."

"It. He. King. Ruler of the world. What difference does it make? It's a tree, after all."

"But a tree with a sentient existence."

"Exactly."

"And Taylynn has really seen it?"

"Yes. Often. For council. As does each queen. The tree shows itself to our queen when it is time for her to take up her mantle."

"Oh."

"Yes. *Oh*." He hesitated as a group of sprites passed and paid him their respects, only speaking again once they moved on. "My mother hasn't accepted that her time has long come. She doesn't trust Taylynn's ability to rule. Doesn't trust that the time is right—which some would argue mirrors her mistrust of the tree. She claims to seek its council even still, if only to reinforce her right to rule. But..." He shook his head. "Dragonwall is out of balance, gravely so. I know enough from Taylynn to know that the tree stopped showing itself to our mother ages ago. If that is not a sign, I do not know what is. My mother will not see the tree again until it is time to die. And believe me, that time has long since come."

"How can you speak of it so bluntly?"

"See?" A smile pulled at one side of his mouth. "Told you you wouldn't understand."

"I lost my mother when I was young. I'd give anything to have her back."

"You're free to have mine, if you'd like. Take her. And good riddance," he huffed.

She shook her head. "Unbelievable."

"Who? Me?" He placed a hand over his heart.

Several sprites took that moment to sit at their table, and soon, nearly all the tables were full, bringing their conversation to a halt. Food was served and voices rose as everyone ate and chatted, excited for the change of the season. As if the forest were any different from one season to the next.

She spotted Jahl sitting with the group of Kaljah villagers. Her skin flushed as his gaze slid over her before it moved on. Perhaps she should have sat with them too. Her people. But were they really? Had they ever been? A sense of untethered freedom seeped into her chest. She was a kite, free to roam where the winds of fate might take her. But where would that be, exactly? And how much did Taylynn know about it?

A change was coming. Of that, she was certain. A visitor was coming to the forest. Someone who would pose a threat to Queen Jade. Someone she had been advised to *watch over* and make a friend of. Whatever that meant. But who? She could only speculate. As Feowen had said, they would know soon enough.

CHAPTER 40

AN ANNOUNCEMENT

Celenore

Tamara tried to ignore the ache in her feet. Each throbbing step was a reminder of the distance they'd covered. Their journey would take them through Celenore to the Scattered Islands. King Talon had ships waiting to take them to Fort Kastali.

The rolling hills of Celenore felt endless, the grass dusted with hues of green and brown. She shielded her gaze against the sun—

"Do you think there will be any unmated drengr in Fort Kastali?" Sophie broke the silence between them.

"I would imagine so," she said, distracted.

"I hope there are." Sophie nudged her shoulder. "I would love another chance to try again."

"I would like that too." She smiled at Sophie, attempting to match her bubbly mood.

"And the capital!" Sophie clapped her hands together. "Can you picture it? I never thought I would see it with my own eyes." Shadows passed overhead. They squinted, watching a returning group of drengr. "Will you and Byron go out flying this afternoon?"

"Gods, I hope so." Her heart leapt at the thought. "I need to get off these aching feet."

"Oh. Well, at least you can." Sophie's voice lost some of its eagerness.

"I..." Her face burned. "That was thoughtless of me. I'm sorry."

Sophie shrugged. "You were lucky enough to find a mate. I was not."

"Ladies?" A deep voice came from behind. Byron fell into step beside them, his gaze assessing. He'd become more watchful of her after the attack, always looking for hidden hurts or wounds, afraid to take his eyes off her as if he might lose her like he did his parents. Or perhaps he expected her to fall apart at any moment. It was a wonder she hadn't. How many women her age were forced into this level of responsibility?

She hadn't even complained.

She wanted to. Gods! Sometimes she wanted to scream at the heavens. It was all so awful. So unfair. She should have been grateful to be alive, but instead, she felt a well of bitterness inside her.

"Lord Byron!" Sophie attempted a curtsy without slowing their pace and giggled.

"Good to see you, Sophie. You look well. And keeping Tamara company, no less. I am glad."

"Of course, Lord Byron." Sophie blushed and turned away.

"Tam?" Byron's gaze fell upon her. He'd taken to using the nickname shortly after the attack. She wasn't sure why, but it gave her a thrill. "Shall we fly?"

She squinted up at him, keeping her gaze shielded with her hand against the bright sun. "You're not too tired?"

"Of course not."

"You've had your wings out all morning."

"So? Scouting is easy work. What do you say?"

"Well, if that's the case." She glanced at Sophie. "You'll be okay?"

"Of course." Sophie bobbed her head. "I'll meet up with the folk from the cookery. They look as if they require some good company. And mine is the best, after all." Her grin was infectious.

Tamara reached for her friend's hand and squeezed. "Yours *is* the best, Soph. You've been a blessing to everyone here." Sophie's eyes glowed with pleasure. "The folk from the cookery will appreciate you. Go."

"All right then," Sophie said. "Enjoy your flight."

"Ready?" Byron held out his hand. His eyes danced as he led her away from the line of trailers stretching out behind them, where he transformed.

The moment she was on his back, their minds melded. A sigh slipped from her lips at the familiarity of it. It was a relief for him, too. He enjoyed being with her like this.

They wasted no time in vaulting into the sky. The people below shrank in size and disappeared. Some waved at them as they departed. Byron took them west for a bit, then turned south. The land sailed by. If only they could afford to leave everyone behind and travel onward. They would have reached the capital by now.

"We cannot abandon them."

She jerked, not having realized how apparent her thoughts were. *"Yes. Yes, I know. Nor do I want to. Just a wishful thought to lighten the burden. I..."*

"You're tired of traveling. I understand. There is no fault in it. I'm tired too. So tired..."

Her chest ached. Byron wasn't fatigued in the traditional sense. He was emotionally exhausted. She saw the heaviness of his burden, day by day, leading the fort to a new—but temporary—home. The loss of his parents, the disappearance of his uncle, the many deaths that had shaken the fort. It was an impossible weight. She comforted him, laying her cheek against his scales, closing her eyes, smiling at the feel of the wind against her skin.

They flew for nearly an hour before Byron spotted a creek and thought to descend. In that time, they talked about simple things. She told him about some of the conversations she'd had that day, while he talked of things he'd spotted during his scouting trips. It was a blessing to have drengr for a journey like this. Each day they were able to fly the heaviest belongings ahead and make camp. When the rest of the fort arrived on foot, weary after a day of walking, they could simply rest.

"This looks like a peaceful place." Byron landed.

He'd brought them to a tree-lined creek, meandering left and right, with gentle curves that took it out of sight. "It's lovely." She unstrapped from the harness and slid down to the ground. Their mental contact broke.

He wasted no time in transforming, falling into step beside her. "Baths are scarce these days. What do you say?"

She balked, glancing between him and the creek they approached. "I imagine it's rather cold, don't you think?" The air was cooling as winter approached, but the sun was still hot, and there were few clouds in the sky. She made her way to the water. It was deep enough to swim.

Byron tested it with his hand. "Not frigid. It will do." She studied him, watching the way his muscles bunched beneath his tunic with every movement.

A bath would be nice, she realized. Refreshing. Exactly what her tired muscles needed.

"I'll leave you for a bit. I know you prefer your privacy. Or..." He hesitated. "I'll join you, if you'd like?" There was a hint of teasing in his voice.

She opened her mouth.

He must have noticed the change in her expression. "Tamara, I know... You have every right to be..." He rubbed the back of his neck, regarding her with a furrowed brow. "You can say it, if you like."

"Say what?"

"'I told you so.'"

Her frown deepened. "Why would I—why would I say that?"

"Because you've been thinking it."

"I have not!" Her voice came out more defensive than necessary.

He took several steps toward her, then paused. "You have. I've read your thoughts. I try not to intrude, but some are hard to ignore."

Heat crept up her neck, flushing her cheeks. "Just because I think it, doesn't mean I'll say it."

"Yes, and for that reason alone, you are too good to me." He took one of her hands in his, folding his fingers around them. "I deserve it—what you've been thinking. Don't think I don't." He hesitated. "I should have listened to you. You told me you were ready. If I had listened, we could have been...my parents would have been...they..." He heaved a breath and dropped her hands, turning away from her.

Sunlight glinted off his golden hair, so like his father's. Her chest collapsed, seeing him unsettled like this. It was unlike him. In all the days since the attack, he had kept these thoughts buried deep in the confines of his mind. He hadn't spoken of what might have been. He avoided it under the pretense of being occupied with his new duties. But she knew what was there, lurking.

She went to him, wrapping her arms around his chest, pressing her front flush to his back. Sparks exploded along the places they met. It felt good—too good. Him against her. Her curves melded with his and it felt...*right*.

"I know what you're thinking," she whispered, barely able to reach his ear on her tiptoes. "But we cannot change the past. If you let it bother you like this, it will wreck you."

"What do I do, then?" His voice came out heavy with emotion —vulnerable.

"The only thing you can do. Your best."

"I'm trying," he growled, his voice rough with emotion. "I really am."

"I know."

He turned in her arms and reached for her face, cradling it. His piercing gaze made her throat feel raw. "I worried that you weren't ready, Tam. That I would dishonor you, even despite the bond. You are young compared to the lifetime of a drengr. I worried that there was still too much girl and not enough woman in you." He bent and kissed her forehead before reclaiming her eyes.

"I'm sixteen now, Byron. Most girls are younger when they are married off. I saw a girl of thirteen, once."

"I—I know." His throat bobbed. Things were done differently among the drengr than the human nobility. "I was wrong about you, Tam. I have seen you these past few weeks. Don't think I haven't." He shook his head. "We should have completed our bond before we left. But...but I will have you now, if you will let me."

She gaped at him, her heart taking off in a gallop. "Right...right now, as in, this very minute?"

"If it is what you wish."

"I..." Her eyes fell to his lips. She wanted to feel everything Claire had talked about. To know exactly what it was like. To put her hands on him. To feel his hands on her.

She exhaled, hating what she said next, but knowing it was right. "We should have the ceremony. It would be good for our people—for our fort. It would give them something to be happy about."

He nodded. "I thought you might say that."

A wide smile spread across her face. "What if we announce it today? We've still got a week before we reach the coast, but that doesn't mean we cannot celebrate. We can get the provisions we need when we pass through the next settlement, set up a party tent, spend a day celebrating. You could ask Fierran to perform the ceremony so that we can speak the words. We ought to do it right. Your parents would prefer it that way. So would I."

His expression brightened. It was the happiest she'd seen him since the attack. He lifted her and kissed her, his mouth moving over hers in a way that spoke of his approval. Heat dumped straight into her belly as his tongue brushed hers. A little mew fell from her lips, swallowed by his. She wrapped her arms around him, sighing, letting their kiss deepen. It went from tentative to hungry. A gasp escaped her.

She didn't stop—didn't want to.

He was the first to break their kiss. She almost groaned with frustration. Almost pulled his face back to hers.

He stared down at her. "I would still like a bath, if you'll allow me to join you?"

"Oh. Uhm..." She blinked the daze from her eyes. A wicked smile threatened her lips. "It could be dangerous, if you leave me here alone and unclothed. Wild animals, bandits, all that. What of my virtue?"

"My dear Tamara, did you just make a joke?" This time, she didn't withold her smile. His low chuckle made her toes curl. "We can't risk your virtue, can we? I must protect you." He kissed her again, making her gasp against his lips, before setting her back on her feet.

They shed their clothes, laughing. Byron helped her with the ties on her gown. Her skin burned with eagerness for every moment that his fingers were occupied, anxious with anticipation. When the dress and chemise slid off her body and fell into a heap at her feet, his hands and lips found her bare shoulders. He kissed her, laying gentle pecks all the way to her neck. She felt the heat of him, radiating against her back.

Her body shivered with delight. No man had ever seen her unclothed. She should have been shy, but the low growl that sounded behind her made her eager, more than anything.

She whirled to find him likewise naked. Everything swept from her mind at the sight of his glorious body. Her gaze traced the lines of muscle along his arms and shoulders, his chest, down his stomach, all the way to....

A gasp slipped from her lips.

His arousal was on full display. Her face burned. She forced her eyes to his. Their gazes met.

"Like what you see?" he growled with pleasure.

She couldn't form words.

"Come—let's swim," he said, taking pity on her. He took her hand and led her to the creek. She squealed as the cold water met her skin. It was a refreshing welcome to chase away the heat burning through her.

"A bit more frigid than I thought," he managed through clenched teeth. "No matter. You have me for warmth." Before she could bite out a response, he took her into his arms and pulled her naked body against his.

She came alive!

Everything sizzled and sparked, sending tingles down to the tips of her toes. She wanted to wrap herself around him, arms and legs, to clutch him. But she knew exactly what might happen if she did that. So instead, she simply let him hold her.

"Gods, it really is freezing," she said through chattering teeth. "No matter how warm you are."

He tried to kiss her but it was no use. Her teeth were clacking roughly together, her skin pebbled with gooseflesh.

He laughed, and she soaked in the sound of it. He used to laugh so much—before everything. "All right then, better get moving before we freeze in here." With that, he released her and splashed away, dunking under the water.

She had no intention of getting her hair wet, so she went down enough to cover her shoulders and rinse her body. "I thought the drengr didn't get cold," she called when his head popped up.

"We get cold," he assured her. "We're at our warmest in our drengr form."

The frigid water chased them out soon enough. She was highly aware of Byron's eyes on her as she reclaimed her chemise. "You are so very beautiful," he said, helping her pull it over her head. "I can hardly keep my eyes off you. Though, for what it's worth, I tried." He pulled her against him, holding her close to warm her against him. Through the gauzy fabric, she felt every touch like a brand, felt the hardness of him against her. It left her stomach curling. She tangled her fingers in his wet hair, bringing his face to hers, kissing him, enjoying him.

Long after they met up with the others, she couldn't stop seeing his naked body. The curves of his muscles, dripping with water droplets. The blonde chest hair that scattered across his skin. Damn Lady Claire for what she'd revealed during those short conversations about lovemaking.

When they made camp, Byron summoned the entire fort. He took her hand and pulled her atop a stack of crates. "Tamara and I have an announcement." Everyone fell silent with anticipation. "We have decided that we will not wait any longer to seal our bond. Too much sadness follows us. Too much hurt. We could use some cheer, so we've decided that we will hold our bonding cere-mony in two days. What say you?" He lifted his voice higher. "Will you celebrate with us?"

Roars exploded all around them. "We are with you!" some shouted. "Seal the bond already!" others called, laughing. Their enthusiasm was infectious. She found herself blushing and smiling at some four hundred people staring back at her. Many of Byron's wing leaders and seconds were fist pumping near the front of the crowd.

He turned to her, grinning. Before she could protest, he took her up in his arms and kissed her in front of everyone. It was long and deep, pulling the very breath from her lungs.

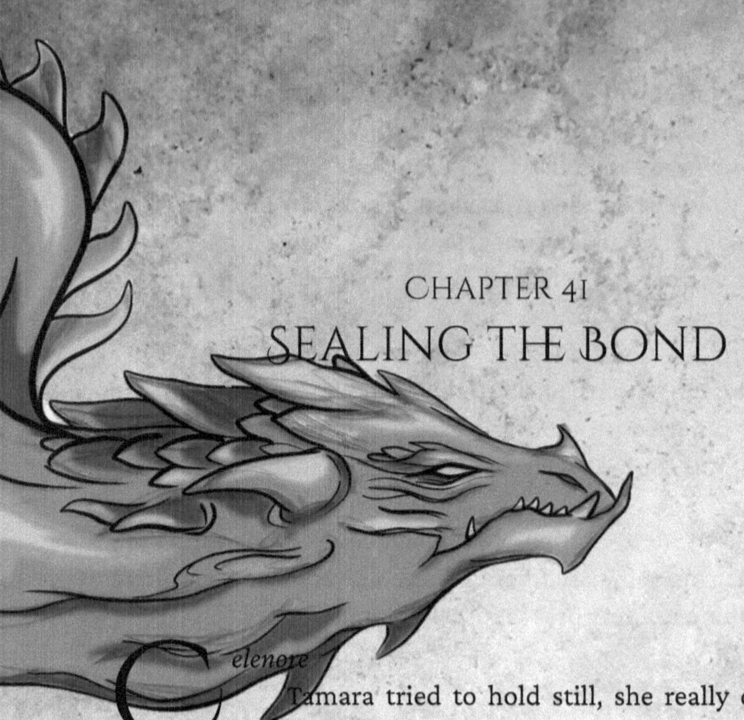

<h1 style="text-align:center">CHAPTER 41
SEALING THE BOND</h1>

elenore Tamara tried to hold still, she really did, but the anticipation was too much. Sophie was alone with her in the command tent, helping her to dress. "Stop shaking!" she said, poking her with a finger. "I can't do your hair if you keep fidgeting."

She'd waited so long for this day. It wasn't happening how she'd imagined it, but that no longer mattered. All that mattered was Byron. They had managed to rescue her belongings, including her ceremony gown and the pommel stone she needed for Byron's sverak, when they'd fled.

"Gods!" Sophie sounded breathless. "Wait until everyone sees you in this."

Lady Emmy's face came to mind. Only a few weeks had passed since her gown fitting, but it felt like ages. Emmy had treated her like a daughter. Her chest tightened and a sob broke free. "I wish Emmy and Davi were here," she whispered. "It's not fair."

"Nothing that's happened is fair, Tamara." Sophie hesitated, her voice turning soft. "I wish they were here too. And Lord Reyr." At the mention of Reyr's name, Sophie's voice turned dreamy. "But we will manage without them, won't we? Because we must."

"We must." Her voice was nearly a whisper.

There was no looking glass to see her reflection. She could only gaze down at herself, at her gown, and admire it. Icy blue fabric cascaded around her, falling over the stool upon which she sat, while Sophie finished pinning her tresses in place. She looked like a frozen waterfall spilling over a rock face.

"There. You look like a queen."

"I wish Claire was here, too," she murmured. "I would have liked that. But...we can't afford to wait any longer."

"Is there a reason you're rushing into this?" Sophie failed to disguise her curiosity, though there wasn't any judgment in her voice.

She hesitated. "We cannot delay any longer. I want him—more than I've wanted anything. It's like something's missing and I'm incomplete. More than that, we must show a united front to our people. We haven't spoken of it, Byron and I, but his father alluded to it some time ago. A vote will happen when we reach Fort Kastali. Our people must vote us in as their leaders. They will be more confident voting for us if we are mated. It shows..." She fumbled for the right word.

"Maturity?"

"Yes, exactly. What would the fort think if he dangled me on a string without solidifying our bond?" She shook her head. "Besides, it's safer for us. We cannot communicate when we are separated. If something happens while we travel..."

"Well, if that's the case,"—Sophie gave her hair a teasing tug— "I'm surprised it took you so long to reach this decision. We've been on the road for nearly two weeks."

"Yes, well, he needed time to grieve. Time for both of us to process what has happened."

"Understandable." Sophie placed her hands on Tamara's shoulders, gently squeezing. "There's naught to be done now but celebrate! Gods, I wish you could see yourself. Come, the others are waiting."

Sophie led her to the doorway of the empty tent. No one was permitted to see her in her gown until the ceremony, which would happen as soon as she made her way to the party pavilion. It was small; most of their audience would stand outside to witness the event. Byron had the idea to set up a makeshift platform using some of the crates they'd brought.

"I'm nervous," she whispered after peeking out at the assembled crowd. An aisle had formed from the command tent to the pavilion, which had been decorated with ribbons. The smell of roasting meat permeated the air. It was only morning, but everyone was eager to feast and celebrate. They would likely spend the full day doing so. She, however, had other ideas of how she wanted to spend her day. Plans that involved flying off into the wilderness with Byron.

Travel bags were already packed for the two of them with everything they'd need. Since the camp would offer little privacy, Byron would fly them to a secluded place after the celebration, somewhere they could be alone.

"Everyone is waiting," Sophie whispered, prodding her in the back. "Quit stalling."

"Okay. Okay. You're right." She took a deep breath, wiping her sweaty palms on her gown. Had it been a traditional ceremony, she'd have had a slew of ladies following her out. Some had offered, but she'd decided that Sophie would do.

Taking the wildflowers Sophie offered, she left the tent. The sun was already racing towards its zenith. It dazzled her. She paused to blink. Gasps erupted around them. The aisle of people waited, watching, whispering about her dress, calling her *beautiful* and *radiant*. She only wished Emmy and Davi were among them, and her family, her mother especially.

She clenched her teeth. There was no use in wishful thinking. She might be a fort leader someday—sooner than she ever imagined. It was time she accepted the world for what it was. Time she made the best of it.

Lifting her chin, she moved down the aisle. Sophie held the train of her gown to keep it from catching on the flattened grass. Her cheeks warmed as the whispers followed her.

The occupants standing under the pavilion came into view. She didn't see Byron at first. Then he loomed into view and she faltered. His attentive gaze was on her, focused on each of her movements. His golden hair was swept to one side, and his eyes twinkled, even from a distance. His hands were clasped in front of him. He stood motionless, shoulders pinched. Was he as nervous as she was?

His manner of dress was similar to hers. He wore a tunic to match, with a pair of beige pants and black boots. The image of his naked body flashed into her mind, distracting her, and she couldn't help the giggle that shattered her tension. He too smiled in response.

She went to him.

"Tamara," he murmured, holding out his hand when she was close enough. She covered the remaining distance and grabbed him like a lifeline, anchoring herself. "Gods, you look incredible. Like a jewel. *My* jewel." He rubbed his thumb over her knuckles. Her stomach fluttered.

"Hello, Byron," she whispered, too nervous to say anything else.

Fierran stood before them, Byron's wing second and life long friend. With a nod from Byron, he began. Everyone hushed to hear his words.

For all the nights spent imagining, nothing could do this moment justice. Nothing could relay the feelings of her nerves while she stole glances at Byron, or explain the feel of her racing heart when they exchanged the drengr pommel stone and rider's bow, to protect each other in their own way. Nothing could illustrate the warmth that snared her body as Byron took her hands in his and turned to face her. They recited the bonding words in unison, staring into each other's eyes:

Rejoice!
A bond is discovered—
a lifetime destined by fate.
A commitment unbreakable,

until Daudagher takes us.
A tender comfort to ease the hardship
the other's labor has brought.
A love that takes root,
encouraged by caring hands and gentle kisses.
A promise is made;
a promise is sealed.
A single mind from two combined:
a drengr and his rider.

As they moved through each step of the ceremony, the rest of the world disappeared. They only had eyes for each other. When their bonding words came to a close, sparks passed between them like shivers, running through her body, humming through her blood.

"And so it is said, so it shall be!" Fierran cried, turning to the audience. His words were far away, as if she were in a dream.

Byron squeezed her hands. "One step closer," he said, keeping his voice low. His eyes darted to her lips. Her stomach swooped. She sucked in a sharp breath at the promise of what was to come.

Around them, the crowd erupted into cheers, bringing her back to the present.

Their audience clapped and smiled and offered words of encouragement as they made their way down the aisle to the command tent, where they would pass several minutes alone before joining the celebration—mostly to catch their breath. "Davi and Emmy would be so proud!" someone called. "About time!" another shouted.

A blush crept to her cheeks at some of the *other* words that were said.

Alone in the tent, Byron wasted no time in pulling her into his arms and kissing her. "Gods, I thought my heart would leap from my chest," he breathed. The look on his face, so open, so vulnerable, melted her insides. "I couldn't take my eyes off you for a single minute." He set her back on her feet and looked down at her. His expression faltered for a moment, smile falling. Almost as quickly, he replaced it.

"What is it?" she whispered, tangling her fingers deeper in his hair. "What's wrong?"

"It's nothing." He was too quick to answer.

"We're mates, Byron. You can tell me anything."

He sighed. "I just wish..." She knew what he was going to say before the words were out.

"Your parents," she finished. He nodded, glancing away from her. She tugged on his hair, bringing his gaze back to her. "They are here," she whispered. "In our hearts."

"You're right." He nuzzled her before kissing her temple. "You're right. They would be so happy for us, my mother especially. She looked forward to having you as a daughter. I'm just...I'm glad she got time with you before...before all this." He took her face in his hands, rubbing her cheeks with his thumbs. "Shall we take a few minutes before going back out there? The crowd is already getting rowdy."

A wry smile twisted her lips. "We'd better not wait *too* long."

Happy shouts filled the air, reaching the tent. Admittedly, she would have been content to sit alone with Byron, with him holding her, cradling her in his arms. She hated to share him on a day like this. But it was necessary. He would never be entirely hers anyway —not if he became Fort Squall's leader.

She tilted her head, listening for a moment before pulling his head to hers. His tongue brushed her lips, sending shivers down her back, like invisible talons clawing against her skin. She opened wider and shivered again when his tongue teased hers. His hands were equally vexing as they roved over her body, exploring her curves through the fabric of her gown. A hint of what was to come later.

"Does it ever stop?" she whispered when he pulled away. "This...wanting?"

A chuckle sounded deep in his chest, more of a dragon's rumble than anything. "Gods, I hope not."

***

The celebration lasted well into the afternoon. There were few tables to be had. Stools were scattered about. Blankets spread across the ground. And not a single complaint about the limited amenities.

Tamara and Byron were seated at what had been deemed *high table*, like a proper lord and lady of the endless wilderness surrounding them. Food was abundant in the form of roast meat, potatoes, and flatbread, so she ate until her dress squeezed enough to smother her. Then they danced to the flutes and stringed instruments that had been pulled from trunks. When the sun fell lower in the sky, Byron made excuses and began saying their goodbyes. It was time to seal their bond.

"Give her memories she'll never forget," someone called as they left the party. "Make your father proud!" another yelled.

Her face lit on fire. Damn them!

Many of the fort's drengr were hundreds of years older than Byron. They'd watched him grow up. This was a happy moment for them, seeing him reach this milestone in his maturity. Seeing him with a mate. It was their chance to tease him with their bawdy innuendo.

She was all but shaking when she climbed up and strapped into the harness. The fort gathered around them, a sea of bodies, offering more congratulations and well wishes. She had planned to change into an appropriate gown for the wilderness, but a few hushed whispers from Byron earlier had changed her mind. He wanted to be the one to remove her gown. The enticing proclamation was irresistible, so instead, she had Sophie bustle it up in the back. It puffed up around her, gobs of fabric the same color as Byron's scales, spilling out over his neck and wing joints.

They took flight and left the cheers behind them, heading east. She embraced the silence of the sky, letting the energy of the celebration die down in her chest. Watching the landscape loosened the knot in her stomach.

"*You need not be nervous,*" Byron said.

"*I'm not nervous!*" Her face colored at her lie. Words from her conversation with Claire had been replaying in the back of her mind, coaching her through what was to come. *"And quit prying,"* she teased. *"These are my thoughts, not yours."*

"They will be mine soon enough." A grumble sounded deep in his chest. She knew exactly what he meant. Her mind. It would be his at all times, soon enough. Not just when they were flying. He swooped low, looking for a comfortable stretch of landscape that might serve them.

Were the drengr always this possessive when a mating was close at hand? His behavior, the frenzy of his mind, his thoughts, had turned from civilized to animalistic. Growls and grumbles driven by instinct instead of logic.

He snorted, sending plumes of smoke from his nostrils. *"Don't expect us to be civilized. We aren't human. And there are plenty of humans that lack the distinction too."* Just to prove his point, he sent her a mental image of how he planned to ravish her, making her skin burn.

They landed on a stretch of open wilderness. "Wait here," he said, rather bossy, already in human form as he moved about constructing a tent with a few quick muttered words. Magic. A thrill raced beneath her skin. She would learn magic once they were bonded. Once his magic belonged to her.

The small shelter wasn't tall enough for them to stand, merely adequate for sleeping. Not that there would be much sleeping. She eyed him as he removed plush furs from the bags—one for the tent and one for the ground outside it, which he cast beside them.

"Hmm." He hesitated, contemplating his efforts. "I think I'll have you right here to begin with. Worship you under the open sky."

Gods above! She placed a hand against her stomach. Had he any idea what those words did to her nerves?

He finished with his task and turned to her, eyes roving up and down her body. Assessing.

"What?" Her voice was barely a whisper.

"Nothing. I'm framing you in my mind so that I never forget. Just as you are here at this very moment." The vein at his neck was jumping. She was certain that his heart, like hers, was racing.

A shiver raced down her spine. She closed the distance between them, her gown whispering over the grass. "And do you like what you see?"

"Very much, Tamara. *Very* much." He wrapped his arms around her waist. "Shall we put Lady Claire's advice to the test?"

She sputtered. "That was...that was private!" As she tried to smack his chest, he caught her wrist, holding her pinned against him with his other arm.

"Feisty, are we?"

"Only when you tease me."

"Mmm. But I enjoy teasing you, Tam." His voice was a low rumble. "I always have."

Memories of the kiss he'd stolen long ago, before she knew they were mates, of the way he'd teased her even then, came to the forefront of her mind. He buried his nose in her neck before kissing the shell of her ear. His silken lips sent shivers across her skin. The fabric of her gown pulled taught over her breasts, leaving her breathless.

"You smell good. Like flowers."

She couldn't find words, and was glad when he captured her mouth in his, kissing her, claiming her. His hands climbed up her back and into her hair at the nape of her neck, releasing the pins holding it in place. It cascaded around her shoulders in an inky waterfall of curls. A gentle sigh fell from her lips, only to be captured up in his greedy mouth as he ran his fingers through her tresses, caressing her scalp. She groaned.

Her hands weren't idle either. They snuck beneath his tunic to the bare skin of his back, relishing in the corded muscle rippling with each movement. He pressed her against him. She flexed her fingers, digging her nails into his skin. He growled, deep in his chest, pushing her away almost immediately.

"Turn," he said, a dark laugh on his lips. His eyes transformed as he spoke, turning into something draconian, pupils to slits. Slits that devoured her.

She shuddered, overcome, as she faced away from him. He fussed with her gown. His fingers worked slowly, until she was convinced that he relished in the act, purposefully postponing their next moments together. A frustrated *tut* escaped her lips. Another dark laugh sounded beside her ear. "Shall I go *faster*?" he asked, his voice a husky growl. Who was this creature?! He took her waist in both hands and pulled her flush against him.

"Yes," she breathed. "Faster."

"Hmm." He began again, this time moving quickly as he finished the remaining fastenings and pulled the gown away, sliding it down her body. His fingers burned through her silk chemise, setting her skin aflame as he trailed down after the gown. When she looked over her shoulder, he was crouched behind her, helping her out of her slippers.

He laid her down beside him on the fur rug, claiming her lips once more. His hands were an entirely different matter. One arm supported her head while the other found the hem of her chemise and began traveling up her leg, sending tingles of sensation to the tops of her thighs. A soft groan built in her chest. She could do little more than wrap her fingers about his neck, tangle them in his hair. When his hand found the apex of her thigh, she gasped. He growled with approval, exploring her, relishing in the effect he had upon her.

The sensations were...unimaginable. Her expectations were entirely unprepared. Warmth and desire ripped through her, turning her into someone she hardly recognized. Nothing else mattered save the way he made her feel and the pleasure he got in return. As his fingers worked, exploring her, slipping into her, a pressure built in her core. At last she was gasping and desperate, her body aching and tense beneath his touch, clinging to him as her muscles tightened. His tongue was against hers, coaxing.

She needed a release. Gods above! More than she had ever needed anything.

Her back arched against his chest. A cry escaped her lips, unbidden, and another, more heightened. Then her world split apart and she shattered around him, letting go. The movements of his hand slowed, then stilled. Her body tumbled down from its high, and her eyelids fluttered open to find his gaze upon her, eyes still draconian slits.

"Here, or the tent," he growled.

She blinked up at him, struggling to speak. "There...there's more?" It was the stupidest thing she had ever said. Of course there was more. Even if she didn't know better, his expression said that clearly enough. Her mind was simply scattered, fragments she didn't care to piece together.

A deep but satisfied laugh shook his chest. "Oh yes, Tamara, there's so, so much more." Without waiting for her answer. He stood and undressed before her. She propped up on her elbows to watch him, blushing as she beheld him for the second time. Her eyes went exactly where they had before, except this time they didn't shy away from taking in the length of him. A pleased rumble in his chest brought her gaze to his. He wasted no more time in toying with her. Instead, he got on all fours and stalked towards her before finding her lips again, enveloping her in a silent promise, one that could not be illustrated with words.

He lifted her chemise up around her waist and united their bodies, sealing their bond as drengr and rider. This time she knew what to expect, and welcomed it, opening herself fully to him. And when her world shattered for a second time, it was to find him riding the waves of euphoria beside her, his mind linked to hers in the throes of passion, permanently fused as one.

CHAPTER 42

THE CAVE EXPEDITION

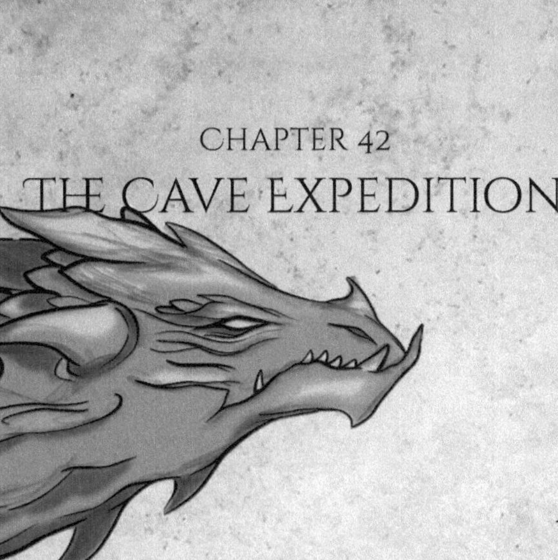

Kastali Dun

Claire signed the bottom of her letter with a flourish, pleased with the improvement in her handwriting. She blotted the ink and tucked her writing things away. Talon's crown glittered beside the sheet of parchment. She picked it up, running her fingers over the stones, weighing it in her hands.

Her heart thumped at the thrill of holding it. At the reminder of their time after the ball. Of their desire, of his frenzy. The memory brought heat to her skin. A smile curved her lips. Talon had left it on purpose. As a game, perhaps, one she was eager to play.

Except, then he'd gone away.

He'd received word of a pirate raid on a coastal town on the northern tip of Galadhal's peninsula. The entire castle had slept late the morning after the ball, late enough for him to slip out unnoticed. His note—simply a few lines of text—had been pushed under her door. She'd found it, still dressed in her ballgown, and by the time she'd read it, he was long gone, Verath with him.

Three days had passed. It bothered her that he hadn't sent someone else. Why did the task require a king, when a shield would do? Why leave the crown behind, if he simply planned to avoid her? Why jump at the first excuse to disappear? Did he want space? Was he running from what had happened between them? Giving her time to consider their discussion?

She missed him. The threads of their unsealed bond tugged on her heart. The separation was almost painful, plaguing her every moment. But not as painful as knowing that he had returned hours ago, without seeking her out. Desaree was the one to break the news. She'd spotted his servants rushing about his tower, delivering messages and food.

Perhaps he hadn't missed her as much as she'd missed him. Three days wasn't a long time. Perhaps it was selfish of her to expect him to seek her out. Selfish to want to be the first thing on his agenda after his return.

So, she had done the only thing she could without appearing desperate.

Dear Talon,

I hope your journey to Fairfay was productive. I have missed our walks together. In lieu of your absence, I have returned to my lessons. It seemed prudent.

If you are not too busy tonight, I plan to visit the cave under the keep, after the evening meal. Perhaps you might count it as our walk tonight? I would recommend bringing your shields. They would appreciate being included.

Oh, and I have a lovely new crown to decorate my quarters. A trophy, of sorts. Would you like it back? On second thought, I think I shall I keep it. I hear the metalsmith in the city does wonderful work. I might have him melt it down into a matching bracelet for my necklace, or even a pair of earrings?

Yours,
Claire

p.s. You owe me a kiss for every day you've been gone.

SHE SMILED, hoping he would see her teasing for what it was. The crown was too splendid to destroy. Besides, she was rather fond of the memories it held.

She folded the note and sealed it. Desaree sat embroidering near the fire. "All done?" She set her things aside and stood. "I'll have it delivered straight away. Do you think he will come?"

Claire shrugged. "I hope so. He was eager to see our secret when I told him."

Desaree took the note and disappeared. She returned a few minutes later to prepare her for the evening meal. "We ought to put you in something bold. Something that will catch King Talon's eye after his absence."

"You *are* the authority on the matter." Claire watched her browse through the wardrobe. "I submit myself to your expertise."

Desaree emerged. "How about this?" It was a red gown with gold beads. One she hadn't worn because it drew too much attention. "It will go well with your hair and eyes."

"Fine, but only because it would be a shame to leave it in there."

Desaree laid everything out and attended to her with care, twisting and coiling her hair into an elegant chignon. While Desaree worked, her eyes darted between her hands and Claire's reflection like a nervous bird.

"What is it?" Claire asked.

"Nothing. I mean, there's something I wanted to speak with you about."

"Is...is everything okay?"

"It's fine. It's about Verath."

"Oh." Claire's stomach dropped.

"We had a talk after the ball. I wanted to tell you sooner, but you were distracted by King Talon's absence."

"That's not a reason, Des."

"Okay, I...you're right. I haven't had the heart to speak of it. Not yet." Desaree fell quiet.

"Well? What did you two talk about?"

"He...we...*I* decided to take some space apart from him."

"What?!" Claire all but jumped from her seat. Desaree had to push her back into it. "And you're only just now telling me this? Explain. Now."

"I..." Desaree sighed but as soon as she started talking, it was like a dam ruptured. After a glorious night of dancing, Desaree and Verath had returned to his chambers together. She had been more than ready to take their intimacy to the next level. Eager, even. "I made up my mind days beforehand. I wanted it to be a special night for both of us." Her throat bobbed. "I was afraid that if I did not act, if I did not make the first move, he might never..." She fell silent.

"What happened?" Claire asked, already sensing where this was going.

"I...I asked him to make love to me."

Claire choked. Desaree had to pat her back. It was rather unlike her handmaiden to be so forward.

"I expected him to be thrilled, but he wasn't. He...he turned all moody. I had to pry it from him but he...he finally explained why. Oh, Gods, Claire. I..." Desaree stifled a sob. "He had a mate, Claire! Verath...there was a woman. Kendra. They..."

"Oh, Des!"

Desaree kept talking, explaining detail by detail, of how Verath found Kendra but never spoke to her, how he'd abandoned their mate bond, how he felt guilty because Desaree looked so much like her, but wasn't her. Desaree spoke until tears streamed down her cheeks and turned into sobs. "I told him it was a lot to take in. That I needed a few days to think about it. So, we...we're taking a break."

"Gods, Des. I'm so sorry." Claire rose from her vanity and pulled Desaree into her arms. "I'm so, so sorry." She stroked Desaree's hair, trying to calm her.

Pieces were falling into place. Verath had gone with Talon. The king could have taken any shield with him, but he'd taken Verath. To give Desaree space. This had nothing to do with her and Talon, and everything to do with Talon wanting to be there to support his shield, his brother.

"I don't know what hurts me more," Desaree was saying between sobs. "Knowing that I'm not his mate or knowing that we can't be together even if I *was*. He's a shield. What was I thinking, Claire? What was I thinking?!"

"I know...shhh," she cooed, continuing to stroke Desaree's hair.

"But I love him, Claire. I love him. How could I possibly be with anyone else?" Desaree's voice came out a strangled laugh. "And here I once scolded you for caring about King Talon. You were right to turn it around on me when I did. I guess...I guess..." Desaree started to hiccup.

"You hoped you were mates," Claire finished for her. "Even if you knew you couldn't be together."

"Yes." It came out as a gasp. "Was I stupid? Stupid to want that?"

"Gods, no, Des. Not at all. Don't hold yourself at fault." She tightened her arms around Desaree's shoulders. "We love who we love. It cannot be helped."

Desaree nodded, then gently pushed out of Claire's arms, wiping her eyes on the back of her sleeve. She spoke through another bout of hiccups. "Kind of like...like you and King Talon. I... I see the way you are...together."

"Right. Like me and Talon." Claire's throat bobbed. Except it wasn't like her and Talon—not at all. Because she and Talon *were* mates. She wanted so badly to say it. To reveal their secret.

Desaree continued speaking, oblivious of her indecision. "You...

there's something between you and King Talon that's stronger than what Verath and I have. Verath loves me. I know it. But King Talon..." Desaree shook her head. "King Talon looks at you like... like he's found something he's searched his entire life for. Like—" Desaree's hands flew to her mouth and her eyes widened.

The room fell silent as Desaree's hiccups stopped abruptly.

Claire's mouth went dry.

"Oh, gods, Claire! Why didn't I see it sooner?!"

"Wh-what? See what?" She stood frozen.

"You are mates—you and King Talon! Oh, gods! Gods! *Gods!*" Desaree slapped her palm to her forehead, forgetting about her vexation with Verath. Forgetting about her hiccups.

Claire's palms turned sweaty. She tried to speak. Opened her mouth. Only a squeak came out. Was it *that* obvious?

"I should have seen it before," Desaree continued. "I spend more time with you than *anyone*. How did I miss it? But it makes so much sense. King Talon swore off women when he got his scars. He never found his mate. He has been alone for so long. It would take more than a pretty face to tempt him—no offense. Do you not see it, Claire? You are his mate. That is why you've been feeling this way about him. That is why you were infatuated with him after the kidnapping incident. It's so obvious."

"I..." Her shoulders fell. She couldn't lie. Not now. "I wanted to tell you," she whispered.

"Wait." Desaree's eyes darted over her face. "You...you knew?!"

"Yes," she squeaked, barely able to get the word out. "I'm sorry, Des. I'm so sorry. He made me swear to keep it a secret. He made me promise not to say a word. I told him how unfair it was. I did. I told him that I wanted to tell you—and Saffra. And...and Jocelyn." She felt awful. Desaree would probably never forgive her. Yet, even as she spoke, a smile broke out on Desaree's face. It was opposite to what she'd expected. "You...you're not mad?"

Desaree threw her arms around her. "Mad? No! I mean, I would have liked to know, but...no. Gods above!"

Desaree's outburst made her laugh. They leaned against each other for support. She swallowed and said, "You know? I think you've said *gods* so many times in the last few minutes it's enough to set a world record."

"I'm just happy for you, is all." Desaree took hold of her shoulders and moved her to arm's length, studying her. "Do you know what this means?"

"Uhm...that Talon and I will probably be mated sometime in the near future?"

"Well, yes, that too. But no." Desaree's face turned radiant. "Claire, I'm going to be handmaiden to the *queen*. Dragonwall's queen!"

Claire opened and closed her mouth like a fish. She didn't have the heart to tell Desaree that she hadn't accepted the offer...yet.

"Gods above!" Desaree gasped, continuing. "Handmaiden to the queen! Which automatically makes me a *lady in waiting* even without my title. I..." She dropped her arms to her sides. "I think I need to sit down. And I need a drink too, if you wouldn't mind? Red wine, please."

Claire burst into another fit of laughter. "Right away, *Lady* Desaree!" she said, sketching a bow.

"You're not queen yet," Desaree teased, flopping onto the sofa, still struggling to contain fits of happy laughter. "This is...so unexpected. Does anyone else know?"

"Nope. You're the first. Not even Talon's shields." She poured Desaree a goblet.

"I'll guard the secret with my life," Des said. "But now that I know, I want the full story."

"I figured." Claire handed her the goblet and sat down beside her. They hadn't much time before the evening meal, so she rushed through the abridged version, telling Desaree about her time with Talon in Brezen, filling in bits and pieces she'd been forced to leave out before. She described in great detail her experience when she entered Talon's mind, the lava field, and the fact that Talon had known and not told her.

"Gods! I *knew* there was something going on between you," Desaree said when she finished, smug at having seen it before anyone else. "I could tell by the looks you shared. Smoldering looks. Like you both might set something on fire. I just thought... well, I thought perhaps it was just infatuation. Now it makes sense."

"Yes, I suppose so. But, Des? We got sidetracked from Verath. Have you decided what you're going to do about him? Mate or not, you have a decision to make. He cares about you."

"Oh..." Desaree's face fell. "I've spent some time thinking. But now that you're going to be queen, this changes everything. I've got a plan, I think—" A knock sounded, bringing their discussion to a halt. "I bet that's King Talon's reply—about tonight." Desaree jumped from the sofa. "We can discuss Verath later." She fetched the note and brought it over.

Dear Claire,

You have discovered my return, I see. All went well. But I have missed our walks, too. Glad you resumed your lessons. I would be delighted to join you tonight. I'll bring my shields. They wouldn't forgive me, otherwise.

As for the crown, since you have grown so fond of it, it is yours. A token of my affection. Unless you decide to melt it down, in which case, I will be quite cross, and most certainly reclaim it.

See you soon.

Yours forever,
Talon

p.s. I would be happy to repay the aforementioned kisses, with substantial accrued interest, and will make good on my promise to do so when we are next alone.

. . .

Desaree squealed, fanning her face. "Another kiss?!" They shared a grin. "In that case, we'd best finish getting you dressed." They rushed through the remainder of her preparations and went down to the dining hall together.

Saffra and Jocelyn joined them at their favorite table beside the fireplace along the wall. They discussed their upcoming venture with hushed whispers so the others wouldn't hear. She found it exceedingly difficult to keep her eyes off the high table.

Each time she glanced up, she found Talon's gaze wandering to hers. He looked pleased to see her, yet troubled, as if the weight of his duties were catching up with him. His brow was furrowed, accentuating his scars. She was left counting down the moments until they were together. The urge to smooth his scowl and make him happier was overpowering, almost annoyingly so.

⁓

"Open up in the name of the king." There was a loud pounding on her door.

Claire recognized the voice. "Or what?!" she shouted, throwing it open.

"Or we'll muscle our way past the guards and break it down," Koldis said, grinning.

"Right!" She rolled her eyes. "You'd love that, I'm sure."

"I'll have you know, Lady Claire, that I'm quite skilled at breaking down doors." He lifted his chin a measure.

Talon and the others stood behind him, holding back grins. She gazed at them, momentarily taken aback. The sight of them together stirred an emotion she hadn't expected. Family. If only Cyrus and Reyr were here to see it.

I'm here, came the gentle reply.

She stepped aside. They filed into her living area, greeting Desaree, Jocelyn, and Saffra. The space seemed to shrink in the presence of five hulking forms. She was careful to notice the way Verath's eyes followed Desaree, never quite leaving her figure.

Talon appeared beside her, brushing a hand down her back while the others talked. Keeping his voice low, he said, "I apologize for my rapid departure the other day. I hope you will forgive my absence—Ahh. I see my crown has already found a new home."

She'd placed it on the mantle, framed in the center.

"Oh yes," she purred. "My new trophy. And you're forgiven, but only once you make good on your delivery." She ticked the days off on her fingers. "By my calculations, that's three kisses, with interest, so a total of six."

A dark laugh rumbled his chest. "Done. When we are next alone, I will make good on my end of the bargain."

"I look forward to it."

"And for the record," he added, "If you would open your mind, I might have told you about my departure without the need for a note."

She opened and closed her mouth. "I like your notes. Besides, you left while I was sleeping. I probably wouldn't have heard you anyway."

"Point taken. Perhaps I was using that as an excuse. I simply wish you'd open your mind to me." He hesitated before adding, "So that I can reach you easier."

"So that you can pester me when you're stuck in council meetings, you mean?"

"Can you fault me?" There was a wicked gleam in his silver eyes.

"Hardly."

She considered his words. With the drengr safely tucked away in Fort Kastali, there was distance between them, and their voices were less of a concern. She could open her mind and go largely unbothered. Admittedly, the idea of sending thoughts back and forth with Talon was appealing.

"I'll think about it," she decided.

"Good. Now, what's this I hear about secret passages and a

cave beneath my castle?" He rumbled, lifting his voice for everyone to hear.

"Yeah." Koldis crossed his arms. "Why didn't you tell us you've been sneaking around right under our noses?"

Verath shot a glance at Desaree, probably surprised she'd kept this from him.

"Maybe we wanted a little fun of our own first, before sharing it with you lot." Claire smiled back at them. "I certainly hope you're up for an adventure?"

"Ready when you are," Talon said, holding out his arm.

She walked past him to the tapestry. "I found it during a storm," she explained, revealing the secret door as she told them what had happened.

"I cannot say I'm surprised," Jovari said, stepping up beside her to study the seam in the wall. "All great castles have secret passages. I'm just surprised we didn't know more about them."

"Well, there was that one you found in the north wing a while back," Verath said. "The one that leads from the courtyard with the stooped hag fountain, and then there's the corridor behind the guest suites."

"Ah, yes. I suppose that counts." Jovari nodded and stepped aside. "But it doesn't sound anything like what our lovely ladies have found."

With the wall hanging pulled back, Claire opened the door. Talon stepped up beside her. He grunted when the stone moved. "I'm not sure I would have spotted it. And there are more, you say?"

"Many more."

"Interesting." He glanced at the others before turning back to her. "Ladies first."

After creating enough light, they proceeded into the narrow passage and down the stairs, assembling on the landing below. They were presented with the three familiar doorways that had once held so much mystery. She explained where each one went. Behind her, she could hear Jovari and Koldis whispering, caught up in a fierce debate. No doubt plotting how they would use this to their advantage in the future.

"And which one leads to the cave?" Talon asked, forcing everyone to hush.

"The middle one." Saffra said, stepping forward.

"Then by all means, Lady Saffra, lead the way." He stepped aside and she accepted his invitation, grabbing Jocelyn's arm as she went. Desaree followed, and Verath fell in step behind her, no doubt hoping to get in a few hushed words.

Claire decided to wait for Bedelth, Koldis, and Jovari so that she and Talon might bring up the rear. He appeared to have the same idea in mind. They stood motionless for several long breaths, watching the orbs of light shrink down the cramped hall.

And then they were alone in the dark.

Talon's movements blurred. Before she could gasp, he pulled her into his arms and claimed her mouth. His kiss was hungry, like he'd been starved these past three days and she was the sustenance he needed to survive. She exhaled against him, sighing, as his tongue roved against hers. The knot in her chest loosened.

He pulled away, breathing hard. "That's one," he said before kissing her again, longer this time. One hand pressed against her back while the other gripped her neck possessively. She twisted her fingers into his hair and tugged, hard, to show her frustration over his absence. A low groan left him. When he pulled away, they were breathless, lips aching and swollen. "And that's two."

"Hmm..." was all she could manage.

"We might get lost down here," he whispered. His voice was a low rumble. "Is it bad if I don't care that we do?"

"Uhm..."

He kissed her again then, this time softly. She fell into him, welcoming the sensation of his body against hers, the heat that scorched all places where their curves met. "Three," she whispered this time, pulling away. "And I won't complain if we get lost." Her mind had grown foggy. She would never be able to find her way like this. Already, the light in the tunnel passage had all but disappeared.

Talon's low, rumbling laugh made her insides clench. "I'm tempted to do it. Disappear forever with you down here in the darkness." He pressed his lips to her forehead. "But I also want to see this cave. Hurry now, or we'll lose them." Taking her hand, he tugged her along. She twined their fingers together. They caught up shortly thereafter, no one the wiser to what had passed between them in the darkness.

Minutes sailed by as they traveled lower beneath the keep, following Saffra's lead. Talon's shields were full of questions, which they posed keeping their voices low. Which rooms led to each of the passages? Had they spied on anyone else using them? Had they explored all of them yet?

The air turned colder and wetter and they fell quiet. Eventually, Talon broke the silence. "I'm almost nervous about what we might find." The light from Saffra's orbs danced across his scars, making him look more beastly than ever, but that only made her want to kiss him again. He must have seen the look on her face because he added, "You may collect the fourth later," and gave her hand a squeeze. It left her grinning.

"Just up ahead," Saffra called.

"Gods, I should hope so," Koldis grumbled. "I feel like we're traveling into the bowels of the earth."

Jocelyn's voice echoed from ahead as she said, "Not quite that far, Lord Koldis, but close."

They stopped and gathered at the mouth of a rocky opening in the passage. "We're here," Saffra said.

Claire closed her eyes. She heard the faint trickle of water and smelled damp, salty air.

"Look." Talon nudged her.

Saffra's orbs flew out into an open expanse. There came a collective gasp. She could see nothing behind the massive drengr forms blocking her view.

"Would you like to go first?" Talon whispered.

She shook her head. "The others can go." She wanted to hang back and witness it in her own time, with him.

"Can we go explore?" Bedelth asked, hesitant.

"To be sure," Saffra said. "It's safe. We have already explored much of it. Follow me."

Claire waited for them to clear out before taking it in. She gasped. Even Talon grunted. A giant cave stretched before her.

"It's incredible!" she whispered, glancing at Talon.

There were formations everywhere, jutting from the ground, the ceiling, from one another, layer upon layer, some monstrous, some sharp, some like works of art. Pools of water were scattered throughout, catching the silver of Saffra's light to reflect it, glittering in the darkness. In the center she spotted the rocky outcropping with the broken gate, and a short distance beyond it was the small building carved out of stone.

"It's all rather...*magical*, isn't it?"

"Hmm..." Talon was oddly quiet. When she turned to him, it was to find a look of awe on his face.

"All this time," she said, "and you really never knew this existed?"

"Here I call myself a king."

She poked him in the side. "No one is perfect, *Your Majesty*."

He glanced down at her, eyes dancing. "Good thing I have *you*." That look left her stomach fluttering. "Shall we?" He lifted an arm as if preparing to parade her through a crowd of people.

"I thought you'd never ask. Lead the way, *my king*." Grinning, she slipped her hand into the crook of his elbow. A king and queen of the underworld.

They moved through the cave. She leaned against him as he guided her past formations. They examined anything that caught their attention. The pools, various stalactites and stalagmites, the greenery clinging to the walls. "Careful, there's a crack here. Watch your step." He was deliberate in his efforts to navigate them towards the rocky outcropping at the cave's center.

She considered all that had led up to this moment, about who she was. About Saffra's visions. About Cyrus's intuition. Cyrus had fallen into *her* cornfield, when it could have been anyone's.

"So, now that you've seen this, do you still doubt my theory about Princess Irelia?"

"That remains to be seen." His words were quiet.

They climbed to the top of the outcropping, Talon carefully

guiding her. She dropped his arm to examine the pieces scattered about. She went to what remained of the onyx pillars, jutting from the rock. They had symbols etched into the features similar to what she'd seen before.

An idea came to her.

"Saffra? Can you come here for a moment?" Saffra was beside her in an instant. She kept her voice low, sharing her thoughts with the king's seer.

Saffra's eyes went wide. "You think it will work?"

"I don't know. The other gate wasn't broken, and I had only set foot in Dragonwall minutes beforehand."

"What's this about?" Talon stepped up beside them.

"Claire is going to touch the gate."

Talon frowned. He glanced at her outstretched hand. A brief nod was the only encouragement she received. She reached for what was left of the nearest pillar and laid her hand upon it.

"Well?" Talon's voice came too quickly. "Is it working? Do you..."

She didn't hear the rest of what he said. He disappeared. They all did, as the light surrounding her vanished. She was plunged into darkness, into the cave as it usually was, untouched.

After several breaths, a new light appeared, the yellow-orange light of a torch. It approached from the mouth of the cave where she'd come in. She blinked. A girl came into view, young, not even fifteen.

"Princess Irelia," she whispered, remembering Irelia's face from the painting in the keep.

The girl moved cautiously, glancing over her shoulder. She climbed to the top of the outcropping and stood, eyeing the gate. When Claire turned to the pillars, it was to find them fully erect and unharmed. She gasped, her eyes growing wide. "Can you...can you see me?" she asked.

The girl said nothing. She didn't so much as look in her direction.

Claire fell silent, frozen in place as the girl stepped forward.

"She's going through the gate," she whispered. "Just as I suspected."

Part of her wanted to reach out and stop Irelia, to warn her that the world on the other side was very, very different from her own. But a deeper realization was solidified in the next moment. If Irelia did not go through, she might never exist. The weight of Princess Irelia's actions struck her square in the chest. It was the only explanation for why she had sprite blood. For why she was so connected to this world when she shouldn't be.

She watched as Irelia took a deep breath and stepped forward, walking straight through the gate. As soon as she passed through the pillars, she disappeared with her torch. The world fell into darkness, swallowing everything up. The darkness remained for some time, as if days, or perhaps even weeks passed. Then a new light appeared, coming from the same place. This one was tinged with green, similar to the magic orbs Saffra had made. The light spread further than Princess Irelia's torch had, so she knew immediately when Queen Isabella came into view.

"Oh my god," she gasped, seeing the great spriten queen in person for the second time in her life. She had once seen her through another mind, a skewed perspective from the eyes of the marble dragon. Now she saw the queen from her own perspective, well aware that connections existed between them. But she wasn't prepared for how deep those connections ran. The similarities knocked the breath from her lungs. Isabella was her same height. They had the same build, same facial features. They were basically doppelgängers. It was like looking at herself in the mirror. Their eyes were different, though. She had remembered that much from the dragon's mind.

The grief etched on the queen's features was obvious. She did not look like the powerful woman who had turned a great dragon into stone. Not anymore. She moved about the gate, inspecting it, muttering to herself. How long had it been since Princess Irelia had disappeared? Did Isabella know her only daughter had traveled through?

A frown materialized on the queen's features. She stepped

forward and put her hand upon the onyx pillar. Her eyes took on a faraway look before her face moved through a range of emotions. "No!" Isabella reached out, speaking to someone unseen. Claire's eyes widened. The queen could see the gate's history as easily as she could. The similarity in their abilities was unnerving.

When the queen pulled her hand away, it wasn't sadness or fear upon her features, it was anger. Rage. Her fists clenched at her sides and she shook her head. "So be it," she whispered.

Claire expected Isabella to go through the gate, to follow after her daughter. She did no such thing. Instead, she threw her head back and screamed, echoing a deep helplessness—and disappointment. Her voice ripped through the cave, sending a shock wave of emotion with it, until Claire's ears felt like they might burst. The air around her exploded. The gate shattered, sending fragments rolling down the steps.

Queen Isabella's face had become a mask. "So be it," she repeated again, then turned and fled. The green light faded and then disappeared altogether. Claire gasped, pulling her hand away.

"Gods above! I think she's back. She's back." Claire found herself blinking into Talon's face. He had pulled her into his arms. "What did you do? What happened? Where did you go? You were here, but not here."

"I..." She gripped her head. Her mind was spinning. "I saw them," she managed, trying to make sense of it. "I saw *her*. Irelia, I mean, and the queen, too."

Everyone had assembled around them with confused expressions.

"What happened?" Talon repeated.

"She saw the past," Saffra said for her. "That *is* what happened, is it not?"

Claire nodded. "It's as I suspected. Isabella destroyed the Gate. But I don't..." Her eyebrows pulled together.

"Why would she do that?" several voices asked in unison.

"I don't know. She loved Irelia. I don't understand why she didn't go after her. Isabella put her hand on the gate and saw Irelia go through it. Instead of going after her, she got angry and screamed, and the gate shattered." She tried to make sense of it. "Irelia was her only daughter. The grief killed her, didn't it? Why didn't she…?" Tears pooled in her eyes. Talon pulled her against him, burying her face in his chest.

"Shhh, slow down." He stroked her hair.

"Maybe she knew," Saffra said, her voice far away. "Isabella was a spriten queen, after all. Spriten queens are gifted with foresight. Maybe she saw how important Irelia would become. That sending her through the gate meant her blood would one day return when it was needed the most. Or maybe it was a price—a price to be paid for her deeds. For the drengr. For the balance of the world. Surely there was a reason."

"That is a wise theory, Saffra," Talon said. "And I'm inclined to believe it, after all of this. It's insane. But I believe it." He kept her head tucked beneath his chin. She was certain he wouldn't have believed Saffra's theory with such ease, if they hadn't discovered their mate bond.

"I need to go train with the sprites," she whispered, only loud enough for Talon. His body tensed against her, but he said nothing.

"Claire…?" Desaree's call brought her from Talon's chest. "I think you should see this."

She nodded, wiping her eyes on her sleeves. Talon gave her a look and she shook her head. She could manage on her own, for now, and retain what little dignity she still had after breaking down so pathetically in front of everyone. The others followed as she and Desaree made their way from the outcropping to the small building beside it.

"We've done some research," Desaree said, "and we believe that this was built by the asarlaí, probably around the same time as the gate. We don't have proof, but it almost seems like this might have been the first gate, and the temple building was perhaps a place of great meaning. Though, we don't know what we will find inside."

"And you haven't been able to open it?" Talon asked.

"I used as much magic as I could," Saffra answered. "No success."

"But look, there are words." Desaree reached the door and laid her palm across it. A scratching sound brought their eyes upward as letters, glyphs, appeared in the rock. "It's whatever language the asarlaí use, but we don't have any translations. Not even Marcel could help us."

"Hmm, curious." Talon's voice was low.

Claire's brow furrowed. She stepped forward and said, "What do you think it means?"

"Perhaps instructions on how to open the door," Talon mused. "Anyone here speak the asarlaí language?"

"Shall I go ask Kane?" Koldis drawled.

Talon's chuckle was humorless. "Let me know how that goes."

"It looks familiar, though, doesn't it?" Claire asked. "Maybe I've seen the writing in a book. Marcel gave me one, you know, on the asarlaí."

"I looked through it already," Saffra said. "There was no way to decipher the glyphs."

"Oh..." Claire's shoulders fell. She continued to look at the writing. The longer she looked, the more familiar it looked, and the more her head hurt. She was still reeling from all she'd seen.

"It's okay." Talon reached over and stroked her back, then took her hand. "You don't have to figure it out right now. Or by yourself. We can work on it. I'm certain we can track down some old texts on the asarlaí language and get it translated." She swallowed and nodded. "As it stands, I think we've had enough excitement for one night?" He held her gaze. He was right. She was drained. The gate had taken a lot out of her. "Shall we return and tackle this another time?"

"Yes." Her voice was barely a whisper. He nodded, understanding.

They made their way back, with Saffra guiding them. Once more, she and Talon took up the rear. He encouraged her to lean on his arm. "I know this isn't the best time to tell you, but I heard from Reyr while I was in Fairfay."

She faltered, coming to a stop. "You...you waited until now to tell me? You know I care about him. What did he say? Is he all right? When is he coming home?"

Talon exhaled. "I should not have waited, but I've been bombarded since my return. I tell you now because when we return to your quarters, I want you to rest. It was now or tomorrow. And yes, he's...safe. Distraught, broken, a mess, frankly. But safe."

"He lost his twin brother, Talon. Of course he's messed up. But..." She struggled to form words. What she wanted to say felt selfish. "Wouldn't Reyr do better around those who love him? Why does he avoid us?"

They reached the landing leading to her quarters. The others were already ascending the stairs, disappearing through the door. Talon stopped, letting them go ahead as he pulled her into his arms. "Claire, Reyr does things in his own time. He might be mine to command, but he is more than that. He is more than my friend or my brother. I love him, but even that does little justice to describe what we share. He has been beside me for hundreds of years, as have all my shields. I trust him to do what is best. He will come back to us, in his own time. When he is ready" He sighed. "Let's talk about this tomorrow?"

She nodded. What she didn't say was how she still carried guilt about what had happened between them. She'd been so angered by his abandonment the first time. Now she only hoped he would return to her in one piece so that she might tell him how sorry she was. Perhaps she didn't need to say it aloud. Talon was well suited to read her. He squeezed her and kissed her forehead before releasing her, seeing the question in her eyes. "I still owe you three. I haven't forgotten. Let's save them for tomorrow." He led her up the stairs and into her quarters where he sent everyone away and bid her goodnight.

CHAPTER 43

THE CITY OF SAFUIL

Safuil

Mikkin devoured a bowl of mushroom soup before going for a second, using a ladle to dish generous amounts from the vat sitting before him. He broke chunks of coarse brown bread from the loaf in his hands, dipping each generously into the broth. With every bite he sighed, relaxing deeper onto the bench. The soup was thicker than the typical broth, still steaming, and flavored with spices. Almost too rich for his deprived stomach.

His companions ate in a similar manner, devouring everything set before them like starved animals. No one spoke, not even Jamie. That was saying much, since the lad was generally the most talkative of the bunch.

They had wandered the tunnels beneath the mountains for days. The dried meat ran out first, and then their carefully rationed water. Mikken was already weakened from his stint beneath Shadowkeep, supported almost entirely between two drengr as they walked. The lack of food and water withered him as nothing had before, not even his worst journeys into the mountains to hunt.

Another day, perhaps just one more, might have ruined them. A party of dwargs found them—saved them, rather—and brought them to this place. This dark, dark place. He'd lost count of the days since he'd seen sunlight. There had been none in Shadowkeep. None in the tunnels. None here.

Safuil. A city of rock and stone, deep under the mountains.

The patrol had escorted them straight to the massive dining room, an empty stone hall filled with stone tables, where they rested and ate. He knew little of the city beyond what he'd seen along the way, but he speculated it was all much the same. Carved from stone, void of daylight.

Thank the gods for Berbik! He'd negotiated on their behalf when the dwargs had considered killing them. Strangers wandering the depths of their mountain tunnels was an uncommon occurrence, especially drengr, but Berbik's quick tongue bought them safety.

They ate what the cook already had simmering on the fire. In this case, mushroom soup. It was the most delicious thing he'd tasted, or could remember tasting.

Once their stomachs were full, they would see Dubrael, Lord of Safuil, who would decide if they were worth killing. At least if they died, they'd do it with full bellies. That was a blessing.

He hardly cared one way or another. He'd been as good as dead already. The others appeared unconcerned, too. All except poor Unka. The goblin hadn't stopped trembling. Dwargs didn't like goblins—no one did, for that matter—but especially dwargs. He'd do what he could to negotiate on Unka's behalf—if it came to that.

He glanced over at the poor wretch who'd hardly touched the bowl before him. "You should eat, Unka," he prompted. Unka's large eyes darted at him, his green-skinned throat bobbed, and he attempted another bite.

The goblin had been true to his word. No, he'd been better than that. He'd appeared when Jamie needed him the most, helping the lad work out a plan to get Mikkin back from Shadowkeep. Lord Averaen and his party showed up just before they were set to scale the mountain walls.

He exhaled and a belch rumbled up his chest. With it came

relief. He was safe. They were safe. For now. Albeit, under careful watch.

Their guards lurked along the wall, observing as they stuffed their faces, making comments in dwargish. He glanced in their direction, studying them now that he wasn't starving. They were as hairy as Berbik, with overgrown beards decorated with beads, bones, and teeth. They were short, too, with bodies that rose not taller than his waist, and wrinkled skin, like it wanted to belong on a taller person but instead, had to make do. Yet, what they lacked in height they made up for in strength.

One of the guards caught his eye and grunted, then turned, commenting to his companion. Mikkin frowned. Berbik could understand them, and no doubt chose to ignore what was said, too intent on his food. After years stuck in the bowels of Shadowkeep, with only gray sludge to eat, was it any surprise?

Two newcomers entered the room. They said something in dwargish. Berbik nodded and answered back, shoving a final chunk of bread in his mouth. He chewed and swallowed before speaking again. "Lord Dubrael will see us now."

Lord Averaen stood first, abruptly, detangling himself from the bench. "I'll do the talking for our group," he advised. "I don't trust our hosts yet, given what we know of Kane. Best to keep our mouths shut and intentions guarded. For now, at least."

"Not sure you have that luxury." Berbik eyed Lord Averaen. "Dubrael will want the truth. And unless you speak the language, don't think you'll be doing much speaking. I'll do the talking."

Lord Averaen's brows drew together. He nodded. "Fair point. Then by all means, Berbik, do your best to get us out of this sticky situation. You agreed to guide us, after all."

They were led through tunnel after tunnel, a maze of them. The walls pulsed with pounding drums and the clang of work from the mines, deep, deep below, reverberating up, up, up. As if the stone itself were alive. As if the mountains had a heartbeat.

The dwargs' world was not dark as he'd expected. On the contrary, the tunnels glowed with life. The walls were lined with loosely woven baskets emitting golden light.

"What do you reckon they are?" Jamie asked, supporting Mikkin as they walked. He had more strength now, but still appreciated the helping hand. "Some kind of magical glow?"

"Hard to say, lad. Hard to say." He tried to get a closer look.

"Glow worms," Berbik answered, sidling over to them. "They live and die in the baskets. Glow worm homes. When they produce offspring, their babies take up the task of lighting the halls. They eat beetles and other insects attracted to the light. Our children take pride in feeding them too, like pets."

"Huh. Fascinating," Mikkin grunted, eying the creatures. "Say, Berbik, what do you know of this Dubrael fellow?"

Berbik shrugged. "Never met him, Master Mikkin. Heard plenty of him, though. Reasonable enough for a dwarg lord, from what I know. But he was a lot younger back then. Can't say much for him now."

"I take it you're not from Safuil?"

"No. Safuil is too far west. I come from Notroic."

Mikkin wracked his brains. "Never heard of it. Where's it at?"

"Wouldn't expect you to. It's near the Ice Mines in the east."

"And how'd you come to be in Kane's dungeon?" He kept his voice casual, though it was a question he'd wanted to ask for a while.

Berbik hesitated. "A story for another time, I think."

They passed through stone halls, each carved with elaborate skill. Some plain, others lined with finely carved murals depicting dwargish life or statues of prominent figures. The dwargs they passed going about their business stopped, setting baskets on the ground to gaze at them, wide eyed. The shock of their arrival swept through the city.

One hall stood out more than the others—an underground market—with stalls for trading goods. Artificial light permeated the space, casting everything in yellow and orange ambience. Smells of food cooking on makeshift fires left his stomach grumbling anew.

"Unbelievable," he muttered, studying his surroundings.

How did they stand the lack of sunlight? How did they manage so far underground? Everything was set within the confines of stone walls and stone ceilings, deep under the mountains. There were no windows. No shafts to let in so much as a sliver of daylight. Despite the vaulted ceilings and roomy spaces, he felt smothered.

Their escorts broke the silence, grunting in their guttural language. "Just up ahead," Berbik translated. Mikkin nodded, glancing at Lord Averaen, whose keen eyes darted about, missing nothing.

"This will be a story for Ma and Pa," Jamie muttered. "If I ever see them again."

They stepped into a vaulted hall carved from the inside of a mountain. It had been a solid space once, hollowed by the Dwargs eons ago. Stone columns, carved smooth but left untouched, while the rest of the rock had been chiseled and removed. The floors and walls were smooth, highlighting impressive skill. More glow lamps had been placed throughout the space, aided by braziers dancing with flames. Dwargs stood around the court, mingling. They stopped to watch. These patrons were dressed more finely than the guards escorting them.

And...were those dwargish women?!

His gaze glided over maids dressed in gowns, just as stalky as the men. They had likely passed others along the way here, but since they'd been dressed similarly to the men, he hadn't made the distinction until now. These females were clearly more refined. Their hairless faces were full of cheer and smiles. Warm. Kind. Though, once they beheld his party, their expressions turned wary.

A stone dais sat at the center of the room just as much a part of the hall as the columns, left behind and carved into existence. A red-bearded dwarg sat watching them, with silver beads stranded into his hair, and a spear in one hand. His fingers were ringed. He had hoops in his ears. Metal jewelry was a symbol of importance.

"Definitely not as young as he once was," Berbik muttered.

"You didn't mention earlier that you'd seen him before?" Mikkin scowled. Berbik remained a mystery to him. How much was there to know about this secretive dwarg?

"Just once, from afar," came Berbik's muted answer. "He came to visit my people when his father was ruling here."

Mikkin nodded. Unka had fallen back, close to him and Jamie, while the drengr and Berbik took up their places in front of the group. Berbik bowed deeply, his nose nearly brushing the floor. He said something in dwargish, his voice echoing from the walls. Dubrael grunted, hesitated, then responded. The dwargish language lacked softness, a perfect complement for those to which it belonged. Harsh intonations for a harsh but durable folk. Berbik and Dubrael's conversation went back and forth.

Dubrael's mood and emotions gave nothing away. "What's he saying?" Lord Averaen growled, growing impatient.

Berbik paused. "He wants to know why we were wandering his tunnels. I'm explaining."

"Seems more than explaining," came the drengr's answer. "And how do we know we can trust him. How do we know he won't turn us over to Kane?" Lord Averaen crossed his arms, eying the lord.

Dubrael began to laugh. His deep bellows filled the hall as he turned his gaze to Lord Averaen. "Dwargs, Master Drengr? In league with an asarlaí sorcerer?" The dwarg's accent was thick, like Berbik's, but his mastery of the common tongue was impeccable.

Mikkin scowled but remained silent.

Dubrael calmed himself and said, "Please, Master Drengr, I can assure you that you are quite safe here. If I were to try anything, you and yours would kill enough of my warriors to leave my people...unhappy. Deeply unhappy. What sort of leader would I be then, eh?" He hesitated, looking them over. "A dwarg's magic is rooted in metal-working. In that, our skill is unparalleled. I see you wear some of our craft at your belt." His gaze fell to Lord Averaen's sverak. "Our skill—great as it is—stops there. Not so for you and your kind, eh? You might even kill me with a few utterances, if I'm not careful." Dubrael snorted as if amused, then repeated, "In league with a sorcerer, indeed! Bah! We humble dwargs are at *your* mercy, Master Drengr. Not the other way round."

Lord Averaen squared his shoulders, perhaps pleased by the compliment. "Forgive me, Lord Dubrael, I meant no offense. It is common knowledge that dwargs and wild dragons had dealings in the old days. The tunnels under these mountains are evidence." He spread his arms wide to encompass the underground city.

Dubrael stood then and spit on the ground beside him. "Tens of thousands of years ago, Master Drengr. Tens-of-thousands-of-years!" He pulled his shoulders back. For a dwarg, he was taller than most. "None of us here were alive for that. Were you?" Dubrael's eyes were penetrating. "No? Didn't think so. We here in Safuil have no ties to dragons nor their asarlaí overseer. We pride ourselves on staying *out* of Dragonwall's business, as we have for most of this age." He slammed the butt of his spear onto the stone of his dais. "We take the sprite approach in such matters. Those *tree-lovers* aren't merely good at growing things. They understand when to keep their noses out of your politics, as do we." He paused before adding, "We may be close to Shadowkeep, but we remain hunkered down in our city. Our patrols are frequent. None cross into Safuil without my knowing. Kane would be stupid to send his goblin minions here." At this, he spared a pointed glance at Unka, who cowered behind Mikkin.

"And the other Dwargish cities?" Lord Averaen asked.

Dubrael resumed his seat. "I cannot answer for my compatriots. Master Berbik tells me he sat in Kane's dungeons for some sixty years. I find myself interested to know why, don't you?"

At the sudden turn of conversation, Berbik pulled at his tattered jerkin, adjusting it, but said nothing.

"Berbik's business is his own." Lord Averaen glanced down at the dwarg. "We made a deal with him. Beyond that, he can tell us or not, of his reasons for being in Kane's dungeon. If he is in league with the sorcerer, I doubt he would have been a captive in such... conditions, as we found him."

Dubrael leaned sideways to look directly at Mikkin, who shifted. "And what were *you* doing in Kane's dungeons, *human*?"

A thin sheen of sweat coated Mikkin's forehead as he stepped forward and bowed. "Hoping to kill as many dragons as possible. The damned beasts slayed my family in Belnesse and I want retribution."

"As many as possible?" Dubrael threw his head back and laughed. "With what, human? Your bare hands?"

Mikkin shrugged. "It was that or nothing. I was more intent on finding them first, before doing much else. Proving that they had indeed come from the mountains. They burned everything. My entire city." Jamie shifted uncomfortably beside him. "I have nothing left," he added.

Let Dubrael see his stupidity for what it was. Better that then consider him a threat. Even if the drengr could do more damage than the dwargs, he wasn't keen for a fight.

"*Humans.*" Dubrael snorted and looked at Lord Averaen. "Are all humans this thick? Been a while since I interacted with any."

Lord Averaen shrugged. "Maybe. Can't say our motives were much better, Lord Dubrael. We went to Shadowkeep too, to see if my theory proved true. I suspected Kane was hiding there. He has indeed been using it as a stronghold. A staging ground. Right under our very noses." He paused, then added, "What we did *not* expect to find, was an empty fortress. The dragons have all gone."

"Well o'course they have." Dubrael waved his arm, like it was old news to him. "They've been sent down to Fort Squall. You been wandering the tunnels long enough to miss that?" Silence fell. Lord Averaen glanced at his companions but said nothing. "Ah. I see you have."

"Tell me." The fort leader's voice was a quiet command.

"Fort Squall has been taken, Master Drengr. Kane flew into battle with his hoard of wild dragons and forced its surrender nearly two weeks ago. Squall's End remains intact, though. I am told a section of it was burned. The fort's occupants have been ejected—sent south according to my informants."

Mikkin's throat went dry. He glanced at Jamie, who appeared just as stricken. If the lad's parents survived the burning of the villages in the north, they would have journeyed to safer ground, perhaps all the way to Squall's End, to be close to the drengr.

"What was the cost of life?" Lord Averaen's posture was rigid.

"Damned if I know." Dubrael brought his spear down again. "We don't get the particulars up here, Master Drengr. Scarcities on the wings of crows. Fort leaders are dead, I hear. Plenty of deaths besides. I don't know the numbers."

Lord Averaen exchanged a hushed whisper with his companions, their faces grim. "This is unexpected news, Master Dwarg. Unexpected and concerning. I am most displeased to hear it. Dragonwall is worse off than I had realized." He paused, his scowl deepening. "With all this, your dwargs wish to remain neutral? What will you do if Kane succeeds? If Kane destroys the monarchy? The kingdom? You really think he will let you hide in your mines? That he won't enslave your people in the same way he enslaves Dragonwall's?"

Dubrael fell quiet. "Dwargs operate independently," he said at last. "We are not ruled by a king. Our decisions are made by councils and votes. If I chose to go to war, it would be a decision that must come from my people as much as me. I could not guarantee any other dwarg lords share Safuil's opinions." He stroked his beard. "However, I struggle to see war as a better option. Why *not* hide out in our halls, hmm? We have no guarantee that Kane will come for us once he has what he wants. Far as I understand it, his fight is with the drengr and King Talon, not the dwargs."

"A cowardly thing to do, and you know it." Lord Averaen's words were loud enough for the hall.

"Oh, aye. Cowardly indeed. You drengr are a solid match for wild dragons and sorcerers. What can we humble mountain folk offer? Ground patrols? Clean up crews? We have no fancy spells to attack our foes with. We have no—"

"You have ice metal." Lord Averean interrupted, growing taller, more frightful. The hall erupted into whispers. "I once served one of the greatest kings in Dragonwall's history, Lord Dubrael. I once called myself a *Drengr Fairtheoir*. I lived through war, hundreds of years ago, when Kalds roved over *your* mountains and attacked the north. You cannot expect me to believe your people have nothing to offer."

The dwargs in the room shifted uncomfortably.

Averaen continued, "You've metal smiths capable of weaving protection into your armor—against dragon fire. You have a lot more than you might think. Your war weapons are more sophisticated than most. Don't think I haven't read the stories from the days of Rage. I've read about the turn of events when all of Dragonwall united against a common enemy. This war will be no different. We need you. We need the sprites. The humans of this world will need *our* protection."

Dubrael slouched in his stone seat, abandoning his composure. He was quiet for a long time. "Fine. I will discuss it with my council," he said at last. "Until then, my men will find you rooms. We will convene in three days. You will have our decision then." He nodded, motioning his escorts forward. "Fikhaul and Groozon will see to your needs. Until then, I advise you not to wander. There are things in my mines unfit for outsiders. Fik and Gro will ensure that you do not stray. Do not make me regret my hospitality."

They were dismissed, but Mikkin did not sigh until they were free of the hall.

"Well, that went better than expected," Jamie mused, grinning.

Yes, it had gone better than he'd imagined. Yet, Mikkin's mind was whirling with intrigue. When the dragons had burned Belnesse, he'd never imagined it as the dawn of a great war. A war that had started with him, in his home. Yet, Lord Averaen compared this to the days of Rage. Circumstances across the kingdom were changing, and quickly. Mikkin was caught up somewhere in the middle, hardly a bystander as most humans were. Others might not have much reason to fight, but he did, and fight he would.

CHAPTER 44

IRELIA ISLAND

Kastali Dun

Claire walked through the streets of Kastali Dun, arm in arm with Dallin, the drengr Verath had asked her to speak with. Her entourage trailed behind, far enough to give them privacy. Verath was there too, leading Desaree, while Bedelth led Jocelyn and Saffra, one on each arm. Lucky him! The king had also sent six of his castle guards. They made quite the party, attracting attention.

She and Dallin were close in age. He was tall, but lacked the layers of muscle seen in a fully mature drengr. His cheekbones were strong, his chin pointed. His pale northerner skin was a direct opposite to those from Austar, like Bedelth. She liked his clear blue eyes the most. They were nervous but determined, darting about, taking in the city with flecks of gold that glittered. He kept his auburn hair at medium length, swept to the side and cropped cleanly at his neck.

They made their way to the city's docks where they would tour the market. Everyone who passed stopped to pay respects. Dallin glanced down at her. She caught his gaze and his cheeks colored.

453

"Forgive me, my lady, I'm not used to escorting someone...so important."

"You flatter me. If it helps, I'm still not used to this kind of attention. And please, Claire is fine."

He nodded. "Where I come from, no one ever offers me a second glance. I've yet to make a name for myself."

"Is that why you're eager to become a shield?"

"The title holds allure, yes." He hesitated, then his eyes widened. "That's why we're out here, isn't it? To discuss my desire to become a shield. I was surprised by your invitation, but now I understand."

She grinned up at him, caught in the act. Casually, she said, "Oh, you know, I wanted to see who was trying to replace Lord Cyrus."

Dallin's throat bobbed. He rubbed the back of his neck. "I...I wish it wasn't necessary—replacing him, but there was an opening."

"The king should always have six," she agreed. "You should know, Dallin, that Cyrus is not really dead."

Dallin faltered. "But his body was—"

"Killed by poison and burned. Yes. I know. But his soul? His soul lives on, within me. They call it a gift, and in some ways, it is. This isn't common knowledge." She pinned him with her gaze. "I trust you won't repeat it?"

"I won't say a word. But...how? I don't understand."

"The *how* is unimportant. What's important is that Cyrus is still alive in spirit. In here." She tapped her temple. "He sees what I see. Knows what I know. He will know if you are worthy to take his place."

Dallin gazed straight ahead, jaw clenched. "That...that makes sense. It's only fair. I do not wish to fill a position I am unworthy of."

Go easy on him, Cyrus told her, right on cue. *I was like him once. Eager to prove myself. His heart is pure.*

Talon's safety is important, she told him. *Besides, you had a mate. He's giving that up.*

They reached the market and the noise tripled. The crowd parted when they spotted her, her entourage trailing behind. To Dallin, she said, "I saw you on the practice grounds this morning, sparring with Lord Verath. You did well." Her words brought a blush to his freckled cheeks. "As a shield, there may come a day when you are all that stands between King Talon and his death."

"I train for hours a day—"

"Yes, but, it takes more than a good sword arm to fill the king's ranks." She thought of Talon's shields, especially Cyrus. There wasn't a drengr alive who could match him or replace him. Yet, it was unfair to expect it. "That being said, Cyrus believes you have a good heart."

"He...he said that? Right now?"

She patted his arm. "He did. But don't let it go to your head." Dallin let out a nervous laugh. She led him to a booth selling seafood and veggie skewers. "Now, I'm famished. How about we get something to eat?"

The others kept their distance, happy to browse the market from afar. She dragged Dallin to various tents, chatting with him about Fort Edge. He was a walking encyclopedia of information.

The sun was warm and soothing. It cut through the chilly sea breeze, making for a fine afternoon. Winter would arrive in a few weeks. Though it didn't snow in Kastali Dun—thank the gods—it would get quite cold. Roaring fires and heavy cloaks would become the norm.

When they'd had their fill of the market, they turned back to the keep, making their way through the city. The streets were quieter here, more ideal for hushed conversations. Like the one she needed to have. Verath wouldn't be happy if she failed to address what he had requested of her.

"You know, Dallin, I feel obligated to point something out. I'm concerned about your eagerness to become a shield." He gave her his full attention. "A *Drengr Fairtheoir* takes no mate. You understand this? Most people search a lifetime for their happily-ever-after." Her mind went to Talon, to their discovery of the bond, to the joy of knowing there was someone the fates had intended for her.

Dallin's jaw flexed. "I understand the...sacrifice. I'll take my chances." He spoke as if finding a mate meant little to him. At her searching gaze, he added, "I'm used to that look."

"What look?" She schooled her features.

"The one you just gave me." A strangled laugh burst from his chest. "It's the same look *everyone* gives me. Like I'm senseless for not wanting a mate."

She sighed. "You know, I didn't fully understand the mate thing when I first learned about it from Cyrus. It all seemed like a big fuss. My world doesn't have anything like it. We love who we love, regardless of the consequences. Some people get married and divorced because it isn't a good match. Others find someone to spend an entire life with. Some don't bother with a marriage, considering it an outdated ritual. But *here* there are mates, and everyone takes it *very* seriously."

He grunted. "You could say that again."

She glanced over her shoulder. "When Lord Verath was young, he joined King Tallek's ranks. Did you know?"

"Yes, he served with Lord Averaen." He barked a laugh. "Want to know what's funny? My father somehow found a mate after retiring from King Tallek's ranks. They said it was impossible. More impossible than someone like King Talon, given his age. He was already old. But fate still had plans for him—for me. I wouldn't be here otherwise, walking this earth. They said my birth was a miracle because of it, because of my mother, Evelyn."

"Miracle indeed! But let's not stray from Verath. Did you also know that after his oath, after he swore it a second time for King Talon, he also discovered his mate? He wasn't as fortunate as your father. He was still a shield." Dallin stopped in the middle of the street. She gave him a moment to process the information before tugging on his arm, spurring him on. "Lord Verath *felt* her, and one day, he decided to find her."

Dallin opened his mouth, only to close it. It was the effect she'd hoped for. She went on, explaining what had happened. She told him about Kendra, and the heart-wrenching decision he'd made. A decision he was forced to live with.

Dallin frowned. "Why are you telling me this?"

"Isn't it obvious? If you are eager to abandon the mate bond, you need to understand the cost."

"You're right. But I *do* understand, perhaps better than most." His face turned a dark shade of red. "The mate bond isn't something I want."

A couple of gentlemen passed on horseback and Dallin's eyes darted towards them before flicking away. They'd reached the Merchant District. The roads were cobbled instead of mud.

"You say it's not something you want. Sounds like your youth talking. How can you be certain?"

He was quiet for a long time. When he did speak, his voice was low. "There is no evidence that mate bonds exist between males."

It took a moment. Then his words hit her square in the chest. She blinked. "Dallin—"

"Wait, please!" He held up a hand, silencing her. "Before you pass judgment, know this isn't something I would share with just anyone. I tell you because I hope you of all people might understand. You come from a different society."

She exhaled, finally understanding. "It's true. My society is more accepting than Dragonwall's, but it's still imperfect. Dallin, I... I'm sorry. I didn't realize." Everything clicked into place. "Thank you for sharing this with me. I think I understand now."

He blinked. "You do?"

They had stopped walking and stood gazing at each other. "I do. I get it." She reached up and cupped his cheek, offering him a warm smile. "You aren't interested in women. Becoming a shield is a way to protect yourself from the judgment of others." He sighed and his shoulders relaxed. She lowered her hand. "Can there really be no bonds between males?"

He shrugged. "None that I know of. I'm not exactly going to ask around about it." She nodded, pulling on his arm to continue their walk.

Verath had been so concerned that Dallin was making a rash

decision, when in fact, he had given this a lot of thought. A knot loosened in her chest. "You've made me realize something."

"What's that?" His gaze was hungry.

"When I first came here, I struggled with Dragonwall's belief system. The people here have a different way of thinking. More old fashioned. It's a deeply flawed society. My world was like that once, and in many ways it still is. Although, we don't have dragons and goblins and sprites." She chewed on the inside of her cheek. "I've been so busy worrying about Kane, that I've overlooked so many other issues. I will speak to the king on your behalf. And I can keep your secret, if you wish, but I believe King Talon will be understanding and accepting, as will his shields." Her lips spread into a slow grin. "If they aren't, you can bet that I'll have something to say about it."

"You would do that for me?" He looked at her in wonder as his entire demeanor transformed.

"Yes, I would. Assuming you're okay with King Talon knowing?"

He hesitated before nodding. "If I am to serve him, he should know me."

"Wise. Very wise. But also, true."

I approve of him.

She faltered at Cyrus's words. *You do? Without really knowing him? What makes you so certain?*

Cyrus was quiet for a time. *Dallin has revealed his greatest secret. It takes courage to be different, and bravery to face uncertainty. In telling you, he displays trust, a quality that will serve him well. Talon's shields are your protectors now too. In this, I believe you have earned Dallin's loyalty.*

Warmth blossomed in her chest.

They reached the keep's portcullis. She bid Dallin farewell and returned to her chambers. "Shall we prepare for the evening meal?" Desaree pulled her from her thoughts.

"Oh, yes, let's."

～

SHE FOUND herself in another beautiful gown, a creation Desaree surprised her with, as they made their way to the dining hall. Desaree had not yet made up with Verath, even though they'd spent the afternoon together, and when pressed for information, evaded her questions.

Saffra and Jocelyn joined them at the table, as did Dallin, when she spotted him across the hall. "You're sure it's okay?" he asked after she patted the bench beside her.

"Absolutely okay!" Saffra answered, graciously making room to allow him.

Dallin gave them a grin before tucking into his food. When she caught sight of Talon, he arched a curious eyebrow in her direction. She shrugged, offering him a small smile in return. He sat nursing a goblet of wine, leisurely studying his courtiers. His face was impassive, which meant something was probably on his mind.

He collected her after the meal, surprising her with the offer to go flying. Her heart raced as soon as he mentioned it. "I thought perhaps you'd forgotten about your promise."

"Forgotten?" He clicked his tongue. "I haven't been able to keep it from my mind. Come." He took her hand and they strode to his tower, to the queen's garden, where he had the most space to transform.

Night unfolded around her, mixed with the briny sea breeze, flooding her senses as she climbed upon his back. The moment her hands made contact with his scales, her mind swelled, melding with his. His excitement engulfed her. A laugh tumbled from her lips.

It was glorious!

He crouched low and vaulted into the air. She squealed with surprised delight. The castle shrank into a series of glittering lights below as the stars greeted them like old friends, nestled in the sky, sharing the heavens with the full moon. The glow lit up the sea, bathing the world in soft brilliance.

A grin fixed permanently to her face.

"Perfect night for flying, don't you think?" There was something mischievous in his tone. For so long, he had seemed nothing more

than a brooding king. Every passing day revealed more of him, deepening her understanding. *"What would you say to a small adventure?"*

"Take me anywhere!" she begged, her heart overflowing.

"How would you like to see Irelia Island? It's best under a full moon." Her breath caught. *"I'll take that as a yes."*

It was absolutely a yes.

The wind was with them, taking little more than an hour to reach the island's closest shore. As they flew, she told him about her afternoon with Dallin. He wasn't surprised that Verath had enlisted her help.

"Now I know why you were so friendly at dinner."

"Yes." She smiled at the sky. *"His honesty impressed me, and Cyrus approves, too. You'll consider him, won't you?"*

"Cyrus approves?" He let his surprise be known. His thoughts turned over, like bubbles of lava oozing up from the lava pools within his mind. Formations writhed and shifted, rearranging. The inside of his head was a moving landscape. She observed the inner workings of his reasoning...and waited.

"Dallin's preferences will not affect my decision," he said at last. *"Not in any way. But admitting him into my ranks must be based on his merit and potential. I admire his truthfulness. Verath says he's a skilled fighter."* A hesitation, then, *"I will take some time to get to know him. Give him a few challenges. Tests, if you will. Then we will decide."*

"Is that how you usually decide?"

Talon's laugh was a draconic rumble, vibrating up through her thighs. *"Hardly. I've never had someone so young. Jovari, Koldis, Bedelth—they were all over a hundred when they joined me. Reyr and Cyrus were easy; they had already had and lost mates and proven themselves in battle. And you already know about Verath."* Talon hummed. *"Dallin's age concerns me. He's not fully mature. But that also means he's a moldable lump of clay. We can shape him as needed."*

She smiled. *"That sounds fair to me."*

The sea breeze was cold against her cheeks. Beneath them, the mouth of the bay slid by. A dark, rolling seascape. Soon a shadow loomed up before them. Irelia Island. The rays of the moon lit its beaches, making the water lapping at its shores glow.

"The island is uninhabited," Talon explained. *"Settling anywhere here was forbidden by Queen Isabella. The law remains intact. You'll soon understand why."*

"It's like a painting." She drank it in.

Talon sailed over the beach and toward the lush rainforest beyond.

"I often come here when I need time to think." He brought them down into a clearing not far from the sand. He transformed, offering her a crooked grin. "Welcome to Irelia Island."

She turned and her eyes adjusted to the darkness. "Gods above!" The whisper slipped from her lips.

They stood in the ruins of what must have been an ancient civilization. Large pillars, chunks of stone, lay broken and scattered about. Some were the size of Talon in his dragon form.

She stepped forward, getting a better look. The ground beneath her feet crunched. She flinched and looked down. Thousands upon thousands of glittering fragments in every color spread out beneath her. In the light of the full moon, the fragments sparkled like pixy dust. Some of it as fine as sand.

She plucked up a fragment the color of topaz and stared at it, confused. "Egg shells?" She glanced over at Talon.

He stood motionless, watching her, then nodded. "Dragon eggs."

"Oh my god!" Her eyes roved over the clearing. "You...you're serious?"

He picked up a fragment too, and walked over to present it. A red shell the color of blood, like Verath's scales. She studied both pieces in her hand.

"This was once a hatching ground occupied by the Sea Clan. Queen Isabella knew that if she allowed people to live here, all of this would be destroyed. It's the only lasting dragon ruin that I know of."

"Wow." She took another step and her feet crunched. She flinched.

Talon laughed. "It's fine. It stretches on and on, well into the trees. Don't worry about the shells. They will endure." He hesitated. "Notice the heat?"

She took a moment. "You're right! It's warm under my feet. Unusually warm."

"The island's natural ability to keep the eggs warm made it ideal. Shall we have a look around?"

"Yes, I'd love that!" Her words were breathless. Talon held out his hand and she took it, but not before trading the two fragments of eggshell for a slightly larger purple one. Her favorite color. "Can I keep it?"

"Of course. Take it with you. People come here plenty. Most are respectful. They believe stealing outright will bring the wrath of the dragon spirits upon them. Or something like that."

The hatching ground continued well into the cover of the trees, as Talon had said. He showed her all the places where the dragons had made their nests. These were areas that had once been large craters, now taken over by the jungle. "It was a perfect location for them," he explained. "A few hours to reach the heart of the mainland for good hunting, or they could catch fish and other sea creatures. We dragons are good swimmers, you know. In fact..." He squeezed her hand. She glanced at him, taking in the wicked gleam in his eyes. He led her through the trees. They found themselves on the beach with sand as fine as sugar. "I think I fancy a swim."

"But...but it's cold out!" She glanced between him and the waves lapping at the shore.

"Yes, but the water around the island isn't." Before she could stop him, he jumped from the ground and transformed, bringing his wings down to carry him out over the water.

She screeched, shielding her face with her hands as sand blew up around her, coating her skin and hair, finding its way into her eyes and mouth. *"You did that on purpose!"* she shouted with her mind, before realizing she'd opened it and removed the barrier Cyrus had put in place.

"Who knew all it'd take is a bit of sand," he teased, smug. She was covered in it, her beautiful gown now gritty. Desaree would have

an absolute fit. "*Guess I'm not the only one who needs a bath. Come. Join me.*" He hovered above the water then dove nose-first into the waves. There was a surge as he disappeared beneath the surface. She watched, waiting, before his large body popped back up. "*Mmm...good eating. Lovely fish.*" He tossed one in the air and opened his maw, swallowing it whole.

"*You're barbaric, you know that you big lizard? Absolutely barbaric.*"

His deep grumble reached the shore.

It wasn't easy getting out of her gown. She watched Talon while she worked, his manner carefree. He spit up fountains of water and dove beneath the waves to pop up in different places. It was impossible not to grin.

She shivered as she raced to the water, sighing the moment her feet were beneath the surf, and plunged into the warm waves. Her hair broke free of its chignon and soon fanned out about her. It was marvelous. Giggling, she half waded half swam out to Talon's dragon form until her feet no longer touched the sandy bottom. He lifted his wings and engulfed her with a torrent of seawater.

"What was that for?!" she screeched, sputtering, splashing him back, a pathetic attempt he hardly noticed.

"*For the lizard remark. Lizards don't have wings.*"

She snorted, dunking beneath the water to come up beside him. Her hands latched onto him.

The moon offered plenty of soft light as they swam about each other, splashing and diving. Talon could see perfectly beneath the surface as he snatched up fish after fish. When he wasn't frolicking, he floated like a buoy. She took the opportunity to climb atop his back and dive in, shrieking and laughing as he surged upward to give her jump air. The saltwater was a balm to her skin, leaving her more rejuvenated than any bath ever could have.

Exhausted, gasping for air, she made her way back to the shallows where she touched the sandy floor. Moments later, Talon's arms surprised her, wrapping around her from behind, pulling her flush to him. His large hands splayed across her bare stomach, covering her, making her toes curl into the sand.

She felt every bit of bare skin between them, every ridge of his hard muscles, even his arousal. A gasp escaped her lips. "Hello," he whispered against the shell of her ear, sending delighted chills down her spine.

"No more dragon?" A playful grin pulled at the corners of her mouth. She turned to face him.

"Not when I can do this." He brought his lips to hers, softly at first, before caressing her with his tongue. She explored his mouth in turn, eliciting a groan. His length pressed into her stomach, sending a rush of heat straight to her core. She sighed, wrapping her arms around his shoulders to stay afloat.

"That's four," he murmured, abandoning her mouth, moving to her neck, his lips feathering against her skin. She took a handful of his wet hair, squeezing enough to hurt, enough to emphasize what she truly wanted, and how frustrated she was about it.

"This is not easy for me either," he growled. His hands smoothed down her back, latching onto her waist, squeezing. He placed his forehead against hers and closed his eyes.

Easy was the understatement of the year, and it wasn't going to get any easier, either. Fate would see them separated before putting them back together again. She didn't want to leave him, but the call of the forest, her promise to Cyrus, was growing stronger with each passing day. She couldn't fight it. Not anymore.

The current pushed them closer to shore as waves gently rolled past them. Talon's shoulders and chest were soon exposed. She noticed the scars on his skin, her eyes trapped by the sight of them. Her breathing hitched. She trailed her fingers across one, feeling the puckered texture of it.

He froze beneath her touch, his wide silver eyes trained on her movements.

They looked like burns, horrific, painful burns. "Why are these different from the ones on your face?" The question was out before she could stop it. His expression shuttered. "I...I'm sorry, Talon. It's not something you have to talk about. I shouldn't have asked."

He placed his hand over hers, pressing it firmly against his chest. She felt the rapid beat of his heart. "This was where it grabbed me," he whispered. He took her fingers and traced them across sections of his skin. She delighted in his touch, in his guidance. "I fought it for hours. I was so angry, so...wrecked. The leader killed my parents and I went into a rage. I saw red and something inside of me *broke*. When I laid claim to my kill, I didn't allow anyone to help." He shook his head. "But no one can fight forever. I got sloppy and it caught me off guard, snatching me from the sky. See here?" He trailed her fingers lower and her breath caught. "This is where it wrapped its hand around me. It's why my scales looked chipped and melted around my chest and stomach. My...my beautiful scales. Destroyed." His voice came out choked.

Anger sent blood pounding in her ears. She wanted to destroy the monster that had hurt him, even hundreds of years after he'd already done exactly that. She wanted to protect him.

A picture invaded her mind, sending fear straight to her heart. She was trapped by a giant made of ice. A Kald. She felt it squeeze her, crush her. Felt the agony as her scales melted. She almost screamed from the pain. Instead, a gasp fell from her lips. She struggled to breathe. An instant later, the projection was gone.

She sucked in a deep, desperate breath and blinked. Around her, the world was back. The gentle shore and warm water. She sighed, all but clinging to him. It was only a memory from his mind to hers, but the terror was still there—fresh as if it were yesterday.

"And...the scars on your face?" She reached up and cupped his cheek. He leaned into her.

"They're different because it scratched me rather than clutched me. It swatted at me like I was no more than a pesky fly." He shuddered against her. "It was agony. My face exploded when it happened. Each scratch ripped me open all at once."

He moved her hand back to his chest, using it to caress each scar across his shoulders and pecs. The gesture curled something deep inside her. She wanted to kiss each scar, run her lips across his body. Taste the salt on his skin. Lick each droplet of water away.

Gods!

"These are by far the worst though," he added. "When it had me in its grip, with its hand wrapped around my body, melting and burning my scales. To it, I was a mere plaything. I...I blacked out before it even dropped me. That...that is why I am like this. Why I am ugly."

Her chest deflated. "That's enough, Talon. No more. Please." She pulled his face to hers and kissed him to quiet him, hoping her lips might brush away the memory. "And for the record," she whispered against him, looking him in the eyes, "I don't think you're ugly. You're the most beautiful thing in the world. When you're in your dragon form, you steal my breath away."

A huff escaped his lips, but he said nothing as he lifted her, holding her flush against him, claiming her mouth. This time their kiss was painfully desperate.

She responded in kind. Her legs wrapped around his waist, anchoring them. She gasped when she felt the length of him against her center. It was torture. To have him and not have him.

Ignoring her body's desperation, she pulled her mouth away and kissed him on the forehead. Her arms wrapped around his shoulders, pinning him against her chest. She laid her cheek against his nose and sighed, well aware she was traversing very dangerous territory. Thank the gods he had better self control than she did. If she didn't detangle herself soon, the agony of not having him would rip her apart.

At last, they made their way back to the shore. A comfortable silence fell between them. He helped her get dressed, first in her chemise and then her gown. She didn't miss his hungry gaze as it devoured every bit of her nudity beforehand. So different from the last time he'd seen her naked. His fingers even brushed her marks, sending shivers across her skin, before her gown found its place upon her body.

He didn't bother with clothes since he would be transforming to take them home.

While it was impossible to rid herself of all the sand, she tried. Talon helped with the ties of her bodice. Her heart thumped with each of his deliberate movements. Temptation drove her to glance over her shoulder. His face was set, lips forming a tight line as he focused on the task.

Seeing him like this did something to her heart. Something painful and desperate. Perhaps she loved him, after all.

"Talon..." Her voice was a hoarse whisper.

"Hmm?" His reply was lazy.

"There's something...something I need to tell you. Something I should have told you weeks ago." His brows pinched together. "I didn't tell you when it happened because we were...we weren't close. Everything was different."

"Another secret?" He finished with the last of the ties and took her waist, turning her to face him.

"This is the last one, I think." Her mouth was dry. Unusually dry. Like sandpaper. She swallowed, trying to find her voice. "There's a reason I'm so determined to train with the sprites."

"Because you are of their blood?" He lifted an eyebrow.

"It's more than that. I made a promise—an unbreakable promise."

The moonlight limned his scarred skin, accentuating his brows as they pulled together. "I don't understand. Like the one you made to Cyrus when he was dying?"

"Yes, exactly. It was careless. I know that now. Cyrus and I were talking—the day of the execution. He said these things and I got caught up in the heat of the moment. I know I shouldn't have been so rash, but..."

"Tell me," he demanded in a king's voice. "Tell me exactly."

"Okay, but, you're not going to like it." She explained exactly what she'd done. Words tumbled from her mouth, desperate to break free, to get this moment over with. This time, she left absolutely nothing out. She wasn't simply playing an important role in the war, she was the one who had to defeat Kane, otherwise the promise would go unfulfilled.

His eyes darted over her face, searching. Perhaps he hoped she'd gotten this all wrong. That what she said wasn't true.

"Say something," she urged. "Please."

"You...you kept this from me? Something this dangerous?" His chest rose and fell with heavy breaths. He glanced about the beach and ran a hand through his hair. "Why would you do this? This is Kane we're talking about, Claire. *Kane*!"

"I...it was an accident," she managed.

His expression crumbled. Emotions passed over his features. Hurt. Disbelief. Confusion. "Maybe it's a misunderstanding. Maybe the magic didn't take. Maybe..."

"It...it worked, Talon. I felt it. There's no getting out of it. The promise is real." She waited, watching him, holding her breath, expecting his beast of a dragon to break free in anger, but it didn't.

He sank to his knees in the sand, still naked, hunched over, and put his forehead in his hands. "Gods, Claire! How could you do this?"

"I..." Emotion slammed against her insides, making it hard to breathe. Part of her felt ashamed, the other part a touch defensive. She steadied her breathing. "I am the best hope Dragonwall has, Talon. Cyrus made that clear. That is why he gave me his soul. With my blood, with his soul, we can defeat Kane." She scrubbed a hand over her face. "Talon, I..."

He didn't look up.

This was bad. Really bad. She would have much preferred his anger to this shut-down version of him. To his open display of vulnerability and hurt.

"There are things about me that I need to figure out, and I think Cyrus knows what they are. He knows something about me that even we don't know. Maybe he knew about my ties to Queen Isabella." She got down on her knees beside him and ran her fingers through his wet hair, trying to get him to look at her. He snatched her hand in his, blocking her caress, and lifted his eyes. His face was unreadable. "Say something, Talon, please."

"I'm not happy about this."

She blew out a breath. "Yeah. That's obvious."

"You are my mate and you...you kept this from me."

She opened and closed her mouth, unable to speak, to move, hand snared within his.

"I do all I can to protect you, Claire, to keep you safe. This need is ingrained within me. It goes beyond what is natural in humans.

It runs deep. It is unforgiving. You remember what happened to your kidnappers?" She nodded, eyes wide. "But this? I don't know if I can protect you from this. Not if you have made a promise. And that terrifies me, Claire. *Terrifies me.*" His expression crumbled. "Gods!" He squeezed her hand so hard it hurt. "Didn't you realize you had already done enough for this kingdom? I'm Dragonwall's king! It should be me. I am supposed to be the one—"

"But Cyrus said—"

"I know what Cyrus said," he all but roared. "You've made that very clear. I have always trusted his judgment. But in this..." He shook his head. "I am struggling here." He released her hand and ran both of his through his hair, then folded in on himself. His form was still a hulking mass, dwarfing hers as she crouched beside him. She was desperate for some form of reprieve. Some form of approval for what she'd done. "There's a good reason why Queen Isabella's descendant has returned to Dragonwall—a good reason why I am here. Cyrus fell into *my* cornfield. I understand that now. What Saffra said last night—"

"Yes, I caught what she said. Believe me." His words came out muffled.

"Then why are you still mad at me?" She hated this. Months ago, she wouldn't have cared if he hated her. She would have welcomed his anger, his scorn, his judgment. "Are you mad because I didn't tell you?"

"Is that what you think?" His glittering eyes met hers. "Really? No. I'm angry because my mate must bear the largest burden of anyone in my kingdom. I'm angry because you're not prepared to do this. I'm angry because I might lose you after—" He let out a strangled laugh. "After having just found you. What am I supposed to do? Rejoice?"

It was like a punch to the gut. She blinked, trying to comprehend what he'd just said.

"I'm sorry." She put her hand on his bicep, barely covering half. His corded muscle tensed at her touch. He glanced down at the contact and then their eyes met. "Talon, I might not be ready yet, but you can help me. You can prepare me. Support me. Get me ready. I can't do this alone. Not without you. I need you. *Please...I need you by my side.*" Tears of frustration blurred her vision. Cyrus knew what he was doing when she'd made this promise, right?

I did. Trust me, it is meant to be you.

"Cyrus says that we have to trust him."

"Of course he does..." he muttered. Without warning, Talon pulled her into his lap, wrapping his body around her in a safe cocoon. "I don't want to lose you. Not when I've only just found you."

Hot tears broke free, a mixture of guilt and exhaustion and fear. "You don't think I can do this? That it will kill me?"

If that was the case, she couldn't blame him for his doubt. Hell, she doubted herself, too. She could barely manage mage magic, and even that was exhausting. Just because she could sing a song and conjure green fire, or work a bit of healing magic, didn't mean she was ready for any of this.

"Claire..." His voice came out calmer this time. "Your capabilities have always impressed me. I know you can do this. I'll make sure that you do. I refuse to allow this *promise*—careless as it was—to claim you. Especially after everything. It's just..." A growl came from deep in his chest. "I hate that you have no choice. That you *must* do this. That I cannot do it for you. I...I don't want this for you. I never wanted anything like this for you." He cradled her against him, pinning her head under his chin. His bare skin was warm and soothing.

They sat like that for what felt like ages, until he said, "Tell me what you need."

"I need to train with the sprites."

"Done."

That single word untangled something in her chest, a knot so tight and smothering she sagged with relief.

"But..."

"But what?" She choked on the word.

"Promise that you will come back to me? That I won't lose you to them. To the forest."

"You will never lose me, Talon. I will come back. I will *always* come back." Even though he might not have known her answer, she had already chosen him.

Silence stretched out between them before she spoke again. "You wanted me to think about becoming your mate, your queen. To think about what it meant. My time away in the forest will allow for that. When I return, it will be to give you my answer."

She felt him nod against her. "That's fair." He tilted her chin up to meet her lips. She felt his fear in the way he kissed her. His lips were tentative at first, but their kiss soon transformed into something that held promise, until she was clawing at his hair, trying to climb deeper into his arms.

"That's...five? Six? I've lost count," he said, when he finally pulled away.

She smiled, brushing her nose against his. A relieved laugh escaped her chest.

Their flight back to the keep was quiet. With their minds entwined, they didn't speak for a long while. Instead, she let him brood, watching the formations of his mental landscape move and transform. She too, brooded, trying to think of a way to fix things between them. With the secret of her promise revealed, there was only one thing left she could give him. She had held back from him for weeks, for fear of revealing this obligation. But it was done.

Relaxing, she pulled down the barriers she'd kept up to keep him out. She let him inside. The gesture surprised him at first. The steps he took were tentative, exploratory. He moved with caution into the confines of her thoughts. She picked out some of her favorite memories, scenes from her childhood growing up on the farm, and shared them. She took him through some of her scariest moments, too. There were tears flowing down her cheeks when she shared the memories of Cyrus with him. Of how she found him, saved him, and lost him, all in the span of a week.

She wasn't sure if dragons could cry, but his chest heaved at seeing his brother in her arms. It broke something in him all over again. *"Thank you for sharing that,"* he said at last, his voice a weak whisper. *"I needed to see it, to see the relationship you built. I wish... It kills me that I wasn't there with him. I wish I could have been with him.*

But you were. You were there. You gave him what he needed, and for that I...I..." He didn't need to finish. She knew exactly what his gratitude felt like without words. Everything between them was twined together now.

There would be no more secrets. No more hiding. Enemy, king, rescuer, friend. He had been many things to her. Now he was the other half of her beating heart, the other half of her mind, of her soul. He was her mate. And one day, he would be her lover. From this point forward, they were in this together. He would never be alone again.

CHAPTER 45

A HUNT

Kastali Dun

Talon found his mate in her chambers. She jumped from the sofa at the sight of him. "Talon!" He liked catching her unawares, the sight of her flushed skin and the way she turned breathless. Knowing he made her feel these things—pleasure over seeing *him*.

"How were your lessons?"

"Good!" she breathed.

Desaree awkwardly cleared her throat. "I'll...just go for a walk then." She darted out the door before he could stop her. Claire's eyes followed her before settling on him.

He covered the distance between them, pulling her against him. Her curves molded perfectly to his, sending a wave of fire through his veins. "Happy to see me?"

"Yes."

"Excellent." He kissed her but did not linger. There was too much on his mind, too much to attend to. He brushed his lips against her forehead, then said, "I came to tell you that I've written to Queen Jade of your impending visit."

"Oh?"

"You leave tomorrow, if that suits you." The words came out thicker than intended. It hurt, the thought of her going away.

"Tomorrow?" she croaked, pulling back with surprise. "So soon?"

"Yes. I can postpone, if you wish?" Part of him silently begged her to say yes. He wanted more than anything to keep her here as long as possible, but the safety he offered was fleeting. He did not want to bring her with them to reconquer Fort Squall. She would insist on going. The more he considered it, the more he realized Claire would be safer in the forest, away from all that. Surely Kane would not touch her there, under Queen Jade's protection.

She closed her eyes. "No, we cannot postpone any longer. We are running out of time. I will need every moment I can get while I'm there."

"I thought as much."

"Do your shields know yet? That I'm leaving?"

"No. We will tell them tonight. The time for secrets is over." He hesitated. "We will tell them what is between us...and of your promise." She sucked in a surprised breath. "It's the only way to justify our decision to send you away. Otherwise, they might not agree."

"You're right. It's for the best. But...Desaree, Jocelyn, and Saffra should be there, too. They deserve to know."

"That's fair. Consider it done."

She blew out a breath.

"What is it?" he asked, studying her expression.

"I promised Tamara I'd show her around when she arrived, and then there's Desaree's trial. I had hoped to be here for it."

"There will be no trial."

"What? But—"

"Caterina has disappeared." With everything bogging him down, he'd forgotten to mention that bit before.

"She—*what*?" Her eyes widened. "*That's* why she hasn't been in lessons?!"

"She missed lessons?"

"Well, yes. After the ball I didn't see her. You were off in Fairfay, but I thought she was avoiding lessons to...well...to avoid me. After she learned what was going to happen to her, she probably hates me even more."

"Hmm." He released her and led her to the sofa. She took a seat beside him, facing him with her legs tucked beneath her. He made himself comfortable, stretching an arm over the back, his fingers close enough to brush her shoulder, which he did, because he couldn't stop touching her. "No one knows when she disappeared. Perhaps it was earlier than I realized."

He wondered if Mage Targa had known of her absence for longer than he'd let on. He made a mental note to look into it.

"When did you find out?" Claire asked.

"Yesterday. I've had my guards combing the city. I suppose she's long gone if what you say is true." He fell quiet before adding, "In her absence, she forfeits her right to a trial. Her absence is an admission of guilt. Her title will pass to Desaree by default."

Claire's throat bobbed. "It's for the best. I don't think Desaree would feel right being responsible for her death—that's how she would see it."

"Yes. But Caterina has mage magic. She could be dangerous enough to cause us problems."

"She's not *that* powerful, is she?" Claire huffed. "No. She'll fade into oblivion and no one will remember her name."

He hoped so, but didn't bother saying as much.

"Can I tell Desaree?" Her face brightened with hope. "She will be relieved, I think, to avoid the throne room."

"No." He shook his head. "I will tell her. It is I who must confer the title, after all. I'll make the announcement tonight at our gathering. She'll like that, I think?"

Claire nodded.

They fell quiet. He watched the flames in the grate but he felt his mate's gaze on his skin, roving over him. Her gaze always gave him mixed feelings. Part of him loved her attention, craved it, was selfish for it. The other part of him was anxious. He hated scrutiny of any kind, from anyone, but especially from her. Like she was reading his every thought.

He considered her words from the night before, when he'd held her and talked of his painful memories better left buried—her claims of his beauty. Did she truly mean it? That she believed he was beautiful? Why couldn't she see what he did? A beast? A monster?

"I suppose I should begin packing this evening." She sounded reluctant.

He turned to her. "I thought you were eager to train with them?"

"Oh, I am. I just... Now it's all so real. Talon..." She hesitated. "It's going to be difficult—leaving you. Our bond. The last time you went into the forest, I struggled to eat. Desaree thought I was starving myself. It didn't make sense. I understand it now. The distance—the tug." She swallowed, placing a hand over her heart. "It was hard to bear."

"I felt it too," he mused. No wonder he'd been moody and morose. A strangled laugh escaped his chest. "My drengr were frustrated with me on our journey." He lifted his arm from the couch and stroked her jaw. She caught his hand and held it against her cheek. The gentleness in her expression, the way she leaned into his touch, sent tremors through him.

"Am I doing the right thing?" he asked before stopping himself. "Letting you go like this?" He almost hoped she might say no.

She opened her eyes, pinning him in place. "Yes." The word was little more than a whisper.

He leaned over and gave her a brief kiss. "I've got several matters to address before the evening meal. You'd best get to packing. At tonight's meeting, we will tell the others."

She followed him to the door, holding his hand like she didn't want to release him. He loved that more than he cared to admit. "Oh, and one more thing." A grin tugged at his lips as he braced himself for her reaction. "Reyr should be home in an hour or two."

Her eyes widened and she shrieked, swatting him in the chest. "You waited until *now* to tell me?! Gods, Talon!"

He shrugged, feigning nonchalance. "Figured I'd leave on a positive note."

A look passed over her features, but it was gone before he could make it out. "I'll get to see him before...before I go."

"I thought you'd like that." He wrapped his hand around her neck and pulled her against his body, kissing her forehead, allowing his lips to linger over her skin. "See you later."

Shutting the door behind him felt like erecting a barrier between them—one he wanted to immediately break down. He exhaled and walked down the hall.

AN HOUR LATER, he was in his study hunched over his desk, hand cramped from signing his name to so many documents. He stretched his tight muscles and reached out to Dallin, commanding him to meet him in the lowest courtyard of the keep.

"I'll be there at once, Your Majesty." Dallin's response was immediate.

He left his tower, striding through the keep, nodding to the patrons he passed. They all paused to bow and stare at the ground. His pace was too brisk to linger over their behavior.

Reyr's voice was a sudden intrusion, making him falter. *"Shall I meet you in your tower, my king?"* He smiled because it was louder and closer than it had been in weeks. A knot in his chest loosened.

He passed through the courtyard with the fountain of King Kendrick and Queen Leonne, sending his answer without pause. *"I've got some business first. Glad you're home. Meet me there in two hours?"*

"Very well. I shall await my punishment until your return." Reyr's sarcastic tone was not lost on him.

There would be no backlash for Reyr's actions. Yet, his shield insisted that his unsanctioned leave of absence was dishonorable. Perhaps it was, but hadn't he done something similar when his own parents died? Hadn't he tried to run away? It was Reyr who reminded him that he was Dragonwall's king—that he had a duty to his kingdom.

Reyr had lost nearly everyone he called family, except Byron. How could anyone find fault with his actions? While they might have been unsanctioned, they were necessary. The last thing he wanted was a careless shield, crippled with grief, making rash decisions under his command. No, he was glad Reyr had taken this time for himself, though he doubted the recovery was fulfilled.

"Good afternoon, King Talon." Dallin stepped in front of him and bowed deeply.

He blinked. Gods, Dallin really *was* just a lad, even in his early twenties. He was gangly, with freckled skin and blue eyes.

"So, you're the one I've heard so much about," he said at last, holding out his arm. Dallin took it with obvious eagerness, turning a shade of red beneath his gaze.

"It's a pleasure to meet you, Your Majesty. Up north, you are a legend."

He almost snorted. "A legend? I suppose my fight with the Kalds makes for good storytelling?" Dallin nodded. "Well, I'm not the only one with a reputation. Seems you've been causing a stir amongst my shields. You've made an ally out of Lady Claire—did you know?" He couldn't resist a toothy smile as it spread across his face.

"Oh!" Dallin flushed even harder and his eyes fixed upon the ground.

It was almost too easy, flustering him. "Come now. No need to be anxious in my presence. Lighten up." He clapped Dallin on the back hard enough to make him stagger. Dallin's eyes widened, stunned by the gesture. "Now, there's an excellent hunting grounds about an hour north of here, full of fat, lazy grazers. Do you know it?" He sent Dallin the projection, just in case.

Dallin nodded. "Verath took me there earlier this week."

"Good. Still know how to reach it?"

"I think?"

"You know? Or you think? Better to know. Uncertainty breeds

more uncertainty." He'd need patience with this one. He sent Dallin a more detailed projection, a flash of images that illustrated which flight path to take.

"Got it."

"Good, because you and I are going hunting."

Hunting always eased his mind. There was something satisfying about wrapping his claws around fresh prey and devouring it. Something that made him feel powerful—reminded him of his strength. It was all he could do in light of Claire's upcoming departure. A distraction to keep him from dwelling on the ache her absence would bring.

To Dallin he said, "I hope you fly fast and hunt well. The first one of us with a grazer in his claws wins." And for show, he offered the lad a smirk.

"You...you want to race?" Dallin opened and closed his mouth.

"Absolutely. Tell you what, I'll even give you a head start."

Dallin's throat bobbed. "And if I lose?"

"You want to become a shield, don't you?" he drawled. Dallin swallowed. "Good. Then you'd best not lose." Dallin's eyes widened with understanding. "Well?" he roared, making the lad jump. "What are you waiting for?! You're wasting your precious head start."

"Oh!" Dallin rushed away and jumped into the air, transforming into the form of a stunning violet dragon. It was Claire's favorite color. A color sure to attract every single eye in the castle. His scales blended to indigo on his underside. Purple was an uncommon color, and beautiful in its own right.

He took a moment to study Dallin's form, the development of muscles along his forearms and hind legs, the span of his wings, the style of his tail tip—spiked—and the way he moved. Like he was appraising a prize stallion that might make a good addition to the stables. Interesting...

Dallin brought his wings down in a mighty sweep and shot skyward. "Happy hunting," he murmured, watching him depart. His movements were graceful, at least. But his body was still young, only about two-thirds the size of Talon's.

Dallin disappeared, streaking across the sky.

Anticipation for the hunt flared in Talon's chest, igniting. This would be quite...enjoyable. The dragon inside him growled, clawed, scratched against his skin. He counted to twenty, more than enough time for a fair head start, then leapt from the ground. Letting his iridescent black scales rip free from the confines of his body as he embraced the broken beast within.

CHAPTER 46

REYR'S RETURN

Kastali Dun

Claire had already searched Talon's tower, Reyr's chambers, the royal library, and the practice grounds, looking for Reyr. She traipsed about the keep, her own guards trailing behind her, no doubt annoyed about following her in circles. Talon's tower had been entirely empty, except for his servants. Reyr's chambers had been recently disturbed, with evidence of his arrival. Reyr himself was nowhere to be seen.

Her shoulders slumped.

He hadn't come to her. He hadn't even told her he'd returned—a simple thought that took seconds. Even though he had no problem doing the same with Talon. She'd heard their short conversation upon his return.

She was tempted to reach for him with her mind, but squashed the idea as quickly as it came. He hadn't, so why should she? Besides, she preferred to speak to him in person, preferably before everyone gathered that evening.

A knot formed in her stomach. Was he still upset with her for not choosing him? The thought of him behaving coldly was fright-

481

ening. Maybe he really didn't want to see her. She tutted, annoyed with herself. She shouldn't have gone searching for him.

She rounded the corner to the *Hall of Kings* and stopped. One of her guards walked right into her. A flash of golden hair caught her eye, disappearing into Talon's tower. "Apologies, my lady."

"It's fine, Connor," she said, hardly aware of her words. Her heart hammered against the walls of her chest. He was there—Reyr was there! She took a deep breath, lifting her skirts, and ran.

"Back again?" Aaron, one of the king's tower guards, eyed her with amusement.

"Was that Reyr?" She stared at the door as if she could see through it.

"Aye. What of it?"

Relief mixed with apprehension warmed her skin. "Let me pass. I need to speak with him."

The guards gazed at her a long moment before uncrossing spears and permitting her entry. She stepped through the doorway and paused in the entryway. The door clicked behind her.

Reyr stood in the main room near the fireplace. He was dressed in a fresh change of clothes, a forest green tunic and beige pants, with boots of brown leather that came halfway up his calf. The sight of him—after all this time—pulled the breath from her chest.

He whirled to face her. His eyes widened. "Claire?"

"Reyr!" It came out as a strangled gasp. She ran across the room and flung herself into his arms. He groaned under the impact, but wrapped his arms around her waist, supporting her against him. "You're back!" she whispered into his hair.

He chuckled and set her down, holding her at arm's length, inspecting her. She did the same, studying his appearance, looking for signs of harm. His face was the same as she remembered, only now it was etched with deep lines of grief. "Reyr, I'm so sorry," she whispered, throwing her arms around him again. "So, so sorry. For *everything*." Her voice cracked as she spoke.

"I know," he whispered. "I am too." A long silence followed, where they simply held each other. "It's good to see you," he said at last, as he pulled away.

The sincerity of his words pierced her heart. A nervous laugh escaped her lips. "I've been looking for you for nearly an hour, you know. You didn't tell me you'd returned. Did you...did you not want to see me?"

He opened his mouth before frowning. "I did. I do. I just believed you wouldn't want—" He cleared his throat. "I thought you might still be upset with me for—"

"I'm not! I'm not upset. Not at all." She grimaced, thinking about what had happened that night. "All I could think about was what I said—about never forgiving you for leaving. I felt awful—I *feel* awful. I shouldn't have shamed you like that. It wasn't fair of me. You were right—what you said about me being selfish." Her chest crumpled. "It wasn't something a true friend would do. That's not the person I want to be." She took his hand in both of hers. "I should have been more understanding. Can you...can you forgive me?"

He huffed. "Claire, I forgave you the moment you said it."

Her heart galloped. "You did?" He nodded. "I didn't deserve that. But...thank you."

"You weren't the only one who said things you weren't proud of that night. I never should have..." He ran a hand through his hair —the same habit Talon had when he was agitated. She almost smiled, wondering who had learned it from whom? "I should not have forced you to make a choice like that. It was dishonorable and unfair. I hated myself for it afterward. But you understand why I had to leave?"

"I... Yes." She squeezed her eyes shut. "Are you better? Are you... *okay*?"

He sighed. "My heart is a wreck. No. I'm not okay. I do not know if I will ever be." He hesitated. "Talon and I spoke briefly when he was near the Scattered Islands, a few days ago I think. We didn't have much time—our words were brief. He told me that when you saw Kane's plans during your mission, you forced your party to turn north to save me. To save us."

She nodded. "I did. I tried." Her throat constricted. "But it wasn't enough."

His face fell. "No, it wasn't, but it was better than nothing. You gave us a fighting chance, Claire. I just wish we..." He blew out a breath. "There's no use in dwelling on what might have been."

She still held one of his hands in hers, unwilling to let go. She squeezed it. "I wish there was something I might say to make things better for you. Seeing you like this..."

It made her chest squeeze painfully.

He ran a thumb across her cheek. "Knowing you care is enough."

She nodded. "I missed you—so much." The words almost came out as a sob.

His face softened. "I missed you, too."

"Is Talon going to be angry with you for running away? You've been gone for weeks."

"Angry? At me?" He offered her a lazy smile in true Reyr fashion, as if he could do no wrong. Though, it didn't reach his eyes. "No. He is too good for that. You should give him more credit—give him a chance. You two aren't still at each other's throats, are you? You've been behaving yourself? I was worried that if I left, chaos would break loose between you. I know how he gets under your skin."

"I..." Her heart skipped. He didn't know. He hadn't been around to see the time they had been spending together, or hear the rumors flying about. Rumors of their closeness, of some wicked affair going on between them. "Talon and I...we don't fight any more. He is a good male. A good drengr. An even better king. Better than we all deserve."

Reyr offered an exaggerated gasp, stunned, and clapped his chest like he'd been shot with an arrow. "Okay, where is Claire and what have you done with her?" She smiled back at him. "You're being serious, then? Here I thought you hated him. What's brought about this change of heart?"

She chewed on the inside of her cheek, contemplating. "Reyr, I should tell you..."

The words stuck in her throat. How would he react? Would this news hurt him?

He frowned, perhaps sensing her inner struggle.

She cleared her throat. "Ahh...there's something you should know."

"Another piece of information from the Queen of Secrets?" He arched an eyebrow, but she could see the desire and curiosity lurking behind his eyes.

She laughed out of nervousness. "Queen of Secrets. Perhaps that's better than Queen of Dragonwall. Assuming I accept the role." Her eyes lifted to meet his. "Talon and I...we...we're..."

There was a long pause and then—

"No..." Realization flashed over his features as his mouth fell open. He shook his head to clear his thoughts. "You...you and *Talon*? Mates?" She nodded. "But...*what*? When? How?"

"We found out in Brezen," she whispered, struggling to get the truth out.

"Tell me everything."

She did. She told him exactly what had happened. He listened in silence, but his face stretched into a smile as her tale continued, until his eyes crinkled for the first time since returning to the keep.

She frowned. "You're not...mad?"

He barked a laugh and pulled her into yet another hug, wrapping himself around her. "Me?! Mad? Gods, no! I couldn't be happier—for you and for Talon."

The pressure in her chest loosened. Thank the gods for that! She'd never been one to worship Dragonwall's deities, but this time she gave them a silent prayer of thanks. She inhaled, smiling. Reyr smelled like sea salt, like the ocean.

"Am I *disturbing* something?" Talon's smug tone came from the doorway. She slowly pulled from Reyr's arms, a sheepish grin on her face. "Oh, don't let me stop you. By all means, carry on."

"Talon." Reyr's eyes darted over to his king, searching, assessing.

Talon stepped forward and covered the distance between them. "Glad to have you back, brother." He and Reyr threw their arms around each other, laughing. The sound of Talon's laugh, of Reyr's laugh, made butterflies flutter in her stomach.

"I couldn't let you manage everything on your own, could I? Where's the fun in that? We've got a fort to take back."

"That we do." Talon closed his eyes, resting his forehead against Reyr's.

Seeing it, her heart bubbled over with happiness. Watching them—witnessing their bond of brotherhood. It reminded her exactly what she was fighting for.

"Claire told me," Reyr whispered, "about the mate bond." His hands were wrapped around Talon's biceps.

Talon chuckled and pulled his forehead away. "Of course she did." He threw her a glare before turning his attention back to Reyr. "And? What have you to say about it?"

Reyr kept a hold of Talon's arms and shook him—actually *shook* him. "I should have seen it! I should have known. It's why you were so...so..."

"*Extra?*" she volunteered, lifting an eyebrow. "I think that's the word you're both looking for."

Talon blinked at her. "*Extra?*"

"Extremely extra." She couldn't help it. A thick laugh bubbled up from her chest. She crossed her arms and lifted her chin.

Talon turned back to Reyr. "You know what they say about hindsight. Clearer than a dragon's conscience. Isn't this how it generally goes with mate bonds?"

"Aye." Reyr glanced between them, shaking his head, obviously struggling to overcome his surprise. "You deserve this Talon. You deserve this more than anyone in the world. Both of you." He turned to her, taking her hands in his and bringing them to his lips. "I will always love you, Claire. But now I get to love you as my queen. It brings me...peace." A few of the lines on his face dissolved.

"Thank you, Reyr," she choked, doing her best to keep her tears in check. A knot loosened and she took a deep breath. "It means a lot to hear that. I just wish I didn't have to leave so soon now that you're back."

"Leave?" Reyr's face clouded. "And go *where*, pray tell?"

"She's going to train with the sprites. We'll be announcing it at tonight's meeting, along with our mate bond. The others don't know yet, so I'd appreciate it if you keep quiet."

"Uh-huh." Reyr's gaze narrowed. "And how long will she be gone?"

"I don't know," she answered for Talon. The uncertainty introduced new knots in her stomach. "I have a lot to learn, but there's not a lot of time."

Talon cleared his throat. "We will be busy retaking the fort. She will be safe with the sprites. Ideally, she will stay until she learns what she needs to defeat Kane."

"Defeat *Kane*?!" Reyr demanded. "I'm sorry, but I don't think I heard you correctly."

"I made a promise," she whispered. She chewed on the chapped skin of her bottom lip—a habit that frequently kept her lips peeling.

"You've got to be jesting." Reyr's expression transformed, darkened.

"Yes. That's essentially what I said when I found out—just last night, mind you." The force of Talon's gaze left her cheeks burning.

"So that's why Saffra..." Reyr trailed off, stroking his chin. "I thought her words were peculiar—that day when we discussed your dreams. She blundered. I knew she couldn't look guilty without reason." He sighed and his hand ran through his hair. Again. "I suppose there's no getting out of it?"

Talon scoffed. "We all know how an unbreakable promise works, Reyr."

"All right, then. But why the forest? Because of the spriten fire and your mark?"

"I'm part sprite," she managed, offering him a half smile by way of an apology for all he'd missed during his absence.

"I see. I suppose that makes sense. And who are you sending her with, Talon?"

"Koldis. And a few pairs from the fort."

"Koldis?!" Reyr frowned.

This was news to her, too.

Reyr crossed his arms. "Why not me?"

Talon hesitated. "I can send you instead, if you prefer? You've only just returned, but if you would rather…"

Claire's eyes widened. The idea of spending more time with Reyr left her warm, almost giddy. But it was Talon's response that surprised her most. When she'd first arrived in Dragonwall, he'd been jealous of her relationship with Reyr, of the ease they shared. All those times he saw them together, arms linked, laughing. All those times Reyr had escorted her to dinner.

That jealousy no longer existed.

Reyr was quiet, perhaps mulling it over. He exhaled and said, "I want to protect her, but you're right. We're at war. There are plans to make. The fort must be retaken. We cannot leave Squall's End under the rule of those beasts." Reyr glanced at her. "Will you be okay with Koldis?" She nodded, hoping to ease his doubt. His gaze lingered over her a moment longer before he turned to Talon. "Why not Verath? Wouldn't he be more adept for a journey like this?"

"Verath is busy training a potential new Shield."

"A potential new…*what*?!" Reyr's shout made her jump. "When did this happen?"

"You have missed a great deal. And, you have been missed a great deal more than that. If you'll wait for me in my study, I will happily fill you in on everything. But first, I'd like a moment alone with my mate."

Talon's smoldering glance left her heart racing.

"As you wish, my king." Reyr bowed his head. "Sounds like I'm in for one hell of a story. Well, Claire, this is where I leave you." He engulfed her in another hug. "I couldn't be happier for you," he whispered. "You've come a long way from the frightened woman I found standing over Cyrus to…to this." He pulled away to look down at her, grinning. Talon cleared his throat. Reyr chuckled. "*That's* my cue. I'll see you later," he added with a wink. Then he kissed her forehead and let her go, offering Talon a two finger salute and a crooked smile before disappearing through the nearby doorway.

Silence followed in his wake. Talon turned to face her. His lips twitched. "Couldn't wait, hmm?"

"I didn't think it was right for him to hear it in front of the others." She twisted her fingers together. Had she done the right thing in going against Talon's wishes? She'd promised him, after all. It was different from what had happened with Desaree, who had all but discovered the secret on her own.

Talon moved over and lifted her chin, planting a kiss on her lips. "You did the right thing, dear heart. He deserved to know." Her stomach fluttered.

"Our...our closeness doesn't bother you? Me and Reyr?"

"Not in the slightest. I love you both a great deal."

Fire shot through her veins. He loved her? She blinked up at him, stunned. He'd never said the *L-word*. But she supposed it made sense. They were mates. Why wouldn't he? Part of her wanted to say it back, but she couldn't summon the courage. Not yet. Only when the time was right.

He rubbed his nose against hers bringing a giggle to her lips. "Now, don't you have some packing to do?"

"Oh. Yes."

"Good. I'll see you at the meal tonight." He copied Reyr's actions, kissing her forehead and offering her a two finger salute before departing through the door that led to his study.

CHAPTER 47

A MESSAGE

Kastali Dun

Saffra scowled, turning away from the sight over her shoulder. Commander Daxton stood exchanging blows with Bedelth, shirtless and glistening. They dove at each other, fists flying, faces snarling. Despite Bedelth's draconian advantage, Dax was a formidable opponent...for a human.

Her scowl deepened.

Maybe if he'd been *more*—more than human—the poison would not have left him in shambles. But he wasn't more, was he? The dark thought frequently nagged her, even before the incident. A human's lifespan against hers, that of a powerful mage. She would live for hundreds of years.

And what of Marcel's concerns? The potential that the poison had reset his body to a stage before...before what? Kane's interference within the keep, his stretch and influence, was unknown to all of them. What if...?

No. She shook her head, pushing away the thought, and fired another arrow.

There was no telling, was there? Who could be trusted and who couldn't? Humans were Kane's vessels of choice because they were

490

easily manipulated. How well had she truly known her beloved? Why did Marcel have any reason to suspect him?

It wasn't raining, but it may as well have been. She glanced up at the sky. Dark clouds sat heavy above her, leaving the air thick enough to drink, even despite the chill of autumn.

Maybe she didn't know Dax at all, even if they were meant to be married. Dax had been eager with her all those years ago—perhaps too eager—when he returned from the Goblin War. He'd singled her out. It had always made her feel special. Women fawned and preened over him, but *she* was the one he wanted.

She avoided another glance over her shoulder. Seeing him with Bedelth didn't help her focus. She'd come here for a distraction, not to be distracted. The practice grounds were usually the one place she found peace.

She snorted. Peace. There was no peace. Not in this world.

Taking a deep breath, she nocked another arrow and let it fly, trying to ignore the memories of Dax filling this place. His time spent training her. The way he often found her here in the early hours of dawn. The conversations they'd exchanged, getting to know one another.

Gods, she'd been so naive to believe in happy endings.

The arrow landed off target. She groaned. Her movements were deft as she repeated her actions over and over. Each time she emptied her quiver, she went to the target and collected her arrows to start again. Twenty. Fifty. One hundred. She lost count. Her arm and shoulder ached. She welcomed the pain, pushing on.

The sun neared the horizon. The sounds died down around her, sharpening her focus. Clashing metal disappeared. Cries of excitement and frustration fell away. The day was coming to an end, and those on the grounds were retreating to the keep or barracks for the evening meal. She didn't dare look over her shoulder again. Dax was there or he wasn't. Either way, she could do nothing about it. So she fired another arrow.

"Still here?" Her arm twitched as Bedelth appeared beside her. The arrow missed its target.

She spared him a brief glance, purposefully ignoring the way his tunic clung to his sweaty chest, outlining the rigid muscle that lay beneath. The kind of muscle a human would never obtain.

She sighed, caring little for the sound of frustration. "Have you come to distract me?"

He chuckled. "I thought we'd already done plenty of that."

She cringed. Had she been that obvious? She threw him a glare but said nothing. Instead, she nocked another arrow, pulled, and released. This one hit the target's center. "Why are you here, Bedelth?"

"Daxton and I always practice in the eve—"

"No. Why are you *here*? Beside me."

He was quiet long enough to make her regret her words. He didn't deserve the sting of her tongue. She had known Bedelth for many years—since coming to the capital. He was one of the few steady figures, like Cyrus, whom she allowed close. She and Bedelth were both from Austar, and perhaps it was that commonality that made him more familiar. Especially after leaving her home and family behind. It created something between them, and while she was rarely one to lose her temper around others, it was all too easy just now.

"Push me away all you like, Saffra, but I'm not going anywhere. It is my concern for you, as always, that brought me here. I wanted to check on you. How are you feeling?"

"Fine, Bedelth." She exhaled. "I'm fine."

His expression softened. The warmth in his eyes, the way he lingered over her, forced her to look away. There was too much concern in his expression.

"Did he...did Dax ask about me?"

"He did not. Nor did I broach the subject. It makes him uncomfortable when I mention you—as you know."

She pushed down a sob, avoiding his gaze. Some words, like these, were near impossible to bear.

"Saffra..."

The sun's low rays bathed his warm skin in a golden glow. She hated herself for allowing her eyes to linger over him, to appreciate him. "I don't want to talk about it. Leave me."

He crossed his arms. "And when would be the right time? In another month? In two? After you've allowed your grief to rip you apart? As if it hasn't already started that process," he scoffed. "You cannot go on like this. I understand what it is to hope. But seeing you like this, seeing you suffer..."

"So I should just give up?!" she hissed. "It that it? I know what you would say, Bedelth, and I don't want to hear it."

He kept his voice low. Controlled. "You think you know, but I'm not sure that you do. You are a mage. Even if, one day, he remembers, the pain will always be there. He will age, grow old, die. You will keep living. Two hundred years. Three hundred. Four. How old was our last seer before she passed? And you are already more powerful. Who knows, you could live nearly the span of a drengr."

"Stop!" she begged. His jaw tensed. "You think I haven't considered the consequences?"

"I am sure you have. Still, it hurts me. To know that this is your struggle—your life. You will hate me for saying it, but I am glad this has happened. It will hurt less than watching him wither away in your arms."

"How?!" she cried. The full force of her rage seared her blood and she nearly reached for an arrow, to plunge it into his eye. "How can you *say* something so awful? He's your friend! *I'm* your friend—"

"As my *friend*, I owe you honesty. How many people have I watched age and die?! Do you forget what I am? Have you stopped to ask if perhaps I am speaking from experience?"

As quickly as the fire roared, it was followed by ice. "You...?"

A flicker of despair crossed his features, quickly replaced by impassivity. His voice came out flat. "I know what it is to love, Saffra—to love and have that love ripped away by the ravages of time. Perhaps I know better than most." He sighed. His shoulders fell.

"I don't want your pity, Bedelth."

He snorted. "What makes you think I offer pity?"

"Because the alternative is much worse."

His jaw flexed. "You think so, do you?"

"Don't think I haven't missed the signs. The way your eyes find me, the concern you've shown, and let's not forget your request to escort me to the ball—a ball I had no intention of attending. But how could I say no in front of everyone?! Not when you put me in such an uncomfortable position. Was that your plan all along? Force me to accept?"

"You make me sound awful."

"I'm *grieving*, Bedelth. I'm still *grieving*. And here you are, trying to take advantage of a *convenient* situation."

But was she? Could someone grieve a person who wasn't dead? It seemed almost silly to say it.

"Is that really how you think of me, Saffra? After all these years? That I'm some vulture, waiting to swoop in and snatch you up in my claws?"

"A dragon perhaps."

"Really…" His voice was flat.

Her chest tightened. "Yes. No." She turned away. She was being unfair. Bedelth had always been a friend, and if he wanted to be more, he had never pushed the matter. He'd been nothing but supportive to Dax and his career. It was Bedelth whom Dax had to thank for the promotion to commander. For every step of his upward rise.

"It is not illegal for me to care for you, Saffra. Hate me for it if you wish."

"I don't hate you." The whisper tumbled from her lips. The hopeless despair of Daxton's situation slammed into her, yawning out before her like an abyss. "I just want him back, Del. I have counted every single day since the attack. Every *single* day. Nothing changes. It hurts." A sob broke free. She stifled the next to keep from crying in front of him. She was the king's *seer*. Not a child. "When do I move on? And why do I feel awful for even considering it?"

For the briefest instant, she craved comfort. She wished he would take her in his arms, even though it felt awful for wanting that. For wanting him to hold her. She missed the feeling.

He merely gazed down at her and frowned. "There is no answer

I can give. You must do what feels right for you." He hesitated. "Know that I am always here for you, if you need me."

She pushed back the lump in her throat and nodded. "I know." But there was something else. Something she needed to know for certain. "Del...do you...do you have feelings for me? Is that why...?"

He squeezed his eyes shut before looking at her again. "It would be unfair of me to say yes."

"But do you?"

He sighed. "Ask me when you have decided what to do about Dax. Until then, I will give you no answer."

Her mouth opened and closed. What he'd just said, wasn't that answer enough? What did she expect? Better yet, what did she *want*?

"I should go. You know where to find me if you need me." He turned to leave, then faltered, turning back. "I meant to tell you, the king wishes for your presence tonight during our shield meeting."

She frowned. "Aren't those private?"

"Claire will be there. Desaree and Jocelyn, too." She gazed back at him, blinking. "I will see you later."

She watched him go, noticing the slump of his shoulders, the way his retreating figure cast shadows along the grass.

She went to the target and retrieved her arrows. Her mind was lost in thought, tortured by the onslaught of emotions Bedelth had dredged up.

"Just what I needed on a day like today," she muttered, growing angry anew. How dare he make her feel so...so...confused! So guilty.

She bent to collect her quiver from the ground and stilled. The edges of her vision faded. "No..." The word was barely a whisper. She blinked, but everything turned black.

A BEAUTIFUL FOREST, drenched in green foliage and mist, swallowed her whole. It was old beyond measure, soaked with ancient magic. She placed a hand over her thumping heart, turning in circles. Her eyes adjusted to the dim light. A chime of laughter split the air, pure and light, but it calmed her.

A trickle of water dragged her forward. She parted the foliage and gasped. There was a woman, covered in sprite markings, sitting upon the gnarled root of a monstrous tree. A tree so tall its top was lost in the mists. The woman laughed again, the picture of resplendence as she brushed her long hair over one shoulder and smiled at Saffra. Her face was familiar—too familiar.

"Welcome," she said, her voice musical.

"You...you can see me?"

"I see all things, Lady Saffra." She reached down and scooped water from the spring at the base of the tree's roots, letting it trickle through her fingers.

Saffra's eyes darted to the pool before returning to the woman's face. "Who...who are you?"

"That is unimportant. You should ask, rather, why you are here."

"Why am I here?"

"To deliver a message."

"For whom?"

"You already know."

Saffra opened her mouth, then closed it. "Is this...am I having a vision? Am I dreaming?"

"Neither. Both." The sprite laughed again.

Saffra swallowed, glancing down at the spring. The water. She was so thirsty.

"Ah, yes. Once you have tasted the waters of the spring, they will always call to you, as they do now. But now is not the time for a drink." Saffra paused. "You must listen carefully, for we haven't much time. Are you ready?"

Her nod was more of a jerk. The world went black. Words rang in her ears, over and over, like the clanging of a bell. Pounding, reverberating. Words she could not forget. Important words. A message. One that must be delivered.

· · ·

SHE OPENED her eyes and found the sky darkening. She was laying in the grass. The sprite's words were still there, echoing in her mind. She groaned and clutched her forehead. Waves of nausea raced through her, like she'd been transported all the way to the forest and back. She turned on her side and vomited into the grass.

The practice grounds were empty, thank the gods. She got to her hands and knees, then stood. The woman's words continued to play through her mind. Her neck and shoulders ached something terrible. From the fall? From all the arrows she'd fired?

A message. She needed to deliver a message. Using the adrenaline pounding through her body, she grabbed her things and sprinted to the dining hall.

CHAPTER 48

THE BIG REVEAL

Kastali Dun

Verath watched their inner circle assemble from the armchair in the corner of King Talon's sitting area. He'd arrived earliest to claim it, but mostly to observe. He wondered if this meeting had anything to do with Lady Caterina's disappearance. The king had already completed the necessary documents to confer Desaree's new title, but why assemble everyone for it?

Lady Desaree.

His gaze landed on Desaree, eyes taking in the curve of her neck and shoulders as she moved across the room, arm in arm with Claire. Saffra and Jocelyn followed in a similar manner. Desaree's chocolate tresses were held in place atop her head, not a single strand out of place. Tonight, she wore a brocade of pink silk.

His hand twitched. He drummed his fingers against the rolled arm of his chair to keep from thinking about the softness of her hair, to keep from thinking about how he wanted to run his fingers through it. If he'd ever again be allowed to.

498

Clenching his teeth, he forced the thought away. He needed to let her go. She deserved more than he could give—a family, marriage to someone who could provide a home and a future. All he had to offer her was his love.

He glanced around the room, taking in each of his brothers as they congregated around Reyr, slapping him on the back, full of questions. He'd already greeted Reyr after the evening meal. They'd spoken at length, in the privacy of Reyr's quarters.

He sighed. What a day it had been. With Lady Caterina's disappearance, he had combed the city for hours. Guards had done the same. There was no sign of her. The only tip came from a down-trodden tavern near the docks, of a woman who sought a merchant ship captain for passage. The same damned captain who had delivered their large order of ice metal not long ago. Reports claimed it had happened the evening of the ball, around the same time she must have disappeared from her classes with Mage Targa.

The atmosphere in the sitting room abruptly changed. He glanced up as King Talon strode in, shoulders back, the picture of regality. Everyone snapped to attention. "Sit, sit," he murmured, encouraging them to get comfortable. The trouble was, there weren't enough places. It was a game of shifting and arguing.

At last, Talon's shields squeezed together on one sofa—Reyr propped on the left arm, Bedelth and Jovari in the middle, and Koldis on the right arm—while Desaree, Jocelyn, and Saffra squeezed together on the other sofa. That left Claire and Talon eying the large armchair near the fire—Talon's usual spot.

Claire positioned herself on the arm, sitting aloof. Not missing a beat, Talon plopped comfortably down in the chair, placing his hand against her back, rubbing down the length of her spine with absentminded ease.

Verath sat straighter, observing. They had grown close, but something seemed different tonight. A distracting change.

"We make quite the merry party," Talon observed, his eyes dancing over them. The fire crackled in the background, warm and inviting. Claire turned to Talon and smiled down at him. Something deeper manifested in her gaze when he returned it, a silent speech without words. The others didn't miss the exchange. Koldis and Jovari shared a pointed glance.

"I called this meeting because Claire and I have something to share, but first, I'd like to address the matter of Desaree."

Desaree twitched, her face going pale under the sudden attention.

"No need to fret," Talon added. "I completed the documentation earlier. It is my honor, nay, my privilege, to confer upon you your title of *lady* and the transfer of all that remains in the Kendall coffers. The Rosens have been removed—entirely." Desaree's eyes widened. She opened her mouth, but nothing came out. "Everything is yours now, Desaree. With Caterina's disappearance, she forfeits all."

Desaree exhaled. "I...she's really gone then?"

"Indeed," Talon said. "From what I understand, we failed to locate her. Verath? Any sign?"

Verath shook his head. "None, my king. A tip confirmed that she fled the city."

Talon nodded. Every eye in the room was trained on Desaree. "The title is yours, Desaree, if you will have it. That is your wish, is it not?"

"Yes." The word slipped out, more of a squeak. Claire beamed, grinning ear to ear. She must have known beforehand. Saffra and Jocelyn both patted Desaree on the back, offering quiet congratulations.

Talon waved a hand, muttered something under his breath, and a rolled parchment appeared, dropping into Desaree's lap. There was a ribbon tied around it. Desaree's eyes widened further. She took the document and clutched it to her chest.

Verath tried to catch her gaze, but she was staring wide-eyed at King Talon. Gods! How he wanted to pull her into his arms. To kiss her. To hold her....

"Good." Talon nodded. "Congratulations, then, *Lady* Desaree." The others echoed his words.

"Thank you, Your Majesty."

"My pleasure." The king glanced between Desaree and Claire. "And as to the matter of your handmaiden duties—"

"I do not wish to relinquish my duties, Your Majesty—forgive me—I did not mean to interrupt."

"Nothing to forgive, my lady."

"Des will stay on as my *lady in waiting*," Claire announced. "I cannot manage without her. She will continue assisting me, even in my absence. She will handle my affairs while I'm away—"

"Away *where*?" Koldis interrupted.

"The forest," Talon answered. "And you will be going with her."

"*What?*" Koldis sputtered. "Me?!"

Verath sat straighter, eyes narrowed. "Apologies, my king. Are we missing something?"

"Yes, Verath. Claire and I will explain. Perhaps it is best to start at the beginning. We have an announcement to make." He looked up at Claire, taking her hand in his. "Would you like to share, dear heart?"

"Me?"

"You." His thumb caressed the back of her hand.

"Okay." She nodded and turned to the group. "So, uh, I guess I'll just say it. Talon and I are mates."

The room was silent. Absolutely silent. Then—"I *knew* it!" Saffra screeched, jumping up from the sofa.

Verath shut his mouth. Judging by the looks of absolute disbelief and confusion, the others were just as shocked. Desaree's eyes found his. She didn't look so surprised. "*You knew*?!" he mouthed. She bit her lower lip before nodding.

Everyone handled it differently.

Bedelth's eyes narrowed as he said, "Talon? Is this true?"

"You can't be serious?!" Jovari roared at the same time. "This isn't just a game to trick us, is it?"

"Right!" Koldis snorted, glancing at Jovari. "Because we all know our king's stance on *love*..."

Talon laughed. "I'm dead serious. We've wanted to tell you for weeks, but we've been waiting for the right moment." To prove his point, he lifted Claire's hand and pressed her palm to his lips. Her eyes fluttered closed briefly. The intimate moment was enough to rip Verath's heart wide open. The abyss of longing and regret stretched out before him—a reminder of what he had lost.

But not entirely.

He still loved. He still had a chance to share that love—perhaps never as strong as a mate's love, but it was still love. His eyes flicked to Desaree again. She was looking directly at him. Her gaze left his skin heated. He wanted so badly to take her, to be with her, to show her what he felt on a deeper level.

"Argh! Get a room, you two!" A pillow pelted Talon in the face. Koldis.

"Oof!" Talon batted it away, laughing—actually laughing! How often did he laugh like that? Almost never.

Jovari snickered. "Gods! It's about time!"

"Guess it makes sense," Bedelth said at last, crossing his arms. His eyes shot over to Saffra who avoided him entirely.

"Gods...I never thought..." Koldis looked at Claire and Talon. Jovari shook his head, clearly struggling to digest the idea. Reyr merely smirked. Out of everyone, Verath expected Reyr to be the most upset, but he wasn't, which meant he must have also known beforehand. Saffra and Jocelyn were grinning so widely their mouths might fall off.

"In hindsight, it makes sense," Talon said. He was all but glowing in the firelight. In all his years, Verath had never seen his king so absolutely and completely happy. The deep scars on his face had practically disappeared behind an unusual smile. "I know it's hard to believe. But Claire and I, we really *are* mates."

Reyr was the first to stand—always the example. He went to Claire and went down on one knee, taking her hand in his. "My queen." The room fell silent. "My allegiance is yours, if you will have it." Her eyes widened. She hid her surprise as he kissed her knuckles and stood.

She glanced at Talon. Their eyes went unfocused. Sharing

thoughts. Even without solidifying the mate bond, Claire's ability to speak with all of them allowed it. "I will have it," she answered, smiling up at Reyr. He nodded and resumed his seat.

The severity of the revelation snapped into place making it difficult to breathe. Talon didn't merely have a mate. They had a queen. After all these years, Dragonwall was going to have a *queen*! Not just any queen either, one of sprite and drengr blood. One from a world beyond. An outsider. Pride flared hot in Verath's chest. He beheld this spirited young female—the perfect complement to Talon's needs.

Jovari was next, then Koldis, then Bedelth. Verath went last, going down on one knee and taking Claire's hand in his. Her skin was already clammy, though she hid her nerves well. "My queen," he repeated, holding her gaze, imparting upon her the seriousness of his heart. "My allegiance is yours. My sverak, my loyalty, all of it—yours." He spared a glance for Talon, who merely nodded.

"Thank you, Verath," she said, breathless. Her eyes glittered with unshed tears. "I'm honored to have it."

He retreated to his seat.

"Well..." Talon exhaled. "That was...unexpected. Welcome, but unexpected." He paused, as if coming to terms with what had just happened. "While we are eager to solidify the bond, I have asked Claire to refrain from accepting me for now. We wish to be together, but the matter is not simple." The others in the room shared confused glances. "Becoming Dragonwall's queen is not lightly done, and she understands this. As such, I will have her answer when she returns from the Gable Forest."

Ahh. There it was again. Confirmation that she was indeed going away.

"But why is she leaving?" Koldis crossed his arms. "And why am I going with her?"

"I'm going to train with the sprites," she answered. "And you're coming because Talon said so. Is that going to be a problem?"

Koldis shrank away from her glare. "Absolutely not, my queen. It would be my pleasure. I just hate sprite food, is all." Claire burst into laughter. The rest of them followed. Koldis offered a sheepish grin. "Well, I do! And I'm not the only one."

Something nagged at Verath, forcing him to ask, "Is it safe, my king? Sending her away like this? Especially knowing she is our queen? Shouldn't she master her mage magic first?"

Talon ran a hand through his hair. "Claire's sprite blood makes that difficult, Verath. She is better suited to master whatever is more comfortable before learning to balance both. We need her as strong as possible for what is coming." He drummed his fingers on the padding of the chair before looking up at Claire. "Would you like to tell them, dear heart, why this is so...*important?*"

Something passed between them. Claire turned bright red. "Uhm?" She glanced at the rest of the room. Her lips flattened into a line.

"I see. Too shy to atone? Well, as your mate, it falls on me then." Talon's expression hardened. "Claire thought it was wise to—how shall I put this?—make a very *naughty* promise."

Claire suddenly seemed very interested in the flames in the grate, in the wall, in anything other than everyone sitting in the room. What was more surprising, she wasn't lashing out at King Talon for his scolding tone.

"What sort of promise?" Verath asked.

"The unbreakable sort," Talon answered, his words clipped.

"I—" Claire opened and closed her mouth. "Cyrus talked me into it."

"So it would seem," Talon said. "Stealing the opportunity right out from underneath the rest of us. Claire promised to defeat Kane, and now she is bound to that. Her words were explicit. The actions of a true queen, I suppose. Already eager for responsibility."

Claire's face turned an even darker shade of red.

Queenly or not, it was clear that Talon wasn't happy. "We all know what will happen if she does not fulfill the promise."

Koldis groaned. "What were you thinking, Claire?! Are you insane? Don't you realize—"

"Enough!" Talon's eyes flashed, pupils narrowing into draconic slits. Koldis snapped his mouth shut. "If anyone scolds her for it, it will be me. And believe me, I already have." Talon sighed. "Mistakes happen—to all of us. What's done is done. We will see her through this. Did you not just pledge yourselves to her?"

"Aye." The confirmation echoed around the room.

Talon nodded. "Cyrus was always the wise one. While I dislike this, I am certain there was a reason behind his madness."

"There was." Saffra had been unusually quiet during this entire exchange. "Mage magic isn't powerful enough to defeat Kane. Not even sprite magic will do, or else the sprites would have taken matters into their own hands. The world requires balance. It will take both bloods to eliminate Kane, and even then, it will not be easy."

"Always the bearer of good news," Koldis muttered.

"Koldis..." Talon warned again.

Saffra hesitated. "Both magics must be in balance. Green and blue. Sprite and mage. And Cyrus will help with that. His sverak and Claire's staff..." Her eyes went unfocused, like she was picturing something, imagining something.

"A staff?" Talon frowned.

"The one I'm supposed to find in the forest," Claire said. She sat up straighter on the chair arm.

"How do you reckon that?" Talon asked.

Claire and Saffra exchanged a glance before explaining everything to the group, detailing Saffra's vision—one she had hidden from everyone but Claire many months before—and the riddle she had been granted earlier that evening.

"What riddle?" Talon asked.

"Saffra had a vision before dinner—"

"Not a vision," Saffra amended, halting Claire's explanation. "I believe Princess Taylynn contacted me. She told me to deliver a message." Saffra hesitated, but when she next spoke, Verath felt his skin prickle at the words.

These answers you will surely seek,
For questions on your mind.

A weapon you will need to wield,
That only you can find.
For in your blood are green and blue,
Two magics intertwined,
But neither can succeed alone,
Though each has been defined.
So if you journey far enough,
To see them both aligned,
A deeper power from within,
Will show itself in time."

"Now you see why I must go," Claire said. "I need their help."

"So we send her to the forest," Jovari decided, crossing his arms. "And then what? Just wait for her to come back?"

"We have plenty to do in the meantime," Talon said.

"We need a plan to reclaim the fort," Reyr added. "Claire will be safer with the Sprites while we do that."

"Well, if that's the case," Jovari said, "I'd like to accompany Claire and Koldis. I am her other trainer, after all."

"No," Talon said. "The last thing I need is both of you troublemakers harassing the sprites, wearing out your welcome."

"Yeah, stand down." Koldis punched Jovari in the arm. "I'm the better shield for the job."

Jovari glared at Koldis. Ever in competition with each other.

"You are needed here, Jovari," Talon said. "And here's why." Talon went into detail about his initial thoughts for reclaiming Fort Squall.

Their discussion continued well into the evening, until Talon lifted his hand to silence the room. "I think that is enough for one night. Claire and Koldis have an early morning tomorrow. My mate needs her sleep." They shared a heated look that had the others looking away, but everyone agreed.

One by one they rose and left Talon's tower. Verath watched Desaree lead Claire away, but not before Claire and Talon embraced. It wasn't until the door closed behind them that Verath sighed and rose. He wanted nothing more than to chase after Desaree, to beat down her chamber door and...well, he wasn't sure what would follow. Desaree had not yet accepted him back into her arms. So instead, he bid his king goodnight and retreated to his room where he might digest all that had been said, well aware that everything had now changed.

CHAPTER 49

A NEW ADVENTURE

Kastali Dun

Claire tossed and turned. Try as she might, sleep evaded her. There was too much to think about. Her secret was out, and everyone in Talon's circle knew what she was destined to face.

"Are you asleep?"

A shiver raced down her spine at the sound of Talon's voice.

"If I was, I'm not anymore," she teased. Someone tapped gently on her door. She sat up, listening. *"Is that you?"*

"It's me." A shaft of light filled her bedroom. Talon's figure was silhouetted in the doorway, filling it entirely. He crept in and shut the door behind him. There was a brief darkness followed by the glow of an orb.

He was dressed more casually than she was used to. Barefoot, a pair of pants that ended below his knees, and a billowing long-sleeved tunic. A deep V showed a generous sliver of his chest.

"It's the middle of the night," she murmured.

"I know." He gazed back at her, staring as if she might disappear. "Desaree was sleeping on the sofa. I did my best not to wake her."

A pang of fondness made her chest tighten. "She wanted to be here in case..." A lump formed in her throat. "In case I needed anything tonight."

The truth was, Desaree was crestfallen over the news of her sudden departure. She'd only just returned, and now she was set to go away again.

Talon still hadn't moved. She tilted her head. "Do you...do you want to join me? I haven't been able to sleep." Without waiting for an answer, she scooted over and pulled the covers aside.

"I do." He climbed in beside her and pulled her against his chest. She found a comfortable spot in the crook of his shoulder before tangling their limbs together. Perhaps if she anchored herself to him, she wouldn't have to leave in the morning.

Heat pooled low in her core at the feel of him.

The orb disappeared, casting them into darkness. "I couldn't stop thinking about you," Talon murmured. "That you should be here sleeping alone, when I might soak up every last moment with you."

"That's...sweet, Talon." She smiled against his chest, inhaling deeply. No matter how long she was gone, she would never forget his scent. "Salt and smoke," she murmured. "That's what you smell like."

He let out a soft snort. "I see."

"I like it," she clarified. "It's what I want to keep with me while I'm away. If I could infuse it into a candle, I would. I'd burn it every day."

He chuckled, the sound tugging on something low in her belly. "I'm not sure sprites take kindly to flames in their forest. Trees and all that..."

"You're probably right. A perfume, perhaps. *Essence of Talon.*"

He gave a soft snort then kissed her forehead. "I like it."

She sighed and fell quiet, snuggling deeper against him. Even with him here, it was hard to chase away the thoughts weighing on her. "I'm scared."

"*You?* Scared?"

She poked his chest. "Come on. I'm being serious."

"I know..." He didn't speak for a while. "I was beginning to think you feared nothing." A soft *tut* escaped her lips at that. "It's true. You left your home behind. You have protected this kingdom at every opportunity. You defeated Kane's wraiths. You even faced me on multiple occasions, without a trace of fear in your eyes."

"Why should I fear you?"

"Why, indeed!"

"Besides, this is Kane we're talking about."

"And you're going to meet him in the forest?"

"I...no. But I must learn everything I can while I'm there. What if it isn't enough?"

He exhaled, his breath rustling her hair. "It is okay to be afraid, Claire. Without fear, there would be no barriers. No mountain to climb. No wall to break through. Everything you want is waiting on the other side. You just have to...get past it."

"Hmm." She considered this. "I never thought about it that way."

He nuzzled her, running his fingers through her hair, massaging her scalp. She almost groaned as something deep in her curled, setting everything on fire.

"Sleep now, little mate." She relaxed in his embrace. "I will stay with you until morning. I will always be with you. Even when I cannot be physically. Right here." He pushed his hand between them and pressed against her heart. She sighed and rubbed herself against him, probably not the best idea, because it only made it harder to resist the desire sizzling between them. He took to caressing her back in lazy circles, the warmth of his palm calming her frazzled nerves. Eventually, sleep took her.

SHE WOKE to gentle kisses and soft murmurs of good morning as Talon detangled himself. This was as it was meant to be. She pictured what their life could be like together, waking up like this every day. She wanted it more than she'd ever wanted anything.

Gray light spilled into her room, casting everything in fuzzy outlines. She tensed, holding him for just a moment longer, before letting him go. He got up to stand beside the bed. "I'll let you get ready," he said, "and see you when it's time to depart." She nodded and watched him go, trying to force back her longing.

Desaree didn't say a word after seeing him leave. She helped her dress in travel clothes, then handed her her pack. She shouldered it.

"I know you're not hungry," Desaree said, "so there's breakfast-to-go wrapped in paper. It's at the top there. Complements of Thomas in the cookery."

She smiled. "Des, have I told you how amazing you are?" Her voice was thick. "If I haven't, then you're amazing. So amazing. I'm going to miss you so much." Tears blurred her eyes.

Desaree's smile was slow and sad. "Just go already, so that you can come back. I'm not sure I can take much more of these sudden disappearances."

"I know." She sighed, taking Desaree's hands. "Promise me you'll work things out with Verath?"

Desaree opened and closed her mouth. "I will...try."

"He loves you, Des, and you deserve to be happy."

Desaree exhaled. "You're right, of course."

"Oh, and one more thing!" She told Desaree about her promise to Tamara, who was set to arrive in the capital any day now. "She's going to need a few friends when she gets here. Plus, I promised to show her around."

"I'll take the best care of her."

"Thank you."

A knock sounded. Koldis popped his head through the door. Seeing that she was ready, he strode into the main room. "Ready for our next adventure? Sorry you can't come, Des."

Claire hid her smile. Had everyone taken to using Desaree's nickname?

Desaree rolled her eyes. "Gods, Lord Koldis, you have far too much energy at this hour."

"So I do!" He shrugged. "Day's-a-wasting. Can't chase the sunrise if it beats us to the horizon."

She snorted.

They followed Koldis out and down to the lowest courtyard of the keep. A group had assembled. Not only Talon, Saffra and Jocelyn, but all of the king's shields, including Dallin. "Training at dawn," Dallin offered by way of explanation, wincing and pointing at Verath, who stood silent beside him.

Pressure built inside her chest. She hated goodbyes, especially when she couldn't promise how long she'd be gone. She gave each of them a hug and heartfelt farewell, fighting against the tears filling her eyes. She lingered over Desaree and Saffra the longest.

Talon was the last to step forward. "I'll follow you to the fort, but I'll take my leave from there," he said, then pulled her into a fierce embrace, lifting her from the ground. "I need not tell you to be careful. Koldis will look after you, but you must remain vigilant. Trust your instincts. They've proven impeccable on every occasion."

"I will," she breathed as he set her down.

There was so much else she wanted to say, but if she said anything else, her tears would start falling. Instead, she took his scarred face in her hands and pulled him in for a deep kiss, showing him exactly how she felt. Letting her tongue caress his, until a groan built in his chest. Someone wolf-whistled. Probably stupid Koldis. She didn't care that passion and fire swirled around them—that everyone saw it. Talon sighed and pulled away.

"Goodbye," she whispered, caressing his face one last time before turning to follow Koldis. He transformed, and she found the familiar harness strapped where his wing joints met his neck. She strapped everything in and got into place. Then she turned and waved a final goodbye to everyone.

When he sprang from the ground, Talon followed them into the sky. She watched his hulking black form beside her. He returned her gaze, watching her with his calculating eyes. She wished it was *his* back and *his* scales she was touching. Wished their minds could meld one last time.

An emptiness opened inside of her. A part of her that was missing. For the first time since discovering their mate bond, her longing for him went beyond words. The incomplete bond left a hole in her chest. A raw hole that chafed.

A few minutes later, the fort came into view. With it, a full wing of drengr rose to greet them. They fell into a V-formation around her, with Koldis at the point.

Talon gave a mighty roar, shattering the heavens. She heard everything in it—everything that she felt. She clutched her chest, trying to breathe, to keep from crying. But the tears came anyway.

A moment later, his voice was in her mind. *"I will miss you more than a dragon misses the sky. More than the sun misses the horizon. More than the moon misses the stars."* She gasped, forcing back a sob. *"Hurry back to me, mate. Please...hurry back to me."* And then he was flying away, banking on his wingtip to return to the city. She watched over her shoulder until he turned into a speck and disappeared among the city walls. Only then did she slap her hand over her mouth to quiet her sobs.

"It wasn't easy for him to say goodbye like that." Koldis said in her mind. *"Letting you go. Frankly, I'm surprised he allowed it."*

She took a staggering breath. *"Me too. And for the record, this isn't easy for me, either."*

"I know." Koldis hesitated. *"But what's done is done. Let's not dwell. After all, we've got an adventure before us! The sky at our wingtips. The land beneath our claws. Let us make the most of it."*

She smiled. *"I'm glad you're with me, Koldis."*

"I am, too. Imagine the trouble we'll get into. Those sprites have no idea what's coming."

She laughed and a weight lifted from her chest. *"Oh, I think they know."*

"Soon enough, yes. If we make haste, we should reach the forest in four or five days."

And what would they find when they did? What magic would she unlock within herself? What power lay dormant, waiting to break free? The possibilities were thrilling. Endless, even. She would miss Talon—oh, yes. She already did. She felt the mate bond tighten between them with each flap of Koldis's wings. But nervous excitement built in the pit of her stomach, rising up, up, up. She was meant to do this, to take this road, this journey. It felt right.

A wing of twenty pairs stretched out behind them. Her protectors. Her companions. She closed her eyes and inhaled, detecting a faint scent of pine and flower blossoms. Scents from the Gable Forest riding the wind currents, calling to her, beckoning her home.

The dawn was crisp. Full of promise. Just like the tip of the sun as it peeked up from the horizon. It drenched Dragonwall with daring ease, calling her to action. Beckoning her into the unknown. This was the start of a new adventure, one she was ready to take. So she stretched her arms wide and leaned her head back, smiling upward, and embraced the sky.

CHAPTER 50

THE GREAT STONE ROAD

Safuil

Mikkin followed his party into Dubrael's cavernous hall. They'd waited three days for Dubrael's council to deliberate. Three days spent hoping the dwargs would band together and fight Dragonwall's common enemy. In that time, Fik and Gro had shown them all over the city. There was something to be said for dwargish hospitality.

Safuil's halls abounded with secrets. Mines that stretched to the center of the earth, vaults of hidden treasures—gems, priceless relics, coin enough to make every citizen in Dragonwall wildly rich—markets for trading, stages for plays and reenactments, underground fields of dirt for growing mushrooms and potatoes with light from shafts in the mountain. But most spectacular was the *Hall of Memories*. Here they found a garden of luminescent plants and statues portraying Dragonwall's history. Giant dragons carved from stone and gems. A stone forest that paid homage to the sprites. Famous dwargen lords. Even a few drengr kings.

Mikkin and the others had gotten lost for hours, wandering its vast depths. Even Unka appreciated it. He asked question after question in his broken language. Fik and Gro required some warming up, but eventually their love for telling stories outweighed their dislike of goblins.

And so it was that they found themselves awaiting Dubrael's answer.

"Welcome, welcome," the dwarg lord said, standing at his stone dais. This time, there were six dwargs with him, three to each side of the stone steps. "Before you, stands Safuil's most prominent council members."

Lord Averaen bowed his head in greeting. "Have you an answer for us, Lord Dubrael?"

"I have." Dubrael took a seat on his stone throne. "The dwargs of Safuil have deliberated. While it took some convincing,"—his eyes darted, scowling, down to those standing before them—"we have reached an agreement. While we would rather hide in our mountainous city, Dragonwall needs us. We will help where we can."

Lord Averaen's shoulders relaxed. "I am happy to hear it."

"Our fastest bird was selected. A message has been dispatched to King Talon. He will be informed of our allegiance. If he chooses to retaliate, our metalsmiths are at his service. Tomorrow, our forges will begin preparation. The drengr will have armor as they did in the days of old. What we make for humans will provide the magic necessary to shield against dragon fire."

Lord Averaen nodded. "Armor would be most appreciated. What of weapons?"

"Oh yes. Of that we have plenty." Dubrael's smile was cunning. "Our vaults are well stocked."

"And what of the other dwargs? Will they take up arms?"

Dubrael hesitated. "As I said before, I cannot answer for my compatriots. However, I think we might have a chance of persuading them. I would recommend those along the Northern Range, from here to Ice Port. Our tunnels connect us." He hesitated, glancing between them. "I will have envoys prepared. Perhaps some of you would like to accompany them? Explain the dire circumstances?"

Lord Averaen glanced over his shoulder and his eyes fell on Mikkin.

Mikkin stepped forward. "Count me in." Jamie did the same. To Mikkin's surprise, so did Berbik and Unka.

Unka had done naught but follow them around like a lapdog. He and the lad had developed an interesting relationship. If Mikkin wasn't mistaken, it appeared that Jamie cared for the poor creature. Something in Unka's willingness to help Jamie rescue him had won Jamie over. He no longer treated the goblin with disdain.

"Hm...an unlikely group." Dubrael nodded, but appeared pleased. "Very well. And what of *you*, Master Drengr?"

"I must return to Fort Edge. We do not know Kane's plans. While the wild dragons are busy at Fort Squall, my own fort could still be in danger."

They talked for a while longer, but it was decided that Lord Averaen and his group would return home. The dwargs agreed to lead them safely through the tunnels and out of the mountains, where they could fly the rest of the way home.

THAT NIGHT, Dubrael threw a memorable feast. All those who lived within Safuil's city gathered in the great dining hall. There was game hunted from the mountains above, roasting on giant spits. Roaring fires that warmed the cold stone. Mushrooms in every capacity, stewed, roasted, baked. Potatoes too. Even a few leafy vegetables and other delicacies from trading were out on the tables in heaping piles.

The dwargs were a rowdy people. They sang and drank and carried on telling their most favored stories. Histories, mostly, of their favorite dwargen lords, inflated to extreme proportions. For a people who claimed to steer clear of politics, they had a fair share of reenactments about great battles spanning Dragonwall's history.

Mikkin and Jamie soon found themselves inebriated, roaring with laughter as Fik recounted—with a heavy accent—a story of

Lord Hendol and how he'd gotten caught with his pants around his ankles. It was during one of the battles against the Kalds hundreds of years past. "It was when the mountain shook," Fik was saying, his voice increasing with every word, "that we dwargs knew giants were crossing over our homes. Out runs Lord Hendol from his lady's chamber, tripping all the while with his pants around his ankles as he struggled to do them up. The guards in the hall had a right time being serious!"

"And did he make it through the tunnels to meet the Kalds in battle?" Jamie's eyes were round.

"Oh, aye." Fik's palm smashed against the table, making the earthenware jump. The sound blended with the rest of the merriment around the hall. "Hendol took a band of clansmen on the backs of goats through the tunnels. Goats—astute climbers, you know. But that wasn't the funniest part," Fik growled. Mikkin chuckled. "His lady came out after him, wrapped in a blanket, shaking her fist at his retreating figure, screaming that he'd left his dignity behind. Dwargish women," Fik huffed. His face took on a soft look.

"Do *you* have a woman?" Jamie asked, eying the Dwarg.

"Aye, a godsdamned difficult one." His soft tone didn't match his words.

Hours later, they stumbled to their beds.

Their morning departure was slow in coming. They were late to rise and gather around a breakfast table. Lord Averaen was there to dole out instructions to Mikkin, words that might help increase their chances of winning others to their cause. "They'll want to refuse," he advised. "Dwargs are damned stubborn about this kind of thing."

Mikkin listened while he spooned porridge into his mouth.

"Make sure you press the importance of the matter. And a little flattery goes a long way where Dwargs are concerned." Lord Averaen's eyes flicked to Fik and Gro who sat two tables over, hugging their heads and groaning as they ate. Dwargs prized ale and were heavy drinkers.

When it was time to depart, Fik and Gro assembled with a

small party. Individuals that Mikkin had met in passing. "This is Bulgrog, Mozzun, Thanduk, Netruc, and Burdus," Fik said, introducing everyone. "But you can call them Bul, Moz, Than, Net, and Bur."

Mikkin and Jamie nodded, glad for the shortened names.

"We dwargs appreciate simplicity when the time calls for it," Berbik said, appearing beside them. "But don't start calling me Ber," he added, eyes narrowed. "I prefer Berbik. Short enough as is."

At this, Mikkin grunted.

Their two groups—the drengr with their guides, and Mikkin's with his—gathered at a crossroads of tunnels. The tunnels running ahead would take the drengr up and then out, dumping them on the side of the mountain where they would depart. Mikkin's party would go deeper, traveling along the underside of the range.

"Well, this is where we leave you." Lord Averaen took Mikkin by the shoulder before grasping his forearm. "Glad we got you out of that stinking hole. I'll report what I've found to my fort and send word to King Talon, though I'm sure Dubrael's letter will reach him first. You take care, and give those damned dragons hell when you face them."

As if summoned, Dubrael appeared to bid their group farewell. Two dwargs accompanied him carrying weapons. "These are for your riders," he said to Lord Averaen. "A gift of goodwill."

While the Drengr already had sveraks, their riders generally carried bows. Dubrael presented each female with a long knife, strong enough to pierce dragon scales. They thanked Dubrael for his gifts, strapping them to their belts. Dubrael also gave Mikkin, Jamie, Berbik, and Unka similar weapons.

"While I don't expect trouble in the tunnels, you never know. Perhaps they will serve you well when we meet again on the battlefield."

Unka eyed his new weapon with glee, and held it against his body, hugging it for a long while before strapping it to his belt. To the small goblin, the thing was more like a sword than a knife. Goblins valued treasure above all else. No doubt the ruby in the knife's sheath would be a prized possession for the dejected goblin. Mikkin almost felt bad for having slain his compatriots.

Almost…but not quite.

The drengr's group departed first. Their guides held torches aloft as they departed down the dark tunnel. Mikkin's group watched until the darkness swallowed them up. Then he turned to Fik and Gro. "Well, that's that," he said. "Lead on, Master Dwarg."

Torches were passed around, and they departed. Mikkin couldn't help the thrill that shot through him. A new adventure but the same goal. Seek vengeance for Mardra and his boys.

"Welcome to the *Great Stone Road*," Fik said after nearly ten minutes. The small tunnel they followed took them to a larger one lined with glow baskets, though these were scarcely spaced. The torches were welcome in the muted light.

The road, as they called it, was much wider and taller than the tunnels they were used to around Safuil. "The dwargen lords of old carved it out of the mountain after settling their cities," Fik explained. "Lords Throstak, Kirsolir, and Wemut decided that all great cities should be connected. They petitioned the city holders across the mountains and it was built."

Thus began their long trek. Mikkin listened to the drone of Fik's voice, on and on, but there was only so much history one could take. After going into great detail about the obstacles encountered in carving the great road into the mountain, Fik went on to talk about each city, and then each city's history of its lords.

"And then there was Lord Akrouth," Fik was saying when Jamie let out a small groan. Fik didn't seem to notice. "He bred a new line of mountain goats that could see in the dark tunnels so they wouldn't bash into the rocky walls."

"I'm going to bash my own head into a rocky wall in a minute," the lad whispered.

Mikkin suppressed his laughter, but said for Fik's benefit, "And how'd he manage that, Master Fik?" This sent Fik spiraling into another long-winded explanation that left Jamie groaning all the more.

He didn't mind the history lessons. Dwargs valued storytelling above all else. While it would be a full day and a half on the road before reaching Kisteg, the first city on their path, he was certain that Fik's stories would keep them occupied all the way and beyond.

He smiled to himself. He'd started this journey without a plan, without much of anything, really. Just a pesky lad by his side, green as grass, eager to see adventure. He spared a glance for Jamie. Now they had a plan and more purpose than before. With help from the dwargs, he would raise an army capable of meeting Kane's forces in battle. He would have weapons. He would have support. But most importantly, he would have his revenge. Yes, in that sense, he'd been more successful than he could have imagined.

CHAPTER 51
HEALING

Kastali Dun

Verath strode through the keep at a brisk pace, deep in thought. He nodded absentminded greetings to others in passing. Claire had departed two days ago and he hadn't seen Desaree since. She was avoiding him. Gods, it irked him that a mere human had the power to get under his skin—that a mere human controlled his emotions. Shouldn't the drengr race be above this sort of thing?

He snorted, earning a startled look from a pair of servants in passing.

He turned his thoughts towards Dallin. It was mid-morning and they'd just finished training. Dallin showed promise—filled with the energy of youth. It was almost too much for him. Dallin's swordsmanship needed work, true. No argument there. But he never complained. He followed orders. He listened with a lack of arrogance that older drengr often displayed.

Talon was right. Dallin was pliable. Perhaps their ranks would benefit from him after all. Even though he hated the idea of replacing Cyrus. Even though it was necessary and inevitable.

At least Claire liked him. There was that.

His mind jumped to his future queen. *His future queen!* He had to repeat the words a few times because the sound of them was so foreign. After hundreds of years, it was nearly too much. And he wasn't the only one struck with disbelief. They'd all been shocked. Things were changing. Times were changing.

The thought of Claire gallivanting off to the forest made him uneasy, filling him with a sense of duty—a need to protect. She'd been sent with Koldis, of all people. Better him than Jovari, though, or the both of them together, which would have been worse.

He gnawed on the inside of his cheek. Would she be safe with the sprites? It was in his nature to mistrust them.

He strode into his quarters, unbelting his sverak before tossing it on the table—

"Verath?"

He froze, his arm outstretched, then whirled around. "Desaree? What are you doing here?"

"I..." She blushed and pushed off the wall where she'd been lurking.

"I mean—" He stepped forward but stopped himself. His thoughts jumbled together at the sudden sight of her. "I didn't mean it like that. I'm just surprised to see you."

"You're right. I...I shouldn't have intruded." She scrambled for his door.

"No!" He lunged for her, wrapping his hands about her waist, catching her. She stilled beneath his touch. Almost as quickly, he released her, afraid to overstep his bounds. "Please." The desperation in his voice was embarrassing. "I don't want you to leave. Tell me what you came for."

She faced him. "I..." Emotions played out across her features, one after another. "I miss you," she said at last, turning an even darker shade of red.

He suppressed a cry of relief and pulled her into his arms, enveloping her, burying his face in her hair. Slowly, she brought her arms around him and he sighed.

"I miss you too," he murmured. "I do not like what is happening between us. Tell me there's hope for us."

She'd told him that she needed time to think things through. Space away from him. He'd given it to her. It should have been easy to let her go, but he couldn't stop having flashes of Kendra and how he'd let her go, too.

"I've made my decision." Desaree's sudden words had him pulling away. "About us, I mean."

He nodded, trying to hide his unease, his fear over what she might say next. "Come, Desaree. Sit with me." She glanced between his hand and the sofa before accepting. Every moment of silence felt tangible. She picked at a stray thread on her skirt, avoiding his gaze. "Why do I get the feeling you are about to reject me?" His voice caught. He clamped his lips shut.

"Reject you?" Her mouth opened and closed.

She ought to. It would be for the best—better for her, at least. He waited.

"Verath, you want me to be happy, do you not?"

He frowned. "Of course I—"

"The problem is, you've got preconceived notions of what will make me happy. You claim to know what is best for me." She shook her head.

"Desaree." A familiar frustration welled up. This was the argument they'd had the night she'd asked for space. He pinched the bridge of his nose. "Can you not see? I would only ever be your lover. Nothing more."

"So? Why is that bad?"

His voice was quiet as he said, "Because I cannot give you a marriage. I cannot give you children. A family. I cannot be a husband to you. It would be improper to take you without offering those things in return."

She scowled. "Says who? All those old fashioned ninnies out there?" She waved her arm. "Please tell me you do not care what *they* think! You—King Talon's shield?!"

"Of course not! I care about your honor."

"My honor!" She snorted. "Love transcends honor, Verath.

Besides, you said it yourself: You cannot give me children. What honor is there to be lost, then?"

His gaze traced the planes of her face, her smooth, flawless skin. "What of my long life compared to your human one?" He hated to bring it up, but crossed his arms anyway.

"You are right. I will grow old and die. You probably won't bear to look at me when that happens. You'll want nothing to do with me then. But until then...we might be happy."

His jaw fell open. "How callous do you think me? I would stay with you till the end, Desaree, and love you long after."

"Then what are you afraid of?"

He stilled. The answer was one he hadn't wanted to confront, one that drove him into this mess in the first place, drove him to push her away. "Regret, Des. I am afraid that you will regret me." The words tasted bitter on his tongue, but they were out before he could stop them. "I fear that when you are older, when you've passed a childbearing age, you will feel I held you back from a family. That you will blame me. And you would be right to do so. I am a selfish creature."

She hesitated, but he could see her thoughts turning over. "Tell me, Verath, you served King Tallek and Queen Ahlessa for a short time, did you not?"

"Yes?" His gaze narrowed. "What's that got to do with it?"

"Queen Ahlessa's ladies in waiting—how often did they take husbands?" She lifted her chin as victory flashed across her expression.

He knew then that she'd won. He sighed, slumping back against the sofa. "Never. The queen's ladies always remain single to serve. Although...there was one who wished to marry. Ahlessa granted her wishes, affording her an early retirement."

"And when Claire becomes queen, will she abandon that tradition?"

They both knew it was unlikely. How could a lady in waiting serve a queen when her duty was to her family? Queen Ahlessa kept her ladies close at hand. They lived in the tower with her, as Desaree would when Claire became queen.

Hope blossomed in his chest. Desaree had backed him into a corner and he loved her more for it, for her fighting spirit. She wouldn't give up on him. Warmth spread through his limbs, left his fingers tingling. "This was going to be your argument all along, wasn't it?" She offered him a slow grin. It forced the breath from his chest. "Well, you've caught me then, Des. I can offer no better rebuttal."

She glanced down at her hands, folded in her lap. "Verath... what happened between you and Kendra is...regrettable. I admit, I foster jealousy for a woman I have never met. A woman who isn't even alive. Gods!" She shook her head. "Kendra is long gone and I still envy the connection you shared, never having met her. I am selfish too, you see."

His gaze was fixed upon her face—upon her chocolate colored eyes. "Selfish...over me?" The rhythm of his heart skipped. A reflection of his growing hope—his growing desire.

"I will not share you with another, for as long as I live. My life might be short, the blink of an eye compared to yours. But for me, it is the chance to be happy." He inched his fingers closer to hers, to where they rested in her lap. She glanced down and ripped her hand away, crossing her arms, pinning him with a fierce, defiant glare. "If you deprive me of yourself, Verath, you will rob me of my happiness. Is that what you want? To be a thief? To rob me the way you—" Her hand flew to her mouth.

He gaped at her. But she was right. "You can say it," he said, feeling the sting keenly. "The way I robbed Kendra." She winced and nodded. "And for the record, I would not dare. You know I would not."

"Then...then you will be with me? You will choose me?"

He exhaled, shaking his head in complete bafflement. "I chose you long ago, Des. The power rests with *you*. Only you. I should have made love to you after the ball. I regret my hesitation. But I needed you to know me—all of me. I needed you to make your choice knowing all the facts." He swallowed.

"I have made my choice, Verath. I choose you." She scooted closer to him and his heart burst, breaking open a deeper part of him, the place where his regret lurked, chipping away at him. "But you cannot hold back anymore," she added. "If you are with me, you are with me fully."

"I am with you fully," he said, reaching across the distance and pulling her into his lap. She brought her lips down on his and he groaned, pulling away. "Shall I prove it?" His words were breathless.

"Yes," she whispered, trembling against him.

He gripped her face, bringing her mouth back to his, exploring the taste of her. A flash of red scales shot through his mind. The rumble of something deeper. The flick of a tail, like an image at the edge of his vision. His inhuman side stirred.

He kissed her deeper, more fiercely, pawing at her gown, working with the ties in the back. Her hands grasped fistfuls of his tunic. She pulled it up and over his head before he could stop her. Before he could stop her fingers as they roved over every inch of his exposed skin, sinking below his waistband.

The dragon within him purred, taking over. He lifted her from the sofa and deposited her beside the bed, where he stripped away her gown until she was down to her chemise. "Are you sure about this?" he whispered against her lips. He searched her eyes for a hint of hesitation. There was none.

"I've never been more sure of anything in all my life," she said. Her hands found the ties of his pants and he froze, unable to pull his gaze away from her efforts. His breathing turned ragged as she unlaced him, undressed him. He pulled her into his arms and onto the bed.

There, he took the pain of regret, the loss over losing his mate, and let it fuel him. Desaree rose to the challenge, filling the gaping holes left behind. With every touch of her fingers, every kiss of her lips, every brush of her skin against his, his beast's purring turned to a roar.

It rang in his ears and sang in his soul, wrapping around him. Tangling with him the way Desaree's body did. Healing him. Until there was nothing left but the two of them. Nothing but the love he proved so deeply, over and over. There could never again be any question between them. He was complete.

~+~+~+~+~+

THE DRAGONWALL SERIES continues in book 4: Koldis the Green
If you enjoyed this book, please consider supporting me by leaving a review or rating on Amazon and Goodreads. These help get my book noticed which is important for indie authors like me.

If you would like to stay up to date with book news, new releases, spoilers, and bonus content, sign up for my newsletter mailing list at https://www.authormelissamitchell.com/newsletter signup

ABOUT THE AUTHOR

Melissa Mitchell is a fantasy romance author and creator of the seven-book *Dragonwall* series. Her love of fantasy began with *The Dragonriders of Pern*, and she now writes stories full of dragons, magic, hidden royalty, and slow-burn romance. She holds a PhD in physics and lives in Atlanta, Georgia with her husband, a husky, and four very spoiled bunnies. When she's not writing, she enjoys baking cookies, bullet journaling, and figure skating—usually while plotting her next book.

Visit her online at: authormelissamitchell.com

Also by Melissa Mitchell

The Arcane Artifacts

Bound by the Blood Ruby

The Dragonwall Series

Talon the Black

Reyr the Gold

Verath the Red

Koldis the Green

Bedelth the Orange

Jovari the Blue

Dallin the Violet

The Lady Witch Series

Wielder's Prize

Wielder's Bond

Wielder's Might

Witch's Ruin

Witch's Heart

Witch's Crown

Royals of Dragonwall Series

For the Crown

Stand Alone Titles

Blood and Ballet